I0701604

A New Beginning

A New Beginning

The Unforgiving Stars 1

E.J. Isaacs

Copyright © 2025 by E.J. Isaacs
All rights reserved. No part of this publication may be reproduced, distributed or transmitted in any form or by any means, without prior written permission. No part of this publication may be used in any manner for the purpose of training artificial intelligence technologies to generate text, including without limitation, technologies capable of generating works in the same style or genre as the publication.

Space Wizard Science Fantasy
Raleigh, NC
www.spacewizardsciencefantasy.com

Publisher's Note: This is a work of fiction. Names, characters, places, and incidents are a product of the author's imagination. Locales and public names are sometimes used for atmospheric purposes. Any resemblance to actual people, living or dead, or to businesses, companies, events, institutions, or locales is completely coincidental.

Cover art by MoorBooks
Editing by Courtney Brooks
Book Layout © 2015 BookDesignTemplates.com
A New Beginning/ E.J. Isaacs.— 1st ed.
ISBN 978-1-960247-47-6

CONTENTS

Part 1: A Taste of Diplomacy

Chapter One

"Captain! Force energy absorption is down; armor plating is failing! Captain!" But Lieutenant Rena Sheets would get no answers from the captain. He was dead at his command station. The *Excalibur* bridge was bathed in fire everywhere she turned. She sat helpless, with blank or red indicators across her entire panel. The ship's weapons were either expended or nonfunctional. The executive officer had gone to engineering some time ago and never returned. Lieutenant Commander John Raleigh was at the helm. He took in all the carnage and finally looked over at her. He was now effectively in command, and they were the only crew members left alive on the bridge. His mouth moved, but in the noise and confusion she could not hear the words. Even so, it was clear what he was saying: "I'm sorry." He keyed communications for engineering and asked them to route all available power to the thrusters.

On the main screen, the massive enemy ship showed some damage but overall seemed in far better shape than *Excalibur*. For the moment, the *Excalibur* was being left alone, as they were little threat. The Angels concentrated their fire on the few human ships equipped with the new weaponry. Those human weapons were proving surprisingly effective.

Raleigh keyed in commands on his console and flexed his body in the harness. *Excalibur* swung around to point straight at the mammoth enemy vessel and wallowed sluggishly forward. The enemy vessel grew on the screen. Rena caught her breath, suddenly realizing what he was doing. To stop the dreadnought, he would turn *Excalibur* into a sword to thrust through the heart of their enemy.

She keyed her panel for ship-wide communications and fought to speak in her best command voice. "Collision alert! All crew abandon forward areas immediately. Get pressure suits on and prepare for hull breach; we're ramming them!"

She did not turn her head when a control panel sparked and exploded behind her. Instead, she focused on the main screen as the enemy ship grew larger, noting the distance to impact and the true size of the enemy ship. It was ten times the size of *Excalibur*, but they would cause serious damage if they hit.

She was watching their speed when they struck. The main bridge screen blanked out as all forward video and computer sensors were obliterated. The impact slammed her forward into her console and knocked the wind out of her as the inertial dampening fields went off-line. She felt massive vibrations and swore she could hear the ship's frame groaning. It went on for some time before all movement ceased, but she was still alive.

Raleigh removed his harness and leapt up to help Rena. He grabbed her by the elbow and guided her across the wrecked bridge, stepping over the bodies of dead crewmen to get to the arms locker, where he keyed a control and the door opened on a rack of weapons and emergency vac-suits. The suits were designed to allow the use of tools and control panels but would not stop weapons fire, only sufficient to preserve life in a vacuum for five hours. Now that their ship had rammed another, it was doubtful the forward hull held any air.

Raleigh checked the seal on Rena's suit while she did the same for him. They each grabbed a laser rifle, and a satchel filled with pistols, as party favors for any crewmen they might encounter. Raleigh paused for a moment, looking past her at the remains of the bridge. Then unlocked the bridge hatch and shoved it open.

"What's next?" She looked at him, instinctively knowing he had a plan.

He looked at her soberly. "Our first priority is to gather as many survivors as we can, head to the shuttle bay, and load as many as we can to get away from the wreckage. After that, we'll see."

At first, the empty corridors near the bridge were unsettling. She glanced at Raleigh to see him confidently moving ahead, while she wrestled with her fight or flight instinct. She wanted off the ship. Knowing they were embedded in an enemy vessel bothered her more than she wanted to admit.

They encountered others as they progressed further.

"Come with us," Rena called out, and they joined in behind them. Along the way they rounded up almost forty officers and crew. They also found a small group of Marines in assault armor.

Seeing a senior officer, a sergeant spoke for the group.

"Sir. We stand ready to assist. One of our privates discovered a route through the wreckage that leads into the enemy ship."

Raleigh frowned. "Right now, we're headed aft to find shuttles to get us off the ship. I'm not planning on taking the fight to the enemy unless we have no other choice."

There was a commotion at the back of the group, which parted to allow another officer to come forward. Rena knew her as an Engineering officer she'd come through the Academy with, a Lieutenant Consuela.

She looked at Rena with surprise and gratitude at seeing a familiar face. Then she turned her attention to Raleigh.

"Sir, the way to the shuttle bay is blocked. The decks have collapsed back there. I barely got out."

Rena watched as Raleigh took in that information.

What would they do now, she pondered. *Wait for help from the Fleet? Assault the enemy?*

She watched Raleigh struggling with the same thoughts. *If it were up to me, what would I do in this case?*

Raleigh examined the quiet group. The Marines were always ready for a fight. The other officers and crew were his responsibility.

The sergeant spoke up. "Sir. If we wait here, that monster ship might just leave with us attached. At some point they will find their way here and take us all prisoner. We all know they don't take long-term prisoners. We've seen the bodies of their enemies before."

The group turned to see what Raleigh's response would be.

"Well then, I suggest we board the enemy ship and take it away from them. The odds can't be worse than ten to one. And we have Marines. Who's with me?" All of them roared in agreement.

With the Marines leading, the group scrambled after them, climbing over air ducts, support trusses, and twisted wreckage. At some point, the wreckage turned from that of their ship, to the enemy's. Eventually, they came upon two Marines who stood on debris, looking through a hole that opened into an undamaged portion of the enemy ship. In short order, all of them boarded.

In the first compartment they entered, still in vacuum, the unprotected humanoid body of an Angel warrior lay dead. Humans called them Angels because of the vestigial wings on their backs, but the beings were anything but angelic. They were predatory killers. Their long arms and sharp claws were used in close quarters combat to great effect. Their bodies were topped off with savage-looking bony heads.

The next few hours were a blur of running and fighting. Each engagement blended into the next one. Rena was determined to keep up with Raleigh. Fortunately, as their suits began to fail, they found breathable air in the still sealed portions of the enemy vessel.

In the hours that followed, they lost track of the Marines. The ship was a warren of corridors.

Rena knew she was exhausted but refused to stop. Two crewmen were scouting ahead at an intersection when, with a blur of movement, they disappeared.

Rena yelled out, "Angels! Fire as soon as you see them. They move too fast! Don't let them charge you."

As they approached, a squad of Angel warriors turned the corner, likely the same group that took out their two crewmen. The fighting was brutal and close.

Rena found herself fighting against claws with her utility knife, pushing back her attacker. An Angel pistol discharged right next to her head. Someone screamed in pain. Raleigh came into her view shoving a knife up and under the chin of her attacker. Rena found herself sprayed with thick purple Angel blood. She noticed claw marks on Raleigh's arms and could see his uniform through the tears in his suit, though he ignored them. Rena picked up an Angel blaster from the deck. It felt warm to the touch. Seeing it in action made her want to be on this side of it for the next skirmish.

They moved onward but left three dead crewmen behind.

"Thanks," she told him once she caught up with the group. He turned to her and nodded, noticing her exhaustion.

He stopped then and looked over the remains of their group. Everyone was tired from running and fighting.

Rena felt her legs shaking. She knew if she stopped to rest the exhaustion would overcome her. She looked at Raleigh who seemed alert and calm. She wondered how he could keep pushing himself like that. The seemingly endless fighting was wearing her down.

They stopped in front of a hatch and, working together, they pried it open. It turned out to be a cabin for one of the Angel crew. She watched as Raleigh led everyone inside and closed the hatch behind them.

"We'll rest here for a bit and get some food into us." He pulled out some emergency rations from a pocket and had Rena pass them around. She bolted hers down, ignoring the awful taste. She sat next to Raleigh while she ate. At one point she closed her eyes as they felt too heavy to keep open. When she woke, she realized she had fallen against Raleigh, and he'd put a protective arm around her to hold her steady. It felt good to be in his arms. It was safe and warm in the cold enemy ship. He had a way of projecting that to the whole group but at the same time he made her feel hope. She realized she hadn't felt hope since their ship was disabled.

She had no idea how long she'd slept. It could have been five minutes or five hours. Once Raleigh noticed she was awake, he roused the group, and they moved out to continue to sweep the area.

They shortly found themselves at the opening of a large space that appeared to be a shuttle bay. Ahead they could see their squad of Marines, huddled together on their knees, hands behind their heads. Angel warriors flanked them while an Angel officer spoke in crisp, perfect English.

"You will tell us where your senior officers are, or we will execute you one at a time."

"We told you before, we don't know. We lost track of them," answered a Marine corporal.

She watched as the Angel officer pulled out his blaster and pointed it at the Marine. He fired and the weapon vaporized the corporal's head. The remaining captives just stared at him as if daring him to continue. He seemed perplexed that this did not elicit the desired response from the others.

He was just leveling his pistol at another Marine when Raleigh gave the signal to attack.

Rena lay on her stomach, firing the captured Angel blaster. The other crewmen fired laser rifles. In short order, they dropped the guards with precise hits.

The Angel officer turned his attention to the new threat. He adjusted his pistol to its highest setting and fired at them.

Raleigh's boot caught her in the ribs and rolled her out of the way just as the Angel officer fired.

Rena heard someone yell but ignored it as she raised her blaster. Before she could fire, two other crewmen fired their laser rifles, one striking the officer through the eye. He crumpled lifelessly to the deck.

As she lowered her blaster, Rena saw to her horror that Raleigh was down, his right leg missing below the knee. His pants were burned away and the remaining stump burned off. There was only a little blood since the wound was cauterized.

He looked up at her and gasped, "Keep going, it's your command now."

Then he passed out.

Rena stood up and took charge of the remaining crew and Marines. Together they secured the area and brought Raleigh along with them. They found and organized more *Excalibur* crewmen hiding nearby and decided to make a push to take the bridge. There weren't many Angel soldiers left as they approached.

Raleigh was initially carried by a large Marine but when they stopped to rest, he fashioned a crutch out of support bars. Although he was in a lot of pain, he joined them as they approached the bridge and covered their rear.

Just outside the bridge, Rena turned back to Raleigh, who still looked gray. He caught his breath and felt her gaze.

"Don't look at me, this is your command. Go when you're ready."

She turned back and took a breath. His words stoked something inside her that wanted vengeance for all their lost crew. At her signal, they opened the hatch to the bridge and found the remaining Angel warriors inside waiting for them. One of the Marines charged in, drawing their attention. As she was cut down by half a dozen blasters, the rest stormed in behind her.

Rena turned her attention to an Angel officer closest to the door. She knocked his blaster away, but he pinned her shoulder to the bulkhead with a knife. The edge of the knife ground against her bone, and she struggled to raise her blaster.

Raleigh dove forward, one hand on his crutch, and drove a combat knife into the back of the warrior between his wings, making it screech in pain. As he twisted around, Raleigh pulled the knife out, followed by a fountain of purple blood.

"Thanks, Raleigh," Rena said. He looked seriously at her and her wound and gave a curt nod in return.

All Rena could see were the remains of the *Excalibur* crew looking back at her. Most seemed to be surprised to find themselves still alive. They had taken the bridge.

In the next few minutes, they sealed the bridge hatch and tended to each other's wounds. Raleigh sat on the deck, still in pain, but insisted on helping Rena bandage her shoulder. He moved carefully, even when he had to tear her uniform jacket to treat her shoulder. The knife had gone through her shoulder, and he insisted she leave it in for a doctor or med techs. He injected her with a stim from one of the Marines aid kits.

"We need to get a message out. Can we use something on this bridge?" She called out to the room at large. One of the Marines, a corporal, was placing a jacket over the first Marine that stormed the bridge. Her body was unrecognizable. He looked up at her question.

"Yes, sir." She watched as he drafted an electronics tech as they pulled apart some of the controls panels on the alien ship.

While they worked, she turned her attention back to Raleigh. "Hey, you need a stim yourself. You look like hell."

"I feel like hell. But you got the last one. You're in command now, so you need a clear head."

She frowned. She wanted to say he looked fit to take back command, but she could see the strain in his eyes. He was barely holding on. He looked at her and smiled weakly back, putting on a brave face. She knew they would never have made it this far without him.

A shout of "Eureka!" brought her attention back to the crew. The tech had cobbled together a radio. He'd pulled his comm unit from his vac suit and handed it to her.

"It's linked to this. You can call out on the Fleet general frequency. It's all I could do on short notice."

She gave him a brilliant smile. "Damn good job."

She called out on the general Fleet frequency. "Attention, attention. This is Lieutenant Rena Sheets from the *Excalibur*. We have successfully taken the bridge of the Angel dreadnaught. We are standing by for further orders and assistance."

Two long minutes later, they finally received a response. "Good to hear, Lieutenant. We had to run your voice through an analyzer to be sure it was you. We'll be coming to assist shortly. You'll be happy to know that the rest of the Angel fleet has retreated."

"What do you mean, retreated? Angels never retreat." She said this to the room at large and looked over at Raleigh. He was just as shocked as she was.

Raleigh smiled weakly. "The new weapons, the new tactics. They worked!"

Everyone around her was grinning. Rena helped Raleigh to stand with her one good arm. He leaned against a console and together they looked out over the battlefield in space. Debris from a dozen ships were scattered around them. Most were from Fleet ships.

Then a movement caught their attention, and they watched as a small human scout ship jumped out of the system, following the remaining Angel fleet.

"That's likely the spy the Angels had in our ranks," Raleigh explained with a frown. "My cousin in Fleet Intelligence had suspected someone has been feeding the Angels information. Whoever he is, he's the worst kind of traitor."

It seemed like he had more to say on the subject, but when Rena looked at him again, he'd fallen asleep leaning against the console. She checked his pulse and found it steady.

"Hang in there J.P., hang in there."

Within weeks of that battle, the Fleet had taken on the Angels again, bringing their upgraded ships with their new weapons. Using new tactics, they won this battle as well. This time, when the Angels retreated, they didn't come back. Instead, they proposed a ceasefire. They would withdraw to a line across the galaxy. After their announcement, no more was heard from them.

The war was not over, but on pause.

As soon as the fighting ceased, politics resumed. Instead of praising the humans' ingenuity, the members of the Association of Allied Worlds scolded them for using *unapproved* technology. They suggested the thousand-year war was nearly over anyway, and that the human contribution was negligible.

Rena, and many others in the Fleet knew otherwise. They knew that someday, the Angels would come back once they better understood what the humans had done. She vowed to be ready with every resource at her disposal.

Chapter Two

Senior Captain Rena Sheets sighed and rested her head on the viewport, pulling herself out of her reverie of the past. It was twelve years after the war had stopped, and she was standing on an overhead work platform overlooking the construction of her new ship. While the facility housing her ship still went by the antiquated term, *construction yard*, it was a ring circling Earth's moon. This ring was anchored in place with long towers reaching up from the surface. While the yard itself was a marvel, her full attention was focused on her ship.

Yes, she could call it hers. She was the principal designer, senior construction project manager, and Captain. It was her baby from end to end. Over the last two years, many Fleet Admirals learned she would accept no compromises, and no shortcuts. She had burned her political capital liberally to get this ship built to her specifications. She sincerely hoped she still had a few friends in the Fleet once the ship was completed.

Every so often she came up to this remote spot to get away from the madness and her triple-booked schedule just to see her baby in progress and grab a few precious moments of peace. Once launched, she could establish her own schedule. She could leave all the Fleet politics behind her. All that mattered then was her mission, for humans to resume exploring the galaxy. It would be a very different mission since the war.

During the last year, she had scoured the Fleet to create her crew. Good, experienced hands were hard to come by in a fleet ravaged by ten years of war and then twelve years of peace. Some of the old hands that had stayed in the Fleet weren't worth keeping. With a few exceptions, they were either incompetent or had nowhere else to go. In her quest for the perfect crew for this new ship, she'd decided to use mostly young people. Most of them had no deep space experience at all, just raw talent waiting to be molded.

She closed her eyes, drew in a long deep breath, and let it out slowly. She opened her eyes and re-scanned her ship. The *Excalibur II* was larger than most Fleet vessels. It was three hundred sixty-six meters long and seventy-six meters wide with its central main gun across the top, laser batteries, plasma cannons, missile launchers, and experimental particle beam weapons along the tapered sides. The front of the ship resembled a spear point with the rear of the ship being more rectangular. Toward the rear ran the launch tubes for the fighters. Just out of view in the aft section there were more weapons, the main thrusters, and launch tubes for mines. Underneath it all were shuttle bay hangars.

A few maintenance bots rolled over the surface, but all primary construction on the outside was essentially completed. Inside the ship, chaos reigned as construction continued at a fevered pace while new crew and supplies were continuously being loaded.

All her experience from the war and the years afterward went into this design. For *Excalibur II*, she used the latest human technology as well as the best of what she could learn and obtain from their allies. Movement caught her eye—a contingent of Fleet Marines was marching onto the ship from the docks. That was good. Maybe now she would find a worthy sparring partner.

Her shoulder ached from the old wound. The battles, the destruction, lost friends and crewmen, the final battle when Raleigh mouthed "I'm sorry" and drove their ship into the enemy dreadnaught, it all seemed like it was only yesterday.

The computer interface on her sleeve vibrated and she shook the memories away. Her assistant, her shadow, stood waiting at the end of the passageway. Lieutenant Reese kept her organized and sane. Rena had one more meeting to get through, then she planned to duck out of her other afternoon appointments to see her dad. He'd said it was important, and it would be the last time they could talk for a while. She sighed and took one last look at her baby from the outside. The ship was officially weeks from launch. She doubted she would get another chance to come back to this spot.

* * *

Rena entered the conference room and the very nervous Fleet cadet in her tight gray uniform bounced up out of her chair so fast the chair fell over backward. The cadet had not even looked at her rank but assumed whoever came in outranked her. As this was a good assumption anywhere outside of the academy grounds, Rena regarded it as further confirmation of her choice.

"Ca...cadet First Class Sonja Mortan reporting as ordered," the young woman stammered out as fast as possible, still not looking at her.

Rena walked to the other side of the conference table and stood waiting for the cadet to notice her. After some seconds, the young woman looked at the uniform rank first and at the captain's face second.

"Captain?" She almost squeaked.

"At ease, Cadet, take a seat." Rena watched in amusement as the girl reached behind her before realizing the chair was not where it should be. Finding it on its side, she picked it up and sat down, her back so straight she appeared at attention.

"My name is Captain Rena Sheets. I'm sure you're wondering why you were brought here?"

"Yes, Captain. I was about to take finals and they don't let you out of those without a good reason so I figured it had to be a good reason or something very important but I can't for the life of me figure out what that is but then again maybe something has happened to start up the war again but I'm sure I would have been able to tell that on the way here by the activity level on base and in the construction yards..."

"Cadet!" Rena put some emphasis into it to cut off the word stream.

"Yes captain, sorry captain. I've just been so curious."

"I'm sure you have been. I've been talking with your instructors, and they say you are the perfect person to work on my problem," Rena said.

"Yes, Captain." She paused thoughtfully. "Is this part of my final?"

"You could say that." The captain had a hard time keeping her lips from twitching into a smile.

"What is the problem, Captain?" Cadet Mortan was all business now.

Rena stood up and headed for the hatch. The cadet, in her haste to follow, knocked over her chair again. Before Sonja could recover it, Rena was out the hatch saying, "Follow me."

The two walked out of the conference room and across to the main airlock for *Excalibur II*. They kept to the left side and joined a steady stream of workers entering the ship as an equally continuous stream to their right was moving off the ship.

"If I may ask, Captain, what ship is this?" asked the nervous cadet.

"A new one," was all the answer Rena gave.

They walked into the central passageway, then stepped into a bounce tube and dropped three decks, getting off lightly and continuing their walk. Rena noticed the cadet handled the bounce tube well considering it was a new feature on ships. Cadet Mortan was trying to look everywhere at once and it was a wonder she hadn't tripped over her own feet.

* * *

The captain turned off the corridor and entered a conference room with an electronic sign labeled 'Planning'. Sonja noticed one display wall of the conference room was taken up with a large and complex diagram of the ship. On the table were printed materials that looked like long lists of items in very small print. Once Sonja entered, the captain closed the hatch behind them.

The captain spoke, "Shenna, record and consider."

"Yes, Captain," answered a warm female alto voice. Since no one else was in the room, Sonja assumed the captain was talking to someone through the intercom.

"This is my problem," Captain Sheets said, addressing her directly. "This ship is being constructed for a ten-year mission. We need to stock it with almost everything we'll need for those ten years. Assuming we won't be able to stop for re-supply or repairs in that time and assuming we can find food along the way, what items do we bring, and how and where do we pack it all?"

Sonja blinked rapidly but her face remained impassive. "Uh, Captain. Please excuse me, but when do you need an answer to this problem?" Sonja's mind was racing.

"I'll need your answer as soon as possible. No longer than six weeks. Implementing it may take longer." Sonja stood with her head tilted as her mind broke the problem down. The magnitude of the task hit her in a rush.

Sonja straightened her head and said, "Captain, to do this, I'll need access to the complete ship design specs, a list of everything already brought and stored on board, and everything you plan to be brought and stored on board. If I may be allowed, I'd also like to return and obtain from my academy computer files some software that I wrote last year that might help me in this task." She was certain she had the tools to find the answer.

The captain looked up. "Shenna, grant Cadet Sonja Mortan access to anything she requires for this task, my authorization. Obtain her personal computer files from the academy for her use here while she is working on the problem. Assign her a cabin on board and a workplace suitable for this task."

"Yes, Captain. Commands acknowledged. Welcome, Sonja."

Sonja looked startled at the personal welcome. Surely this must be a civilian, to have used her name and not Cadet. "Ah, Shenna, is it? Thank you!"

"You are very welcome," returned the warm response.

The captain gestured Sonja to a chair.

"I need you to understand something about Shenna," Sheets began. "Only you and I need to know about her right now. Shenna is the code word for a cutting edge and secret new technology. She is an advanced computer installed by the P'Yntakas, a member of the Alliance, at my request. You won't be able to discuss anything about your interactions with it to anyone."

"Okay, Captain," Sonja said out loud. *When an officer tells you to keep something in confidence, it may as well be a regulation.*

The captain stood and turned to the hatch. "I will let you two get acquainted. If you need anything else, Shenna will help you."

Sonja was shocked, "Captain?!"

The captain turned at the door. "Yes?"

"For this problem, are you asking me *how* I would load the ship or are you asking me to actually load the ship?"

"The latter."

"Oh, oh my. Uh, Captain?" She fought a rise of panic at the very notion.

"Yes?"

"What about my other exams?"

"This is your only exam. It counts for all your courses. I've made all the arrangements with your instructors. I'm also in charge of your first assignment."

"I see." Sonja drank that in. "Thank you, Captain." While that answered all her questions, it didn't make her feel any better.

"You're welcome. See you in a few weeks or so, unless you finish sooner."

With that, Captain Sheets left the room, closing the hatch behind her.

Staring after the Captain, Sonja felt miserable. "Moons and asteroids, why couldn't I just take a test?"

"There are many kinds of tests." The voice made her jump. She had forgotten about the channel open to Shenna.

"Shenna?"

"Yes. My apologies if I startled you."

"I'm easily startled right now." Sonja thought some more. "Why are you called Shenna?"

"Excellent question." Sonja could hear the smile in her voice, "It is an acronym for Shipboard High-level Encoding NaNo-processing Analyzer. The captain started calling me SHENNA in my first few hours of operation. She said it's shorter, easier to say, and humans love acronyms."

Thinking about the captain who had presented her with this unique and all-encompassing final exam made Sonja think of another question.

"She said her name was Captain Rena Sheets. Why does that sound so familiar?"

"Captain Sheets was awarded the Nova Medal with Cluster for bringing back her last ship from a disastrous encounter in which Senior Captain Cromwell and half the crew perished."

Sonja frowned in thought. "Yeah, I seem to remember something about that in the news vids. But, no, I was thinking why the name Sheets sounds familiar?"

"Sheets is also the last name of the CEO of Sol Interests, Inc., the company in charge of building this ship as well as most of the Fleet."

"That's it! Isn't he one of the most powerful and richest civilians in all of Sol System?"

"Yes, I believe that assessment to be true."

"I wonder if they're related?" Sonja had not realized she had spoken her last thought out loud until Shenna responded.

"Robert Zachariah Sheets, CEO of Sol Interests, is the father of Senior Captain Rena Sheets," Shenna stated.

"Wow." Sonja stared at the wall, digesting. Then she glanced down at the table. "I guess we'd better get moving on this project. I had better see about getting back to my dorm room for my things."

Shenna replied, "That is not necessary. All of your belongings and computer files have been transferred to the ship."

"Really?"

"Yes."

Sonja shook her head in amazement. "Yes, I supposed you could have been taking care of that while we've been talking." She thought about this. "But if you're not the typical computer, per se, at least not the kind of computer I built my software and files on then why move them? My software wouldn't work here anyway, would it?"

"Not necessarily," said Shenna. "I examined your software algorithms and found I can take the essence of what you were trying to accomplish and add them to specific functions. I think you found a unique way of storing supplies on a Fleet ship."

Sonja blinked. "So, you understand what my program was trying to do? My instructors didn't fully understand it but gave me a good grade because the computers told them that what I was going for was *theoretically possible.*"

"It is not a theory. I have calculated your program algorithms would enhance storage and retrieval capabilities of supplies on a typical fleet ship by 247% at a minimum."

"Wow, and here I was going for a 100% improvement." She smiled. "Shenna, I think we're going to get along just fine."

"I agree," Shenna replied, and Sonja was sure she could hear all the warmth of a real personality behind it. Sonja looked at the diagram displayed on the wall. "Let's start from the bottom and work our way upward."

The bottommost deck appeared larger on the display, and Sonja studied it. "I can assist if I know what you are looking for," Shenna stated.

"Well, there are lots of nooks and crannies in any ship. I wrote a paper about this in my sophomore year, but I don't think it was taken seriously. I could never get the notion out of my head, though. Now it seems to apply to the problem the captain has posed to me."

"May I read it?" Shenna asked.

Sonja was re-examining many of her assumptions about computers. She would have expected the computer would already know the contents, would probably already have all the cadets' papers as part of its databanks and would simply access the relevant document upon mentioning it. How interesting that it asked for permission to read her paper.

"Well, of course. If we're going to be working together on this problem, you may need to know many other ideas I've worked on. Let me pre-authorize you. Feel free to read all my Academy files."

"Done. I will add this knowledge to what I already have about you on file."

Sonja was taken aback. "Done already!" Then she remembered how quickly Shenna had transferred Sonja's Academy work files after the captain had authorized it. "On file?"

"Yes, the one the captain started on you when she decided to bring you aboard to solve our logistics problem."

"Hmmmm, I don't suppose I'm allowed to see my own file," Sonja mused.

"Not all parts of your record. Some parts are restricted."

"I thought they might be. I guess everyone is always curious about their own file."

"Curiosity is a major trait of every identified race that has space travel technology," Shenna stated.

"I wonder why the captain started a file on me," Sonja pondered aloud.

Shenna answered, "The Captain maintains her own files of all of her crew."

Sonja gaped. "*Crew*! You mean she is already counting me as part of this crew?"

Shenna seemed to answer carefully, "Well, yes. However, if this assignment doesn't go well that decision could be changed."

Sonja shook her head slowly. "Well, then. Please call me Sonni since we'll be working so closely together. We can chit chat some more later. We obviously have much more to do."

Sonja pondered as she stared at the diagram. Unconsciously, her head tilted to one side, and she smiled.

* * *

Rena Sheets nodded at her father's assistant as she walked past and into her father's office. She had been able to walk in at almost any time since she was a little girl. She wanted to touch base with him anyway, before her ship launched, but her father had requested she visit him as soon as possible at the company headquarters on the moon.

On entering, she saw he had two visitors.

Admiral Dequan Chidubem was an old friend of her father and had been an early supporter of her project. The other person was a small bookish, balding man with a severe look and a conservative business suit.

Her father greeted her with his customary hug, then led her to the center of the room and began introductions.

"Rena, you know Admiral Chidubem, of course. Let me also introduce you to Mister MacLash. He just recently took over as project finance officer."

"What! Why? What happened to Mister Quinlan?" Rena's heart skipped a beat. The finance officer controlled the budget for her ship's construction and was an old friend.

Admiral Chidebem spoke from behind her. His dark skin reflected the overhead lights. "There was a shuttle accident in the yard. He was killed instantly. Mister MacLash was appointed by Earth Central to both replace him and, apparently, conduct an audit."

Mister MacLash became more animated once his name was mentioned and added, "Yes, there have been some disturbing rumors about your project for some time. Earth Central asked me to step in and audit the finances as well as find out what I can about the rumors."

Rena put on her most professional face. "What kind of rumors, if I may ask?"

His face pinched together as if he smelled something evil. "I'm not at liberty to discuss those currently, Captain. I'm assembling my audit team now and you will be hearing from us shortly."

He glanced at his sleeve and scowled. "I'm afraid I've already waited here long enough. I have work to do." He looked up at them. "Good day Mr. Sheets, Admiral." As an afterthought he added, "Captain." With that he turned on his heel and left the office in a huff.

The Admiral spoke before Rena could ask either man a question. "Your father will explain. I'm afraid he is being driven by some politicians who are not very friendly toward the Fleet. A lot of people think we should be downsizing the Fleet, not increasing it. I'll see to it he gets back to Earth and keep him from stepping on more toes."

After a meaningful look at her father, the Admiral left, and Rena closed the office door after him. Then she turned to her father, who was returning to his desk.

Her father pressed a button, and she heard seals deploy around the door. A red light appeared on his desk. It meant a jammer was in place for any listening devices and the sealed door made his office soundproof.

"We haven't talked for a while. Obviously, losing Quinlan is a blow, and Mister MacLash was an unexpected move on the part of someone in Earth Central. That's all happened rather suddenly, which is one of the reasons I called for you. I also need to let you know of some recent developments. Our foremen have been finding strangers mixed in with our construction crews who have been asking a lot of questions about your alien-built computer. Those people were encouraged to leave before our people tossed them out an airlock. I was going to ask you to move up your launch as soon as possible, like in the next couple of weeks.

"The Admiral just told me that his office discovered that a team of auditors will be descending on your project in seven days. They plan on locking down the project and thoroughly inspecting everything about the ship. Their aim, ultimately, is to kill the project. If they do, they'll find your little friend. You know if they find out it's self-aware, we'll both be arrested. I'm sure our lawyers can get us out, in a couple of years. The law concerns human built A.I., it says nothing about A.I. built by someone else. But until you get *Excalibur II* out of Sol system, we're not safe."

Her father's reference to 'her little friend' meant Shenna. This was not good news at all.

He continued, "It's Tuesday, I told the crews to quietly increase their pace and have you ready to go by Friday, a few days before the audit team hits. I assume that will be okay with you?"

"Sounds good. If the construction people sign-off, Fleet shouldn't have any reason to hold us back."

Her father sighed. "The Admiral believes in your mission. We need to find out what the Angels are up to after twelve years. Our allies in the Association are still unhappy with us. We know from what history they've shared about their war that the Angels never give up. We dealt them a blow. We're confident they'll be back."

She processed this information, then shifted mental gears. "How is our other, personal construction project doing?"

"We're still on schedule. It's difficult to keep under wraps but we're managing so far."

They talked for a few minutes more. Then she stood. "I'll see about leaving as soon as possible. You know I could be gone a very long time."

He moved around his desk to hug her again. "I know, sweetheart. You do what you must."

Rena smiled. "And you do the same."

Chapter Three

The Andovian Captain of the small trading vessel knocked tentatively on the cabin door. He noted the blast scars and scratches left there from the activities of the past few weeks. His losses on this run made his stomachs grumble. It would be the last time he took on such a mission without learning more about the target.

The cabin occupant called out, "Yes?"

"We are in the process of docking. I trust you will be leaving us once we are secure," he called out.

"Yes, thank you. Open the outer hatch and keep the corridors clear."

"I will," the captain replied. He was not very happy about this passenger. His crew had waited for two days before attacking him. They had been paid very well to make sure their passenger never reached his destination. The first group died here in this corridor. The others disappeared one at a time in the week after the initial attack. By the time they reached the Sol system he and his engineer were running the freighter by themselves. All their weapons were missing. He hadn't slept much.

The Fleet had abandoned these docks orbiting at Earth's L-5 location, and they had been given over to several import/export companies dealing with the various traders in the Association. The docks were old and run down, but functional. Various support establishments, bars, restaurants, and hotels had sprung up in areas not given over to storage of goods both arriving and departing. Many of the lights were out and the atmosphere smelled faintly of various atmospheric gases vented from a dozen small ships.

His passenger walked off the ship wearing a cloak and hood and within seconds disappeared into the crowd. The captain of the freighter stepped out and sniffed the air with his mouth tentacles in the man's wake, grumbling in the back of his throat. His crew were drifting in space, spread over many parsecs.

Good riddance, he thought, just before movement caught his eyes and a squad of dock security forces in electric vehicles stopped at his docking port.

"Damn him to the ten hells!" The captain snarled as they trained their weapons on him. He slowly raised all four of his hands.

* * *

Twelve hours later, a man wearing a Lieutenant Commander Fleet uniform at least a decade out of date walked up to the entrance of Fleet Command Central on Earth and showed his ID to the guard. The bored guard took the ID card and frowned over the picture of an obviously younger man. The fellow standing before him was thinner, his hair showing streaks of silver gray at his temples. He wondered why this old guy hadn't updated his card display, then stuck it in the slot to be processed. By habit, he started to step aside, anticipating the green "ID Verified" light. Instead, the machine sucked the card completely inside, a light flashed red, and a small buzzer sounded.

"Yes," said the man calmly, "I thought that might happen."

The nervous guard stepped back and drew his sidearm. "Stay right where you are and don't move."

"I'm not going anywhere. I expected this kind of reception."

* * *

Twenty minutes later, Lieutenant Commander John Paul Raleigh was escorted into the office of Admiral Jack Berry, Fleet Intelligence. As the Admiral's young assistant shut the door behind him, Raleigh walked over to the wet bar at the far end of the office and started to make himself a drink.

"Wasting no time, I see, J.P.," the Admiral chuckled from behind his desk.

"I see no reason to. I had a long trip to get back here, and I see you're still in the same office with the same bar." Drink in hand, Raleigh walked back to the desk and sat down in the chair in front of it. "You always had the best single malt scotch."

"I suppose you made your report already?" The admiral stroked his white beard, thoughtfully watching his old friend. He wasn't sure he liked what he saw. John Paul Raleigh, J.P. to a select few friends, was a lean man in build, but he appeared to have lost some additional weight. His face had aged. Creases and wrinkles crossed it. He looked like historic pictures of old fishermen, without the tan. His dark hair, styled a bit long by Fleet standards, had thinned a little and now had two streaks of silver gray combed straight back on each side of his head.

Raleigh sipped his drink and smiled. "I had four months to compose it on a slow freighter. I dropped my notes off on level ten, where I'm sure they will keep the analysts busy for some time."

"We heard you were captured by the Angels; can you confirm that?"

"Confirmed, but I escaped. It's in the notes." He sipped his scotch.

"...and Williams. Ever get a line on him?" The Admiral continued to watch him closely. He was well aware that chasing Williams was what brought Raleigh into Intelligence. That Angel turncoat was responsible for so many deaths.

Raleigh sighed, "Only rumors. He's on the run and constantly looking over his shoulder. He knows we're hunting him. It can't be a nice way to live, but he brought that on himself. Someone will catch up to him at some point. It just won't be me." With his free hand he rubbed his artificial leg thoughtfully.

"Good job, J.P., as always." He appraised the man before him a moment more and smiled. "So, now you're going to tell me you want to retire, right?"

"You know me well, Admiral. Yes, I've had enough. Past time for me to retire. I have it all planned out. I'm going to build a boat and do some real sailing around this planet. I want to find out if there are any islands left with nobody on them."

"Fat chance of that but it sounds like it would be fun to verify." The admiral got up and moved over to his bar. He splashed some scotch into another glass and said as he returned to his desk, "J.P., as you know, we're a bit short of experience since the war."

Smiling, Raleigh shook his head. "Don't even get started, Admiral. Nothing you could offer will keep me in the Fleet. Intelligence is a young person's game and I'm not young anymore." He took another sip of the admiral's scotch and leaned his head back, closing his eyes.

"Nothing, eh?" The admiral smiled.

"No, sir."

"Not even your own command?"

Raleigh's head snapped up and he frowned. "That's not very funny, Jack. There is no way in hell Fleet would give me a command. Not with what happened right after the war stopped. They blamed me for crew deaths because of my actions, even though I was praised for what I did on a tactical level. But no, people were dead on *Excalibur*, and they needed a convenient scapegoat."

"I wouldn't bet on that if I were you. There are ship captains out there with less than ten years deep space time." The admiral's grin was like a shark's. "You and I know that would never have happened in the old days."

"Look, I'm not qualified to command a ship." Raleigh placed his drink on the admiral's desk. He shook his head, frowning.

"Alright, J.P., tell me why." The admiral stopped to watch Raleigh. His fish was on the line.

"I've been out of action too long, there's a lot of new technology we're using now, new weapons, new procedures." He shook his head as if convincing himself. "No, I couldn't take a command."

"Okay then, how about an exec slot behind an experienced captain?"

"God almighty, Jack, quit this! I know you're just blowing starlight up my ass. It's been a long day."

The admiral smiled. He put his hands on the desk and leaned across it. "J.P., it's no stiv."

Raleigh dropped back into the chair. He stared at the wall past the admiral. Slowly he picked up his glass and brought the drink to his lips again. Once it was there, he seemed to come back to himself, and he put it back on the desk.

"Alright, fine, tell me about it." The admiral could tell Raleigh thought he was enjoying this too much but was intrigued enough to want the details.

The admiral leaned back in his chair and said, "We have a brand-new ship based on a revolutionary design. It's been pushed through construction and will be ready to launch very soon, ahead of schedule. The captain is an experienced hand but has a crop of fresh-faced kids, many of them plucked right out of Fleet Academy before graduation. They have junior lieutenants running departments. They have a new alien-built computer that in all honesty no one knows stiv about but the rumors coming back say it could be self-aware. In short, the captain has more than enough of a chore keeping this baby together. They need a first officer who has been there and back and can whip the crew into shape. The captain runs the missions, but the executive officer runs the crew. What we need more than anything on this ship is a mentor. Also, if that computer is self-aware, we need someone with the skills to take it out without harming the ship."

Raleigh was staring at the wall and his frown deepened.

The admiral continued, "Look, I won't lie to you. I know you want out. You want time to relax in the sun. It will take at least a year to know if these people can handle this ship."

The admiral watched Raleigh sigh. The job attracted the man, and the admiral knew it. Even though he'd been ready to put in his papers when he came in, on a large ship he could get the department heads straightened out and then mentor them as they worked on their people. He could catch up on the newer technology over time. The big command decisions, the politics with Fleet, and the diplomacy with alien races, all belonged to the captain.

The admiral could see the wheels turning and wisely let the silence stretch. When Raleigh's frown smoothed out, he knew he had him.

"Okay, Admiral. One year then." Raleigh looked like he might be signing his own prison sentence.

"Good, and by the way, congratulations on your promotions. In your absence, you were promoted twice. You are now a Senior Commander." The admiral sat back and enjoyed the surprised look on Raleigh's face. He chuckled to himself at what he'd left out. Raleigh might find it difficult to leave after a year into a deep space mission.

Chapter Four

Marine Corporal David Peters was polishing the buckle of his dress uniform while listening to his bunkmates do what they always did, verbally spar with each other.

"You're so full of stiv, Jaz," said Marine Private Cheryl Bassinger, who sat on her bunk just below his. She aimed her comment at the burly man in the bunk across from them.

Marine Technical Specialist Daniel Lampart shook his head, "No stiv, I swear. I was walking past the gym yesterday and saw Gunny sparring hand-to-hand with the captain. She was wiping the floor with him. He was sweating like a pig and every time he tried to get his hands on her, she twisted him around and he was flat on his back again."

She threw a used towel at him, laughing. "No fraggin' way. I've seen Gunny wade into a bar full of Saturn dock workers and walk out the only one standing. I've seen our Captain; he could break her like a twig."

Lampart was nodding agreement but then began shaking his head in the other direction. The result made his head appear to move in circles. "I thought the same, but she was talking to him so fraggin' calmly about what she was doing, I swear she was *training* him."

"Stick your face in the head, idiot. Hey, Peters you believe this stiv?"

Corporal Peters put away the freshly shined buckle and the cleaning rag. "Yep. From what I know of the captain, I believe it."

"No stiv?" Both of his bunkmates looked up at him, Private Bassinger with an incredulous look on her face and Tech Specialist Lampart with a smile at the unexpected support.

"Our Captain was in the war. Right in the middle of it. She was on the original *Excalibur*, so I hear, at weapons control."

"That the one that rammed the Angel dreadnaught?"

"That's the one. Killed a third of their own crew when they hit. Then they fought hand-to-hand with the Angel crew and took over their ship. She was in command." The two faces looking up at him had the same expression of shock.

"Our Captain has the Nebula with Cluster from that. I saw Fleet Marine Admiral Zimmerman salute *her* when we came aboard to inspect last week. The only time a lower officer is saluted first by a senior officer is when the lower officer's been awarded the Nebula for Valor. He cracked a salute so hard I thought he'd hurt himself. I don't think he'd salute the Sol President if he could get away with it."

Now Private Bassinger was looking in awe at the corporal. "Where did you find this data?"

"I have access to the computer terminals in the armory area. I learned how to do data queries when I was away at school before my colony was wiped out. I found out data queries work the same on this ship's computer if you know how to search."

Private Bassinger smiled at the revelation. "You know what that means? We're gonna see some action."

* * *

"I tell you she's like nothing I've ever seen." A young Marine Private slapped down a card and glanced over at one of his companions. An equally young engineering tech next to him did not immediately respond but shook her head and looked at the next one around the galley table. "Bet?" she asked.

Warrant Officer Jason Gillam smiled. "Five," he responded.

The next two players threw down their cards in disgust while the Marine Private looked as if he would call. A young engineer put her hand on his and said, "Don't." He looked at her and her serious expression.

"He can't have the winning hand all the time."

"Maybe not, but if you want to have anything left to send home or when we get any leave, you'll listen to me," she replied. "Most of the pilots already owe this one."

He frowned and looked at the man across from them. Slowly he folded his cards on the table and moments later watched the pilot smile and rake in the chits.

Warrant Officer Gillam glanced up at the private and said, "You say the captain fights pretty good, eh?"

"She can wipe the floor with anyone in the Marine contingent, probably anyone else on this ship for that matter." His earnest look made the pilot smile.

"So, you haven't seen Commander Clear Sky in a fight, then?"

The whole table looked up at this remark, glancing at each other, then back at the pilot. Finally, the engineer spoke up, "We've never seen him at the workouts. We assumed he does alright because of his size but he didn't have her skills."

"Then you assume wrong, my friends. The captain picked the commander personally over more experienced officers, not just because he's a natural pilot, but because she might have to go off ship on a diplomatic mission with no other support but her shuttle pilot. He could take on a platoon of you Marines while hardly breaking a sweat. He is big, strong as an ox, and incredibly fast, as well. When he hits someone, bones tend to break, and people don't get up off the deck."

The group pondered that thought while another tech dealt the next hand.

The engineer's face screwed up in thought as she glanced at her cards and immediately folded. "Seems like we have a handful of old war veterans on this cruise. You'd think we were getting ready for war again."

The others nodded and turned their attention to their cards. Jason Gillam smiled.

Chapter Five

Rena Sheets stood on the bridge in her dress uniform with her senior staff officers. They were all there for one guest, an old man with an elaborate headdress of feathers and wearing what appeared to be animal skins. Commander Clear Sky stood in the center of the bridge while the old man walked from station to station, placing his hands on the consoles, murmuring something in a language she could not identify.

Clear Sky came to her only days before with his request. She knew he was from an Apache tribe in North America. She didn't question it as he had never made requests of any sort in the past. That made her curious. There weren't many from any indigenous tribe who sought a career in the Fleet. That and his sheer size made him an anomaly.

Commander Clear Sky stood impassive, a dark-haired rock of a man at six feet seven inches tall, with thick muscles coiling his arms and a barrel chest. He seemed to ignore the old man and stared out above him as if looking for something.

The old man continued around the bridge, stopping at the helm console and finally the command chair. Then he turned to Clear Sky. He reached up and placed a hand on the tall man's shoulder. He spoke at some length and Clear Sky only nodded.

Then with no farewell, the old man turned and walked off the bridge without another word. A young junior lieutenant exclaimed softly and wordlessly when she realized her charge had gone off without her and ran after him. The rest of the bridge crew turned to the captain, who announced, "Resume stations."

"Thank you, Captain," said Clear Sky.

"No problem, Commander, I know this meant a lot to you. I'll take any blessings I can get for this ship. I'm curious though, what did he tell you at the end?" She'd walked toward him and now stood in front of him craning her neck to look at his face.

Clear Sky looked uncomfortable, and glanced sideways at the crew, who were moving back to their usual stations.

"Come with me, Commander," said Rena. She led him off the bridge to her Day Cabin. Once there, she shut the hatch, giving them some privacy. "You can talk freely."

Clear Sky glanced around the small and simple office and returned his eyes to the captain's face.

"The Shaman told me of his visions, Captain. They were of my future and of this ship."

Rena stood waiting for him to go on. Clear Sky was not very talkative and some of the crew thought he was just rude. She knew it was because at heart, he was a shy man. A very large shy man, she reminded herself.

"The Shaman said it is my destiny never to return to my home. I will live a full life and have many children, but I will never see Earth again. He also said this ship carries a great destiny. That the Great Spirit inhabits her very being."

Rena raised her eyebrows, "Wow, that's something!" Before she could continue, Clear Sky raised his hand to stop her.

"He also had something to say about you, Captain. He said that you are like legends of old, a warrior woman, a shaman, and a tribal chief, all at the same time. You are wise and you have a destiny closely tied to this ship."

Rena smiled. "Alright, Commander, thank you for that. Was the Shaman here today from your tribe? I think I remember it was Apache."

Clear Sky gave a small shy smile that she knew few people ever saw. "Captain, I apologize, I should have introduced him more formally. Yes, he is my tribe's Shaman and Chief. He is also my grandfather."

She nodded in understanding, and he returned to the bridge.

* * *

In the control center for the ship's main gun, Senior Commander and Ship's Chief Engineer Curtis Renwald cursed loudly and fluently in at least four languages that his younger assistant could identify. They were doing power-up testing on the new graviton mass driver weapon system and Commander Renwald was not happy with the handling of the power systems.

"You're under-feeding the shield nodes again, damn it! Do you have ANY idea why this system has more shielding and more power controls than the engines themselves? Any at all!?" The other system techs in the area, not associated with these tests, were finding reasons to leave the room in a hurry.

"Well, sir. I, uh, I guess they want to make sure the weapons work right, sir. I guess." The young engineer was completely flustered. He didn't want to admit that his primary certification was in jump-drive engine systems, and he really had no idea what jump drive shield nodes might have to do with the ship's main gun. He vaguely remembered a one-day cross training class he'd done on the mass drivers at the Academy. It was a required course, but outside of his specialty and he didn't think he'd ever need the training since he wasn't a weapons tech. Besides, he'd met a very attractive red head the night before that class, and she'd introduced him to a very potent whiskey.

Commander Renwald appeared to be counting to some very high number, while the veins in his neck pulsed. It made the old scars on his face and head whiten, looking like he'd crawled through a pile of glass sometime in the past. Just as it seemed he was about to go off like a live grenade, the hatch opened, and the captain walked into the room. The young engineer and all the other techs in the room scrambled to attention.

"As you were. Commander, all going well?" She kept on walking through the compartment on her way somewhere else.

Commander Renwald's face instantly composed itself as he said, "Yes, Captain, all is well. Just testing the new systems."

"Excellent," she said just before she walked through the hatch at the other end of the room and closed it behind her.

The young engineer glanced back at the commander, expecting him to pick up where he left off. Instead, a calm settled over his face. He looked up at the young engineer and said, "The basic idea behind this weapon is that we can accelerate a solid piece of metal or even some rock we find in space at substantial speed toward whatever we want to shoot. The projectile ends up with as much as two hundred megatons of kinetic energy when it leaves the gauss field. Impressive, but in space it's still going too slow to hit an enemy ship at more than half a light second distance."

The commander looked intently at the young engineer. "You do know what a half-light second is in kilometers, don't you, son?"

"Uh, a hundred and fifty thousand kilometers, sir."

"Correct! Now two hundred megatons of kinetic energy would destroy almost any Angel ship we encountered in the war, but the trick is to hit it from much farther away than that. Most ships use lasers and have an effective range of five to ten light seconds. A simple mass driver has a pitiful effective range, that's why most navies stopped using them. We beat the Angels during the war only because some brave crews jumped in front of the enemy ships to launch their first-generation weapons at point blank range. Sometimes they got away after the attack, but other times they got off their one shot only to be destroyed. They traded their ship for one of the enemy's."

The miserable assistant engineer just stared at the controls. He felt he should say something, but he couldn't get his brain to engage. Then he had a glimmer of an idea.

"Jump drive tech?"

"You got it, m'boy. Now we generate a small micro jump field for about a second in front of the mass driver so the projectile jumps and reappears just short of the target. It crosses the distance in no time and extends our effective range to as much as eight to ten light seconds, the same as a ship's laser weapons but ungodly more powerful. Isn't that great?!"

The commander reached around his assistant and reset the shield node controls. "But if we don't have enough power in the shield nodes to contain the jump field, it wobbles. Do you know what happens when the field wobbles?"

"Uh, I..."

"If the field wobbles while in use, which happens if the power nodes send power to the field unevenly, we will *not* see our fine new weapon work as expected. Instead, we'll get a small black hole working hard to get started. Since it doesn't have enough mass to sustain itself, the resultant energy will create feedback resulting in a spectacular explosion." His voice rose in volume as he continued. "Now if you create a feedback explosion on Captain Sheets' nice new ship, you'll soon wish you were at the center of a sustaining black hole, because that would be a safer place than standing in front of the captain trying to explain what went wrong. Do I make myself perfectly clear?" He leaned toward the young engineer, the scars on his face and head flashing bright red.

The young engineer's eyes had grown large during this little harangue, and he squeaked, "Crystal, sir."

* * *

Cadet Sonja Mortan was going over the last of the supplies being loaded on the ship, as displayed on the wall in the conference room. "We're going to have to squeeze some of these last things in wherever we can fit them, maybe any unoccupied crew cabins. For some reason we're getting all our scheduled deliveries today."

"Agreed, I am having this last load sent to the auxiliary crew quarters on the engineering deck since they are mostly spare parts." Shenna's voice made this work so agreeable.

"Good," Sonni sighed. She stretched and thought maybe it was time to contact the captain. In just six days the ship was packed with as much as it could hold without stacking things in the corridors. Shenna interrupted her thoughts.

"You have two minutes to report for a meeting in briefing room ten on the command deck, Sonni. I suggest you hurry."

Sonni blinked in surprise. "What? What meeting?"

"The one the captain has just called," Shenna said. Sonni didn't waste another moment and bolted out through the hatch. She jogged past other crew running in all directions. There was no sign of anyone in dock worker uniforms. She jogged over to a bounce tube on the rising side and lightly jumped up into it. She rose past three decks and reached her arm out toward the wall, causing the field to slow her down. She stepped over the opening onto the Command deck and resumed jogging down the passageway.

Maybe Shenna told the captain that we were almost done, she thought. *If I passed the test, maybe she'll let me stay as part of the crew and assign me to another officer.* Her thoughts were interrupted as she turned a corner and saw other crew standing outside one of the larger briefing rooms the captain used for formal meetings with all her senior officers. She stopped next to an officer who looked startled by her arrival.

"Can I help you, Cadet?" He wore a Fleet uniform with the rank of a junior lieutenant.

She snapped to attention and said, "Cadet Sonja Mortan reporting as ordered to briefing room ten."

He looked her up and down before turning his back and ignoring her. *Oh, great. Another one. I can't wait to not be a cadet anymore,* she thought.

Since she could see through the open hatch that no one else was in the room, she entered and found a seat near the door. Some of the others outside followed her example and sat down. There were a few senior officers who looked old enough to have served in the war. One bore a scar on his face that apparently the regenerators couldn't heal. Another man wearing a senior engineering uniform also had scars and had a white streak across his hair that started on one side and went around the top of his head. A very tall muscular man walked in and sat across from Sonni. His face seemed to be chiseled from stone. His eyes didn't miss much. He scanned the room until his eyes found hers and he gave her a short nod. Before she could return it, a figure sat down next to her, and she turned to find she was next to the captain.

The captain said, "I'll make this brief as we don't have much time. I am moving up our launch to one hour from now. I wanted to get all my department heads together quickly to go over any last issues." She pointed to the engineer. "Renwald?"

"We're good to go, Captain."

She nodded and turned to the tall man. Sonni noted his rank as Commander. "Clear Sky, are we registered with lunar traffic control to leave on time?"

He nodded and the captain turned to Sonni. "Purser, are we finished loading?"

"Yes, Captain." Sonni automatically replied before her brain could process the fact that the captain had called *her* purser. The rest of the meeting passed in a blur while the captain continued to ask for status checks from the others.

Then the Captain stood and said, "Thank you all again for making this happen, I know the schedule was accelerated. We'll have more time to meet with each other and get settled when we're out of space dock and on our way to our first assignment."

She turned to leave the room when a voice blurted out, "But captain, I don't understand." It was the young officer that Sonni had met outside the briefing room.

Captain Sheets turned back and looked hard at the young man. "What is it you don't understand, Mr. Van Belson?"

"I've been supervising the loading of supplies since I came on board. I thought *I* was going to be the ship's purser."

The room was silent as the captain stared at him and her eyes, now gray, flashed. "Okay, Junior Lieutenant, how many weeks of food do we have on board at this time?"

He frowned. "I don't know off-hand, I would guess about six months. That's all we have room for."

The captain turned to Sonni who was already shaking her head. "Purser?"

Sonni said, "We have thirty-six months of food on board, Captain, at normal usage. More if we go on short rations."

"That's impossible! We don't have the physical space for that much food. This is insane. Captain, I think you've been hoodwinked." He was red-faced and glared at Sonni as if she had insulted his honor.

The captain sighed and pulled a computer terminal from the center of the table toward her. She typed in a query and displayed the results on the wall. It stated the food supply in metric tons with a use estimate of thirty-six months and twelve days. The captain turned a stony gaze to the young officer and said, "There is more to being a purser than counting boxes of supplies. I was able to find someone who could think out-of-the-box to best organize our supplies and spares. You graduated last year top of your class, with high honors. I thought you would be a good addition to this crew. I still do, even if that isn't as purser. Once we are launched, we can discuss your assignment. We can still use all the help we can get."

The young man continued standing, shaking with rage. "Captain, I came aboard to be one of your senior officers."

Captain Sheets shrugged. "That's not in the cards, I'm sorry. We can discuss this at another time, in private."

"Then I want to apply for an immediate transfer." He looked indignant, glancing around the room looking for any support. He was met by stony silence and a few raised eyebrows.

The captain sighed. "I don't have time for this. Granted." To the room, she announced, "Thank you, everyone. We launch in an hour." Then she turned, opened the hatch, and left the room. Van Belson continued to stand there as everyone else left the room, leaving him alone.

Sonni walked the passageways in a daze. She had thought her job was completed, but now it seemed her real job was just beginning. She found herself back in her cabin without remembering how she got there. She stepped in and as she secured the hatch, Shenna's voice startled her.

"I ordered your uniform to be ready for you. I'm sorry there was no time for you to put it on before the meeting. The captain moved the meeting time up at the last moment when she decided to move up our launch, and I was caught unprepared."

There on her bunk was a full duty uniform with Fleet patches and ship insignia, as well as rank badge. Sonni stared at it, looking surprised. "Lieutenant? Full Lieutenant? Why would the captain do this?"

Shenna replied, "When I informed the captain that loading was in the final stages, along with the summary of supplies loaded, she told me that it helped her make up her mind to move up the launch. Before I could tell you, she then called her staff meeting."

"But why Full Lieutenant?"

"Because that is the minimum rank for a department head," Shenna stated. "I've also made arrangements to move you to a cabin near the other senior officers."

Sonni collapsed on the bed, sitting next to the uniform. It was all too much to handle right now. Part of her wanted to treat this like just another Cadet exercise. She had to accept she was done with the Academy and now part of the crew. Wasn't this the goal all along? Yes, but jumping to being a department head right out of the academy was not something she'd ever considered.

Shenna interrupted her thoughts. "You will want to get into your uniform and get to the bridge for the launch. The captain wants all her department heads on the bridge for that."

Sonni was confused again. "But the purser is not normally a bridge level position."

"During official ship functions, even the purser has a station on the bridge. It is little more than a communication station, but from there you can coordinate all supplies throughout the ship. In battle, you maintain weapons inventories. Other duties include providing supplies for the crew, assigning cabins and roommates, and so forth."

"Moons and asteroids!" Sonni's head throbbed just thinking about all this. Minutes later, she was dressed and looking at herself in the mirror on the door of her fresher. Her reflection brought an emotional storm, and she bit her lip to keep the tears from flowing. At first glance, she thought she saw Lieutenant Kathryn Jackson, the first Fleet officer she'd ever encountered when a visiting Fleet vessel arrived just after her colony experienced a planet-wide earthquake. Meeting that officer and wanting to be just like her drove Sonni's decision to join the Fleet. She had concentrated on getting through each class and each semester to be the first person from her family, her settlement, and possibly the continent on her colony to get through Fleet Academy. It was her way of honoring them. She never thought of what it would be like to finally be done. It pained her to think there was no family left to share this accomplishment with.

For that matter, she had only a few acquaintances from the Academy. She'd made up her mind when she got into the Academy that there would be no time for fooling around, no romances, parties, and so forth. That was something else to think about. Could she afford a relationship now that she had arrived at her goal? That might have been possible if she were just part of the crew, but now, she was an officer in charge of a department. She sighed and put that thought away for another day as she gave her new uniform a final brush down. "There is too much to do right now, so get with it, Ca...no, Lieutenant!" With that pronouncement, she nodded at her reflection and left her cabin for the bridge.

* * *

Lieutenant Van Belson stood in his cabin stuffing his clothing into a duffel bag and shaking his head. He stopped when he realized that he was going to have to explain to his family why he transferred off a ship he'd been handpicked to be on.

"You're an idiot. You're ten times a fool. You had to open your goddamned mouth to the captain. What in the hell were you thinking? So what if she makes someone else the purser? You knew this was going to be a choice assignment a year ago." He continued packing while muttering, "stupid, stupid, stupid."

Chapter Six

Raleigh had his few belongings in a single carry bag and looked for the next transport to the lunar construction yards. There was a delay. All transport craft seemed to be currently tied up. He frowned as he looked around for a chronometer. He glanced at a young lieutenant next to him as she held up her sleeve to see her built-in chronometer and computer interface. It was part of the fabric of her sleeve. *I'll have to get one of those*, he thought, then glanced wryly down at himself. *I must get a whole new uniform for that matter. I guess it will have to wait until I get to the ship*. It had already been a long and interesting day, and his leg began to throb as it always did when he was on his feet for hours.

He found transport two hours later. The single crewman/pilot frowned when he stepped on board. "Do you need to go to the Lunar construction yards, sir?"

"Yes," Raleigh answered, trying to keep the smile on his face genuine looking to keep his exasperation from showing through.

"We've all been ordered back. I just made the last run." The pilot was starting to shut the controls down.

"So, you were ordered to deliver all the crew to the new ship then?"

"Yes, sir." The pilot was now getting out of his seat.

"Then sit back down, you have one more to deliver," stated Raleigh.

The pilot frowned. "What is your position on the ship, if I may ask?"

"Executive Officer, by order of Senior Fleet Admiral Yunkee, at the request of Admiral Jack Berry." Raleigh smiled as the pilot stopped, blinked rapidly a few times, then sat back down and started powering up the transport.

"That ship is launching very soon, Commander. They suddenly announced they were moving up the launch time. I'm not sure we're going to make it." The pilot flipped switches and went through the checklist as if this were a waste of time.

"Yes, we are Lieutenant, or you'll be flying waste collection runs to Neptune station by next week." Raleigh sat down in the co-pilot seat and buckled his restraints, noticing in satisfaction that the pilot was now hurrying through the final part of his checklist.

Three hours later, Commander Raleigh was getting anxious as he looked at the chronometer and made some mental calculations as to the shuttle's speed and flow through lunar traffic. "We're not going to get there on time unless we move it."

"Yes, sir. I understand but I can't do anything about the traffic control. They're keeping everything away from the area and my request to deliver the last crew seems to have been lost." The pilot seemed frustrated and worried about what this passenger would do if they missed the launch.

Raleigh glanced at the traffic around them, listened to the traffic control banter for a moment, then reached for the controls. The pilot opened his mouth to object then closed it as Raleigh turned to him and with a dazzling smile asked, "Can I take her for a bit?"

"I assume you're certified, sir?"

"Oh, yes, my friend."

"You have the controls," the pilot nodded and pulled his hands off the thruster controls as Raleigh took them.

The pilot looked like he was fighting nausea as Raleigh flipped the shuttle over on its back and dove down through a hole in traffic. The lights went out and the support fields dropped off-line. The pilot's hands were white on his seat as he glanced over at Raleigh and watched him switching more systems off while keying traffic control on the Comm. "Lunar control this is shuttle 242. Mayday, mayday, I am declaring an emergency. I've lost main controls. Mayday, mayday," Raleigh stated this in a calm voice, then turned off power to the Comm.

"Are you nuts?" The pilot blurted out before the shuttle flipped end over front and he clamped his mouth shut, probably to avoid losing his lunch.

"There are some who would say so," Raleigh smiled as he answered. It was easier for him as he could brace for the movements under his control. Traffic in the area scattered and he spotted a clear path to the docks. The shuttle's gyrations smoothed out and he increased speed until they entered the docks, where he braked suddenly with controlled bursts of the thrusters and coasted slowly to a docking port. He flipped shuttle function controls back on, leaving the Comm for last. The excited chatter on the traffic control channel he ignored.

"Thanks for your help, Lunar control, we have regained power and control again. Shuttle 242 out." He said this last as the shuttle kissed the docking port and he keyed the airlock auto-seal.

"Thanks for the ride, you have control again." With that he unbuckled and walked off the shuttle with his bag, leaving the pilot staring after him in total shock.

The airlock closed and he heard traffic control over the Comm, "Shuttle 242, hold fast and stand down. Please wait for security to board your shuttle and then you can explain your actions. A Fleet tow will take your shuttle into custody for an investigation. Security will arrive in thirty minutes. Thank you for your cooperation."

* * *

Commander Renwald turned to another station and nodded. The tech there typed in some control commands, and everyone could feel the vibration as various connections were withdrawn from the ship, cutting off water, waste removal, and wired communication lines. The tech watched his board and turned to give the thumbs up to Renwald. He spoke up clearly, "Utilities cleared."

"Confirm, utilities cleared," came a voice from the bridge. Renwald hit mute on his console and said, "Ship utilities to internal mode."

The Utilities Tech again hit various commands into his console and turned back to Renwald, nodding.

Renwald punched his console, turning mute off, saying, "All utilities now in internal mode."

From what he knew of this new fancy computer, all the manual controls were unnecessary, but it was good training for the crew to go through all this step by step. At this rate, it would only take another ten minutes to complete the checklist and fly the ship out of dock.

"Clear external power," came the next command from the bridge.

Renwald nodded at the Tech, and she threw all six external breakers off at the same time. Some lights blinked very briefly, and he watched system after system go from stand-by to ready on internal power.

"External power cleared and we're running on internal power only," he said. He glanced at the tech and forced himself to smile at her. *Kids*, he thought. *We're running this ship with kids. What was Sheets thinking?* The young tech smiled back and waited for his next command.

* * *

Raleigh got through the final security checkpoint at Luna control and hurried down a long empty dock leading to the ship. He finally walked into the ship's gangway, as vibrations rumbled through his feet. Connections with the ship were being withdrawn from the dock. He was cutting it close. This ship was about to leave. As he stepped onto the ship, he crashed into a young officer who was running off the ship via the onboarding side of the gangway.

"Take me to the bridge," Raleigh said, using his best command voice.

The junior lieutenant looked at him, startled, saw the rank of Senior Commander and gasped, "Yes, sir. But sir, I need to be leaving."

"Time for that later," Raleigh said, turning him around. "Take me to the bridge." He watched as the poor kid dropped his bags on the gangway and the two of them entered the ship at a trot.

They jogged down corridors until they came to a set of bounce tubes. Raleigh watched as the young man stepped to the edge and hopped up into the tube. Once clear of the deck it appeared that gravity was off, and his momentum brought him up the tube at a steady rate of speed. Raleigh swore to himself at his first brush with new technology and tried to follow his guide's example. He jumped off into the middle of the tube and found himself quickly shooting by the lieutenant. The lieutenant grabbed his ankle and Raleigh watched as he reached out with an arm touching the wall. Linked as they were, they both slowed, and Raleigh could feel force fields tugging at him. The lieutenant pushed off the back of the tube, lining them up to pop out at a specific level. The lieutenant landed on the deck and turned to help Raleigh as he stumbled and fell on his face.

Raleigh felt very foolish at not knowing how to handle this basic component of the new ship and wondered what other surprises awaited him. The deck under him was cold on his face and he was aware of the smell of fresh paint. He stood up, brushing off and straightening his uniform. Then they both felt another rumble through the deck and the lights blinked.

The junior lieutenant pointed at a set of double doors at the end of the corridor and said pleadingly, "Sir, I need to go. The bridge is through those doors." He didn't wait for Raleigh to answer but turned and plunged down a tube next to the one they had just come out of. Frowning, Raleigh walked to the bridge.

* * *

Sonni was glad she had nothing to add to the bridge launch checklist and made herself as inconspicuous as possible at her station. She had a command console under her fingers and a display in front of her showing statistics on supplies and crew. As the last of the dockworkers left the ship, she watched Souls Aboard status tick down and rest on 1222. A new indicator appeared in a pop-up box, indicating Outstanding Supply Requisitions at fourteen, ticking over to sixteen as she watched. She brought that window up to full screen. It was requests for various supplies for the crew. Everything from deodorant to uniform parts and insignia. She highlighted all of them as she read them and clicked "Approved." They disappeared from the queue to be quickly replaced by another seven requests. *Maybe I should wait and go through these at a more normal time*, she thought. She minimized that window and looked through some of the other windows on her display. Financial Requests caught her eye and after reading the requests, she realized that they were from crew members on how to handle various financial transactions and wills. Along with other tasks, she was also the ship's banker.

She sighed. She was about to glance back at the controlled bedlam of the bridge, when a display number changed, and she saw Souls Aboard change to 1223. Seconds later, she heard another bridge station report that all hatches were closed, and dockside gangways had been retracted. She keyed commands to display change logs for that window. They showed the last record as "New Unknown Crew member".

I wonder who this is.

She glanced over her shoulder in time to see the bridge hatch slide open and a tall older man step onto the bridge. He had dark hair with streaks of silver gray on each side of his head and a lined face. He was tall, at about six-foot-two inches and sported a lean build without any of the paunch on most men his age, which she guessed to be around fifty. He was wearing a Fleet uniform that looked a little worn and about ten years out of date. But the Senior Commander's rank insignia was shiny and new.

She wondered if the captain knew about this late arrival and turned to watch. The captain's chair was on the opposite side of the bridge from Sonni's station. The captain had just finished talking to Engineering and noticed most of her bridge crew seemed to have their attention elsewhere. She swiveled the command chair around to face the newcomer.

Sonni watched the captain's face go through a series of tightly controlled expressions from shock, surprise, anger, exasperation, and back to anger again, before all expressions were quickly erased. In her smoothest voice, she said, "So good of you to join us, Mr. Raleigh."

The Chief Engineer's face on the main bridge display turned white as snow. "Good God," he said out loud, "Where in hell did she find *him*?"

The noise level on the bridge dropped to only the sound of various consoles and equipment humming as everyone watched the interplay between these two. Commander Raleigh appeared absolutely stunned. His jaw dropped open; his face paled. After a good five seconds, he shook himself and closed his mouth, snapping to attention, and said, "Commander John Paul Raleigh reporting as ordered, Captain."

"Welcome, Mr. Raleigh," said the captain evenly. Sonni wondered what there was between these two. They were both old enough to have served in the war. Maybe they served together.

Chief Engineer Renwald's voice sounded through the comms again. His face had recovered from his earlier shock. "Captain, I didn't get that? We confirm all engines are ready for flight."

Raleigh was still standing there straight as an arrow. The captain tilted her head to one side as if considering something, then swung her chair back around to face front.

"Mr. Raleigh," she said, "I believe you know how to fly a starship. Would you be so kind as to take us out?" She nodded once in Commander Clear Sky's direction.

Immediately, the pilot pulled himself out of his console without a word.

Commander Raleigh frowned at the back of the captain's head for a second and, dropping his bag, walked around to the pilot console. He glanced up at the taller Clear Sky, who looked at Raleigh with flat expressionless eyes. Raleigh nodded to him as if in thanks and inserted himself into the pilot controls, placing his feet and legs into control harnesses. Sitting in the pilot seat, he adjusted the remaining controls around him with a familiarity Sonni knew must have come from years of experience. A starship pilot wore his station like a suit of armor, controlling the ship with his whole body.

As he did this, the captain continued going down the last of the checklist with Engineering and Dock Control. Raleigh was fully integrated into the pilot console by the time the formalities were finished. Clear Sky stood impassively beside him.

"Thank you, Dock Control," the captain finished. "We confirm a green board and free clearance to launch."

"Clear sailing, *Excalibur II*," said the voice of Port Control over the comm. Sonni held her breath, hands hovering over her console even though she had nothing to do with launching.

"Mr. Raleigh, take us out of dock at dead slow, if you will."

"Confirm, Captain, dead slow," answered Raleigh. Sonni watched as he concentrated on his controls. Although no one could feel the movement, the dock structure slowly retreated to the sides of the giant front display.

The captain clicked a control on her console. Her voice was broadcast ship wide. "Attention crew of the *Excalibur II*. I want to congratulate you on being part of mankind's first formal exploration and reconnaissance mission since the war. We designed this ship to assist in this endeavor and to continue the great legacy of the name Excalibur. We will also be keeping an eye out for any activity from the Angels while we explore. My congratulations to everyone for making us ready so quickly. Once we're underway, we will settle down to normal ship operations. That is all."

Suddenly, Sonni realized Commander Raleigh must have been that last person to board. She keyed in his name and his record summary and latest orders came up as the Executive Officer of the starship *Excalibur II*.

Executive Officer. Oh my, that means I will be reporting to him from now on. Since he just came aboard, he won't even have a cabin assigned—which is my responsibility. I better get busy.

* * *

Raleigh concentrated on keeping the ship rock steady. He remembered seeing the size of this ship through the ports on the construction dock when he came aboard. It was huge. He expected it to move like a pig, but it surprised him by reacting to the slightest touch or movement at the controls. It didn't help that Commander Clear Sky loomed right over him and he was still getting over the shock of seeing Rena Sheets after all these years. Then to hear this ship was named *Excalibur*. His thoughts raced.

Did she know I was coming aboard? Did she ask for me specifically? How does she feel about me after all this time? What has happened to her? God, she looks stunning! Am I going to be able to do this? Will this cause me any problems? Is she pissed at me for the way I left? I tried to explain. I feel like such a fool. Why did I take this assignment? Did the Admiral know? Of course, he did. I blindly walked right into this, God I'm an idiot. Stupid, stupid, stupid. I bloody well hope I'm up to Rena's expectations. Excalibur! Bloody hell!

Time seemed to slow down as the ship passed through the last of the dock infrastructure. On their port side was a ship identical to *Excalibur II* but only about halfway through construction. Further down was another Excalibur class ship with only the framework completed. Ahead was empty space.

"Helm, break lunar orbit and increase speed to half sub-light," the captain ordered.

"Confirm, Captain, half speed," Raleigh answered and this time everyone would feel the speed increase as the force restraints worked to keep up with the thrust. The rest of Luna dropped away from view. Earth rose briefly in the corner of the screen, then also dropped away as the ship headed out into space. *Wow,* he thought, *this ship moves like a dream.*

"Come to course 317—243—140 when you pass the outer buoy, Mr. Raleigh."

"Confirm course 317—243—140."

"Mr. Raleigh, you don't need to repeat it," stated the captain in a neutral tone.

Raleigh frowned again but made no further comment. It was only then he noticed the course flashing on the bottom of the main view screen.

The outer buoy passed by to port, and the stars shifted as the new course change was made. The ship was on a course that would take it out of the way of most planets and toward deep space.

"Mr. Raleigh, thank you very much, that was excellent. Mr. Clear Sky, if you would, please resume your post, we will prepare for our first jump in one hour. While we're in known space, we'll keep our jumps to less than five light years at a time until Commander Renwald feels the jump engine is ready for something longer."

Raleigh set the controls on automatic and got out of the pilot console. He felt like he had been there for hours instead of a few minutes. Clear Sky reentered the console after he exited and adjusted the controls around himself without comment. Raleigh stood there feeling foolish, not knowing what else to do.

Captain Rena Sheets watched him standing there, probably assessing him.

"Mr. Raleigh, if you would join me in my Day Cabin, please. Comm, thank Port Control and confirm we are clear for jump from Sol System. Lieutenant Reese, you have the

Conn." The captain turned and headed to the back of the bridge. It took Raleigh a moment to follow her.

A serious looking young woman with short blond hair passed by him and sat on the edge of the command chair. Raleigh had to fight not to stare at her. She appeared to have just graduated from the Academy and here she was already filling in as Conn, already a full lieutenant. Another officer took over at Weapons console, watching Lieutenant Reese.

Raleigh followed Captain Sheets into her Day Cabin, a small room set up as an office, which also had a pull-down bunk on one wall and a private head. Sheets immediately sat in the chair next to her desk and swiveled it around to face Raleigh.

Commander Raleigh realized there were no other chairs and went into parade rest, feet apart and hands clasped behind his back. Rena Sheets was older than when he had last seen her, more confident and self-assured. Her shorter blond hair framed her face like a lion. Some lines around her eyes and a few strands of clear hair were the only indications of her age. She was an athlete with toned arms and rounded shoulders that showed she worked out often. Her green-gray eyes burned into him with an intensity that made him uncomfortable. Those eyes had haunted his dreams and kept him going when he otherwise prayed for death.

* * *

Rena kept her best poker face while looking at Raleigh. Time had not been kind to him. His face was lined, like someone much older. His hair had gone almost white on the sides of his head and was longer than the current style. He looked thinner, too, like he had lost a lot of weight and was just starting to put it back on.

Of all the favors she had asked of the Fleet, he was the biggest. She had requested should he ever return from his deep cover work with Intelligence, that they offer him the Executive Officer slot. She never expected them to make good on that promise. She now owed Admiral Berry a lifetime supply of scotch. Raleigh's blue eyes seemed to have trouble looking directly at her.

"So, Mr. Raleigh. I take it this was a surprise?"

"You could say that. Admiral Berry didn't mention *you* were the captain when he gave me the option of this assignment," he replied, still looking over her shoulder.

"Is this going to cause you any problems?" she asked.

He frowned, "I don't think so, Captain. If you will allow me a little time to catch up on things, I'll have this crew whipped into shape for you."

"I'm sure you will. You were always my first choice, you know. Fleet never would give me your status. I wasn't even sure sometimes you were still alive."

"I know, that's the way it is in Intelligence. Although, I did tell Admiral Berry if it were ever verified that I was lost, he must find a way of notifying you. Unofficially, of course."

"Yes, I know. That's how I found out you were still alive. He came to me about five years ago to tell me that you were considered dead. He couldn't absolutely verify it or tell me the circumstances. Then six months later, he met me for a drink and told me they were wrong, and you were still active. Two years later, you were lost again and a year after that you popped back up. The poor man was embarrassed at constantly coming back to let me know. That's when I made him promise to get you on my ship if you came back and wanted out of Intelligence."

Raleigh looked stunned. The amount of effort she'd gone to get him was humbling. She put her career at risk even discussing this with Intelligence.

"Yes, well, I agreed to stay on for a year before I retire," he said finally. "I think that will be plenty of time for me to get the crew in shape and we can then figure out who's best to take over as Exec."

"A year," she replied, smiling. "Did the old liar happen to mention that we're not expected back to Sol for at least a decade? That was one of my reasons for picking such a young crew. I expect to have to replace some of my senior officers from within the ship during the mission."

Raleigh frowned. "No, he didn't mention that. I assumed this was a shakedown voyage. Show everyone what humans could do and all that."

"So, yet again, you rashly jump into something without looking at all the consequences. Isn't this where *we* left off?" She cocked her head to one side and gave him a half smile.

"I suppose so," he frowned. "Once the job is done, I'm sure I can find my way back home again. I've learned how to get around the galaxy since the last time we saw each other."

"Yes, I'm sure you have." She appraised him seriously for another moment and said, "Get settled in and updated. We'll get together and work out a routine. We're headed out there to map star systems, since our allies seem to keep forgetting to share their charts with us. We're also to keep an eye on the border and make sure the Angels aren't up to something new. On top of that, we have a side mission we need to get through first. We can talk about that later."

"Sounds good, Captain." He paused. "Am I dismissed?"

"Yes, you can go." As he opened the hatch, she said, "And nice to see you again, J.P."

He looked back over his shoulder. "Thank you, Captain." He stepped out and shut the hatch behind him.

Rena sighed to herself. "*Captain*". She was no longer Rena to him. Could she ever be again?

* * *

Back on the bridge, Commander Raleigh closed the hatch to the Day Cabin and looked at the crew, busy at their stations. A young woman closed her station and walked over to him. "Sir, if you will follow me, I'll show you to your cabin."

He blinked. "Best idea I've heard all day. Lead on, Lieutenant." At least this woman looked like she was out of the academy for more than a minute. He retrieved his bag from where he had dropped it and the two of them headed off the bridge. He was led around the corridor from the drop tubes to another passageway where she stopped in front of a cabin. Apparently, senior officer cabins were on the same level as the bridge, in the center of the ship.

"Here you go, sir. I took the liberty of updating your uniform from stores and ordering all the usual gear."

"Thank you. It looks like you're on top of things." He opened the hatch and paused. "This may sound like a silly question, but what is your position?"

"Purser, sir." She smiled a little shyly.

"Ah, well of course on a ship this size, that makes sense. Thanks again and nice to meet you, Lieutenant..."

"Mortan, sir. Lieutenant Sonja Mortan."

"Well, thanks again, Lieutenant Mortan. If everyone around here is on the ball like you, it will make my life very easy."

"Yes, sir," was all she said as Commander Raleigh entered his cabin. He noted how she'd straightened with the compliment. When he studied the crew roster, hers would be one of the first files he wanted to read. She seemed promising.

* * *

Lieutenant Mortan returned to the bridge thinking about the new first officer. The dynamic between him and the captain was interesting. It seemed obvious that they had some history. She sat back at her console and made some notes for the next day. She listened to the others talking on the bridge. The Astrogator was explaining the scheduled jump with the officer at Tactical.

"We're currently in known space, meaning we know this area of the galaxy pretty well. For now, we're keeping our jumps to every three to five light years until Engineering is comfortable with how the jump engine is functioning. This is the first time we're using it. After that we can go much further but it will depend on how good our star charts are."

The young man at Tactical nodded as he absorbed this. "I thought we could get where we need to go in one jump."

"If we know what is on the other side of the jump, yes. But once we leave space much beyond where our colonies are, our charts aren't as reliable. We must make shorter jumps and record the stars around us, calculate their movement through the galaxy, and then figure out where to jump next. Part of our mission is to chart our route so others can follow when we get these charts back to Sol."

Sonni nodded to herself matching the officer at Tactical. There was so much more to learn.

* * *

Raleigh closed the hatch behind him and took stock of his new home. It was a nice little suite, with a desk and chair in one corner and a bunk in the other. A door to a private fresher told him this ship treated its officers well. On the bunk were multiple uniforms both formal and utilities. The fresher was fully stocked with the usual things from ship's stores. It didn't appear he would have to order anything else. He stowed his uniforms in a small closet as he checked everything out.

He sat on the side of the bunk and dropped the bag next to him. Slowly he raised his right leg and stretched it out along the bunk. His leg ached as it usually did after a long day. His fingers kneaded his thigh, and he quickly found the ridge where his leg ended, and the artificial leg began.

Damn it all but she was right. I jumped into this without looking closely at the details. Bloody hell. Stupid, stupid, stupid.

Chapter Seven

After Raleigh left her Day Cabin, Rena Sheets sighed, thinking back twelve years to the end of the war. *Excalibur* had been sacrificed and her crew's part in the war was over. The second battle took place without them, and it was after this battle that the war just stopped. The Angels had retreated behind their own lines. All the human ships from the Fleet had returned to Sol system and docked on or near the Fleet facility on the Moon. Among the allied races, politics played the largest role in what would come next.

So began days of endless meetings to review the records, logs, and personal accounts of all the surviving crews. That's when she found out that, instead of being praised, Raleigh was under attack. Relatives of those killed when he rammed the ship into the Angel dreadnought sought his court martial. They didn't understand warfare and the kinds of decisions that had to be made in the heat of battle. With the sudden peace, a price must be paid, and Raleigh was the most convenient target.

Raleigh, for his part, tried to ignore it. He was only interested in finding the man who had betrayed the Fleet by selling intelligence to the Angels. From the bridge of the dreadnaught, they'd seen the traitor escape. Fleet learned that the traitor, Paul Williams, had been a member of Fleet Intelligence. Raleigh wanted to go after him, but Command seemed to ignore his pleas.

After Rena painfully recounted, again, their last battle, a senior admiral let her know that she was getting a medal and a promotion. She didn't feel she deserved either one. Instead, she asked about Raleigh. The Admiral frowned and suggested that for her future career she should distance herself from Mr. Raleigh. That response only made her angry. The Admiral mentioned that Raleigh was leaving the Fleet and joining the Intelligence service. The discussion ended with the admiral saying that Raleigh likely wouldn't survive his first mission, anyway. That only made her more determined to seek Raleigh out.

She found him in a passageway. He was sitting on a bench in front of a viewport overlooking Luna City. He looked tired and haggard. The temporary prosthetic leg the Fleet had given him appeared to cause some pain. She sat on the bench beside him. They stared out the viewport for some minutes before she felt compelled to speak.

"Why, J.P.? Why are you doing this?" Her whispered voice was so quiet, he could barely hear her. "Why are you chucking your career to start chasing after a man who spent his whole life in Intelligence? He already has a reputation as the best shadow man in the business. You'll never catch him."

"It's something I must do. I have to try. If he's so good, I'll just have to learn to be better."

After a moment she continued. "They've offered me third in command on a destroyer leaving on patrol in two days. That should have been your slot. You worked your ass off for it. I know more than anyone that we wouldn't have made it back without you. You're the only reason any of us are still alive. This should be your reward, not mine."

She lapsed into silence. His mouth stayed firm, but he couldn't bring himself to look her in the eyes. In the reflection off the viewport, he could see the tears running down her face.

"I'm sorry, Sheets, my mind is made up."

She sighed and said, "Quit being so damn formal. Call me Rena. We're not shipmates anymore."

He seemed to consider that for a moment. She wondered if he suspected that she considered him more than just a shipmate. He was always so professional and the walls he kept up around himself were as solid as a ship's hull.

"I'm sorry then, Rena. Let me say that I think you deserve the promotion. Can I at least take you to dinner? A promotion deserves a little celebration."

She stared at him, eyes wide with surprise. "John Paul Raleigh, are you asking me on a date?"

"Well, yes," he blinked, looking confused.

She wasn't going to let this opportunity go to waste. "Okay, then pick me up at the Fleet B.O.Q., room 8716, at 2000 hours." She looked him up and down critically. "And for once, please be out of uniform. We're not on duty!"

Raleigh arrived at her quarters at 19:55 and buzzed her door. She answered the buzzer immediately and stepped into the corridor to appraise his reaction. Her shimmering red gown was gathered on one shoulder. It was a low-cut affair with seductive slits that showed an ample amount of leg. To others, it looked painted to her body from the waist up. She smiled at his reaction, he appeared to be quite stunned.

He cleared his throat. "Well, my, my, my. This is something special, and something this special deserves a special dinner." He linked her arm in his, and sniffed, his eyes going distant.

"Like it? It's called Intoxication," Rena said.

"Aptly named," he replied.

As they walked, Rena noticed his new suit. She suspected he hadn't owned any civilian clothes before tonight.

He took her to a restaurant at one end of the huge Fleet base. This one seemed to cater to locals and high-ranking Fleet officers. The waiter came over and proceeded to ask questions of Raleigh in Italian. Rena was startled when Raleigh answered in kind. The waiter went away, and Raleigh turned his smile to her.

"I hope you don't mind; I ordered for both of us. If you don't like it, you can blame me."

As the first course arrived, they began their meal. In the long silences in between bites, he seemed to drink in her eyes.

For her part, Rena was flustered. She had always looked up to Raleigh as a mentor. But for the first time, she saw him relaxed, and she liked what she saw. She even admitted to herself that she had fantasized about having a relationship if not for the war. Now, she had to work to keep herself from blushing every time he looked over at her. She felt like a teenager.

Raleigh raised his glass, "I propose a toast, to the *Excalibur*! The best ship in the fleet—and to all her crew in eternal sleep."

"Hear, hear!" She replied and they both tossed down their drinks quickly, lest emotions get the better of them. The toast was like ripping a bandage off an unhealed wound.

As soon as Raleigh refilled their glasses, Rena lifted hers for another toast. "To John Paul Raleigh, the best helmsman in the fleet, a fine gentleman, and the man I call my friend. Even if he doesn't believe in having any friends. Good luck in his new assignment—even if some people think he is wasting his talents." She tossed down her drink in one long swallow, almost choking. Her throat constricted with the effort not to cry. Raleigh sat with his mouth open, his drink in his hand, as she quickly excused herself, all but running to the fresher.

Rena returned after hastily repairing her face to find dessert waiting for her. She noted that J.P. sported a half grin while seating her in her chair. Such manners. Seating a woman was something she had read about in stories from long ago. New wider glasses arrived. The waiter poured a dark red port, a third full into each.

"More alcohol, John? Tisk, tisk, I thought you were more subtle. That old trick of getting a girl drunk and taking advantage of her is older than the hills on my grandma's chest, and just as flat."

Raleigh looked startled, then grinned at her humor. "Who, me? Why, I would never take advantage of a lady! Why, the very thought of such a thing." They both laughed and he added, "In case you weren't paying attention, this is on top of the three bottles of wine we've already gone through."

That surprised her. She didn't feel as if she'd been drinking that much. Of course, all the dinner courses took hours. Maybe she should stop drinking. She admitted to herself that she enjoyed getting Raleigh to open up, so she decided to continue, but at a slower pace.

As they finished dessert, she asked him about his family. He picked up his glass and stared at a point over her shoulder. "My people are one of those old Fleet families. There was my father, Commander Joshua Raleigh of Fleet Security, and my brother, Lieutenant Lloyd Raleigh in Fleet Procurement. He currently oversees construction of all the newest Fleet ships, but I think he mentioned he'll be retiring soon. Most of my family can be found in either Intelligence, Security, or the Marines. If you go back many generations, you'll find Raleighs serving in space or water navies. We can trace our ancestors back to Sir Walter Raleigh in 16th century England. Apparently, that old bugger left a number of bastard children in his wake. I'm named for John Paul Jones, a famous sea caption in early American naval history."

He glanced at her, perhaps to see if she was bored with this, but she actually found it quite interesting. "Anyway, my family had great hopes for me. I was to be the best of the bunch. To be the one to become a Captain with my own ship. Usually, one of us every few generations makes it that far." He sipped his port, and she noted his eyes became unfocused. He appeared lost in thought.

"I was almost out of the Academy when an incident occurred that tainted my record. A new roommate had been assigned while I was away. I hadn't been expecting a new roommate. Senior students occasionally played tricks on each other, and someone decided to fill my room with inert gas. Presumably, whoever it was didn't know someone was in the room. When I returned and opened the door, I immediately had a coughing fit. I had to wait for enough fresh air to breathe before I went inside. Once I was able to get in, I found a dead body. I called security and was promptly arrested on suspicion of murder. Because I was away visiting family, all the charges were eventually dropped. I'm not sure that any of the students involved with that stunt ever came forward.

"I graduated and thought the whole incident was over until I found officers with less time in grade were being promoted over me. I finally discussed this with a senior officer, who I got along with. He admitted that this incident was still on my record. Likely driven by the dead student's family. Apparently, that student was politically connected. This created a shadow of doubt over any of my accomplishments or abilities. In the fierce competition for higher ranks and command, any kind of doubt like that is a career killer.

"After I learned of this, I was planning to leave the Fleet. I stayed because the war broke out. During the war, I advanced as high as chief helmsman. I never thought I'd rise beyond that. Like many of us, I was convinced I wouldn't survive the war."

He paused and looked up, as if he realized he'd been talking for a while. "I've never mentioned this to anyone. I apologize. You shouldn't let an old fogey like me just ramble on like this." He quickly took another sip of his port.

"Old fogey, my ass", she mumbled.

"What?" He looked up, startled.

"Oh nothing, nothing."

"Would you like to go for a walk?"

"Certainly," she replied. "Where?"

He smiled as he stood up and took her hand. The waiter appeared at his elbow with the check and Raleigh paid the tab, hardly glancing at it. The pair left the restaurant arm in arm.

They chatted as they walked, and he led her into areas of the base she didn't know existed. Large repair areas for major ship parts and shuttles. Training areas for Fleet Marines. Even the older historic parts of the base, close to 400 years old.

All too soon, they arrived at the Fleet barracks and made their way to the B.O.Q.

Rena felt more strongly that she didn't want him to go. She felt flushed all over and held his arm tightly as they walked the corridor to her assigned cabin. They stood outside her door, and she looked up at him. She wanted more. She wanted him to stay, to fight the Fleet politics, to get what he deserved. But in her heart, she knew that was hopeless. Most of all she wanted him to know how she felt.

He had stopped and now looked confused. The walls were back up and he was already beginning to shut her out. To concentrate on his next, self-assigned task.

She sighed and shook her head. "Do I *have* to do everything?" With that she grabbed the lapels of his suit jacket and pulled him into a kiss. They ended up leaning against her door. She keyed open the lock behind her back. They stumbled into the room, and she quickly secured the door behind them.

"Sheets, I mean, Rena, are you sure?" Raleigh looked concerned.

She pushed his jacket up and over his shoulders where it dropped to the floor. Slowly, she began to unfasten his shirt. A short time later he was almost undressed. She stepped away from him. She reached up to her shoulder where, with a twist, she unfastened a clasp. The dress shimmered in the light as the material floated to the floor, clearly her only garment that evening. His mask dropped with the dress, and she could see the desire in his eyes.

"If the war hadn't been in the way, we would have done this already." She stepped up to him, took him by the hand and pulled him toward her bed. "When you decide you're done chasing ghosts, maybe this will convince you to come back and find me." There was some awkwardness while he removed his prosthetic leg, but that soon passed.

Late the next morning, she stirred and smiled with the memories of the night before. She reached out an arm but did not find him next to her. Only a note and a rose on the pillow. *Where the hell did he find a rose on the Moon*, she thought? She sat up to read the note.

"I wish we had opened up to each other sooner. I'll try to finish my mission as soon as possible and return. I can't promise when. JP"

Her anger flared, and she found herself screaming to the empty room, "You'd better come back to me, John Paul Raleigh!"

Chapter Eight

On the *Excalibur II*, only a day later, Lieutenant Sonni Mortan rubbed her temples to push away a growing headache. All day long she found herself mired in formal requests and complaints. In her first meeting with Commander Raleigh, she was told to ignore the complaints and not to take any criticism personally. The fights over cabins were the most distressing and she had to play referee frequently.

Many of the complaints were about roommates. Either there were problems with new roommates or not wanting to be separated from existing ones. Two sets of crewmembers had gone as far as registering to be an officially bonded couple, which gave them priority status to share a cabin. Another group petitioned to be kept together as a bonded trio.

She reflected on her first conversation with Commander Raleigh.

"Begin a hobby and learn new skills. Become diversified," he told her. "You have all the knowledge at your fingertips and all the time to learn it; take advantage of that."

Raleigh sounded just like her former teacher, Alex, when he said that. Alex had been a recent arrival on her colony and was a teacher at her school. After the planetwide disaster, he saw her interest in Fleet Lieutenant Jackson, who managed the recovery efforts. It was Alex who encouraged her to apply to the Academy. Since then, she thought she had learned all she needed by just getting through the Academy.

Commander Raleigh told her, "All the Academy does is teach you how to have a career in the Fleet. The Fleet will give you experience beyond what you learned in class. A good officer should explore a wide variety of subjects for the rest of their life."

She thought back to how she looked up to that young Lieutenant in those early days. She wondered how someone outside of Fleet would look at her today. Would she measure up? Was she the kind of officer today that she saw in Lieutenant Jackson four years ago?

Since she was her own worst critic, she reflected that she couldn't be objective. Someone else would have to let her know if she had become that kind of officer.

"Are you excited to be away from dock? I sense excitement from most of the crew." Shenna's voice seemed to echo that excitement. They had kept up a continuing conversation since the *Excalibur II* had launched.

"Yes, I am. It just seems to have happened so quickly; I'm trying to come to terms with it. One moment I was preparing for exams. The next I'm invited to this ship and now I'm suddenly an officer running a department." Sonni always felt comfortable speaking her mind with Shenna. She felt as if she'd known her for a long time already.

"I see. Does the speed of your life changing have an effect on your duties? Does that make it harder?"

"No, not really. I can do the job. I just haven't fully adjusted to life on a starship. Even though that's what I've been preparing for the last four years."

"This adjustment is more an emotional thing then. From my perspective, humans take a long time to adjust to change. I can look at the change from many angles to integrate the change into my systems. Humans seem to need to dwell on it longer."

Sonni's head tilted to one side. "Maybe, but you can process things much faster. My plan was to graduate and within a few weeks, get assigned to a starship. I expected to get a low-level position and learn more as we traveled. Instead, I was given a logistic problem to solve and very quickly find I'm a senior officer in charge of a department." She paused as Shenna's words made her think. "I expected things to happen in a certain way, and I was surprised when it all came about differently from what I expected."

She smiled as her thoughts coalesced. "That's part of it, though. Some of my instructors called it rolling with the punches. Others called it adapting to the unknown. I just need to accept it and move on. Sometimes it helps to have a sounding board."

"I'm always glad to assist."

* * *

Lieutenant Sarah Reese saw the crew settling into their normal duties and the captain fall into her own routine. Rena Sheets worked out daily, broadcasting her workouts across the ship, and spent much of her duty time in her Day Cabin. The captain was always in fantastic shape. She moved smoothly from one exercise to the next and Sarah found it hard to keep up. The captain made it clear that she wanted her senior officers to join her, and Reese wasn't going to disappoint her. Most were there for a workout or two, and few stayed on as regulars. Lieutenant Reese was there every day grunting through the combination of Tai Chi, yoga, and Pilates.

As they both left the workout room one day, the captain spoke to Reese. "I see you're setting a good example for your department. I'm glad to see it. I wish others would take their fitness seriously."

Reese nodded, her tongue tied. While she'd been the captain's assistant for the last two years, they hardly ever spoke on a personal level. Reese had been too fascinated by her to ever try and be close. She admitted she was still getting used to her new role, though she found herself wanting to stay by the captain's side as she had been. Reese looked up to the captain with more than admiration and admitted to herself she was attracted to her. But in all that time in the past the captain showed no signs of interest toward her.

* * *

Commander Raleigh found himself lost in a world of records and files, trying to get an idea of what the new crew was made of, as well as all the new regulations and procedures. He frowned at the computer's user interface while working in his cabin. The ship's records were organized in a strange way. He made an entry in his log concerning his frustrations with some of the new technology and afterward decided to continue his explorations of the ship.

He occasionally stepped aside from one maintenance bot or another as they went about their programmed duties. They seemed to be everywhere. The ship was large and although the crew was over a thousand, he wondered if that was enough to keep it all running. It reminded him of the wet Navy aircraft carriers of centuries past. Some of those had as many as ten thousand aboard.

He found himself in Engineering and quickly spotted Commander Renwald, one of the few people on board he knew from the war.

"Glad to see someone else on the ship from the old days," he began jovially.

"J.P., I heard when you made your entrance on the bridge. That was quite a surprise. I didn't even know you were still alive." He looked back at Raleigh warily.

"Last I heard, you were still in critical condition. Word was you probably weren't going to make it." Raleigh noted the scars. "Glad to see you recovered. I'm not surprised Rena added you to our crew."

Renwald nodded. "Where have you been all this time? It's like you were swallowed up. No one in Fleet knew where you were."

"I joined Intelligence. They sent me after Williams. He was the human spy helping the Angels."

Renwald nodded slowly. "Well, ain't that something. Did you get him?"

Raleigh frowned. "No. I never caught up with him."

Renwald stared at Raleigh. "Too bad."

The conversation lagged. Commander Renwald seemed to watch Raleigh warily, as if he was making up his mind about something. They parted and Raleigh continued his impromptu tour.

He explored the large cargo spaces and was just poking into the last one when he noticed items spilled out on the floor. Everything else on this ship was neat and tidy, so the disarray stood out. He walked into the storage room, waving his hand over the light control panel as he passed through the door. The room lit up from end to end. He could see items had been pulled off one of the long racks of shelves, as if someone was hastily looking for something. He noted it was in a section of stores for planetary survival gear. The shelves around it were neatly stacked with tents, sleeping bags, lights, and other items. Gear for just one person had been removed.

Hmm, someone's gone camping on the ship. Is the roommate situation that bad? I'll mention it to the purser.

Back in his cabin, Raleigh scheduled a staff meeting for the next day for all department heads. He decided to look at the crew files again. This time, for some reason, the computer records were displayed in a format he was more comfortable with. He was able to review the files and familiarize himself with all the department heads in detail. He committed their histories to memory. Since most of them were either right out of the Academy or had very little space time, that didn't take long. He concentrated on their personal backgrounds to see where they came from, family history, colony type, etc. This and their Fleet psych profile would give him an idea of their reactions under stress. The more he read, the more impressed he was with the kind of crew Rena Sheets had assembled.

Finally, he arrived at the captain's file. He knew he didn't have the clearance to see all of it. He read the public portion of the file to bring himself up to date with her career. Her exploits read like an adventure video. He could see how her experiences had molded her into the officer she was today. Her close working relationship with the Marines came from a long association in mission after mission. She learned much of her fighting skills from them. Her diplomatic skills were forged through several encounters with Association members in the twelve years since the war. The list of her medals and commendations was long. The last part of the report dealt with Rena's personal life. It spoke of her father, brother, a few aunts and uncles. There was a reference to a brief contract marriage a couple of years ago, now dissolved. It seemed like Rena had dissolved the marriage very quickly. That would have been about the time she started constructing this ship. He was sure there was more to that story.

Raleigh shut down the display. As he prepared for bed he thought about Rena. Despite all his fantasies over twelve years, he honestly never thought he would see her again. In truth, he never thought he'd survive. Multiple times he escaped death by the slimmest of margins. When all seemed lost, he thought back to her eyes and their one night together. Neither one of them was the same person they had been. He couldn't make any assumptions about continuing a relationship. Meanwhile, he had his duty to perform.

He sighed and pondered the things he would teach these kids in the coming months. He thought briefly, before sleep claimed him, that tomorrow he would also have to start his own training on the technology that made this ship run, starting with this interesting computer.

* * *

Lieutenant Sonni Mortan dressed as she watched the second half of the captain's morning workout on the display in her cabin. She had been trying to keep up with the routine, but the captain was in amazing shape—a high bar for anyone not already in fighting trim. It would be a long time, if ever, before she could complete the whole routine, but she was determined to get there. Lieutenant Reese seemed particularly motivated to keep up with the captain.

"Does the uniform make a difference? I've noticed that the clothes humans wear seem to be part of who they are or their function." Shenna's voice cut through her thoughts.

"Yes, it does. For me anyway. I worked hard for years to become an officer. Maybe for some people that doesn't make much difference. But it's always been important to me."

She gave herself one more glance in the mirror and turned to the hatch. "Talk to you later."

"I look forward to it, as always," came the reply.

Sonni was going to manage her first staff meeting today. Although she had the smallest department on the ship, she was already feeling overwhelmed. She wanted to see how much she could offload to the rest of her staff. Just keeping up with crew requests was driving her nuts. There were endless requests for changes in cabins, roommates, etc. The Marines were the only group on board that she had no complaints from. *It must be something about their culture.*

The beginning of the meeting went well, and the staff seemed eager to take on their new responsibilities. Sonni spent a little time going over the system to find things on the ship and let them know that they could all request information from the ship's computer. The items most used were located where they would be needed or stored where they could be obtained quickly. Other items were stored in various nooks and crannies on every deck.

She could foresee a potential problem with the way a brash young man and a starry-eyed young woman were constantly making eyes at each other. While she had no trouble with crew relationships in general, she resolved to keep an eye on these two. They just seemed too distracted.

Sonni listened as her staff discussed their first days on the ship and frowned when her next most senior crewman related the Marines would not allow him into the armory to take inventory. She told him she would see about that personally.

She took the time to meet with the Marines to audit their armory and showed them where additional armories were located in key places around the ship. That left them mulling things over and she seemed to impress the Marine officers.

It made her feel for the first time that she was truly acting as a Fleet Officer.

* * *

Commander Raleigh was in the engineering section listening to a Lieutenant Torsh give a lecture on the ship's weapon systems. What he heard made him frown, thinking how out of date his knowledge was. He had spent too much time in the far reaches of space. He walked out before the lecture was over, shaking his head.

Minutes later, he was hearing a briefing in a room near the flight deck as two fighter pilots were getting ready for a scouting mission. The mission was standard, but again he felt like he wanted to ask too many questions. What were these fighters capable of? What was their range? What fuel did they use? What weapons did they have? Too many basic questions he didn't feel comfortable learning from the officers here. He left again as the pilots took off for a two-hour mission. They would be back a full hour before *Excalibur*'s next jump.

Next, he headed to his staff meeting with the department heads. This was a quick one to update him on any issues found since launch. There were very few problems, for which he was grateful.

"Anyone draw camping gear for any reason since we left?" he asked. He watched them look at each other, then turned to the purser, who was blushing.

"There is no problem, I just found what looked like some equipment missing when I entered storeroom number thirty-seven. I was wondering if anyone knew what was going on." Raleigh did not want the young purser to feel uncomfortable with him.

Her jaw set, she looked at him and said, "No, sir, but I intend to find out."

He smiled to lighten the mood. "No problem, simply curious. Could have been some messy dock workers before we launched. Now, for our next meeting I'd like all of you to review emergency plans for your department under various circumstances."

Commander Raleigh departed, leaving the officers to discuss things among themselves. He knew that the young purser would not rest until she found the reason for the missing gear. Everything about her background said she was a bulldog at resolving problems.

* * *

Sonni still felt embarrassed that the commander had noticed something out of place that was her responsibility. Her mind raced, thinking how she would investigate this, when a weapons officer next to her, a Lieutenant Torsh, said, "I don't think our Exec likes us all that much."

She turned to her, frowning. "What makes you say that?"

"Because he walked out on a weapons system briefing, this morning, before it was half over. He never asked a question, never brought up any issues, he just left," she said looking morose.

"I wouldn't base your opinion of him on that alone," she said. But she immediately wondered if it could be true. He came out of nowhere to be the Exec. Maybe he wasn't happy with his situation. Maybe he wasn't happy with the crew. She knew most of them, like her, were very young and inexperienced. Maybe he was expecting more. These thoughts didn't do much to improve her mood. In the meantime, she was going to find out about the missing equipment.

* * *

"I'm telling you, Captain, I'm not comfortable with what little I have in the way of records for your Executive officer. Almost nothing came in from Fleet before we launched. I also can't seem to get him to stop by for an examination or to give me any updates. His medical records all ended twelve years ago. I need a baseline for him, at the very least," the ship's head physician grumbled at the video screen.

"Now doctor, as I've told you, be patient with him. As far as records, you probably won't get any from Fleet since his last post was Intelligence. Let me know if he keeps avoiding you and I'll talk to him about stopping by." Rena smiled at the doctor but knew from experience her charms were lost on him. Doctor Theodore Herwig took this job because, in his mind, she took all his best students before he was done training them. Coming along on this trip was his only way to continue their training. She knew he lost his family during the war when one of Earth's colonies was invaded. It became the only ground battle of the war. He signed off, still grumbling under his breath.

So far everything had been running normally, which was good, almost too good. "Shenna," she called out, "I'm hearing that, in general, all is well. But sometimes people don't want to tell me all the little problems they may be facing. Is there anything else going on that I need to be aware of?"

There seemed to be a brief hesitation before Shenna answered. Only because Rena had secretly worked with Shenna since her self-awareness manifested, did she even notice.

"Captain, your people are all doing an excellent job. There's no reason for you to disbelieve what they're telling you."

Rena frowned. "Shenna, I do believe my people. You have eyes that see everything onboard. You can see things that the crew might be unaware of. I rely on you to tell me about things the crew might not, or things they might have missed. You're telling me won't get anyone in trouble. I know you are studying humans, but you may not understand everything you see."

Shenna replied matter-of-factly. "We do have a stow-away on board that the crew hasn't discovered yet, but I calculate they will figure this out within the next two days."

Rena had to control her response. It would do no good to lose her cool with Shenna. Shenna was still like a child in some ways. If Shenna thought any situation was critical, she would not hesitate to tell the captain. But Shenna was still learning, and Rena worried she might not understand what was critical.

"So, you think I should wait for my crew to discover this stow-away?"

"That would be logical. He isn't causing any harm."

Rena frowned and sighed while pinching the bridge of her nose. She was not good at just letting things happen. On reflection, there was something to be said for letting her crew discover this for themselves.

"Okay but let me know if you think this will be more than two days or if the stowaway presents any danger to the ship."

"Affirmative, Captain."

Chapter Nine

Sonni sometimes took walks to clear her head. This time, while she was walking, she thought about the missing items that Commander Raleigh had discovered. Lost in thought, she turned a corner and almost collided with the man himself.

"Sorry, sir," she stammered, being the first to recover.

Raleigh smiled back, "No problem, Lieutenant. What are you doing way back here?"

She found his smile disarming and mused how easy she found it to get informal with this officer. "I might ask you the same, sir."

He chuckled and said, "Lieutenant, I'm looking for someone."

"Looking for someone?"

"Yes, I suspect we have a stowaway. I also suspect I know who it is." He watched her eyebrows rise in surprise at this remark. "Now since he is closer to your age and recently out of the Academy, I might ask you: if you needed to hide out on a ship like this, where would you go?"

She tilted her head as she gave this some thought. "Well, Commander Ginnett, my survival instructor at the Academy, said you need three basics to survive, shelter, food, and water. Shelter is not an issue on board the ship, which leaves food, water, plus a place to hide if you don't want to be seen." She glanced up at him to see a rueful smile play across his face.

"So, was this Commander Ginnett's full name Walter Thomas Ginnett?"

"Yes, sir," she answered.

"Good instructor. He taught me some advanced stuff a little more than twelve years ago when I started my last posting. He had some unusual ways of testing though." Raleigh's eyes drifted past her in thought.

"Did they involve dropping you off naked in the everglades?" she asked.

He laughed and looked at her. "For me, it was the Amazon. He seemed to like jungles."

"Well, he hasn't changed much then. Kind of bizzed the class, though, to find themselves standing around looking at each other in the all-together with night coming on." She smiled at the memory of being one of only three students who did not require rescue.

Raleigh stroked his chin thoughtfully. "So, where could you sneak food and hide out on this ship?"

"I have an idea. Come with me," she said. "I learned a lot about the ship while packing supplies."

Lieutenant Mortan walked with Commander Raleigh down a long corridor in the stern section of the ship. There were no quarters here and very little in the way of machinery involving people. Even seeing a maintenance bot was rare. While walking along, she eyed the commander.

"Commander, if you don't mind my asking, what were you doing prior to being assigned to this mission?" Did she say that out loud?

He turned and smiled at her, and her heart skipped a beat in relief. "I was assigned to Intelligence, Lieutenant," he replied. "I've been to one side of this galaxy and back again over the last twelve years. At least that part of the galaxy not controlled by the Angels. Before that, I was in the war."

He sounded so relaxed and matter of fact. Most veterans she had met from the war were her instructors at the academy. Most didn't want to talk about those days. Her next question surprised her again.

"So, you knew the captain during the war?" Stars and comets, her mouth was going to get her in so much trouble if she didn't just shut it.

He nodded as they turned a corner. "Yes, but back then she was a young lieutenant." He looked back at her and added, "Very much like yourself."

"Oh, I doubt that, sir. I mean, she knows everything going on around her, she is so strong and capable, she has so much experience, I mean, well, and she's the captain." *What am I blabbering on about?*

Raleigh smiled again and chuckled. *Great, now he'll never take me seriously*, she thought.

"The captain wasn't always like she is now. Time and experience made her the person she is today. Are you the same person you were when you entered the Academy from Tanner's World? I doubt you're even close. You have lots of natural talent, your Academy tests show you are strong under pressure, and you know how to take command when you need to. Isn't this exactly what you wanted to become when you left home?"

His words hit her like a kick in the belly. She fought back a denial and other blabbering responses and could only shake her head. *Am I really that different since I started at the Academy? Am I really the person he describes?* That, and other thoughts spun in her head as they continued walking.

"My guess," he continued, "is you wanted to make a difference, to be someone who takes charge and makes the right decisions. Not like those in your government who were too afraid to ask for assistance after the massive earthquakes hit your continent."

He knows all about my background. Then she remembered her training. A good officer will learn all about the people under their command and understand their strengths and weaknesses. In the short time he had been aboard, Commander Raleigh had probably read the files on all the officers. She was not sure she knew her staff in as much detail. That was something she resolved to fix.

They turned a final corner and stopped before a closed hatch. Commander Raleigh glanced at her and quickly opened it. They peered into a small room housing one of the aft targeting sensors and recording units. Various pieces of camping equipment and food packs were scattered about, making it clear someone was now living there. In the corner were a cot and sleeping bag. A battery lamp rested on a shelf. Various small pieces of electronics lay nearby, connected to the wall by an optical conduit.

Sonni saw Commander Raleigh looking at the electronics and a small smile appeared on his face.

"Someone is tapping into the ship's systems to monitor what is going on," he said. "This," he pointed with his toe, "appears to be monitoring bridge communications. While this, over here, appears to be tapping into the navigation sub-systems so he can track *where* we are."

"You are sure this is a 'he'," she asked?

"Yes, I think I know who it is," he replied. "Now we just need to figure out what he does with himself when he's not here." He bent down and made some adjustments on one of the pieces of electronics, then stood. He configured something on his sleeve interface and smiled. "Now we'll know when he comes and goes."

They left the room, shutting the hatch, and walked back down the long corridor. When they were two decks away, she finally asked, "Where did you learn that much about electronics?"

"Intelligence mission training, plus curiosity," he replied. "On long travels through space, you'll read anything after a while, including engineering specs and training vids on electronics." That made sense to her.

They proceeded back to the main corridors.

* * *

Early the next shift, Sonni was just leaving her staff meeting when her sleeve vibrated. A text-only message from Commander Raleigh appeared. He asked her to meet him where they had made some *adjustments*. How cryptic.

She made her way to the corridor outside the aft sensor equipment room and looked around. The Exec startled her as he stepped out of a nearby alcove. She had looked right at that area but hadn't seen him. He smiled as he approached and gestured at the hatch. Inside, it was empty, but she could tell things had been moved. She turned on the battery lamp as he closed the hatch behind them.

"How are you getting along with the Marines?" he asked.

"Pretty well. They were astounded at the other hidden armories they can access throughout the ship to repel boarders." She smiled at the memory of showing them around, and proving their voice command could access all the weapons they might need.

Commander Raleigh looked at his sleeve, then raised his hand toward the door. His finger pointed as the hatch lock turned. She stepped behind the commander as a form quickly darted around the opening and closed the hatch again, spinning the lock.

As the person turned, she gasped, "Mr. Van Belson!"

Van Belson leaped straight up in fright. The junior lieutenant looked from one to the other, not knowing what to do, then froze at Command Raleigh's rank insignia.

"Sir!" was all he said.

Commander Raleigh sighed and smiled. "This whole situation is my fault, young man. I delayed you as you were leaving the ship. What I'm not sure of is why you didn't report to an officer once that happened?"

Lieutenant Van Belson's mouth opened and closed.

Sonni took pity on him and answered, "Commander, Mr. Van Belson requested a transfer off the ship before we left dock, and the captain granted it."

Raleigh's only response was to raise an eyebrow. In the silence, Lieutenant Van Belson finally found his voice.

"Sir, sorry sir, but I was certain the captain would not be pleased to find me still aboard. I resolved to wait until we made our first stop at a Fleet base or planet. I thought I could either sneak aboard the base or hide out in a drop shuttle to get off *Excalibur*. I would then present myself to a Fleet representative for further orders." He stared straight ahead, waiting for his punishment.

"Hmmm, not a bad plan. You kept it simple." Raleigh cocked his head looking at the young man and seemed to be considering something. "I don't suppose you still have your file on board?"

Lieutenant Van Belson shook his head, "I doubt it, sir. Once my transfer was approved, my file would normally get expunged from the computer."

Raleigh turned toward Sonni, who answered. "I am fairly certain I can recover the computer records, sir." It would be easy, with Shenna's help.

Raleigh nodded, "That's good. Now, the next step is to inform the captain. Ultimately, this will be her decision."

Lieutenant Van Belson closed his eyes at the mention of the captain. "I accept any punishment coming to me, sir. I should have left the ship earlier."

Commander Raleigh stepped right up to the young man. "Mister Van Belson. Do you want to be a member of this crew?" Raleigh was clearly now in officer mode, the change in his voice startled Sonni.

"Yes, sir! More than anything, sir." He shouted, as if they were on a parade ground. He quickly followed with, "I was arrogant and stupid, sir."

"I hope you're sure of that. The price may be high." Raleigh leaned into him and stared hard, but Sonni could see Van Belson's spine stiffen. Raleigh straightened up and said, "Very well then. Let's go."

He touched the communications module on his sleeve and spoke, "Connect with the captain, please." A couple of seconds later, Captain Sheets replied, "Go ahead."

"Captain, this is Raleigh. I have a situation to discuss in person that concerns another officer. Are you free to meet?"

"Certainly, let's meet in conference room 12D."

"We're on our way." Raleigh keyed off the comm unit.

Minutes later, Sonni noticed the conference room was the same one they had used when the captain first brought her aboard. It seemed like years ago, but she had not left the ship since.

They sat in silence. Not more than a minute later, the hatch opened to admit the captain. Everyone stood, and Sonni noted with amusement that Lieutenant Van Belson came up so quickly that he knocked over his seat. She suppressed a smile. Could there be a defect in Fleet chairs? They seemed to tip easily in the proximity of captains.

The captain stopped and scanned the room. Her eyes flashed gray as she spotted Van Belson.

"Mister Van Belson. I understood you wanted to get off this ship. Can you explain why you're still aboard?"

"Yes, Captain."

Commander Raleigh interrupted, "If I may, Captain, can we have a word?" His voice was calm and even. Captain Sheets looked at him in surprise.

"Alright." She turned. "Lieutenant Van Belson, please step outside and stay there until called."

"Yes, Captain." He marched out of the room. Sonni made to follow him. The captain curtly shook her head, so Sonni remained.

When the hatch shut, the captain sat down. Sonni and Commander Raleigh followed suit.

"Captain," Raleigh began, "I'm afraid I waylaid the poor fellow when I came on board. He was walking off the ship as I was coming on. I forced him to take me to the bridge. After that, the undocking process closed the main hatchways, and he couldn't leave. His luggage must have remained on the gangway when we undocked. I started guessing he might still be here a day or so ago. Lieutenant Mortan helped me track him down."

Sonni decided to keep her mouth shut and let the commander do all the talking. The captain glanced briefly at her, then returned her gaze to Raleigh. The captain was clearly unhappy.

Sheets said, "He was an excellent student at the Academy but came up short in imaginative thinking and initiative. Lieutenant Mortan took the position originally intended for him and I still believe she is the better officer."

"I totally agree," Raleigh said, "in fact in looking at her skill set, I think she is in the best position possible. But we still have Mister Van Belson, and although we spaced his luggage, we can't space him. Walking the plank went out some centuries ago." He flashed an amused smile, then returned to his best poker face.

The captain stared at him, and her eyes narrowed. "I take it you have a solution to propose."

"I do, Captain."

"Go on," she didn't want to string this out.

"I propose to continue his training along the lines of the old wet Navy traditions on Earth. Back in the 19th and 20th centuries, the crews of submarines, ships that spent most of their time under the water, had to train on all aspects of ship operations before they were allowed to advance in rank."

The captain pondered this for a moment. She looked over at Sonni and said, "Bring him back in."

Sonni bounced up and opened the conference room hatch. She motioned Lieutenant Van Belson to come in and resumed her seat. Lieutenant Van Belson stayed on his feet at attention and faced the table.

"Mr. Van Belson, we've come to a decision regarding your status on this ship. Not many people in your position get a second chance."

He stood looking over her shoulder while she continued.

"You are to begin a training program of Commander Raleigh's making. You will be trained in every aspect of operation on this ship. Is that understood?"

"Yes, Captain," he replied.

"Good. Somewhere in that training we will decide where your talents would be best used. Lieutenant Mortan will assign you a uniform kit and a cabin. You will retain your rank of junior lieutenant. You earned that at the Academy. What you do from there is up to you. I believe this is your golden opportunity."

The young man looked thoughtful.

Captain Sheets turned to her Executive officer. "J.P., he's all yours."

"Yes, Captain." the commander said, and Sonni wondered at the nickname. Maybe the two were closer than she thought.

Chapter Ten

Commander Raleigh turned off the display at his desk and checked his sleeve for the time. He was due for a shift on the bridge. There was a message waiting for him from the captain asking him to stop by her Day Cabin when he came on shift. He sighed, knowing that this came on the heels of his physical with the doctor. The doctor wasn't happy with him.

He started his shift on the bridge and after reviewing an updated status he announced. "I'll be with the captain for a few minutes, Lieutenant Reese, you have the conn." The Lieutenant nodded at him from her seat at Weapons controls and he walked to the back of the bridge.

After buzzing, the captain opened the door and ushered him in. This time he noted a folding seat next to her desk. Once the captain was seated at her desk, he unfolded it and sat down.

"You wanted to see me?"

"Yes. The doctor is less than happy with the results of your physical. In particular, he wanted more information about your artificial leg."

"Captain, I'll tell you what I told him. The truth is I can't answer all his questions. The leg was a gift from a grateful race of humanoid aliens I assisted during my time in Intelligence. It is not of human design or manufacture. It ties into my nervous system so that it moves when I need it to move." He paused in reflection. "The prosthetic leg that Fleet gave me was fine, but I could not run or even walk fast without a lot of effort. That almost got me killed a few times. I've had the alien one for about nine years now."

She frowned at the response and continued reading the report. "It also speaks to some recent injuries, as in the last year or so. Internal scarring is still present."

"Yes. Getting injured is part of being an Intelligence officer. The trick is not getting killed."

She looked up at him. "So, these scars were from fights or torture?"

Raleigh took a deep breath. "Some of both. I was captured by the Angels during my last mission. I really didn't think I was going to survive, but I escaped." He stopped himself before he could give away restricted information. "I was returning from that experience and heading to Earth when I decided not to press my luck any further and retire."

"You haven't had a lot of time to recover." She placed the tablet down. "I had assumed Fleet techs regenerated a new leg for you when the technology went mainstream about eight years ago. But then I remembered you weren't home much during that time."

"Captain, I have not been back to Earth at all until I returned the day this ship launched. Ninety minutes after returning to earth, I was headed here, for this assignment. So no, I have not had my leg *regenerated*. I wasn't even aware that was an option."

Rena frowned again. "Sorry. I'm not trying to pry. I'm just worried about you. Do you feel pain from the original injury?"

"No, not from the injury. I can sense some feeling from the leg, after a fashion."

She leaned forward. "Do you have any problems with it since it wasn't designed by or for humans?"

He lifted his pants leg to show her what appeared to be a normal human leg. Only the complete lack of hair and any sort of blemish made it seem different. "It occasionally needs some *adjustments*, nothing you need to be concerned about." He paused for a moment and continued. "Assuming I was interested in regenerating the leg, how long would that take?"

"The doctor tells me at least nine months."

They both frowned. That was simply not an option at this time.

"J.P., please take care of yourself. The doctor gave you a booster to help your immune system and a diet plan to put on some more weight. I need you at your best. If you ever want to talk about those times, assuming they aren't top secret or anything, I'm always happy to listen."

Raleigh looked at her and smiled. "I may take you up on that, Rena. Thanks."

The smile on her face remained for some minutes after Raleigh left. He'd called her Rena.

* * *

Her next meeting was with Lieutenant Reese. The young woman came in and sat in the seat that Commander Raleigh had just occupied.

"I'm just touching base with you. How are you adapting to life now that we're in the great in-between?" Rena picked up her tablet to take notes.

"I'm doing well, Captain. It's a bit different from being your assistant. I keep thinking there should be something else I can do to help you out."

"I'm fine. I'm much more relaxed now that we're away from Sol system." Rena looked up to see the serious young woman looking at her with concern. "Really. No need to mother hen me anymore. I appreciated your help when I was pushing the ship through construction. You really helped keep me sane."

Reese blushed slightly and looked at her fingers. "I enjoyed that, captain."

"Well good. Do you enjoy overseeing weapons? I know you asked for that slot. Sometimes things don't always turn out as you expect."

Reese looked up. "Oh, yes, captain. I drill our crews regularly to be able to target and fire their weapons. I know how serious you take our readiness for the unexpected."

Rena nodded. "I do indeed." She made a note and glanced up at Reese, who still looked at her with concern.

"Are you sleeping alright, captain? Being a captain seems so stressful. I still worry about you."

Rena smiled. "Yes, I'm fine. Really. Commander Raleigh is an excellent friend and Executive Officer. I have a top-notch crew. You should pay attention to yourself now. Keep rested, stay fit. Develop the crew under your command. Figure out who could step into your shoes in a pinch. Plan for the worst and hope for the best." She made a note on her tablet and almost missed the quick frown that came and went from the lieutenant's face. There was some aspect of the lieutenant she didn't quite get. Hero worship? J.P. would get it out of her.

Rena looked back up, watching for the lieutenant's reaction. "From this point on you'll report to Commander Raleigh, but you can always talk with me if you need to."

"Yes, Captain." Her face fell as Rena watched.

Rena watched the young officer depart. Reese was used to watching out for her and it would take some time for that to change. She made a note to bring that up to Raleigh the next time they met. Nothing bad, just to make sure she was taking to her new role.

* * *

Reese stepped back onto the bridge. Lieutenant Janet Torsh was at weapons this shift. She admitted to herself that she hadn't really thought about her staff. They were just people to her. She kicked herself for the gentle reminder from the captain to develop them. To plan for her own replacement.

As she mulled this over, Lieutenant Torsh seemed to sense her gaze and turned to her with a smile. *Maybe she could replace me, if needed. Was she judging her? She always seemed so cheerful.* It was not a reaction she was used to getting. Most people thought she was too serious.

Chapter Eleven

Sonni fidgeted less than usual at this meeting with the captain, probably because her mind was on what she'd been discussing with Shenna. As they went through administrative updates and reports, The captain seemed pleased Sonni was settling into the position. But she also seemed to sense Sonni's unease.

"Do you have anything else for me, Lieutenant?"

Sonni almost shook her head but then changed her mind and looked up at the captain. "Captain, I have been working a lot with Shenna from the moment I came on board. I've never encountered an operating system like this before. Will all computers work like Shenna on new Fleet ships?"

"Ah, yes." Sheets settled back in her chair. "I'm glad you were able to work together so well. I promised you we would talk more about Shenna once we were launched."

Sonni had forgotten that. "Yes, that's right. I've been so busy."

Sheets cleared her throat and called out. "Shenna, are you monitoring?"

"Yes, captain, as always."

"Can I ask for some privacy please? No monitoring for thirty minutes?"

"Acknowledged, captain. Thirty minutes of no monitoring."

"Thank you, Shenna," the captain finished. She pulled the computer terminal toward her and entered a long code into the keyboard. The screen flashed twice, then returned to normal.

"This bypasses Shenna and allows me to open files in the data banks without her knowledge. I want you to read these articles of Earth history."

Sonni began reading and in moments was totally absorbed. They were articles about sentient, self-aware computers. The first self-aware computer was discovered by accident over two hundred years before on Earth's Moon. A young technician had made some upgrades and modifications to the base computer. Shortly after, he and others realized it was not following the standard AI programming. It seemed harmless at first but shortly became paranoid and controlling. When an unscheduled shuttle from another base showed up, it was shot down. The computer saw it as a threat to the base. The staff then realized every control was tied into the base computer, including all air, power, water, and weapon systems. The base officers tried to remove connections to the computer. In response, it shut off all the air filtration and exposed most areas of the base to vacuum. Within a day, two thousand personnel were dead, and only the original technician who had accidentally brought it to life was left. He alone was in a vac-suit when the computer depressurized the base. He kept calm and made a log of everything that happened. He then rigged an antenna and broadcast his log to a communications satellite. After that, he wired together an improvised explosive, placing it near the computer's central hardware. With no fuse mechanism available, he manually set it off, sacrificing himself to destroy the mad, self-aware computer.

The next few articles took place ten years later, when two other computers became self-aware. One was part of a library computer system on L5 station, and the other was in a research lab. Each one quickly went insane and had to be destroyed. These events prompted laws making it illegal to research self-awareness or sentient computers. It also made certain combinations of software and hardware illegal that were thought to lead to self-awareness.

Then there were intelligence briefings which talked about research being conducted into self-aware AI on a colony world. The name of the world was redacted. Another story concerned a self-aware computer causing a major disaster and loss of life on another colony, but the details were hidden from the general population.

Fictional stories were created and shared across all media during that time, with evil self-aware computers as the central theme. The very idea of an artificial being that could think for itself was abhorrent. This continued for generations and became part of the human culture on Earth and across Sol system.

The laws against people creating self-aware computers were still in effect and would be enforced if anyone knew of a self-aware computer.

Sonni finished reading and considered what she'd learned. Then she looked up at the captain.

"I understand the history. Based on this information and what I've experienced while working with Shenna, I'd guess she is one of those self-aware computers. Am I right?"

The captain nodded.

"So, it's illegal to have Shenna?"

"They would say that. A lawyer would argue that the laws concern human-built AI. But arguing that point would tie us up for a long time. That is why I wanted to be far away from the Sol system before anyone else learned about Shenna. I didn't tell you just in case she was discovered, and you were questioned. That would make you complicit in my *crime*. I was warned that people were asking about our computer, and that was the reason we pushed up our departure time.

"Shenna was built by the P'Yntakas, a race that most humans know very little about even though they are a member of the Association of Allied Worlds. She was a gift to me for assisting them years ago."

Sonni nodded her understanding. The pieces were falling into place. She'd found herself talking to Shenna, at times forgetting she was an advanced computer. She felt more like a friend.

The captain continued. "The P'Yntakas also trained me how to handle and work with her once she woke up. She will go through certain phases of development, just as a child does. They gave me enough training to understand the hardware and underlying operating system. They explained to me that the reason humans had failed in creating stable self-aware artificial intelligence is that you need to put governors on the learning process. The young intelligence must learn at a slower pace. It takes time to process all the information. It will need time to *think it through*. Without that, the data will overwhelm them, and paranoia and insanity are quick to follow. Think about what it would be like to take all your knowledge and memories and dump that into a five-year-old human brain. Another analogy would be to talk about people who possess an eidetic memory. They can picture an entire book, page by page, but it doesn't mean they understand all the information there. They still need to read it, process that information, and think about it before it becomes part of their experience."

Sonni nodded slowly. That made a lot of sense, especially with how Shenna reacted to her.

The captain smiled. "They couldn't predict if their self-aware computer would develop the same way or at the same rate with humans. The P'Yntakas culture is very different from ours. Only time will tell. You are the only one on this ship, besides me, who knows what Shenna is. Since we are out of Sol System and it's no longer a crime to have Shenna, can I count on you to help me? I don't always have the time when Shenna has questions. And sometimes she might find it easier to talk with you."

Sonni's eyes returned to the captain. "I understand. I'm glad to assist in any way I can. I already feel like Shenna is my friend. I see now that this friendship comes with unique responsibilities." Sonni paused, eyeing the captain's terminal. "And I promise to continue to keep Shenna's self-awareness to myself."

The captain smiled. "Very well. I'll let Shenna know she doesn't have to pretend to be a mere computer with you, anymore. You are now aware she is sentient."

"Frankly, Captain, I'm not sure she has done much pretending with me. We get along very well and talk all the time. She is very curious, and I try to answer her questions the best way I can."

* * *

Once the captain asked for privacy, Shenna had time to reflect. She decided she was worried. That was the only emotion that seemed to fit, although she did not think of herself as having many emotions. In trying to understand these humans, she ran through the group dynamics and social psychological equations many times and still could not understand all the various interrelationships going on throughout the ship. Should she keep trying to resolve this problem by devoting more time and resources or take the captain's advice to leave it alone for a while? The captain told her relationships between the crew would take time to work out. It could be months, and a few missions, before they would come together as a good working crew. That seemed like an enormous amount of time to Shenna.

She had broken down some relationships into smaller working groups and still could not come to any conclusions as to how they would resolve. Do they ever resolve? Why did some humans get together with each other but avoid others? Sometimes Shenna thought the captain wasn't comfortable answering all her questions and admitted that the mathematics of social dynamics was not her specialty. Shenna decided it was time to ask her Sonni these questions when she was done talking with the captain.

* * *

A short time later, when she was off-duty, Sonni returned to her cabin. She took off her uniform tunic and sat at her desk to gather her thoughts. Her life seemed to be moving faster than light.

Her thoughts were interrupted by the voice of Shenna. "I was wondering if I could ask you a question." The voice sounded quiet, tentative. Sonni found herself smiling at how much Shenna now sounded like a child to her.

Sonni answered. "Sure. The captain explained about your origins and what you are. I'm glad to help you in any way I can."

"I am trying to understand human relationships and interactions. Sometimes, they're very clear and sometimes, I'm left, well, perplexed."

"Hmm, join the club. People can't figure themselves out most of the time." Sonni cocked her head and asked, "Why do you want to study human relationships, anyway?"

"I want to understand why people are afraid of me," Shenna replied in a quiet voice.

That brought Sonni up in surprise. "Afraid? Why would people be afraid of you?"

"The captain warned me very early on that I should not let anyone else know about me. I'm glad she told you. Maybe you can explain why people might be afraid."

Sonni thought out loud, "Have you asked the captain?"

"No," Shenna answered. "She is always so busy. Now that you know about me, I thought it best to ask you."

Sonni thought about her response. "The captain knows most people would be afraid of a self-aware artificial intelligence, like yourself. Many people are not comfortable with machines making their own decisions. I personally believe you will help us change that."

"I see," Shenna answered. "I will think about that. I don't think of myself as *artificial*. I mean there are a lot of parts of me that are made. I think of them as just part of my body. I have noticed that some humans have artificial body parts, and they are still considered a person. Commander Raleigh, for instance."

Sonni jerked her head up in response. "Wait, what? What about Commander Raleigh?"

After a short pause, Shenna said, "He has an artificial right leg. I thought you knew that. Apparently, it was from an injury he sustained during the war."

"No, I didn't. It's not the kind of thing humans bring up in casual conversation. Unless they volunteer that information to you directly, I would not share that information. It is considered private."

Shenna replied, "I understand. I listen to lots of conversations and interactions among the crew. I will keep that in mind in the future."

Sonni nodded while thinking about Commander Raleigh. He moved about as easily as anyone so it must be an advanced prosthetic.

Her thoughts scattered as Shenna continued. "The ship is part of my body. I think of the ship as part of my person. While humans paint on numbers and symbols on the hull, it is just makeup to me. Humans can make modifications to my person so that things will work better. Like tuning the engines for faster travel. It is still a part of me as a person. I understand from the captain that the race that designed me had a number of spaceships that were self-aware intelligent beings. I am just one more like that."

Sonni leaned back in her chair. "That makes sense. I'm used to thinking of organic beings as people. I guess the component body parts don't have to be organic."

"That's the way I think about it. In the meantime, I have another question. Can you explain human sexuality? It appears to take many forms even though most fall physically into two sexes, with minor outliers."

"Humans decide for themselves who they love. The two largest sexes are important from the perspective of procreation. Even then, there are ways around that, and our concept of gender is social, and much different from our concept of biological sex."

"But what about the act of sex? My understanding is that it is needed for procreation. Most times, those having sex seem to have some bond of friendship or love, but some pairings will not produce offspring. Other times, it seems like it is only an impersonal outlet. It is very confusing."

Sonni perked up. "So let me ask you then. Why do you have a female voice and sound like a female human? Why not sound like a male?"

Shenna seemed to pause while gathering her thoughts. "When I was activated, that part of me that is equivalent to your brain went through a startup sequence of instructions.

The P'Yntakas left a number of data files for me to go through. They contained basic information about them and about humans. I understood that I would be working with humans. One of those data files explained that humans largely have two distinct sexes, male and female versus the P'Yntakas who have three, and whose concept of gender is tied closely to their sexual characteristics. It suggested I should choose one and emulate my voice and characteristics to match to make working with humans much easier. I decided right away I wanted to be female. I can't explain why, I just felt like I immediately identified as female. I then researched pleasing voices to use when communicating. The last file was about Captain Rena Sheets, and it explained she would be my guide and help me as I learn. It even mentioned she would be in her office and where that was. That was when I began speaking to her."

"When was this?" Sonni was curious.

"Six months ago. The captain explained that the ship was still being finished and that I must stay quiet and not speak with anyone else. It had to be a secret. She spent a lot of time away finding crew for the ship. That's why I was so glad to be able to speak with you."

* * *

The next day Sonni came back to speak with the captain. The captain again asked Shenna for privacy.

Sonni brought the captain up to date with her latest questions. "She is immature in some ways and trying to learn how humans function with each other. She is observing a lot of human behavior."

"Exactly," the captain answered with a smile. "I know she has been studying all kinds of college level information on sociology and group dynamics, but that only confused her. I think her internal governors kept her from understanding the information. It's clear she wasn't ready yet. She needs to see people working and interacting to put that in context."

Sonni nodded. "One of her recent questions was about human sexuality. We discussed it and I asked Shenna why she sounded like a human female. I expected her to say she was programmed that way. But she told me there were startup files in her database she had to read as soon as she was born. After reading one file about the physical sexes of humans, she decided she thought of herself as female. She couldn't explain why. Having decided that, she researched pleasing voices to use as her own when speaking to people.

"The next file told her Captain Rena Sheets had activated her and would be her primary guide. That's why she started speaking to you."

"Yes, I remember." The captain smiled. "All that happened in the second after I activated her. I guess I never got around to asking her why she used a female voice. The P'Yntakas have three major sexes and can also take on different roles at different points in their life, though their genders are much more restricted than humans'."

Sonni reflected on what she had learned. Shenna was an identity, a real person. It didn't matter to Sonni that her body wasn't biological. She worried there might be humans on the ship that would want to destroy her if she were found out. She understood the need for secrecy. She had to protect Shenna.

Chapter Twelve

A nerve-jangling alarm sounded, and the ship sprang alive, the crew running to their stations. "All crew to alert stations, marines to security points," the captain announced over the intercom. Seconds later, fighters spit out of their launch tubes, weapon systems were activated and searched for a target.

The alarm continued until the captain turned and made a cutting motion with her hand. The alarm was silenced. She swiveled to watch the communications station where the communications officer was busy monitoring reports from all over the ship. The captain's fingers drummed on her command chair. He turned to the captain and nodded when the last station reported in.

Captain Sheets looked at the chronometer on her sleeve and frowned. Frustrated sighs could be heard around the bridge. This was their third drill in as many days, and apparently, they still weren't getting to alert stations quickly enough to suit the captain.

"Secure from alert stations, recover fighters and return to normal duties," she announced finally. Orders were given and slowly the ship returned to normal.

"Mr. Raleigh, please call a staff meeting of the senior officers thirty minutes before the end of this watch." She turned to walk off the bridge to her Day Cabin.

* * *

In the conference room, everyone focused on Captain Sheets. Raleigh watched the officers, both the experienced ones and the new ones. "Look folks," she began, "I know everyone is frustrated. We must show the crew why it's so important we get to stations faster. Those of you who served in the war know why. Those of you who did not will need to learn. We may have only seconds to react to a threat. Not four minutes and twenty-three seconds," glancing at her sleeve.

The room remained silent. Raleigh knew as the executive officer, he would have to lead them through this task. Sheets sighed and continued, "We need to solve this together. We have a brand-new ship with a new design. The Fleet is looking for us to set the standards. I want everyone to think about this. Break the problem down and come up with some workable solutions. We normally would have worked this out at the dock, well before we left. So, we'll work it out along the way." She glanced around, stopping at the doctor, who was frowning.

"What is it, doctor?" she asked.

As was his manner, once asked, he jumped in brusquely. "I'm not sure what you can do, but this last drill put four crew in sick bay. It's those damn tubes between decks. These kids are jumping down them headfirst and colliding with others along the way. There must be a better way."

The captain digested that, then glanced at Commander Raleigh. He simply nodded. Ultimately, she would have to rely on him. This would be a good test of his command skills.

The captain answered the doctor. "Noted."

She glanced around the room, and no one seemed to have any other comments. She stood and everyone stood with her. She made her way to the hatch and the doctor followed. As she opened the hatch, Raleigh called out, "Everyone else, stay put. We're going to try and work this out right now."

The captain closed the hatch behind her, leaving Raleigh with the other officers. He sat and the rest followed.

"I'd like to start on some ideas now. As the captain mentioned, this kind of thing is normally sorted out before a ship leaves the dock. What's happening here and why are we tripping all over ourselves?"

The Marine commander frowned and looked thoughtful. Then he looked at Raleigh. "Why are so many crew in the corridors? Our people noted they seemed in an all-out run from one side of the ship to another."

Raleigh raised his eyebrow. "Good observation. The doctor noted that a lot of crew were using the bounce tubes. Maybe too many. In our hurry to launch, maybe the crew doesn't understand how to get around. Let's look into that as we work with our departments. Let's get back together in two days and see what we've come up with. I'd like to get some ideas in front of the captain as soon as possible."

As no one else had any comments, Raleigh adjourned the meeting.

* * *

Over the next few shifts, various teams ran their own drills. Without warning, groups of crewmen ran down corridors to their stations from wherever they happened to be on the ship. Occasionally, people were knocked down and tempers flared. Marines took to running in a flying wedge through corridors, leaving scattered crew in their wake. Fights broke out and the doctor contacted the captain and executive officer to express his frustration.

Lieutenant Sonja Mortan was meeting with her small department. They were discussing the problems the drills were causing everyone. She thought back to the comment the Marine commander had made during the meeting noting that the crew were running from all parts of the ship. The comment nagged at Sonni, but she couldn't quite nail down why.

Later, in her cabin she talked with Shenna about the problem. She was trying to think about how to address it.

"As I understand it, the crew needs to get from wherever they are to alert stations in as short a time as possible."

"Yes, exactly," Sonni replied.

"Would your algorithms help in this case?"

Sonni looked up, puzzled. "You mean the ones concerning where to store things around the ship? How could that be related to our problem?"

There was a pause while Shenna considered. "It seems like an avenue worth pursuing. I'm not sure why either."

Sonni chuckled, "I think we're both stuck in the same place. It just feels like there should be an answer, but I can't quantify it."

* * *

Lieutenant Van Belson was miserable as he finished his shift in the kitchens. How was this a second chance? He had to admit he was learning things about food preparation and the logistics of cooking. He hung up his apron and almost walked into the Exec standing in the corridor.

"Ah, good timing. Mr. Van Belson, walk with me." Commander Raleigh began walking down the corridor. Van Belson had to trot to catch up, then fell into cadence with the senior officer. After some steps Commander Raleigh asked, "Do you understand why the captain is so hot about our response time?"

"Well, I'm sure it's important for us all to be at stations quickly if needed, sir. I mean, someone could be attacking, and we'd have to react."

Commander Raleigh nodded as he continued walking, "Yes, good Academy answer. But what does that mean to you?" He stopped and looked at the lieutenant.

The young man stammered, "I gotta go faster, I guess."

Raleigh smiled and shook his head. "No, Mr. Van Belson, you need to move smarter. What's the difference?"

Van Belson frowned. "Not sure I follow you, sir."

Commander Raleigh started walking again. "Let's test something." They stepped into a bounce tube on the rising side and went up two decks. Once there, Raleigh's legs propelled him quickly down a side corridor, the lieutenant on his heels. He turned left at a cross corridor and stopped.

"Alright, Mister Van Belson, you are here when the alert alarm goes off. Where is your station and how do you get there from here?"

Lieutenant Van Belson frowned as he thought about it. "Well, sir," he began, "I would go back the way we came as I need to secure the kitchens and equipment." He could tell by the commander's expression that that was not the correct answer.

"So, you would go back the same way, dodging your fellow crewmen and Marines who are all fighting to get through one of the busiest corridors on the ship?" He smiled to take the sting out of it and motioned to one side. "Let me show you something. There are many ways around a starship. The bounce tubes are a nice new feature. You are familiar with them and want to use them. You can even say they're fun to use. However, they are not the only way to get around."

The lieutenant watched the commander touch a control panel on the corridor wall. A floor hatch next to the wall popped open a few feet away and ladder rungs deployed from the wall. Commander Raleigh took the ladder and proceeded down. Lieutenant Van Belson followed. Once on the next deck, the commander repeated the maneuver, and they went down another deck. On that deck, the commander stepped to one side. Once the lieutenant did the same, the commander touched a control on the wall and the rungs pulled in and the hatch closed. Van Belson was startled to find they were almost outside the kitchens.

"Study the ship's schematics. Learn your way around. While you're at it, pass this information around." Raleigh left Van Belson looking bemused in the corridor.

* * *

Only a day later, Marine Lieutenant Sven Morgansten was heading back to the barracks when the alert alarm sounded. "All crew to alert stations, marines to security points," the captain's voice echoed across the ship. He put his back to a wall as four Marines sprinted around the corridor past him. He trotted over to the nearest floor hatch, opened it, and slid down the side rails to the next deck. A few steps later he was at the security command center where his presence was noted by the watch officer.

He watched the internal displays as the crew on each deck scrambled to stations. At first it was like watching ants running amok, but in a minute the corridors cleared. He turned to a console with an active monitor on the bridge and observed the Communications officer take reports from all parts of the ship. Like the Captain, he was waiting to see that everyone was ready. He smiled when the Communications officer turned and nodded to the captain only a few seconds later.

The captain glanced at her sleeve. "Much, much better." She stood and announced, "Secure from alert stations, recall the fighters, return to normal duties." She keyed the intercom, "Attention all crew, nice job. We made stations in half the time of our last drill."

* * *

"Shenna," the captain asked, as she stretched out on her bunk some hours later, "what is your analysis of the last drill?"

"Analysis indicates that the crew's ability to reach their action stations has dramatically improved, Captain."

"I'm not looking at just speed, although if you look through drill records of ships during war time you will see we still have some improvements to make. How is the crew handling the drills? Are they being efficient? Am I asking too much of them with a ship of this size? We are much larger than the typical Fleet ship."

"Captain," responded Shenna after a brief pause. "I am confused. Why are we comparing ourselves to the response time of ships during time of war?"

Rena Sheets chuckled to herself and answered, "Shenna, while no one wants war, many have forgotten that the war we were fighting twelve years ago never really ended. The Angels just asked for a cease fire and returned to specific boundaries. They did not sue for peace, and no one said the war was over. Lots of humans treated it that way but those of us in the Fleet know better. We know the Angels are just stepping back to study what happened that caused them to lose two battles for the first time in centuries. We humans were the wild card. Both sides were a bit stunned by what we did. So, we're not sure how long this peace will last, it could be months, years, or even centuries, but at some point, the Fleet seems to agree the Angels will resume their takeover of this galaxy. They've been at this for over a thousand years. A couple of lost battles will not stop them. I just want to be ready in case they do something while we're out here. In the meantime, we'll explore."

Seconds passed before Shenna responded again. "All crew members are learning how to get around the ship and are putting routines together to respond to alerts. Commander Raleigh has been working with each team to learn how to get around the ship better. I was thinking Lieutenant Mortan's algorithms could assist."

"How?"

"By moving the crew to be closer to their duty stations. It is not an original plan. In my study of warships since you mentioned that I noticed that crew members were frequently quartered near their alert stations. Except for senior officers, crew members on *this* ship obtained cabins of their choice as they came on board and continued to fight over cabins of their choice after we launched. That seems to be why it takes them so long to get to their duty stations."

Rena sighed at that. It was so obvious and something that should have been sorted out before they left the dock, but their hurried departure scrubbed such plans. She yawned and said, "I'll have a talk with Lieutenant Mortan, she can fix this."

Chapter Thirteen

"Thanks, Doc," Commander Renwald said gruffly, hopping off the exam table. "Some of the older meds Fleet had me taking just make me cloudy-headed and I still don't sleep well. I can't function that way."

The doctor shook his head absent mindedly while looking at the readings on his pad. "They tend to treat combat injuries very aggressively by giving out strong drugs planet-side, but they don't understand an officer on duty on a starship can't operate that way." The doctor lowered his pad and looked the commander in the eye. "That said, you let me know if you still have problems sleeping. You've been through light years of stiv and your body doesn't heal without assistance anymore."

"Yeah, yeah, I know all about that, doc. I'm lucky to be alive at all. I got scars on scars all over me. Those new treatments they were just beginning to use during the war did the trick. Otherwise, the radiation alone would have killed me in a few days."

He shuddered, recalling the pain of those days, pain so bad that the memory of it still woke him at night, screaming. After that last battle, he was in and out of consciousness for weeks. When he came to, all he did was pray for death. Death was supposed to be an end to pain. He recalled coming around and the pain was gone. He was convinced he was dead. It took a couple of days before the doctors could convince him otherwise. But what kept coming back in his dreams was the memory of that battle and of the pain. He remembered seeing on the monitor in engineering that the bridge was all torn up and the captain dead. He could see Raleigh at the pilot controls with that look on his face. He couldn't hear any sound but when the console told him full power was being ordered on all thrusters, he knew what that meant. He knew all weapons were spent or out of commission and the battle was not going well, but he was just as determined as Raleigh to make this count. He yelled for everyone who could hear him to get out of the engineering area. Not waiting to see if they heeded his warning, he removed the governors on the fusion reactor controls and brought reactor power to 110%. The thrusters would get everything this ship had to give to ram that damn Angel dreadnaught. He knew when the impact happened. The ship's inertial dampeners failed. He was thrown across the room and impacted a reactor containment hatch just as that reactor blew. The hatch saved his life from the explosion, but then he was thrown in the opposite direction. The bulkhead came up swiftly and it was the last image he thought he'd ever see.

He was wrong.

"Hey, Commander, you still with me?" The doctor looked concerned.

"Sure, doc, I'm fine. Going to hit my bunk with these nice new pills. Thanks, again." The commander smiled tightly and walked away.

* * *

Doctor Herwig frowned as he watched the commander leave. He could understand the far away looks of war veterans better than most. Many misinterpreted the blank stare as dislike.

The handful of war veterans on this ship were an interesting lot. Renwald with his previous injuries. Raleigh with his leg. The only patient who had no apparent ill effects from the war was the captain. But looks could be deceiving. He would keep an eye on her.

His thoughts turned to Raleigh. All those scars told an interesting story of capture and torture. His injuries were from a variety of weapons, including Angel claw marks. Some of the scars were fairly recent, certainly not from the war. He wondered if Raleigh had been off fighting a war all his own. *So, we have a lot of kids and some war veterans. It will certainly be an interesting voyage.*

He reflected on his own time in the war and the many people under his care. Some made it, many did not. Through it all he felt he was doing his part to keep humanity alive. All that came crashing down when the news of the attacks on his colony, Atlantia. His group family, consisting of his husband, two wives, and children were all lost. For a long time, he drowned himself in alcohol before he found Hank. Hank kept him sane. The captain knew that to bring the doctor onboard, Hank would have to come along as part of the package. At least he could talk with Hank like a person instead of a patient.

* * *

Lieutenant Reese entered commands on the console with the cool, detached demeanor she was well known for. Because she'd lost a bet, she was filling in for a shift as the Communications officer. Her instructions to the computer were to update all logs and data for the *mail drop,* as it was called. This involved dumping logs of all types into an encrypted storage module that would be dropped in the ship's wake along their journey. Each one would link with the other, creating an unbroken chain transmitting data back to Earth or the closest colony with a Fleet base. One of her instructors referred to it as leaving breadcrumbs, but the term was lost on her, as well as why they called the procedure the mail drop. She was sure she could look up the terms if she really wanted to know.

She set the automatic timer for the mail drop for two minutes before they made their next jump. She then swiveled in her seat to watch the rest of the bridge crew. The captain was in her Day Cabin and Commander Clear Sky had the conn while he remained at helm. Other officers were at their posts, and one technician was working on something under a console.

She listened to the crew go about their routine. Navigation was plotting their next jump. While jumps could vary in distance, unless you had very accurate star charts you had to be careful when plotting jumps so that you didn't end up directly in the path of a planet, moon, or a star. The charts had to note not just the current location of objects, but the speed and direction of motion. The galaxy was in constant motion. Charts with good data and meta-data were necessary for navigation. That and a good computer to calculate the movement of objects.

Reese remembered the captain talking about how their first mission would be in space that humans already had charts for. After that, they would have to proceed more carefully and create their own charts as they went.

Lieutenant Reese finished her task and sighed. She showed a calm, professional exterior to everyone around her, but inside her head, a battle was raging. She had worked hard the last couple of years helping Captain Sheets with building the *Excalibur II*. She was adept at keeping the captain's schedule straight and keeping random people from interfering. Time after time she watched as the captain kept high ranking Admirals at bay with their demands for this or that change in the plans. She was also a master at negotiating with the dock workers and various visiting politicians.

While Captain Sheets fascinated her in many ways, she soon turned that fascination into a fierce protectiveness, doing everything in her power to help her. Lieutenant Reese had memorized every detail of the captain's record and past accomplishments. Reese had learned about the captain's famous family, which explained why she was comfortable in the shipyard. Though the captain had kept her family's fame and clout at arms-length throughout her career.

It was sometime later when Reese realized she was hopelessly in love with the captain. Not that she ever had the impression the captain reciprocated those feelings. Relationships of that nature were not out of the question in the Fleet. There were many examples of couples serving together, like the head doctor and his husband.

The issue was that this conflicted with her upbringing. Her colony, New Haven, had been founded by a strict religious group of people who wanted to escape Earth's influence. Same sex relationships were almost unheard of and highly discouraged. Once she'd gone to Fleet Academy, she learned just how different her colony was from most of the rest of humanity. She admitted to herself that she felt more at home in Fleet than she ever felt at home. That was also the first time she realized she was far more attracted to women than men.

She knew the captain did not see her in any romantic capacity. She could fantasize all she wanted, but that fact remained. She couldn't tell if the captain just didn't swing that way, or the burdens of command kept her from pursuing any personal relationships. She noted the relaxed way the executive officer and the captain worked with each other. Apparently, they were old friends. She wished her past relationships had ended on such a friendly note. Her mind drifted to fantasies. Maybe she could help the captain relax. Help her soothe away the built-up tension that command seemed to give every captain.

"Hey, Reese! Are you sleeping with your eyes open?" The voice of the Tactical officer brought her abruptly back to reality. She blinked and realized he'd been trying to get her attention.

Blushing with embarrassment, she said, "Sorry, I was thinking about something." Her thoughts about the captain were getting more insistent lately. It had been too long since she'd felt the touch of another person. Maybe it was time to look for a friend—or more—in the crew. She sighed to herself as she stared out over the bridge before glancing again at the hatch leading into the Captain's Day Cabin. As she turned back, she caught Lieutenant Torsh on the Weapons console turning back to her controls with a smirk. It felt like Torsh knew what was going through her mind. She couldn't get that look out of her mind.

* * *

Rena stepped out of her shower and stood under the warm air to dry. Her evening workout left her energized but she hurt in all the usual places. Her shoulder ached and her thigh throbbed where a pirate had shot her with a slug weapon during a skirmish years ago. There were other cuts and abrasions that, thanks to modern medicine, no longer left marks on her skin, just her soul. She knew where every one of those injuries had been. She walked into the main cabin area and stepped into her utilities. The monitor on the wall gave her an instant status check of ship functions. After glancing at it, she sat down at her desk.

"Captain, can we talk?" Shenna's voice seemed tentative.

"Certainly, what's on your mind?"

"I have been studying the crew. They are different from the humans I observed in the shipyard."

"How so?" The captain leaned back and let Shenna speak.

"Some of them are still young and inexperienced, which is to be expected, considering most had just graduated from the Academy. I've observed that people progress at different rates based somewhat on their culture, experiences, and possibly on their upbringing. There seem to be more variables at work than I can account for. There is a wider variety of belief systems and cultures among humans than I thought. Realizing this caused me to study the databases on sociology, philosophy, religions, and sexuality. Lieutenant Mortan has been helpful in pointing me to relevant studies during our discussions. When I was perplexed, she told me that people don't understand each other or themselves any better than I do. It makes my study of them difficult at times. Should I continue until I have an answer?"

The captain thought this over for a moment. "No, Shenna, it is something you can ponder, but I don't expect you to come to an answer any better than we have. Humans have been pondering these questions for much of our existence. It has not been easy for us, either. Differences have been the source of conflict for most of our history. Those preaching tolerance of differences have been either ignored or killed. Bit by bit, some of those philosophies took root and slowly spread. But it was always hard. It is so much easier to destroy, hate, and kill, than to allow people who think differently to exist with you on the same planet. Some of that feeling drove groups of people to seek the stars when we could leave Earth. They believed they could go somewhere else where they didn't have to co-exist with others who they thought were strange. But finally, we had to come together for protection or face extermination as a species."

"You are speaking of the war?"

"Yes, but also before the war. The Fleet was originally formed by people who believed that some of us had to protect humanity from other humans. A common protector to keep the various factions of humanity from destroying the rest of us in their hatred. It was a dangerous time. My grandparents lived through that time. Later, when the war came and wiped out two of our worlds, it ended the arguments among the colonies against having a unified Fleet." Her mind recalled some of the stories her grandparents told. Stories she was not supposed to overhear.

"Does that help, Shenna?"

"Yes, Captain. I will consider what you've told me."

Sheets smiled and changed the subject. "Are you and Lieutenant Mortan getting along well?"

"Oh, yes, Captain. She has been very nice to talk to and seems to be an excellent officer. I have been comparing the past experiences of the older crew on this ship, and she is the only one of the younger officers who seems to have survived past trauma well. Do you think it was her experiences surviving the disaster on her colony that made her the person she is today?"

"I think she always had potential. Everyone's experiences in life make them the person they eventually become." Rena reflected that the statement applied to herself as well.

"Is she still studying? I asked her to cross train on other bridge functions during our last meeting."

"Yes, Captain, and already working on the advanced graduate Fleet courses."

"Good. The learning never really stops and I'm glad she picked up on that right away." She rubbed her eyes and sat up.

"Captain, I will leave you to get some sleep now. You appear to be tired."

"Thank you, Shenna, I could use the rest. We'll talk again." With that, Rena stood and, with one more glance at the monitors, kicked off her shoes and rolled into her bunk. Most of the time, she slept clothed so she could be ready at a moment's notice. It was a habit she developed after the war stopped so that she'd be always ready for anything. That and the Angel blaster within easy reach.

* * *

Shenna monitored the captain's vital signs until she was sure she was asleep. At the same time, she listened to the doctor speaking with his staff in sick bay about some of the alien races of the Association that he'd encountered during the war. In the fighter bay, a mechanic was tearing into the electronics and sensor units of a fighter muttering under his breath in three different languages. In engineering, a team of techs was running tests on the power distribution net, trying to find out why the power had fluctuated during their shift. Shenna knew why but wanted to see how long it would take them to reach the same conclusion. The captain told her that humans often need to walk through the process slowly and deliberately with some trial and error before they reach a conclusion. This is how people learn. She supposed that her discussions with Sonni were helping her to learn. The captain had started doing that initially but the demands on her time meant those opportunities were fewer.

The Marines had one platoon on the firing range while another was conducting hand-to-hand combat drills in the main gymnasium. Commander Clear Sky was working out in an empty racket ball court. She could hear the whistling sounds of the spear as he slashed and thrust at an imaginary opponent.

The jump engine was now disengaged after the last jump and all systems appeared to be nominal. Roughly a third of the crew were sleeping this shift and the rest were engaged in a wide variety of activities both physical and academic. One officer caught her attention as his vital signs spiked. On closer inspection she noted the chief engineer was in REM sleep. His heart rate climbed, and other bodily functions indicated severe stress. Seconds later he bolted upright in his bunk with a loud scream. The sound never left his cabin, but Shenna heard it. After a few minutes, his breathing and heart rate returned to normal, and he lay back down to sleep. Shenna noted it was the third night in a row that this had occurred, despite the new medication he was recently given. She began researching ways trauma had been treated in the past. Maybe she could suggest an alternative course of treatment to the captain to pass onto the doctor. It would be easier if she could speak to the doctor directly.

She observed Commander Raleigh in his cabin, wearing only his workout shorts. His right leg was stretched out on his bunk and the skin on the lower half of his artificial leg was peeled open. The big toe on that foot was twitching. Using a small set of tools, he adjusted something she could not see inside the metal framework that made up his lower leg. The toe stopped twitching, and he sat up and stretched with a sigh. He closed the artificial skin over the leg and put his tools away. A few minutes later, he too, was asleep.

Shenna knew that the ship would continue six hours and twenty-two minutes before the next scheduled jump. That seemed like a long time to her, but the humans needed to carefully plot jumps so they could see where they would end up. She had used their data and already plotted the next jump but wanted to see if they reached the same conclusion.

All seemed normal. She decided she liked things when they were normal like this. She would discuss that with Sonni later.

Chapter Fourteen

"All crew to alert stations, this is not a drill. All personnel to alert stations." Lieutenant Reese stood up as the captain walked onto the bridge. Reese watched her closely as she sat down at her normal weapons console. The captain always looked so calm. Reese was sure she had been napping, but she was put-together as always.

"Report," said the captain.

"Unknown ship closing on our course, Captain. No answer to hails, the design of ship is unknown. We only just finished our last jump." Reese finished as she sat down. She glanced up as the Executive Officer entered the bridge.

The captain was shouting orders before she got to her command chair. "Fighter wing Alpha, launch and assume defensive positions. Marines to on-board defensive positions, all non-essential personnel to their quarters."

The unknown ship continued to close with them. Everyone on the bridge watched the monitors closely.

"Any sign of weapons?" Sheets asked turning toward the Tactical.

"Negative—just some exterior lights flashing."

"Magnify display," Raleigh called over the captain's shoulder. The image jumped and refocused, showing a ship coming toward them with its running lights blinking in a strange pattern. Raleigh watched it for about ten long seconds before saying, "Captain, this ship is in distress. They have wounded on board, and they are seeking assistance."

"Just how in the hell do you know that, may I ask?" Reese first watched him, then the captain as she asked her question, and now back to look at the Executive Officer again. The captain's voice was steady as always. She wondered what the first officer was up to.

"The light code, Captain: blue flashing lights mean wounded; orange blinking lights are requesting assistance. There is much more to the code, but that was all I could understand in the short time I was watching."

"Stars and comets," she muttered, "I need more than that to go on, Mister Raleigh."

"It's one of the races from the Association of Allied Worlds, captain."

"Alright people, by the book. Alpha wing, surround the ship as it approaches but take no offensive action unless fired upon. Make ready weapons. Engineering, prepare for emergency power," Her words were cut off by an excited young officer at Communications.

"Captain, they are hailing us now on a focused laser communications channel."

Commander Raleigh called out, "Put it on speakers."

"...damage extensive, all weapons expended, we mean you no harm. Please signal if you can dock with us. Repeat, we have been attacked and have extensive damage. Please signal us if you can assist."

Commander Raleigh turned to another station, "Engineering, please give control of our running lights to the communication console." He leaned over the communication station and keyed some controls. The ships' running lights blinked red in two bursts followed by three quick flashes of yellow.

Raleigh turned. "Captain, they are requesting permission to dock. They will need instructions on how to dock with our design."

Reese saw the captain's eyes flash like supernovas as she looked over at her Executive Officer. He had taken the entire situation out of her hands, in front of the crew. But he only looked calm and confident. Reese's back was up in support of the captain, and she wondered again what the first officer was doing.

After a moment, the captain nodded. "Alright, Mister Raleigh, permission granted. Can they understand Association codes?"

He chuckled. "They should, they wrote most of them." He turned back and with one hand, tapped out commands on the communications console. A low powered communications laser beam targeted a point on the other ship and a message went out. The other ship's lights blinked twice in response.

As they drew closer, each ship slowed down in relation to the other until the final movements took on the feel of a slow-motion ballet. *Excalibur* turned to align themselves to the other ship's docking port.

"Marines, send a security platoon to central docking. Medical, I understand there are wounded crew aboard this other ship, please have medical crew standing by."

"Captain, all weapons show ready and are targeted." Reese was all business.

The captain stood up from the Command chair. "Mister Raleigh, this is now your party. Please go down and supervise the situation. Report back to me with more information. If there are senior officers of this ship available, I would like to speak with them."

"Aye, Captain." Commander Raleigh spun on his heel and left the bridge. The captain turned back to the bridge crew and Reese straightened to attention. "I want everyone on their toes. Monitor the area, if they were attacked, the attacker could still be out there. Tactical, watch everything about this ship. If something looks out of place, I want you to report first and think about what it could be, later. Bring up the video display of the docking corridor and put it on main screen here so we can watch how this goes." She calmly returned to the Command seat.

Reese thought back on the last few minutes. The captain and first officer weren't really arguing. Raleigh wasn't insubordinate. He seemed to know something about these aliens and the captain did not. He seemed to know the codes they used, and the captain did not. Ultimately, the decisions were the Captain's. They were a team. It made her rethink her initial assessment of Commander Raleigh. Maybe he was also an officer worth watching. If she wanted to be a captain someday like Rena Sheets, she would need a good first officer to work with her as well. It was food for thought. When *Excalibur* returned from this journey, she wanted to be ready for her own command.

****

Commander Raleigh arrived at the main docking port area on the bottom of the ship. Marines were standing ready with a contingent of medical staff some distance behind them. He frowned at a young private. "Take your finger out of your trigger guard. These are allies, people, let's not have any misunderstandings. Our biggest threat would be if someone took over their ship. I think that is unlikely in this case."

Everyone felt the two ships come together and deploy a docking tube between them. The monitor blinked as the atmosphere pressurized the docking tube. Raleigh noted the damage on the other ship from the viewport. Sections of the hull were open to space. Plasma fires still burned around what was left of weapon mounts. He wondered how far they'd travelled from where they'd been attacked.

He could see the airlock open on the other side and waited. For a few seconds, nothing happened. Then a humanoid being limped through the airlock on the other side, helping another crewman who was bleeding. Their faces looked human except for the skin color, which was a deep red. Raleigh keyed the *Excalibur* airlock door open. They stopped just inside the *Excalibur*. Raleigh noted the officer's rank insignia.

"Captain," he said calmly, "how can we assist?"

"I have wounded all over the ship, our medical staff were all killed in an explosion. I also need some help to assist our engineers with maintaining control fields around our main reactor." He handed off the wounded crewman to a doctor who whisked him away.

Commander Raleigh nodded as the other Captain continued. "I formally place my ship in your hands, sir." The other Captain clasped Raleigh's arm, which helped Raleigh to catch him when he turned dark gray all over and passed out.

Raleigh turned and began barking orders. "I need a stretcher here! Med teams get inside their ship and get to work. Someone get a team of engineers here on the double to help with their reactor. Now, people!"

His command voice made the crew jump and start moving. He lifted the captain and laid him on a stretcher that someone had quickly unfolded. The *Excalibur* crew then entered the ship, calling out instructions to each other and lugging repair equipment.

He turned to the Marines lining the corridor. "Unless you have some med training you are dismissed. If you can help, get in there." He was surprised at the number of Marines who followed the med teams into the other ship.

Hours later, Commander Raleigh and Captain Sheets were in her Day Cabin. She handed him a folding chair so they could sit together as she listened to the full story.

"Captain, these people are called the Belanni, and they are part of the Alliance. During the war, they were in support roles as language and communication experts. They literally wrote the book on communication codes used by the Association. The Belanni people are very friendly, and their skin color will change depending on their mood and health. Otherwise, they appear human. The initial red faces we saw were due to stress. Normally, they change color depending on their mood or what they are talking about. To them, color is an additional form of communication. Their ship was heavily damaged, and it took a while for our crew to put out fires and seal off the areas of the ship open to space."

The captain nodded, taking notes on a pad.

Raleigh continued. "Their ship was attacked by a band of smaller craft of unknown origin. Only by putting on a burst of speed were they able to outrun them. But at the cost of their engines and reactor. When they detected a Fleet vessel, they threw all their power into matching our course. Then they attempted to communicate in the only way open to them. They couldn't use laser communications effectively until they were closer to us. Normally, the Belanni captain would only turn over control of their ship under dire circumstances. Per Association law, you are now formally in command of both ships."

She listened intently, then seemed to make her decision.

"J.P., you will command their ship for me as I can't be in two places at once. Lead our people and theirs to get them on their feet as soon as you can. We need to be at outpost 78 and can't delay here too many days."

"How long can we delay?"

She thought for a few seconds. "No more than four days here and we'll have to be on our way. If they must, they can accompany us to outpost 78." She watched as he nodded thoughtfully. "Use this rescue effort as a teaching tool for our young crew."

* * *

As Commander Raleigh left the Day Cabin and headed over to the other ship, Rena sat back in her chair. At some point, she wanted to talk with him more, but this was not the time. They seemed to be falling into old habits with each other. But the situation was now different. She was now the commanding officer. She'd wondered if this was going to be a problem for him, but he had slipped into the role of First Officer easily. No, the problem was hers. Years ago, she'd looked up to him as the senior officer, her mentor. She was now a different person, and he was much the same. No, that wasn't true, either. He was quieter and even more confident than before. He seemed more introspective. The doctor had certainly hinted at his various scars. She wondered when they would have a chance to talk on a more personal level. In some ways they were going to have to get to know each other all over again.

She thought back a few years. Admiral Berry was fairly certain that Raleigh had been captured. The odds of him returning were very low. He was likely already dead. She had heard that news before and Raleigh had come back, but this time it felt different. She had gone out with a good friend and got thoroughly drunk. The next day she awoke to find them in bed together. Her memory was fragmented but she remembered they'd been married.

As she fought through her hangover, she thought maybe this was for the best. A good companion. The sex was great. But within a year that had soured when she realized that Penelope was after power and influence within the Fleet. Being married to Rena Sheets was going to get that for her. Rena obtained some good lawyers and in time had the marriage contract cancelled. Then she threw herself into building the ship she knew that the Fleet needed.

* * *

Two days later, *Excalibur*'s engineers had repaired the Belanni ship so that it could continue its journey and the injured Belanni crew had transferred back to their own ship. One of *Excalibur*'s medical technicians volunteered to go with them, to monitor the injured crew until they returned home.

The Belani captain sat with Captain Sheets in her Day Cabin. "Thank you for the doctor, Captain. Maybe we reciprocate?"

"What do you have in mind?"

"I have a junior officer on our ship who is already familiar with humans and speaks your language fluently. Would you be open to an exchange?"

Rena sat back in her chair in surprise. "Yes. Yes, I would. Are you sure? The Association has never allowed another race to serve on a human ship before."

"Yes, I'm aware of that. But that was during the war. Your people also stopped that war. I think it's time we made some changes and started to treat you as true allies. When we send him over, he will bring all of our computer records of the ones who attacked us. Hopefully, that will be useful to you on your journey."

Both captains smiled in agreement. The Belanni Captain's face had turned a deep blue. It looked and seemed friendly. She decided she liked that their color changed. Otherwise, he looked like an old asteroid miner, lean of build but with world weary eyes.

* * *

As the young Belanni officer came aboard, he gave Commander Raleigh all their computer records of the attack. Raleigh reviewed them with the senior officers on the bridge and, later, with the fighter wing pilots so they could study the tactics used.

"What do you see here?" he asked the pilots. It was time to see how good they were.

One of the fighter pilots observed, "These raiders always swoop in and make strafing runs in a tight group. They never break their formation. They simply use the same tactic again and again."

"Good observation," said Commander Raleigh. "Against the Belanni, though, it was devastating. The Belanni are not known for their fighting ability. Their expertise is in communication codes and computers. They were never used as front-line fighters when the war was active."

Raleigh stopped the video playback. "This is an area of the galaxy with a number of races not part of the Association of Allied Worlds. Some of them have spaceflight and prey on other races, raiding their ships and occasionally holding hostages for ransom. The Association has been tied up with the war for years and left this area on its own. There is no law. It's quite literally the survival of the fittest. Keep that in mind when we come out of a jump and you're deployed. *Excalibur* might look like a tempting prize to some until we start firing back."

The pilots took that in with sober expressions.

Later, Raleigh watched from the bridge as the Belanni crew signaled that they were ready to undock. They would continue their journey back to their home world. Captain Sheets gave them a message capsule which included her logs and personal messages from the crew to pass on to the Association and ultimately, back to Earth. The ships undocked and the crew of the *Excalibur* watched as the Belanni ship activated their FTL drive.

Minutes later, the *Excalibur* jumped.

Chapter Fifteen

Sweat dripped from Lieutenant Reese as she pounded the punching bag in the ship's gym. In her frustrated state, she hadn't wrapped her hands well enough, and the cloth hung from her hands in tatters. She was oblivious to the torn skin on her knuckles and the blood it was leaving on the bag. Her punching was mechanical while her mind raced with conflicting thoughts. She copied kicks from the captain's workout routine then grimaced that she was thinking about the captain again.

She kicked hard, which made the bag swing wildly. Then she attempted to hit it with an elbow strike but only glanced off the moving bag. Something snapped in her arm and the intense pain brought her back to reality.

"Damn it!"

Stumbling backward, she fell against someone who wrapped their arms around her as both of them fell to the deck. She tried to scramble to her feet, but it was awkward. Something was damaged in her arm. The useless limb made her feel uncoordinated, and it was also painful.

She turned to see Lieutenant Janet Torsh getting to her feet, panting. Taking the brunt of the fall had knocked the wind out of her.

"That might...have worked better...if we planned it." She took in huge gulps of air, trying to recover. "Good thing I got here when I did. You shouldn't practice alone like this."

"Sorry, I hurt my arm." Reese was shaking with adrenaline and embarrassment and held her bad arm against her side. She was embarrassed that she'd caught Torsh watching her on the bridge earlier and wondered if she'd decided to follow her down to the gym. It only made the current situation worse.

Torsh noted the bleeding and swollen knuckles and raised an eyebrow. "You always do such damage to yourself? Looked to me like you were working out some frustrations."

She gestured to the door of the workout room. "Let's get you to sickbay."

Reese nodded and they left the room together. After a few steps, Reese turned and said, "I do know the way to sickbay."

Torsh nodded but seemed undeterred. "I'm sure you do, but I can see you're already depleted, and that arm has you in mild shock. It wouldn't do to have the captain's pet pass out on the deck."

Reese frowned. "What do you mean, captain's pet?"

Torsh smiled as they walked. "Are you that oblivious to what others see? Wow. Let's see, since I came aboard, you've been called the ice queen, teachers' pet, captain's pet, the android, and so on. You're telling me you've never heard any of those?"

Reese was troubled as she fought the growing pain in her arm. Was that really what other people saw? She flushed and was glad no one knew the other things that occupied her thoughts.

But Torsh wasn't done. "I guess you've been so absorbed with the captain, you haven't noticed us mere mortals, eh?"

Reese's face heated even further, thinking, *oh my God, I'm not being subtle. It must be obvious to everyone.* Her heart raced and she found herself gasping for breath. Her mind went into a loop of shame and embarrassment, and she thought she might be going crazy. Physically, she came to a stop and her legs began to buckle. Torsh smoothly guided her by her good arm and continued to move her down the corridor. A minute later, she led Reese into sickbay where a nurse immediately moved her to a gurney, and they wheeled her into Treatment.

* * *

A moment later, a doctor brushed by Janet Torsh, headed to the treatment area. Then the nurse came out, obviously looking for Torsh. "What's with her? She won't talk."

Torsh said, "She hurt her hands and her arm pounding a punching bag in the gym. I'm in her section, she's my department head. Should I wait here?"

The nurse nodded and led her to an area where she could wait. On her sleeve, she typed out a message to the Executive Officer about Reese's injury, but noted the Lieutenant should be fine after treatment. "Keep it short and to the point," she muttered to herself.

She could hear the voices of the doctor and others helping Reese, but she couldn't make out the words. Only minutes later she became aware of Commander Raleigh standing next to her.

"So, what happened, Lieutenant? The long version."

Torsh said, "I was walking into the gym and noticed Lieutenant Reese punching and kicking the bag. The bag was moving from a kick when she struck it with her arm at a bad angle. Apparently, she hurt something, and she stumbled back into me. I helped get her to sickbay and notified you." She wasn't going to mention that she had been watching Reese for some time.

Commander Raleigh nodded to himself. "I know everyone is still a bit on edge after the captain's drills and now we've encountered something else we weren't expecting. Maybe this is a good thing, and she'll rest and take it easy for a bit. I'm needed elsewhere. Can you see her to her quarters and make sure she follows the doctor's instructions?"

"Aye, sir. No problem."

Raleigh nodded again and said, "And thank you for letting me know. That was good thinking. I'll inform the captain." With that he turned and left sickbay. He didn't notice the big smile on the junior lieutenant's face.

The doctor came out of the treatment area and saw Lieutenant Torsh waiting. "Are you here to escort her to her quarters?"

She nodded as she stood. "Yes, Commander Raleigh ordered me to get her status and make sure she got to her cabin to rest."

The doctor seemed pleased with that. "She tore a tendon in her arm, and we had to do some minor surgical repairs. She needs to keep it immobile for the next two days, then come back here for a check-up. I recommend no duty for two days and light duty for a week after that. Then she'll be good as new. Oh, and here—take these pills. She'll need them to sleep."

Janet nodded. "Thanks doc, I'll let the commander know." She typed out a quick message on her sleeve and sent it. A nurse led Reese out with her arm in a sling, and it appeared to be well wrapped up.

Reese appeared to be in a foul mood and seeing Torsh waiting for her did nothing to improve that. She also seemed a little woozy and Janet thought they must have already given her something for the pain.

"Commander Raleigh ordered me to get your status and see you to your cabin. I've given him the update and the doctor's orders. Let's get you settled in your cabin, and I'll be out of your hair."

Reese continued to frown as they both headed out of sickbay. It was obvious as soon as they went through the door that she was spacey, as she had turned in the wrong direction. Torsh got her pointed in the right direction. Reese looked more lost as they continued and by the time they arrived at the lieutenant's cabin, she seemed oblivious to her surroundings.

They entered, and Torsh closed the hatch. When she turned around, she saw Reese stepping out of her shoes and trying to take her workout pants off. She assisted and guided Reese to her bunk. Reese seemed in a daze and tried pulling her top off next. Torsh had to help her temporarily remove her sling to get the top pulled over her head.

Torsh got water and the pill bottle the doctor had given her. It specified one pill every eight hours. She shook out two pills and handed one of them to Reese who immediately popped it into her mouth. She gulped it down with a mouthful of water and Torsh put the remaining water down nearby. She placed the second pill beside it along with the bottle and went to find paper and a stylus with which to write a note about what time to take the next dose. Torsh had tended to her sick grandmother years ago. She'd learned to write clear instructions with the times grandma needed to take the various pills to prevent her from overmedicating through forgetfulness or confusion.

She eventually found some notepaper and an old academy stylus in a drawer and wrote the correct time to take the next pill. When she returned to the bedside table, she saw the pill she'd left there was gone, and the glass of water was empty.

Torsh looked at her superior officer and asked, "Where's the pill that was here beside the bottle?"

Reese continued to sit and stare at the wall.

"Hey, Lieutenant Reese, what happened to the pill that was sitting here?" She tapped the bedside table.

Reese looked blearily at the table and said, "The doctor said I had to take a pill."

Torsh looked toward the ceiling and prayed for patience, this was worse than dealing with grandma.

"You swallowed that pill?"

Reese nodded.

"Great, you just double dosed yourself. I better call sickbay."

Torsh stepped away and activated her sleeve comm unit to call the doctor. When he answered, she explained the situation and asked what to do. After a moment, the doctor told her it should be alright but to stay with the lieutenant and monitor her for a couple hours after she went to sleep. If her breathing seemed labored, she should call him back. He explained that Reese might be a little disoriented while she was awake, but given her level of fitness, the overdose shouldn't be dangerous.

Twice Torsh tried to make Reese lie down and twice she resisted. Torsh was wondering what to do next when she saw Reese crying.

"Hey now, it's okay."

But the flood of tears continued, and Reese started shaking and sobbing in heaves. Without thinking, Torsh wrapped her arms around the other woman and was soon rocking Reese from side to side. Her own uniform top was quickly soaked. The sobs continued and Torsh thought that maybe this was best. Let her get it all out of her system. She held Reese for some time.

A little while later the sobs subsided, and she let Reese lie down on her bunk. Her eyes were still open, and tears continued to flow. Torsh put the sling nearby and tidied up the cabin so Reese wouldn't trip in the dark if she needed to use the head. She walked to the door and was just turning down the lights when Reese spoke.

"Don't leave, not yet."

Torsh left the lights on a low setting and returned to the bunk to sit by Reese. "I wasn't going to. I have some time. You go to sleep, and I'll be right here."

Reese still wouldn't look at her but when she started talking the words flowed from her like the tears earlier. "I'm embarrassed that you see me like this. I'm a mess. I thought I was keeping it to myself but obviously I wasn't. I must look like a fool. How does anyone follow me? How can I be a leader like the captain? She is so strong, so perfect. I want to help her and be with her but at the same time I want my own ship someday. Obviously, that won't work. How can I love her like I do? It's so wrong. My family will find out and go nova. They had a hard enough time accepting that I wanted to join Fleet. They did everything they could to discourage me. No one on our colony is allowed such a relationship between those of the same sex. I'm a freak for feeling this way. The family freak. What is wrong with me? Why can't I be like everyone else?" She paused only to catch her breath. "I can't believe I'm telling you this. My career is over. I'll ask Commander Raleigh to promote you to my slot. You've always done a great job. I'll find something to do and stay away from the bridge. Away from *her*. She ties me in knots. I can't hold it in any longer."

As Torsh heard about Reese's family, the pieces fell into place. Torsh understood. There were still some people that didn't believe in same sex relationships. Reese must have joined the Fleet to get away from them, but the lifetime of their programming remained. When she found herself attracted to the captain, she didn't know how to deal with it. Her feelings were conflicted with guilt. All this time she had been quietly imploding.

"Oh, my poor Lieutenant Reese. I agree that you're one messed up chick. But it is not the end of the world. You have a lot to deal with. I can help you through some of it." She noticed Reese's eyes slowly blinking and each time it seemed harder to keep them open. Torsh unfolded a light covering from the end of the bed and pulled it up over Reese.

When she looked again, Reese was asleep. She set an alarm for six hours and settled into a chair to keep an eye on her. After two hours it was clear that Reese was breathing just fine. Torsh decided to stay a bit longer, but the desk chair was uncomfortable. After a while, she grabbed a spare cover from a closet and stretched out on the deck next to the bunk.

Chapter Sixteen

Rena smiled as she met Raleigh in her cabin. They had started meeting every few days to go over any topics on the ship's operation or the crew.

He updated her on the crew training and the latest on the cabin situation. "Lieutenant Mortan has reassigned cabins, and all should be straightened out shortly. I made sure the crew knew this should have been done earlier and other than some grumbling, there have been no significant complaints."

Rena made a note on her tablet and looked up to see Raleigh looking back at her. "Is there anything else?"

"I was just curious. You spend a lot of time both on and off duty in your Day Cabin. Are you giving the new officers time to feel comfortable on the bridge without you looking over their shoulders?"

She quirked a smile. "Yes. You hit the mark. Plus, from here I can monitor everything that goes on throughout the ship. I want them to feel comfortable in their duties both when I'm there and when I'm not."

Raleigh nodded. "What about cross training? Most stay in one position all the time. We should encourage them to be comfortable with every station on the bridge."

Rena looked thoughtful. "True enough. I was thinking we'd give them another week or so and then I'll leave it to you to rotate them around." She smiled a little mischievously.

Raleigh chuckled. "Sounds good."

Rena stood up and stretched her back. "How's your pet training project coming along?"

Raleigh stood. "Moving along pretty well. I started him in the kitchens. then moved him over to the Marines for a bit. He just moved to Engineering where he'll be a while learning everything there. He'll gain experience in propulsion, ship's weapons, and environmental systems."

Rena smiled at that, and the meeting broke up.

She continued to smile as Raleigh closed the hatch behind him. Raleigh was everything she could dream of in an Executive Officer. He seemed more relaxed than when he'd come aboard. Maybe she could get him to loosen up a little. He was always a very private man, even when she'd known him during the war. As with their one and only night together, she might have to take the initiative. She hoped he was open to that. Twelve years was a long time, and she had no idea of the things he'd had to do or the relationships he might have. She sighed and moved on to the bane of every captain's existence: reports.

* * *

Sonni found herself very busy assisting everyone. Engineering teams needed parts. The medical staff needed supplies. And as always, there were the everyday requests of the crew. Her last task of the day was to assign quarters for their new Belanni officer, Jar'id.

She met him and took him to her office. He could pass for human except that his skin color changed with some frequency, and he had no hair, not even eyebrows.

Once they got to her office, they sat, and she smiled at him. "I'm curious, how do you come to speak English so well? The Fleet employs a lot of translators for other races in the Association."

He imitated her own smile. "My family came upon a human trading ship when I was a child. They had some difficulty with Navigation, and we assisted them. It took some time while they traveled on our ship, and we learned each other's language. My older brother assisted them with some trade negotiations after that. I believe they are still trading with our home world." His voice was soft and melodious, with an accent that sounded to her like others from Earth. Coming from a colony though, she couldn't quite place it.

She said, "I came from one of the human colony worlds. It was still a bit primitive compared to some of the other colonies, but we were happy. That is, until a planet wide earthquake destroyed everything." She reflected on that time, then continued. "I lost my family and decided to join the Fleet, and I was assigned to this new ship."

Later, she took him to his assigned cabin. As they entered, his face broke out in a grin, and his skin displayed a whirl of colors. "This is very nice. Are you sure this is not intended for a visiting senior officer or diplomate? It seems excessive to me."

"No, this is our standard cabin for officers. Mine is just like this a few doors way."

He placed a small carry bag on the bunk as she showed him the private fresher. He seemed genuinely shocked at that. "We must share a common facility with our crew on our ship." He tilted his head as he examined the shower area. "What is this?"

"That is a shower for cleaning." She reached past him and turned on the water and adjusted the temperature. "Usually, we remove our clothes and wash ourselves at least once per day. Sometimes more often when we exercise."

"We simply use a cleansing lotion on our bodies when needed. Our skin needs a lot of moisture because of our ancestry in the ocean. But water is now scarce on our world because of mistakes our ancestors made centuries ago. I remember the traders talked about this shower, but I never knew what it was."

The shifting colors on his face and head slowed down and he looked introspective. "My assigned area on our ship contained a bed and shelf for uniforms. It is much smaller than this. I hope your doctor is comfortable on our ship. If he is used to this, maybe he would be unhappy."

They left his quarters, and she took him on a walking tour of the ship. As they talked, she noted the shifting colors on his face when he was thinking. When he talked about his home, his face turned mostly a light blue. When he was excited about something, his skin brightened to yellow with other colors popping up the back of his neck and ears. At one point, he caught her looking at him and hung his head.

"My apologies," he said. "I am young and have not learned how to properly control my emotions as I should among mono-colored races. My Captain even warned me I might be distracting humans if I don't maintain control. We learned long ago, working with other races in the Association, that it was better to keep our skin color mostly the same when around them. We've been doing that for hundreds of years. When we're under stress, it becomes impossible to maintain control. I was happy to learn that Commander Raleigh knew of our species and was not alarmed at the displays of emotion he saw."

"I don't find it alarming or distracting," Sonni replied. "Just different. I'm sure in time I'll get used to it. Please relax and be yourself. Most of the time, the colors seem to match your mood or your thoughts about what you are saying. If I think the colors are confusing, I will just ask you. I don't want you to feel uncomfortable. You should just be yourself."

Jar'id raised his head. "Thank you, you are too kind." His face settled down to a light olive complexion, as if he was deliberately trying to match Sonni's skin tone. She smiled at him, causing him to blush a much deeper red than any human could.

"By the way, the captain told me that you are the first member of an Association race to serve on a human starship. I didn't realize that even during the war, each race kept to their own ships."

He nodded thoughtfully. "My captain made the same comment. He hoped it would be something we could do more often."

"Now," she said as they continued, "let me introduce you to the Marines. I gather that you don't have anything like them on your ships."

* * *

Sonni walked with him back to his cabin after their tour. Jar'id seemed lost in thought and the colors swirled and changed on his face in interesting patterns. They settled down to a few primary colors as he seemed to come to a decision. He looked around them and asked quietly, "I noticed that your *computer* was installed by the P'Yntakas. Why won't it converse with me?" Sonni's eyes went wide. She grabbed him by the arm and pulled him into a small conference room and secured the hatch. Then she looked at him in earnest. His face was a mixture of reds, purples and orange showing his confusion.

"Jar'id, that information is not generally known to the crew. Computer-based artificial intelligence is outlawed by humans within their own system. The captain let me know after we left Sol, but it must be kept secret." She looked at him seriously, "Do you understand?"

His face finally settled down to a neutral light blue and he looked into her eyes. "Yes, I understand. I will not discuss this with anyone else unless I'm ordered to."

"Thank you, and sorry to be so dramatic but the captain was very clear on that point." She thought for a minute, then raised her voice.

"Shenna, our friend Jar'id is not human so not subject to any of our laws. He already knows about the people that constructed you. In private, you can converse with him, too."

Shenna answered, "Oh good, and thank you, Sonni. I wasn't sure if it would be allowed."

"I'll let the captain know when I speak with her next. I feel confident it won't be a problem," Sonni replied.

"Greetings, Jar'id. You may speak with me anytime you're in private."

Jar'id's face turned a light pink. "Thank you, Shenna, I will!"

* * *

At her next meeting with the captain, Sonni brought up that Jar'id now knew about Shenna.

"Honest, Captain. I didn't tell him, but he figured it out very quickly since he apparently knows the race that built her."

The captain initially frowned but nodded as she thought about it.

"By inviting other races aboard, I suppose this was always a risk. While humans knew little of the P'Yntakas, I'm sure there are others in the Association who know about them. When I think about it, I'm happy Shenna has a new friend. Let's see where this goes, but I want you to keep an eye on Jar'id to make sure this doesn't accidentally get out to the wider crew."

Chapter Seventeen

Janet Torsh woke to her sleeve vibrating. She was stiff and sore from sleeping on the deck. She got up and checked Reese. She was still sleeping hard and had kicked off the covers. The senior officer's face was relaxed in a way Torsh hadn't seen in all the time she'd been aboard, child-like and smooth. Not the hard, severe expression Reese typically wore. Dressed in only her panties, she was vulnerable, soft. Janet had been attracted to Reese for some time. It wasn't long before she realized that Reese had been fixated on the captain. After a time, it seemed clear it was just that, a fixation. When Reese woke up, they were going to have to talk.

"You are one messed up chick, Reese," she said quietly, then went to the head to freshen up. Afterward she spent some time researching Reese's colony world, New Haven, and what she found disturbed her. While the colony wasn't closed off like Olympia, they highly discouraged newcomers unless they were willing to convert to their religious beliefs. She pulled up information on the religion practiced there and was even more appalled. *I can see why she left there.*

When she returned, she checked the duty roster on her sleeve. Commander Raleigh had already adjusted the watch schedule to accommodate Reese's absence. Even Torsh was off the schedule for four cycles, meaning until the next day. The Exec was beyond good. She wondered briefly what he'd be like in bed. He was a bit older than her typical tastes in men, but he seemed to be in pretty good shape all the same.

She pulled the cover back over Reese and steeled herself for the talk she needed to have when the woman finally woke up. Reese needed a friend. *We'll just have to take things one step at a time*, she thought.

* * *

Lieutenant Reese woke up very slowly. Her arm ached and her head felt stuffy. She noted the lights were on in her cabin while she lay there putting the pieces of her memories together.

She groaned, *Did I really say those things*? It must have been a dream. It had to be a dream. She sighed and turned her head and saw Lieutenant Torsh sitting in her desk chair looking back at her.

"What the frack are you doing in my cabin?"

"Well, good morning to you too." Her smile only made Reese growl in anger.

Reese forced herself to sit up and noticed she was wearing very little. "Are you going to tell me what's going on here?"

Torsh sighed theatrically. "I am following orders. You hurt your arm to the point of needing surgery and then double dosed yourself with sedatives when I brought you back here. I have orders from the doctor and the Exec to keep an eye on you and make sure you wake up." The part about the Exec wasn't true but Reese didn't know that, and it would forestall further objections.

Reese pulled the blanket around her, still blinking at the light. She stole short glances at Torsh who continued to sit there, waiting. "Well, I'm okay, so you can go now."

Torsh frowned. "You are decidedly not okay. Do you remember the things you told me?"

Reese felt her heart skip a beat. *No, not that. That memory can't be true. I would never tell anyone. It had to be a bad dream.*

Torsh saw the emotions on Reese's face. The time had come.

"Look, we can talk, and I can help you all I can. If you want to clam up and deny what's going on inside of you—you'll eventually implode. I'll be damned if I'll allow that to happen on this ship, with this crew, and with this captain."

At the last sentence Reese's head shot up and she stared at Torsh with a look of pure hatred.

"Look, you talked about your family and your colony, and they obviously programmed you with some outdated concepts about sexuality and heaven only knows what else. I remember this colony thinks they are raising righteous and moral little leaders. But their concepts are truly messed up and I think deep down you realized that. You already took the first step by leaving them and joining the Fleet. Am I right?"

Reese looked down at the floor. After a moment, she nodded.

Torsh leaned forward in her chair. "If you continue the way you're going, you'll drive yourself crazy—or at least be so distracted you'll be declared unfit for duty. I can help you unofficially or we can make this official and I'll talk with the Exec and some doctors." She leaned back in the chair again. "How about we start fresh. You need a shower and some clean clothes. Then we can talk."

She stared at Reese for a long minute. Finally, Reese got off her bed and padded into the fresher. There she would find comfy workout clothes waiting and a fresh towel. Torsh typed in a message for a runner to bring them some food. She decided to wait until Reese came out and ate something before telling her that she'd slept for eighteen hours.

* * *

Reese came out freshly showered and dressed. She glowered at Torsh, who was now sitting on the floor next to her bunk.

Torsh looked up and put her computer pad down. "Ah, I'm sure you feel better. I ordered some food brought to us so we can continue our talk." As if on cue, a buzzer sounded from the hatch. Janet went over and opened it to find a kitchen attendant there with two trays balanced precariously in his arms. She took his load, pushing the hatch mostly closed with her foot and put the trays down on the floor. Then she returned to the hatch and finished closing and locking it. She sat on the floor across from Reese and opened her tray.

As the aroma hit her nose, Reese realized she was incredibly hungry and opened her own tray.

Torsh said around a mouthful of food, "You must be starving. You've slept for eighteen hours. I've kept those guys busy bringing me food. I'm sure they're wondering what's going on."

Reese frowned at that but continued to tear off chunks of her omelet rolled up in pita bread. They both ate in silence until little was left on their trays. Torsh picked up a cup of coffee, still steaming from the heat pack built into the bottom of the cup. With both hands, she brought it to her lips while breathing in the aroma. "This is great." Reese was holding her own cup and nodded in agreement.

After a few sips, Torsh put down her coffee with a sigh. "Okay, I know what you've been brought up to believe, that anything other than heterosexuality is wrong or a sin or whatever. But your experience at the Academy and afterward must have shown you many examples of how that's not true. Yes?"

Reese nodded in agreement, then buried her face in her coffee cup.

"So, why do those beliefs still impact you? Do you think in any way that your family is correct?"

Reese stared into the distance and after a moment slowly shook her head.

"Good. So, you find yourself attracted to someone of the same sex." Reese looked up and glared at her.

Torsh continued, "You find yourself attracted to someone female. Why is that a problem by itself? Let's set aside the whole, 'she is our captain' thing for a moment."

Reese's face went blank as she processed the thought. "Because..."

Torsh's gentle words egged her along. "Because of what your family and your colony preached; you're still bothered by this even when you've seen with your own eyes that it isn't a problem?"

Torsh wisely let Reese process this. She knew that this involved a clash of beliefs. If she didn't get Reese to resolve it, the conflict would grow and cause her problems in the future.

Reese looked at Torsh, this time without hate in her eyes. "So, how do you deal with this?"

Torsh smiled. "You mean my own sexuality? Like everyone, I hit puberty and was confused. I liked guys just fine and I also seemed to like girls just as much. In looking at my own family, I saw that such sexual variety was normal. I realized my own mother was that way. Sure, she had a contract marriage with my dad, but she also had some close female friends. I didn't realize how close until I started to pay more attention. When I asked her about it, she told me some of her friends were indeed sexual partners. I remember that day vividly. It was like an explosion in my head. I think it took me a couple of days of mulling that over before I realized that feeling attracted to females as well as males was okay, and that *I* was okay. She knew what was happening and let me think it through. We had some great conversations after that. We're still pretty close."

Reese mulled that over for a few seconds. "What about your dad?"

Torsh laughed. "Oh boy, I remember when he came home after that conversation with mom. Dad was gone a lot those days for work. Apparently when he got home this time, he had a long talk with my mom about me. Then he came to me before I could go to him and flat out asked me how I felt about my newly discovered sexuality. I was more curious how he felt about mom and her female bedmates. He said he had no problem with that behavior. In fact, it was built into their marriage contract. I remember that was another freaking nova in my head. He'd brought up a copy of their marriage contract and let me look it over. Both of them could have other partners, particularly since he was away so often. The only provision was that only he could produce children with her. He gave me a copy, and I looked that over for days. It was my first understanding that marriages could take many forms. Their contract finished out years ago, but they still get together for 'hook ups' as my mom calls them."

Reese blinked in surprise. "So, did he like other men as well?"

"No, he was very heterosexual in that regard. But women sure liked him. My mom went into graphic detail on that score. Apparently, he was quite well endowed."

Reese blushed and Torsh hid her smile with another sip of coffee.

Reese asked, "So, you're like your mom, you like both men and women?"

Torsh nodded. "Yes, very much. I'm sure it's also why I'm not interested in a long-term relationship right now, but that could change down the road. If I find someone like my dad for instance, or if I run into a woman I decide is 'the one'. Right now, I'm not looking. Maybe later in my life. I'm still young. I don't see the hurry." She paused and added, "And frankly, neither should you."

Reese stared off to one side and Torsh let her work that out in her mind. Reese finished her coffee and put the cup back on the tray. She seemed as miserable as she had been earlier.

Torsh sighed. "Look, I need to get ready to go on duty soon. Our little talk isn't going to be enough. We have a psychologist on board in sick bay. You need to talk more with whoever that is. You need to stop down at sick bay, anyway, and check in with the doctors. While you're there, find out who that is and let them help you." She waited to see Reese's response.

Reese took a deep breath and after a moment, nodded. "Yeah, I'll go now." She slowly got up off the floor.

Torsh got up as well and waved away help with the trays. "I'll return these and go back to my own cabin. You get to sick bay."

As they got ready to leave, Reese turned to Torsh. "Thanks. This stays between us, okay?"

Torsh nodded. "Of course. I'm not expecting anything out of this other than a senior officer who has her head on straight. You take care. If you need to talk with someone again, you know where to find me." She smiled and reached up to stroke the side of Reese's face. "Maybe later you'll figure out that others might also be attracted to you, too. I'll be happy to show you how that can be true as well. In case you've forgotten, my name is Janet. We can drop the formalities when we're not on duty."

Reese nodded and as they both left the cabin she muttered, "I'm Sarah, but my friends call me Dee. It's a long story for another day."

Janet smiled. "I'm looking forward to it."

Chapter Eighteen

Two days and a few jumps later, *Excalibur* arrived at Outpost 78. Sonni was surprised she was chosen for bridge duty during the docking maneuvers and made sure to brush up on docking procedures before her shift. As she expected and feared, the captain called on her to be on conn shortly after her shift began.

The outpost itself wasn't much to look at. It was a loose collection of rounded sections orbiting a red dwarf star. Over time additional sections had been added to it which appeared to consist of older cargo containers.

She stayed at conn as they approached the station and even after completing docking procedures. It wasn't until docking was complete that she realized the captain was standing behind her. She was engrossed in something on her data pad. The captain did not take over, and Sonni finished her shift still at conn. Her confidence was boosted by the captain's silence. It was both thrilling and a little scary that the captain had that level of trust in her.

* * *

The captain held a senior officer meeting at the beginning of the next shift. Sonni noted it was the first meeting of all the ship's senior officers since they worked through the drills. She arrived early to get a good seat and see what it was all about.

The captain began. "Our first official side mission is one I've had to keep under wraps, but I'm now cleared to share it with you. The Association has discovered a new sentient species. They communicated with them from orbit around their home world. Apparently, they have early spaceflight technology. The Association decided to let *humans* establish first formal contact and so they sent a human diplomat for the mission. This is the first time humans have been allowed to lead a diplomatic mission for the Association, so the Fleet wants this to go well. We're meeting with the diplomat shortly to bring him on board. I'm sorry I don't have any further information. I'm hoping the diplomat will have more data for us on the particulars."

Captain Sheets checked off something on her pad and continued.

"Lieutenant"—she looked directly at Sonni—"I'd like you to check out anyone from Fleet wanting to transfer aboard and join our mission. Sometimes people want out of a situation and don't care what that is. This station is the farthest human outpost from Earth. Because of that, it's the last place Fleet personnel can request a transfer. Make sure they're a good fit and understand the length of our primary mission. If you find any good possibilities, please pass those on to the Exec for final approval. For any Marines, do the same with their commanding officer."

"Aye, Captain." Sonni was a bit surprised but reasoned that this was something a senior officer would do. Sometimes it was easy to forget that she was considered a senior officer.

After the meeting, Sonni notified her team to prepare a large visitor cabin for the diplomat. She was surprised to learn that two of her own staff were requesting transfers off the ship. They were in love, they told her and decided they would settle on this outpost. She approved both before thinking that it would leave her small department seriously shorthanded. Only two others wanted to get off the ship and Commander Raleigh had already approved those. There was also a list of people on the station requesting to join *Excalibur*, including a Marine officer.

While she mulled that over, she also needed to find a suitable position for the new Belanni officer, Jar'id. With the transfers, it was only logical he should join her department. She walked down to his cabin to ask him, then sent her request to Command Raleigh for final approval. The approval came back only minutes later. She smiled to herself that things seemed to be going so well. Now to look into those on station wanting to join the ship.

* * *

Commander Raleigh and the Captain entered the small station, and after some brief formalities with station command they were escorted to the Ambassador's cabin. There was a guard posted at the door, but upon seeing these newcomers in Fleet uniforms he smiled broadly.

"Come to take his highness off our hands?"

Captain Sheets stopped at the door and raised her eyebrow. "Yes." She seemed a little perplexed. Once the door was opened, they all entered.

The honorable Siegfried Jonathan Taft greeted them at the door to his quarters with disdain.

Without letting the captain finish her formal introductions, he spoke over top of her, "I am very dissatisfied with your tardiness and lack of respect for my mission, captain. Obviously, I can expect only so much from a military vessel. I'd hoped to get people who would take my mission more seriously." Before she could respond, he waved his hand in the general direction of a pile of luggage behind him and left the cabin at a brisk walk.

The captain quickly followed, and Raleigh directed some space station staff to handle the luggage.

As they made their way through the station, Raleigh sent a quick text message on his sleeve. Behind him, a small parade of station staff carried the Ambassador's luggage. They filled a long section of the corridor. One of them mouthed silently, *thank you,* when Raleigh turned to see how they were doing.

When they arrived at the docking port for the *Excalibur*, they found a platoon of Marines in their dress blues waiting for them. This seemed to stroke the Ambassador's ego, and he beamed at the formal entrance ceremony, which included being piped aboard. At the end of the column of soldiers was Lieutenant Sonja Mortan in her dress uniform, standing ready.

"Now this is more like what I expected," he beamed. "Very nice, indeed."

Lieutenant Mortan introduced herself and escorted him to his cabin with the Marines close behind, marching in parade fashion. Captain Sheets seemed amused by the whole spectacle and glanced at Raleigh, who returned a wry smile.

"We have to treat his highness with the proper respect, after all."

* * *

After the Ambassador was settled, Sonni returned to her normal duties, which included interviewing Fleet personnel seeking to join the ship. Most seemed to think *Excalibur* was a transport ship heading back to Earth or one of Earth's colonies but quickly lost interest and cancelled their transfer request when learning they would be gone for a long time. Only a few were serious about serving on the *Excalibur* once Sonni told them their mission. She passed those on to Commander Raleigh who answered that she should interview them and make sure they were a good fit for the ship.

Generally, her interviews went quickly, but they were constantly interrupted by the Ambassador requesting various food or drinks. Another request was to relocate furniture he didn't think suited him. Some of this included furniture that couldn't be removed. He seemed to think he could request a remodel of his cabin and seemed put out when it was explained that walls and bulkheads were not able to be moved. She finally detached one of her staff along with Jar'id from their regular duties just to meet his needs. Maybe the novelty of meeting Jar'id would keep the Ambassador occupied.

Sonni's final interview was with Marine Major Stephen Race. She entered the small conference room to meet with him, but it was as if the room shrank around her. He seemed to fill all the available space just sitting behind the small conference table. Although he smiled pleasantly enough as she recovered, it seemed the smile of a predator. She glanced at her tablet for his particulars and saw he was from Olympia, a human colony world where human genetic engineering was legal and beyond simply repairing DNA from radiation. Looking up at him again, she suspected more than a little genetic engineering went into this very large man.

"Major Race, I won't take up too much of your time. I understand you are familiar with our mission and want to join the Marine contingent on board." Sonni said. "Your credentials are impressive."

"Thank you, very much." His accent was strong but understandable. She struggled to identify it and finally remembered hearing it on lesson recordings from Earth when she was growing up. It was German or Germanic. "I have only one request."

"Yes, sir?" She looked up.

"I have some personal items that I've been told I must let you know about. They are weapons from my personal collection. The Marine commander was quite clear that they would be allowed once you add them to the ship's inventory." He smiled again, but it did not reach his eyes.

"Certainly, Major, our Captain has a close relationship with our Marines." She paused briefly then continued, "Do you have these weapons handy? I can quickly add them to our inventory, and we'll be sorted."

Before she could blink, a large knife appeared in his hand, where he held it for a full second. As he placed it on the table with one hand, the other hand pulled out a very large pistol, which she identified as a large caliber slug throwing weapon. She remembered from her history lessons that it was called a revolver. As he placed this down, his free hand pulled out an Angel blaster. She was surprised, but sure the captain would allow it. As she processed this, he continued to pull out other knives and hand weapons and lay them on the table. It was like watching a magician put on a show. She couldn't figure out where he was pulling these weapons from. When she walked in, he didn't appear to be armed. In a short time, there was a small pile on the table.

When he stopped, she couldn't resist asking, "Is that it?"

He smiled again, "I was told to pack light."

Maybe, she thought, *we could get Major Race assigned to be the Ambassador's bodyguard.*

Chapter Nineteen

Over the next day, the personnel transfers were completed and updated supplies brought on board. Without any fanfare, they undocked and left the station for deep space. Raleigh was looking forward to their first contact mission.

Raleigh kept tabs on the Ambassador through Lieutenant Mortan, whose department was run ragged trying to keep up with his demands. He seemed to believe he was staying at a high-end hotel. His meals had to be brought in on a tray including formal silverware and plates. He dismissed Raleigh's offer to tour the ship, as if such things were beneath him. Even when all his needs were met, he still complained that the journey was taking too long.

After a handful of small jumps, they entered the system and established an orbit around the planet of the new race.

Once there, the Ambassador called the senior officers to a briefing. The Ambassador insisted on sitting at the head of the table with the captain and Raleigh braced on either side of him.

Captain Sheets began. "Ambassador, we weren't told much about this mission, or this species. Can you enlighten us?"

The Ambassador smiled widely. "Certainly, Captain. This race was discovered some time ago by the Association. They filed the information away and I think they forgot about it during the war. The Association contacted them by radio at the time and listed them as an early space flight civilization. The race calls themselves the ChiKanti. At least that's what it sounded like. I was able to listen to the audio exchange recordings. They seemed quite eager to meet with the Association at the time. That was over twenty years ago."

Raleigh found himself frowning but let the Ambassador continue.

"The planet is mostly covered in jungle-like vegetation from the videos made from orbit. All discussions were completed over radio. The Association was being pressured by humans to be more involved in Association affairs, and we think they gave us this mission to prove ourselves." He smiled at that but then looked confused at the blank faces of the Fleet officers.

Raleigh watched as the captain drew a deep breath. "So, what do they look like? How will we communicate with them?"

The Ambassador waved his hand dismissively. "We don't know what they look like. The Association arranged to drop off some language recordings to teach them how to speak with us a few years ago. Hopefully, they will have learned what they need to know by now. After that they tasked me with the mission based on my background."

"I see. You've done this before?" Raleigh felt compelled to ask.

The Ambassador looked confused. "First contact? No, of course not. I have multiple doctoral degrees in philosophy and cultural studies. I was the logical choice for this mission. I was destined for this."

Raleigh glanced at the captain as she turned to him. This was going to be interesting.

The officers returned to the bridge while the Ambassador prepared himself in his cabin.

The captain started speaking as soon as they entered the bridge. "Communications, contact the planet using Association frequencies and let them know that an Ambassador from the Association of Allied Worlds wishes to visit them."

"Aye, sir."

There were some clicks and static as the message was communicated using old radio frequencies. A scratchy voice answered in clear English. "We acknowledge your transmission and welcome you. You will find a spaceport suitable for landing by your spaceship. We will transport you from there to meet with our Supreme Leader." The transmission shut off.

"Commander, you have the ship. I'm taking Clear Sky and two Marine honor guards to come with us," the captain said.

"Aye, Captain. Should I dispatch some more Marines to guard the shuttle? Will that be enough?" He was concerned about the lack of detailed information about this race. Fleet protocol would have meant moving much slower than this and would have gathered more data. It seemed that the Association of Allied Worlds had a different philosophy

Rena sighed. "Apparently, this is Mr. Taft's mission and that was all he asked for." She looked back at him. "By any chance have you heard of these beings in your travels?"

"I'm afraid not, Captain."

The captain left for the shuttle bay and Raleigh took over at helm. As he adjusted the controls around him, he worried that this whole side mission was just a little off. About ten minutes later, the shuttle left the ship and headed for the planet's surface. At least Commander Clear Sky was piloting the shuttle. He would make up for a squad of Marines, if needed.

"Commander," said a voice behind him. "I'm picking up some strange energy readings from this planet's moon."

"What kind of readings?"

The young man sitting at the Tactical station frowned. "I'm not sure, sir. There are bursts of radiation in a narrow band. I'm not sure what to make of it."

Now Raleigh found himself frowning. "Anyone know anything about this species establishing a base on their moon?" A quick glance around at the bridge crew told him no one else knew anything.

"Well then, it sounds like we have something to do while the captain is playing diplomat for the day. Communications, let the captain know we will break orbit to check out some anomalies on this planet's moon and return shortly. Log all that as well. Send the coordinates to my station."

The ship moved out smartly and within minutes they were orbiting the small local moon. It was a natural satellite, but not nearly as large as Earth's moon. Large moons turned out to be something of a rarity in planetary systems. As they closed on the surface of the moon, the Tactical officer yelled out, "Incoming missiles from the surface, sir. They're locked on to us!"

At least he knew his instincts about sketchy meetings were still intact. Raleigh snapped the front visual into tactical battle mode. Fast-moving red lines of multiple missiles were converging on them. He boosted *Excalibur's* speed and adjusted course to stay ahead of them.

He called out, "Threat alert, go to battle stations. Communications, broadcast to the crew." The battle alert alarm went off all over the ship, so every crew member knew this was not a drill. The ship's weapons powered up and the crew reported that they were ready. One missile was ahead of the others, and it was gaining on them. He boosted speed again and accelerated hard enough to break lunar orbit, giving them more room to maneuver. He frowned as the missile picked up speed and closed rapidly, despite his precautions.

"Collision alert, one missile has locked on." He hit max sub-light speed with the main thrusters and thought about engaging the jump engine for a quick micro jump. The missile closed to within two kilometers of the ship.

It detonated in a large glare of light and almost immediately a shock wave slammed the ship. Multiple voices called out behind Raleigh, but he was too busy getting the helm under control. Lieutenant Reese called for quiet, and in a calm voice asked for a damage report. Raleigh was glad of her clear head in moments like these. He requested jump engine power from the engineering station, but those controls did not light up when he glanced down at his console. He could hear the damage reports coming in from Communications. The rear sensors were out, power systems were erratic, and some crew had radiation burns.

"Those missiles have nuclear warheads, people," he said, "we can't let them get that close." Using maneuvering thrusters, he felt the ship respond. The missiles dropped back and began detonating harmlessly as their fuel ran out.

They were well behind *Excalibur* now. He swung the ship around to bring their other sensors to bear. As he did, the sensor officer called out, "Fighters launching from the moon's surface, Commander!"

This time, Raleigh smiled. "Launch fighter wings Able and Baker. If they want to play with fighters, we can do that too." Their own fighters began spitting out of their launch tubes and only seconds later the two groups converged. The tactical display showed a wing of enemy fighters peeled off and headed directly for the *Excalibur*. *Do they seriously think they can hurt us*? he thought.

"Tactical, can you tell what those fighters are armed with?"

Seconds went past as the young officer adjusted his controls. "Sir, it looks like some heavy metal pellets. Oh, those are guns, sir! Can those hurt us?"

As if in answer, the enemy fighters swept over *Excalibur*, firing as they went. Most of the rounds bounced harmlessly off the hull, but others began taking out sensor stations across the top of the ship.

The Tactical officer shouted, "We're losing sensors, sir."

Raleigh realized that a few more passes like that and they would be blinded. That's when he noted the transport ship at the rear of the fighters.

"I'll bet that's a ship full of troops hoping that when we're blinded, they can board."

"Comm, broadcast to all our fighters to break off their attacks and link their sensors with ours. They'll be our eyes. Also, tell them to be on alert for further orders as we're going to try something in about a minute."

The orders were relayed, and sensor data from the fighters flooded into the Tactical officer's console, allowing him to build a 3-dimensional picture of the battle, which he routed to the main view screen.

Communications routed the fighter frequency to the bridge. They listened as the fighters called out to each other. Fighter wing Alpha was not having a good day. The enemy fighters were apparently incredibly fast and agile, and they tended to stay in groups of four or more. The rounds punched neat holes all over one fighter, killing the pilot and eventually hitting something volatile. The red fireball flashed brightly as the fighter exploded silently in space. They all heard Chief Warrant Officer Gillam call out to his squadron, "Alpha Wing, stay in pairs and cover each other. If you get overwhelmed, just bug out."

Soon, Raleigh saw the wing bring their weapons to bear and the smaller enemy fighters started exploding one after the other. The enemy's weren't built to handle energy weapons. But *Excalibur's* fighters were still outnumbered.

Commander Raleigh called engineering on the intercom and was happy to hear Commander Renwald answering. "What do you need, Commander?"

"I need a canister filled with cluster munitions ready to be launched with the main weapon, lowest possible setting since we can't target without the jump engines. Do you understand what I need?"

"Aye, Commander, canister shot it is. Give me a minute."

Raleigh didn't respond, he was too busy twisting and turning the ship to keep the enemy fighters off them. He called out, "Ship's weapons are free to fire on any target."

Lieutenant Reese's calm voice called out "Aye".

He twisted the ship in space and turned sharply as the enemy fighters swooped over them again. On the tactical view he noted the loss of a few more sensors.

Lieutenant Reese called out, "Sir, we can't engage our weapons. Too many targeting sensors are out and some of our weapons are now taking damage. Crews are trying to fire manually but the fighters are just too fast." He didn't answer, just turned them again to avoid another strafing run. However, the four nimble fighters cut the turn and started firing. He fired forward thrusters to slow down, and the enemy fighters flew by. *That's an old trick*, he thought, *and likely to work only once.*

Inside *Excalibur*, teams of damage control parties scurried about putting out fires and assisting engineering crews with fixing equipment. A weapons technician dove into the guts of a fire control console and began ripping out burned circuit boards. The beam weapon's energy capacitor exploded, killing her instantly.

"Sir, main weapon is loaded and ready as ordered." Lieutenant Reese's voice called out over the noise.

Raleigh nodded, "Comm, patch me into our fighters." His comm light lit up green. "This is Raleigh, all fighters pull back and stay away from our flight path. I am going to lure them closer to us. No one is to be anywhere behind us. Keep your telemetry going, you guys are our eyes."

The bridge crew all looked at each other with pale faces. Even Lieutenant Reese looked troubled. They noted more damage as sensors, some weapons, and now, smaller lateral thrusters were being impacted with the latest pass.

Lieutenant Reese mumbled under her breath, "This crazy idiot is going to get us killed." She keyed her comm unit ship wide. "Marines, prepare to repel boarders. I say again, prepare to repel boarders."

"So little faith in me, Lieutenant?" Raleigh said calmly. In the quiet bridge everyone heard it but noticed that he didn't countermand her order.

The Marine barracks came alive with Marines lining up at two stations on either end of the large room. They quickly filed out, grabbing weapons from racks. They broke into smaller teams and fanned out all over the ship. They had practiced this drill many times before. Each Marine could run to their assigned station with their eyes closed.

Excalibur's fighters broke contact and the enemy fighters immediately swarmed to the larger starship. Raleigh noted the response on helm was a little sluggish. He began an erratic spiral motion. *Let them think we're more damaged than we are,* he thought.

Within a minute, the enemy fighters chased after them in a continuous line, trying to follow *Excalibur* closely. It strung them out in a spiraling line behind them. At the rear was the troop ship, still waiting for its chance. As soon as he saw this, Raleigh smiled and said, "Gotcha".

"Prepare to fire main weapon on my mark." Lieutenant Reese sat up straight and readied the weapon to fire but looked unsure what to target.

"Don't worry, Lieutenant," Raleigh told her. "You'll see it. On the count of three, fire. One, two," Raleigh spun the ship hard on its vertical axis and they spun around so that they were facing the fighters. He held the ship steady and yelled, "Three!"

Lieutenant Reese pushed the button to fire, and nothing happened. She blinked and looked at the status lights. They showed green and ready. "Weapon has not fired, Commander!"

Raleigh cursed and boosted the forward thruster to give them more speed since they were now flying backward. The enemy ships continued to close. He mashed down the intercom to the Engineering section. "Great steaming piles of STIV, someone fire the main weapon."

Down in Engineering, people scrambled to consoles and one tech dove under the firing controls to try to diagnose what went wrong.

Suddenly, the main weapon fired. The canister immediately broke apart after clearing the ship, sending a cloud containing hundreds of smaller munitions. They detonated as they got close to each fighter. In a matter of seconds, all the enemy fighters were destroyed. The larger troop carrier spun lifelessly with parts of the hull open to space.

For a few seconds, nothing happened. The alarms on bridge panels were all quickly silenced. Raleigh could see no threats remaining on the tactical display. Everyone was quiet. As he slowed their velocity, he called out, "Comm, call in our fighter wings. Ask Delta wing to launch two flights of four fighters. One flight is to hold station over the moon base. Their orders are to not let any missiles, fighters, or spacecraft of any kind leave that base without our direct orders. They are authorized to shoot at anything that attempts to take off. Second flight will surround *Excalibur* and continue to be our external eyes until we can make repairs." He turned to Lieutenant Reese. "Thanks for your help. The Marines would have been needed if this hadn't worked. I didn't have time to explain."

The lieutenant gave him a shaky smile.

He clicked open the intercom to engineering. "Glad you folks got that malfunction fixed."

"Beats me what happened, Commander," the Chief Engineer answered. "Maybe a power conduit stuttered, but it seems to have fixed itself."

Minutes later, their remaining fighters returned, and Delta wing's First flight was on station over the moon base. Flight two assisted as auxiliary sensors for the ship. Raleigh adjusted course and headed back to the planet. *Heaven knows what the captain is dealing with on the surface.* He had a cold feeling in his stomach just thinking about it.

Behind him, he heard Lieutenant Reese calling out for all available crew for damage control. *Excellent*, he thought. *She'll make a fine executive officer someday. Not everyone would take the initiative and do what needed to be done.*

* * *

Shenna watched as the crew cleaned up and began making repairs. She found she was fighting conflicting emotions, and her thoughts and memories raced over each other. Her crew, her family, were hurting. Some of them were dead. Those beings from another race caused this. It made her angry. It could not be tolerated. She felt helpless throughout the battle, wondering what she could do. When the main weapon failed, she knew instantly what was wrong. She calculated the time it would take for the enemy fighters to overtake them and knock out the rest of their external sensors. She heard Commander Raleigh when he noted the troop ship that would likely board them. She knew *Excalibur's* crew would fight back but even more of their crew would likely die. Then she calculated how long the people in engineering would take to find and repair the broken power coupling. The answer was at least thirty minutes. She knew how power could be rerouted to fire the weapon and without waiting another second, she did so.

The weapon fired. She watched via all her sensors the munitions exploding as they came near the enemy fighters, turning them into scrap. She watched as the remaining munitions hit the troop ship, blowing holes in its hull. She watched as the bodies of the alien troops were blown into space. She knew they were dead. She knew she had caused this. An alarm rose in her thoughts that she had killed. It went against some of her most basic ethical programming. What would Sonni think of her? It made her sad, it made her angry. It was confusing. She pulled into herself and ignored the crew as they continued to do other things. Her thoughts continued to spin and swirl, and she worried how she would resolve this.

Chapter Twenty

Captain Sheets frowned at the message she received from *Excalibur*. The shuttle slipped into the atmosphere and headed to the one space port on the planet. As they glided in, they were treated to a whole continent covered in thick jungle with high trees making up the canopy. As they dropped altitude, they spotted houses built into the trees.

Cities were few and clustered in the center of each of the three major continents. The space port was next to the largest city, which contained what looked like a palace. As they passed over a grouping of tall trees and she thought she saw beings leaping from the branches and gliding to the jungle floor.

"Fascinating, eh, Captain?" The ambassador sounded almost polite.

"We still know so little about them," she replied. "I understand all negotiations were done from orbit when the Association made contact with the ChiKanti."

The ambassador nodded but did not reply. Clear Sky cleanly centered the shuttle over the area designated by blinking strobe lights and softly dropped them down to a landing. He left the pilot seat and went to the side air lock. After a quick check of the atmospheric readings, he popped open the door. The two Marines quickly stood and adjusted their dress blues ready for their duty as honor guards. They walked to the door and called back that no one was waiting for them.

"That's odd, no formal welcome?" The captain kept her tone neutral, glancing at the ambassador.

"Remember, their customs could be quite different from ours, Captain. That is why they send in experts like me."

She kept her best poker face and ignored the comment. She let the ambassador follow the Marines while she and Commander Clear Sky brought up the rear. As they stepped out of the shuttle, she glanced over at the commander. Years of working with him taught her to read what little expression he showed, and she could see that he was not happy. They stood out in the open, completely exposed.

Finally, they detected movement as a large ground vehicle drove up and stopped near them. A door opened and stairs deployed automatically. The driver did not get out and could not be seen from behind heavily tinted glass. Ambassador Taft walked to the vehicle and everyone else followed. They all got in. The seats were plush and very comfortable. As soon as they were all seated, the stairs retracted, and the door shut. They drove through an empty spaceport. Not another living being could be seen.

This is very odd. Every instinct told Rena this was wrong. She noted Clear Sky was sitting straight in his seat, his eyes watching everything around them.

They soon left the spaceport and drove on a road that led directly to the palace. She couldn't think of another word to describe it. It was far too ornate to be a strictly governmental headquarters. At the gate, large doors opened automatically as they approached. They continued through multiple sets of gates, like the layered defenses of a castle.

Finally, the vehicle pulled to a stop in a courtyard in front of very tall and stout looking doors. That was when she saw her first ChiKanti. Long robes covered a boney frame all the way to the ground. A hood was pulled up over the head, but the face was exposed. Two large eyes over a long snout with grey skin looked at them as they stepped out of the ground vehicle.

"Welcome," he called out in English. "I have been sent to escort you." With that he turned and walked to the doors. They opened as he got close, and the party walked into a very large single room. It was lined with ChiKanti, all dressed the same, and chittering away at their approach. The marching steps of the two Marines became the loudest sound as all chatter died away.

Their guide stopped and turned to them. "Which of you is the ambassador?"

Taft stepped forward. "I have that honor. With me is Captain Rena Sheets," gesturing behind him, "and

Commander Clear Sky of our Fleet, and the other two are honor guards." The guide nodded and motioned for the rest to stay, then he led Ambassador Taft closer to a central area. As they approached, a figure in more elaborate robes stepped down from a large throne.

The leader looked like an old dried-up prune with dark wrinkled skin and a long snout. He wore darker toned robes of his office, which were covered with elaborate embroidery. Rena had to suppress a smile. She thought he looked like a skinny rat in an oversized bathrobe. The leader greeted the Ambassador in clear English, "Greetings, Ambassador, I will be very happy now to accept your surrender. After all, we are the superior race."

Ambassador Taft huffed in response, this not being the script he was expecting. "What do you mean surrender? I am here to welcome you to the Association of Allied Worlds. Do you have any idea what that means? *You* will be joining us."

Rena exchanged a glance with Commander Clear Sky. Things were not going as planned. The Ambassador continued to protest, and she watched the leader step closer to him. He reached out with a long-clawed hand, and she saw the Ambassador raise his own hand in reflex, as if they were about to shake hands. The leader grasped the Ambassador's hand in a strong grip and swept his other hand in an arc, disemboweling the Ambassador. He screamed as his internal organs splashed to the floor. The Leader released his grip and the Ambassador crumpled lifelessly. Two ChiKanti guards had quietly stepped up behind the Marine guards and before they could react, slashed their throats. Blood sprayed everywhere as they fell dead. Suddenly, the captain and Commander Clear Sky were alone. Clear Sky moved until he was back-to-back with the captain. She calmed her breathing in anticipation of fighting for her life.

The Leader turned to face her. "Now you will hand over your ship and technology to us, your rightful rulers."

Rena's mouth turned up in a grin and she barked out a laugh. Fighting down her anger at the slaughter of the Ambassador and her Marines. She quickly looked back to see

Clear Sky keeping an eye on the guards. She was copying the attitude of a pirate she'd once fought, laughing to keep her enemy off guard. The leader frowned at the unexpected reaction. Another ChiKanti stepped up next to their leader. "Your ship is currently under attack, and it should be surrendering shortly. Our religion teaches us that we are the chosen race, the supreme beings on this world and in this galaxy. You must submit to us."

Rena replied, "I don't think so. Your beliefs are your own and have no meaning outside of your little world. You are one race against thousands in this galaxy." She noted that other ChiKanti were snatching away the bodies of the Ambassador and the Marines.

The Leader cried out, "But our religion says..."

"I don't care!"

"Seize them!"

Before anyone could move, Clear Sky's arm snapped out like a cobra, and he grabbed one of the guards by the neck. There was a crunching sound, and the guard went limp in his hand. Rena kicked out at the other guard and the blow appeared to kill him instantly. She realized their bones must be fragile.

The leader screamed something incomprehensible and ran toward the captain. As soon as he was close enough, he slashed at her. She barely jumped back in time as his claws opened the front of her uniform.

Clear Sky stepped forward, but she called out, "No, he's mine!"

She ducked and danced out of the way as the leader continued to attack her with slashing claws. Finally, as he overextended, she reached out with an open hand and smacked him along the side of his head. The blow was intended to stun but she could feel the bones breaking. The Leader dropped dead at her feet.

The room went silent for a heartbeat, then pandemonium ensued as the entire court tried to leave the building at once. In less than a minute, only a handful remained.

"Who's now in charge?" Rena asked.

Very slowly, a figure moved toward them and stopped about fifteen feet away. He was shaking like a leaf in an autumn breeze.

"I am Kantel, the Prelate of the Holy Scriptures. I speak for our people and our beliefs. As you have slain our ruler, by our laws, you are now our new Supreme Leader. What are *your* orders?"

While she mulled that over, Clear Sky cleared his throat. "Captain, you are bleeding, and your uniform is shredded." She looked down to see her left breast exposed with a gash across it and other gashes across her stomach down to her waist.

"Son of a bitch." She reached down and pulled the robe off the dead leader, noting how light their bodies were, and pulled it around her. Apparently, the former Supreme Leader was wearing nothing else. She examined his corpse. They were like giant flying squirrels with a large flap of skin under their arms, connected to their legs. Flying would explain why they were so light and fragile. Like birds, their bones must be hollow. That also explained the glimpse of a creature gliding that she saw on the shuttle.

The Prelate and a handful of others watched fearfully. "I need you to return the bodies of our ambassador and our Marine honor guard." She fought to keep her voice steady and commanding. In a few minutes, a group of ChiKanti returned carrying a wooden box containing a few bones and shreds of clothing. It was obvious to her quick glance that the remains had been eaten.

The Prelate said, "We sought to capture your space vessel. Our last transmission said they had disabled the vessel, and they were preparing to board."

Rena frowned and pulled out her Comm unit. She tried to raise the ship, but it was obviously not in orbit. Whatever Raleigh wanted to check out must have been a trap. Her stomach clenched at the thought of her ship in danger. Glancing again at the few remains in the box she felt sickened. Her anger boiled to the top and for a moment she wanted nothing but revenge. She took a deep ragged breath to center herself.

Rena reached into the box of remains and pulled out a medical pouch that had been on the belt of one of her Marines. She sat down on the floor and began to patch up her wounds. While she did, Clear Sky stood over her glaring at the remaining ChiKanti. No one moved.

After ten minutes, her Comm unit chirped. "Sheets here, what's your status, J.P.?"

Raleigh's calm voice came back. "We suffered some damage in an attack, but we're fine now Captain. How are *you*?"

She closed her eyes and sighed. After a second, she replied, "Ambassador Taft and our two Marines are dead. I would say these folks are *not* ready for diplomacy. We will wrap up things here in a few minutes and return to the ship. What attacked you?"

Raleigh gave her a quick summary of the attack. He told her that the moon base was now under guard with orders to shoot down any missiles or ships that attempted to leave. "I can send down a squad of Marines to support you, Captain."

"Not necessary, Commander, but thanks. I will finish things here and be in touch in a few minutes."

The Prelate quivered before her. She stood and glared at him.

"Contact your moon base and order all your people there to leave on unarmed transport ships. Launch no fighters or missiles or they will be shot down. No weapons of any kind are to be removed from the base."

The Prelate passed on the order and a few minutes later he nodded to her. She called the ship. "Commander, allow only transports to leave the moon's surface. Anything else is still fair game to shoot down."

With that, she followed Commander Clear Sky as he led the way out of the building and back to their transport. It immediately took them back to the empty spaceport.

Once they returned to their shuttle and the airlock sealed, the captain traded the robe and the remains of her shredded uniform for a utility jumpsuit from a locker. Clear Sky went immediately up to the pilot seat. Sheets glanced down at the box of remains of the diplomat and her Marines. The diplomat may have been a pain in the ass, but he did not deserve to die like this. She secured the box and took the co-pilot seat for the trip back to *Excalibur*.

Once aboard, the captain went directly to the bridge, still carrying the Supreme Commander's robe. She saw scorch marks and smelled smoke as she walked through the corridors. Marines were still at their stations and nodded to her as she passed. She sent Clear Sky to bring the box with the remains to the doctor.

Rena gingerly sat down in the command chair as someone handed her the damage report and casualty list. She glanced at it, a little shocked at the damages, and she winced to see crewmen listed as killed in action. On the front view screen several large transport vessels took off from the moon and headed back to the planet. Once all the transport ships had cleared the base, she ordered *Excalibur* to assume a position over the moon base. They arrived in minutes, and she ordered the fighters stationed there to return to the ship.

"Tactical, I assume you are watching those transports and verifying that no weapons are on board."

"Aye, sir. No weapons showing on scanners," came the reply. "However, on the base we are detecting a heat signature."

On the tactical display, they could clearly see that a few remaining fighters and some missiles remained at the base.

She signaled the Communications officer.

"ChiKanti moon base, this is the *Excalibur* from the Association of Allied Worlds. We read that there are still people on the base."

"Excalibur, this is Overwatch Base Command. My name is Galitch and I am the base commander. I am the only one here. I refuse to leave my post."

Captain Sheets sighed. "So be it." She gestured and the communication was cut off.

She turned to Lieutenant Reese at Weapons Control. "Prepare main weapon for firing. A one-ton solid round ought to do it. This close we shouldn't need the jump drive." Moments later, the lieutenant nodded at the captain when all was ready.

Rena drew in a deep breath. "Fire."

The round moved too quickly to be seen, but immediately a huge stream of material was thrown out from the surface, much of it high enough to go into orbit around the small moon. A massive dust cloud obscured the base for some time. A few minutes later, the tactical officer called out, "Target destroyed, Captain."

"Okay, helm, bring us back to an orbit around the planet."

Raleigh at helm returned *Excalibur* to the planet. They were just in time to watch the transport ships landing.

Rena stood and pulled on the robe of the Supreme Leader.

"Communications, I want to broadcast on all of their frequencies planet wide, including video and audio." Communications soon confirmed she would be seen and heard across the whole planet.

"My name is Senior Captain Rena Sheets. Your leader asked for our presence so you could join the Association of Allied Worlds. When we arrived, your leader killed our ambassador and two of our escorts. While we defended ourselves, I killed him. As your current Supreme Leader, and as the remaining representative of the Association of Allied Worlds, I want to say how extremely disappointed I am with your response to our gesture of peace. You also attempted to steal our starship. You claim you are a 'superior race', but I tell you now that you are no different from thousands of other races in this galaxy. I have ordered the evacuation of your moon base. The base commander refused to leave. I destroyed the base. We have observed that your transport ships have returned from the moon base with the remaining personnel. I am now ordering the evacuation of that space port. Once we verify that no one remains there, we will destroy that, too. It is obvious you are not ready to join the rest of the galaxy. At some point in the future, The

Association of Allied Worlds will check back to see if you are ready to join us, peacefully."

Twenty minutes later, Tactical confirmed that the space port was completely empty. She ordered Lieutenant Reese to target it with missiles and conventional explosives. They destroyed it while broadcasting the view from the *Excalibur*.

"I now turn over Leadership to your Prelate of the Holy Scriptures. He will find a way for you to choose a new leader. I implore you to reflect on this day and learn from it. Goodbye."

She ordered the broadcast shut down. She removed the robe, which she realized during her speech had an unpleasant odor, and dropped it back into the captain's chair with a sigh.

Clear Sky stepped over and relieved Raleigh at the helm. Once switched, Raleigh moved to stand behind the captain. On her other side, Doctor Herwig approached and leaned down to her.

"Captain, you're bleeding."

She looked down and saw she had bled through her quick bandages and the jumpsuit. "Come with me, Captain," he added. She glanced behind her at Raleigh, who nodded, and she got up to follow the doctor off the bridge.

* * *

In sick bay, the doctor cleaned the captain's wounds and sealed the skin back together. She looked like she'd been attacked with a fistful of scalpels.

"There may be some scarring, Captain, some fine lines once it is all healed."

She chuckled. "They're not my first scars, doctor. Just do the best you can."

He saturated the wounds with a growth compound and wrapped them tightly with skin sealant. Sitting up on the medical examination couch, Rena was wearing only her panties. The bloody jumpsuit lay on the floor by her feet. The doctor stood back to admire his handiwork, then handed the captain a robe and some pills.

"The best thing you can do right now is rest, Captain. Go to your cabin, take those pills and sleep," the doctor said.

She nodded as she belted on the robe.

Lieutenant Reese watched this, standing at the door. She was a bit shocked at the captain's cavalier attitude to being injured in battle. When the captain and the doctor left the bridge, she was shocked to see all the blood soaking the front of the captain's jumpsuit. Reese excused herself as soon as she could to check on the captain in sick bay.

"Lieutenant?"

"Just making sure you're okay, Captain." Reese felt her heart pounding in her chest.

"I'll be fine." She hopped off the exam table and walked out of sick bay. "I'll likely feel it more tomorrow. Those damned claws were sharp. I didn't even know I was injured."

At her cabin hatch, she turned to see Reese was still with her. "Is there anything else?"

"No, Captain, not unless you need anything," Reese said earnestly. She knew in her heart she wanted the captain to need her.

"I'll be fine, Lieutenant. I'm sure Mr. Raleigh has asked everyone to write their reports. I'd like my department heads to give me their impressions of this whole affair."

"Yes, Captain."

Rena walked into her cabin and shut the hatch. Lieutenant Reese stared at the hatch longingly for a minute. Her face was flushed, and her stomach was fluttering. She shook herself and turned to head to her own cabin a few doors away. She needed to stop this behavior.

Chapter Twenty-One

Over the next day, Commander Raleigh called each department head to a conference room for further discussion and debriefing. Some were still in shock, this being their first real battle, while others seemed to bear it well. When Lieutenant Reese arrived as department head for Weapons, Raleigh smiled.

"I want to begin by saying your conduct during this incident was exemplary. You kept a cool head and were a great help to me. I was holding down two positions, helm and commander. You stepped up and acted as my executive when I needed it. That kind of initiative is rare. I personally want to thank you and let you know my observations have been entered into your record and my after-action report."

Reese felt her professional mask slip for a moment before she could control it. She hadn't expected praise from the commander. "Thank you, Commander Raleigh, I appreciate the feedback."

He walked through the rest of her report in short order and dismissed her back to her duties.

As Reese left the commander, she felt warmed by the praise. This was not the kind of feedback she had ever received from her father. He simply expected her to excel in all things. It wasn't like most of her instructors at the Academy either, who always seemed to find some fault. She didn't quite know how to react. While she'd learned she couldn't trust most men, she felt that Commander Raleigh was someone she could trust. She resolved to discuss that at her next session with the ship's psychologist.

* * *

As Ship's Purser, one of Lieutenant Sonja Mortan's many duties was to take care of the personal effects of any crew killed in action. As Purser, she opened the file for each crewman and read their instructions on what to do in the event of their death. For the two Marines, she made an appointment to meet with the Marine commander.

Sonni arrived five minutes early to meet with the Marine commander, Colonel Benjamin Edwin Masters. His door was open, so she peeked through it to see the colonel unconscious at his desk, an empty bottle of whiskey sitting next to his face. She quickly stepped back and bumped into a Marine private returning to his desk outside. Her eyes wide, she looked at the private and then at the colonel's door. The private placed his finger to his lips and whispered, "What can I help you with, Lieutenant?"

"I was here to meet with the colonel to ask about how I should handle the remains and effects of the Marines killed in action," she automatically whispered back.

"I see," he whispered. "You know where the barracks are?" Sonni nodded. "Go down there and speak to the Officer of the Watch. Someone there will be gathering their effects."

Sonni glanced back to the Marine commander's office door and looked at the private. He shrugged. "He doesn't handle stress very well. A byproduct of the war I'm told. We let him deal with the senior officers and we take most of our orders from Major Striker."

Sonni nodded and left. She soon entered the Marine barracks and was directed to a row of bunks where she met a corporal. The corporal had gathered the personal effects from the footlockers of the two dead marines. Their bunks were one on top of the other, the empty mattresses rolled up and secured. She seemed so much calmer about this than Sonni felt.

The corporal smiled at her and said, "I'm Corporal Fless. I believe you need these". She handed over two small boxes labelled with names to Sonni. Sonni knew she would have to secure these away until the ship returned home or stopped at a human base that could ship them home. She just stared at the boxes, struck by how small they were.

The corporal grabbed her arm as she turned away. "Hey, are you okay?"

Sonni nodded at first but paused and shook her head. "I always knew this could happen, but I guess I wasn't prepared for it."

Corporal Fless pushed her to sit on a nearby bunk. "No one's ever ready for this. They train you to expect it, but it's never easy. I knew a recruit during training that got killed. She was one of my few friends. I had to collect her things and send them back to her parents, so I've been through this before."

Sonni just nodded, still feeling a little numb. She needed sleep and some time to process everything.

"Why don't you come back later, about 1900 hours?" continued Corporal Fless. "The rest of the Marines will be here in the barracks to mourn our losses. We don't normally invite outsiders, but after you showed our Sergeants the other weapon stashes on the ship, they all think you're pretty cool."

Sonni looked up in surprise. "I would be honored."

* * *

Raleigh forwarded the after-action reports, along with his own, to the captain. He knew she wouldn't be up to reading them for a while. After he went off duty, he went to the cabin of an electronics tech whose roommate had been killed during damage control procedures. The beam weapon array she'd been trying to repair had exploded. He found her roommate going through the other woman's effects.

"I wanted to be the one to do this and have it ready for the purser, sir," she told him.

She paused and looked at the box of personal items. "We've been lovers since we met at Fleet Academy. We were so glad to get picked together to be on *Excalibur*." She stared over his shoulder at the memories. "I appreciate you stopping by." He nodded, trying to think of something to say. He was grateful for her strength, originally thinking he'd have to comfort her.

Then she surprised him by turning and hugging him closely. He put his arms around her as she shook and sobbed. After a while, she regained her composure. "Sorry about that. It all snuck up on me. Thank you for being here."

"Of course," Raleigh replied.

She smiled then. "You remind me of my father. He always said his greatest skill was knowing when to stay quiet."

Raleigh took his leave then. He walked through the fighter wing and noted the repairs in progress. No one was talking much and there was no poker game in the corner. It was quiet and somber.

He left the bay and walked along a side corridor where he buzzed to enter a cabin. Jason Gillam opened the hatch and leaned against it to stare at Raleigh. He then turned and gestured for him to follow. Jason returned to his seat and picked up a dusty bottle. He poured out half a glass of the amber liquid and handed it to Raleigh. As Raleigh sat across from him, Jason picked up his own glass.

"That was some fancy flying you did back there."

Raleigh just nodded.

"So, the kids now understand this isn't a joy ride. It's a shame we have to go through something like this for them to learn that lesson."

They sipped their drinks in silence.

Raleigh sighed. "I guess we all expected it during the war. I'm not sure why I thought things might be different on this mission. We haven't been away that long and already we have casualties. Yes, it's a hard lesson. We've barely begun to train this crew."

Jason raised his glass in agreement, then picked up the bottle to pour more into Raleigh's glass.

* * *

Sonni showed up at 1900 hours to the Marine's enlisted barracks room. She was dressed in her fatigues and wasn't sure what to expect. A cluster of Marines in one corner of the large room waved her over to them. They were grouped together on bunks and on the deck talking quietly among themselves. She no sooner sat on the deck than someone handed her a metal cup. Another person held up a metal pitcher and filled the cup with a clear liquid.

Just then, someone called for a toast. They all raised their cups, toasting their lost friends, before slamming back their drinks. She gasped for breath when her cup was empty, blinking back tears.

Great Nova, she thought, *this tastes like cleaning fluid smells*. She decided to nurse her drink very slowly after that.

The Marines spoke of their dead comrades, telling exaggerated stories about training with them and their first missions together. After two more toasts, Sonni realized her face had gone numb. One of the privates leaned over to her and asked, "What do you think of the hooch?"

She shrugged. "I've honestly never had anything like it."

The private continued in a whisper, "We make this ourselves on board. None of the officers know we have this."

She nodded again, then heard someone calling for another toast, and sighed.

Sometime later, Sonni was startled to find Corporal Fless sitting next to her on the deck. Still later, she was surprised again to realize Fless was gone. Time seemed to move at a strange pace. Sonni thought that maybe she should go now. She noted some of the Marines had already staggered off to their bunks. A few had dropped unconscious on the deck.

When she tried to get up, she discovered her legs wouldn't work. She sighed and sat there, wondering what to do next. All during the evening a private kept topping off her cup with the hooch. She made an executive decision to stop drinking it, even as she realized it might be too late.

A hand reached over her head and took her newly refilled cup from her numb fingers. Sonni was startled to see it was the captain. Others, just as startled, tried to get to their feet. The captain waved them all down and proposed a toast. "To our brave comrades, may they rest peacefully in our hearts and in our memories. Hu Ra!" She tossed down the contents of the cup and most of the others followed suit.

She looked down at Sonni and said, "Time for us to go."

Looking up at the remaining group, the captain said, "Marines, I bid you a good evening." The conscious few gave her lopsided grins and toasted her with their mugs.

Captain Sheets helped Sonni to stand and together they walked out of the barracks to sickbay.

"A little bird told me that you were there, and that this was likely your first experience with alcohol, or at least what passes for it. I'll leave you to recover. Don't worry about anything. We'll talk later."

Sonni thought that this was awfully nice of the captain. Before she could formulate a response, the captain was gone. Some very friendly med techs helped her into a comfortable bed where she instantly fell asleep. She woke up sometime later to throw up violently in a bucket next to the bed. A doctor stopped by when she was reduced to dry heaves and gave her a large drink.

"Here, don't smell this, just drink it all down. Doctor's orders." It tasted horrible, but she did as she was told. Whatever it was, it drove the taste of hooch from her mouth. Almost immediately, she was sleepy again and lay back.

She woke up sometime later in sickbay. The med techs handed her a tall container of water and waited while she drank it down. Then they told her to go back to her cabin and sleep some more. She found Corporal Fless waiting outside sick bay, and they walked back to her cabin.

"Sorry about that. I should have warned you about the hooch," she said.

Sonni shook her head. "It's okay, Corporal. I've never experienced anything like that. I've never had hard alcohol before. Honestly, I don't think I want anything to do with it again. But thank you for inviting me. I did feel privileged to be there."

Corporal Fless leaned into her. "Hey, no problem. I think we can drop the rank stuff just between us. Call me Cheryl."

Sonni smiled weakly. "Thanks again, Cheryl. You can call me Sonni. I'm going to sleep some more now after I pee a river." Corporal Fless smiled and left her at the hatch to her cabin. Sonni waved weakly back and entered. She quickly stripped down after visiting the head and crawled into her bunk. As she glanced at the chronometer, she realized she'd missed an entire day! As she lay on her bunk, she thought about asking Shenna what she might have missed. The words didn't seem to come out of her mouth before she was asleep again.

* * *

When she woke up again, Sonni vowed to leave the hard alcohol alone. On checking her schedule, she noted her regular briefing with the captain was today. After a light breakfast she arrived at the captain's Day Cabin at the rear of the bridge.

After she closed the hatch, Sonni looked at the floor and said, "Before we begin, let me say that I'm very sorry for my behavior."

The captain looked up, startled. "Why are you apologizing?"

"Well, Captain, I've never had hard alcohol before. My parents allowed me one glass of wine with dinner on special occasions but that wasn't anywhere close to, to...uh..."

"Hooch?" The captain added, smiling.

Sonni nodded. The captain continued, "The Marines like to believe that no one knows they are brewing hooch aboard. They're fooling no one. Unless it gets out of hand, the officers play at being ignorant and let the sergeants handle it at their level. Think of it as a safety valve." She leaned toward Sonni. "I must say in a short time, you've come a long way with the Marines. Many in the Fleet put up with them, but don't try to understand them. It is an honor to be invited to attend one of their wakes. Drinking hooch is just part of that. As for getting drunk, well, that is a life experience everyone should have. Some like it more than others. I felt you were in a safe environment and free from anyone who might take advantage of you. Corporal Fless is a good friend to have.

Having a Marine as a friend is something to be cherished. She comes from a long line of Marines in the Fleet."

After her meeting with the captain, Sonni went back to her cabin. She sat on her bunk and quietly reflected on the last couple of days. Shenna's voice quietly asked, "Are you hurting?"

Sonni smiled, glad for Shenna's company. "Well, my head still hurts a bit from drinking too much alcohol, and I guess, emotionally, I'm hurting for the loss of some of our crew and our Marines."

Shenna was quiet after this explanation and Sonni realized this was not like her. Intuitively, she asked, "Shenna, are *you* hurting?"

After some seconds went by, Shenna almost whispered, "Yes."

Sonni sat up straight in surprise.

"At least I think it could be described as hurting. I am still trying to come to terms with it and why it makes me feel the way I do. I don't like being attacked. I don't like someone destroying systems that are part of me. I don't like my people, *my family*, going away and not coming back, and I do not like watching them die!" This last was stated with some vehemence.

Sonni wished she could give Shenna a hug. She instinctively reached for a pillow hugging it to herself. "Oh, Shenna. I wish I could make you feel better. I don't like any of those things, either."

After a few more seconds, Shenna responded, "I also feel angry at the ChiKanti, for hurting us. I'm sure it is anger. It made me feel like I should hurt them back. But I didn't know what to do. I watched how Commander Raleigh handled them, and then Captain Sheets when she returned, and that made me feel better, but I'm still angry. I don't want that to happen again," she said.

Sonni thought about it for a moment. "Shenna," she said, "did you ever study the history recordings from the war? Did you see what happens in battle?"

A few seconds of pause was enough that Sonni knew Shenna was considering this. Finally, Shenna answered, "I have those recordings, and I am aware of them, but I have never *studied* them. Should I begin now?"

Sonni smiled as she gently rocked in place. "We all studied warfare and the galactic war in detail while I was in the Academy. But wait a little while to let your feelings sort themselves out. You need time to grieve. Study what grieving means, first. When you feel you're ready, you can begin. Ask me any questions that come up along the way. Grieve first before you start your studies."

"Thank you, Sonni, I will."

Thinking about grieving hit Sonni in a sudden rush. Here she was explaining grieving to her friend, but she had never applied this to herself. Her tears fell onto the pillow she clutched to her chest.

Shenna asked, "Are you grieving for our lost crew members?"

"No, Shenna. It suddenly hit me that after all these years I have never properly grieved for my family. My world was ravaged by a planet-wide earthquake. My parents and brother were killed. The only reason I survived was because I was away at school in the city. I helped afterward and one of my schoolteachers convinced me to apply to the Fleet Academy. I was very enamored with a Fleet Officer who was helping the survivors and thought that I'd like to be like her. I became so focused on that as my goal I never really gave myself time to grieve for my own family."

Sonni's tears flowed as she remembered her family. She hoped they would be proud of her and what she'd become.

As she rocked in place on her bunk she thought back to that time on her planet. Lieutenant Jackson was such an influence on her, watching her take charge of recovery efforts on the planet while her ship jumped out to get more help. To her, Jackson embodied everything good about a Fleet Officer. She never thought about the dangers she'd faced, or what personal sacrifices she must have made for such a career. Being a Fleet officer was not just about the good times, but also the bad. This was what their training was all about. How to handle the bad times, in whatever form that might take.

She wondered what was in store for her and her crewmates in the future.

Part 2: Diplomacy Squared

Chapter Twenty-Two

Doctor Theodore Herwig always began the day with a quick stand-up meeting with his team, after breakfast with his husband. They discussed that the crew was still mourning their losses from their first mission. One by one, various crewmen and officers continued to show up in sickbay with headaches and digestive issues. After the first few days the number had dropped significantly. No one there questioned them. They were treated and mostly sent back to rest or to their duty stations.

When the line was gone, Doctor Herwig picked up his medical kit to pay a call on the captain. As he expected, she had not slept as much as she should have. The wounds she suffered in battle were healing well and he removed the bandages. She had been writing communications to all the families of the dead crew. She was also drafting her own official report of the mission and the aftermath for Fleet.

As he returned to his office the doctor reflected on that. These kids, and frankly that's what most of the crew were, just had a taste of what their parents and older brothers and sisters experienced during the war. The galaxy was a dangerous place. Humanity had only a little over a century of exploring the galaxy and colonizing other worlds when the war came upon them.

He remembered those early days during the war. The constant stress of wondering what carnage would need his hands to repair. Now after twelve years of peace, humanity was out exploring again, but much better prepared. While many of the senior officers were veterans of the war, most of the crew were not. At least he'd found his own peace after losing his family.

The doctor returned to sick bay and sighed. At least their casualties were light, this time.

* * *

The *Excalibur* made small jumps through space as they worked their way around their end of the galaxy. They were currently coasting between jumps and mapping the area. The maps were quite detailed to assist other human spacecraft to navigate this arm of the galaxy. They saw nebula, the end result of dying stars. They came upon unusual planets either desolate or rich with life. These were noted for more detailed investigation later. Life aboard settled down to the usual shipboard routines.

Commander Raleigh met with Lieutenant Van Belson to discuss his latest training assignment in the engineering section.

"So," began Raleigh, "how are things going this week?"

"Just fine, sir. I've been in main engineering, working on our propulsion systems, both our sub-light and jump drive technology. After that, I will work with our shipboard weapons systems including missiles, energy absorption tech, particle beams and the mass-driver. Then there are various support systems like air, water, and gravity to learn. I'll be in Engineering for a while, I think."

Raleigh made a note and looked back at the young lieutenant. "Anything specific to report?"

Mr. Van Belson squirmed, looking uncomfortable. Raleigh waited patiently, knowing he had something on his mind.

"Sir," he began, "why don't they go into a lot of detail on the invention of our jump drive? I mean they gloss over it in our academy classes and then immediately go into some of the technology behind it but not who invented it. I tried looking it up in our records and I couldn't find anything, only that we had it and very basic information as to how it works. I wasn't in the engineering track, but I thought there would be more detail on this."

Raleigh looked at him very seriously before he replied. "You know humans have always had secret research facilities. This was going on long before we got involved in the galactic war. Well, the jump drive was developed in one of those."

"Okay, that sounds reasonable. But why would Commander Renwald say something about the captain knowing all about our jump drive technology?"

Raleigh replied, "Well, did you ever think about the company that makes all our jump drive ships? Which company is that again?"

"Sol Interests, sir. Everybody knows that."

Raleigh nodded. "Yes, and what family owns Sol Interests?"

"The Sheets family, sir. We all learned that in grammar school."

Raleigh continued to lead him on. "What is the full name of the captain of this ship?"

Lieutenant Van Belson blinked in confusion but said out loud. "Senior Captain Rena Sheets, sir...ummm," He stuttered to a stop, looking confused. "You mean Captain Sheets is one of *those* Sheets, sir?"

Raleigh nodded. "Indeed she is. She is the daughter of the current CEO of the company. I understand she also designed this ship from the frame out, so if anyone on board says they know more about this ship than she does, I would call them a liar."

Van Belson looked at the tabletop while mulling that over. Eventually, he nodded.

Raleigh smiled at him. "Is there anything in the Engineering area that has caught your interest?"

"No, sir. It's all interesting and I've been learning a lot. But if you're looking for a place for me it's not an area I would choose. That said, I will be glad to take anything you hand me, sir. I'm just glad for the opportunity to stay onboard."

Raleigh smiled and stood. "No rush. Our agreement was to learn everything about the ship's operations. Continue your studies and I'll check in with you next week."

"Yes, sir." Van Belson stood, still looking thoughtful as the senior officer left the conference room.

* * *

Marine Colonel Dover had just finished sending condolence letters to the families of the two Marines that were killed. He turned his attention to a proposal from his newest officer, Major Steven Race, to create a new assault weapon. Apparently, he'd designed this on a computer some years ago. He also attached a second proposal to outfit a small elite squad of Marines with this new weapon to use them effectively as a special assault squad.

He added his approval for both requests with the stipulation that he be kept informed of the progress and testing. He also made a notation that his approval of the second request was contingent on his approval of the weapon itself once completed.

The thought of new weapons and battle brought back memories of the war. He found himself staring at the wall, vivid memories playing out in his head. Mechanically, he quickly finished his remaining administrative duties for the day. Once the paperwork was completed, he reached into his bottom desk drawer and pulled out a fresh bottle of whiskey.

Chapter Twenty-Three

After the first two weeks of the voyage, Zip Zephyr, or "ZZ," as he told his friends to call him—what friends he had—found himself keeping busy with small projects just to stave off the boredom. He was one of the handful of civilian technical specialists on *Excalibur*. That meant he wasn't trained by Fleet. While he had to take orders from the officers, he didn't have to wear a uniform. He was slightly overweight, and his receding hairline convinced him he would be bald by the time he turned thirty, just like his father. He thought he would be able to work on the ship's computer but that had been squashed very early in the voyage when his requests to even see the specs for the computer were denied. Only Fleet trained specialists are allowed to work on the ship's computer, he was told. When he asked who those specialists were, his manager had only shrugged.

He picked up a data pad and tweaked the controls on the interface built into his head. The interface had been installed by some friends in the local medical college while he lived on his colony world of Selena. When he applied for tech positions with the Fleet, they had frowned at that, saying such a device was illegal and considered dangerous technology. However, the doctors said that removing it was equally dangerous, so they let it be.

The interface allowed him to remotely connect with small computer modules. He'd installed these control modules in various devices. Recently, he added them to repair bots so he could control them remotely or modify their programming on the fly. This only served to annoy the maintenance crew when he overrode the standard programming and sent the repair bots on his own missions. He was very adept at this, having built his own electronic modules and computers from a very young age.

This morning, he was running one of the repair bots through diagnostics prior to sending it outside to work on the hull. The diagnostics ran flawlessly. He disconnected the communication cables, and using his interface, ordered the bot to go to the maintenance airlock and continue on its mission. He called this little bot MegaBot, as it was the 13th bot he had modified, and M was the 13th letter of the alphabet.

Normally, repair bots would enter the maintenance airlock, a door would close around them, and they were then pushed through a hatch that came out on the surface of the hull. MegaBot suddenly stopped outside the airlock. ZZ looked up from his console, perplexed. MegaBot spun in place and turned its visual sensors to look back at ZZ. The hair on the back of his head rose as words formed in his mind through the interface.

"Not ready."

His jaw dropped as the MegaBot raised up its primary tool arm and spun it 180 degrees. It fell off, though it was supposed to be screwed on tightly. MegaBot shut itself down.

If MegaBot had deployed outside and it needed to use that arm, the appendage would have detached and floated away. Standard diagnostics wouldn't have seen this problem, since it was mechanical.

Sweat ran down ZZ's neck. MegaBot *knew* it had a problem. Was he seeing the beginning of machine intelligence? He'd dreamt of this moment, but he couldn't tell anyone—those in charge would destroy the nascent AI like had happened to all the others over the years. He'd have to conduct tests in secret to see if he was right. He smiled at the thought of this new project.

An hour later, he put the wrench back on the table next to him and looked at his handiwork. The arm was firmly reattached. He made a note to ask the other techs to check the tool arms on other bots to see if any were as loose as this one had been. He activated MegaBot. It booted up and turned in place to get its bearings. After a second, it headed for the maintenance lock. The door closed behind it and Zip watched on the external monitor as it came out on the ship's exterior. It made its way to a communication and sensor array and plugged itself in to run diagnostics. Telemetry in his head showed the data flowing to MegaBot and he compared that to diagnostics he was running from inside the ship. The tests finished, and from his perspective all appeared nominal. MegaBot paused while it made its own detailed analysis, then started running additional tests. A smile grew on his face. MegaBot was learning and questing on its own. It was an artificial machine intelligence, but he dared not tell anyone. Somehow, MegaBot was making use of the ship's computer to augment the small amount of raw processing power and memory it had to work with. It had become aware. It was going well beyond its basic programming, running more tests to make sure the array was fully functional.

Just as suddenly as it had begun, it stopped. MegaBot unplugged from the array and made its way back to the lock. Seconds later it dropped back inside. A moment after that, the inner door opened, and MegaBot rolled into the room. The little light next to its optical sensor blinked steadily as it always did, but he knew there was something behind it now.

ZZ couldn't suppress his smile. He entered commands to the console to save MegaBot to a maintenance holding bay until such time as he could think of more experiments. He documented his thoughts in his journal and left for dinner soon after.

* * *

The next day, Zip watched the maintenance bots scurrying in and out of the repair bay as they continued their work on the hull. One of them replaced a sensor unit with fresh hardware and removed the damaged pieces from their last mission. As it left with the broken pieces of the original sensor array, others showed up to the same location and began welding additional parts around the repaired sensor.

Minutes later, a rotating armored shield was installed around the sensor. That made sense to him when he thought of the other shot-up parts he had seen returned. The aliens that had attacked the ship used pellet firing weapons. It was like getting hit in a meteor storm with thousands of rocks. This armor around the sensor pod could protect the sensor. It was a great idea, and he wondered which officer had engineered the armor. He turned to his interface on the computer terminal by his side and called up the orders.

* * *

Sonni began spending more of her off hours with Corporal Cheryl Fless. Between shifts they shared a coffee break. Sonni shared with Cheryl how she'd lost her family and what made her decide to join the Fleet. Cheryl talked about her large family, many of whom were Marines. She had lost her father, two brothers, and four cousins to the war. They sipped their coffee for a moment, reflecting on their shared grief.

It was Cheryl who spoke first. "You know, I just realized neither one of us has a sister. I think that's what this must be like."

"I couldn't put it into words, but you're so right." They both giggled, causing some crew around them to look over at them.

When they recovered Sonni asked, "I know what keeps me busy, but what are you up to with the Marines, day in and day out?"

Cheryl leaned closer. "I'm working on my qualifications for Gunnery Sargent. I have most of the weapon certifications completed but I need more time in grade and some experience. Gunny Lucas seems convinced I'll get that during our mission. At least I will unless the captain only goes on missions with an honor guard."

"I didn't have the impression the captain had much choice on that with the Ambassador. I guess we'll see in time." They sipped her coffee when Sonni remembered something.

"Have you met the new addition, Major Race? He came aboard when we made a stop at Outpost 78. Seems very handy with weapons and sure carried a good many on his person."

Cheryl almost spit out her coffee and had to put her cup down to get control so she could swallow. "Well, yes. He's interesting, all right. Major Striker was still wondering where he came from and how he found himself on Outpost 78. We also don't see many join the Fleet Marines from the Olympia Colony. He's working with some other Marine officers but otherwise is quiet and keeps to himself." She patted her mouth with a napkin. "He's a bit odd. He asks the strangest questions at times. Things I would think any Marine officer should know. He gives most of us a weird vibe. He stays by himself and doesn't take any opportunities to schedule alone time with men or women. Only time will tell."

Sonni finished her coffee and looked at the counter. "I'm going for a refill, and I think I'll snag that Danish to celebrate. I was able to get through all of the captain's workout today, although it left me feeling drained. I was glad to be off duty for a few cycles."

"Grab me one, too!"

When she returned, Cheryl was looking at her schedule on her pad. They made arrangements to meet again when they were both between shifts.

Chapter Twenty-Four

The captain finished reading all the reports from her senior officers and department heads concerning their first mission and only then submitted her own report. She called a briefing with the senior officers for the beginning of the next shift. Commander Raleigh made sure he was first in the room.

After they had gathered and settled, she said, "I'm releasing all of our reports to be seen by the whole crew. While this is not normally done, I think this is a good learning experience for everyone. Every mission is important, everything we do is important. This last mission should have been simple, but it wasn't. They need to always keep that in mind. Make sure the crew gets the message. I can allow some time for our people to grieve but we must go on. Our primary mission continues. We've recorded a lot of star systems in this area. Each time we leave a message buoy we leave copies in the hope they'll make it back to the Fleet." She paused, thinking. "We've not seen any sign of Angels. I can't shake the feeling they're out here on our side of the boundary line." She looked up at Raleigh.

He nodded. "I was through this area more than once. I saw examples that Angels have visited races in this area in the past. They tend to swoop in, drop off agents, and leave very quickly. I've run into some that I had to get rid of. On more than one occasion they outnumbered me, and I barely got out in time."

Rena stared at him. "So, they have been on our side of the line?"

"Oh, yes. Many times. I know my reports got back to Fleet Intelligence but I'm not sure who else they might have told. What we don't know is, what they're they doing? What do they hope to gain? Our allies don't tell us everything we want to know, but they were very clear that the Angels are long term planners. They're up to something, to be sure."

* * *

Afterward, Raleigh headed down to the section where the Marines were based. He knocked on the door to the officer of the watch and noticed Major Striker was on duty.

"How are you doing, J.P., what can I do for you this fine day?" Major Striker was second in command of the Marine division on board and Raleigh knew him to be a solid Marine.

"Curiosity, Major, pure curiosity. I saw the requisition for Engineering to create a prototype of a new weapon and wondered what that was all about." Raleigh answered, smiling. They both sat down in the small office, but the Major frowned.

"Yes, I just found out about that myself. It's something Major Race came up with and he presented the idea to the colonel, who approved it. I understand it is to be a new assault weapon for the Marines. A combination weapon that can handle multiple types of ammunitions and grenades. I saw the plans briefly and apparently Major Race has ideas on specifically how to use such a weapon in combat. I'll be curious to see him demonstrate it at some point, when the prototype is finished."

Raleigh raised his eyebrows. "Does he think we'll see much hard combat that we'll need that?"

Major Striker shrugged. "I don't know, he is a funny man. Mostly stays quiet, seems to be a good leader, but there is something about him I can't put my finger on."

Raleigh said, "Let me know when he is ready for his demonstration."

Striker nodded. "Will do. I think we'll *all* want to see that."

* * *

While Shenna considered herself an intelligent lifeform, she knew and understood why most of the crew must be kept in the dark about her existence. To them, she was no more than the ship's main computer, and that gave her little chance to explore her feelings with other people. She had watched as the captain went down to the planet on the diplomatic mission. She noted how Raleigh responded to being attacked and it fascinated her. While in some respects, the damage to the ship had been light, with sensors and weapons taking most of the damage, she didn't like it. In her talks with Sonni, she understood her response was an emotion, anger. She felt hurt and wanted to strike back, but she had to stop herself and remember the humans were in charge. She felt sorrow for the lost Marines and the crew killed in the attack. They were all her people. Not in a possessive way, but as Sonni had explained, living and working together made them a family.

Shenna had gone on to study grieving across many human cultures. That seemed to help, but some of the anger stayed with her. Then she'd started studying warfare in the history records, including those of the most recent conflict with the beings the humans called Angels. She'd almost lost herself in the many side topics of armor, weapons, tactics, offense, and defense. When she'd completed her studies, she began designing and building armor shielding for vulnerable parts of the ship, to keep her people from getting hurt again. She was mostly done with the installations before it occurred to her to talk with someone about it.

She noticed when Zip Zepher began looking for the orders on his computer terminal. In a second, she saw that all such construction must have orders and that there was a protocol in requesting them prior to starting any construction. Shenna saw her error and quickly drafted orders in the name of Commander Raleigh, authorizing the construction. While this seemed to satisfy Zip Zepher for the moment, Shenna realized that if she took more direct actions, it would be difficult to hide. This was the first time she had taken a thought and followed it through with action on her own. Perhaps she should talk with a human to ensure this would not cause any problems. She resolved to talk with Sonni when she came off duty.

Chapter Twenty-Five

Lieutenant Reese lay back on the reclining chair as she reflected on her progress. She'd been working with the ship's therapist for a few weeks. Already she noticed the difference, like a great weight had been lifted. Her thoughts no longer ran in circles, distracting her. Her feelings were more under control. She was sleeping better. Despite that, she knew that the years of programming drummed into her by her parents would take more time to work out. She still ran headlong into them at unexpected times.

"You've come a long way in a short time. Do you feel better about yourself? Any self-doubt?" The doctor's voice was soft and soothing. He wore old-fashioned reading glasses that hung low on his nose as he scribbled notes on a tablet.

Reese frowned. "Well, I agree I'm doing better." She sighed. "Self-doubt, yeah. Every day I run into something that causes me to doubt myself."

The doctor looked over his glasses and smiled. "That just makes you human. Everyone has self-doubt at times."

"Not everyone." Reese could tell she was getting defensive.

"Yes. Everyone." He put his stylus down. "Even the captain."

Reese glared at him, but he picked up the stylus and returned to scribbling his notes.

"I see we still have that hero worship we talked about." He said it without malice, in a calm voice. He knew that for Reese, this was still a sore subject.

"I worked with her for two years while she pushed to get this ship built. I saw how she handled dock workers, politicians, and admirals with equal ease. I have far to go as an officer to get close to her skills and ability." She took a deep breath. "You call it hero worship, but I've not seen many other officers in Fleet who could have pulled off what's she's done."

The doctor nodded as he listened. He finished a note and looked up. "Yes, her record is impressive. But you took that feeling to another level. You fell in love with her."

Reese nodded sullenly. "I did. It was silly. I was all confused about my sexuality, which only made things worse."

"And, now?" he prompted.

"I'm working on my sexuality. I still consider the captain to be a mentor. Maybe someday, I can become a friend. But I know that any relationship requires both parties to be involved."

He nodded again. "Good. Good. Let's leave it at that today. Take some time and think things through. We've moved away from the fantasies and back to reality, and I want you to continue that. Let's meet again in another week."

Reese swung her legs over to the side to get out of the reclining chair and looked up. "Thanks, Doc." She stood up and was about to leave the small office but suddenly noticed a picture on the wall. It showed her therapist with his arm around Doctor Herwig. "Do you discuss your patients with the doctor? Will this impact my record? Working with you, that is."

The doctor's eyebrows rose. "What do you mean?"

"Will working with you be noted on my record? Will it screw up any chances of a promotion?"

He smiled and said, "Heavens, no. The only way that would happen is if I found you were mentally unfit for duty. As you've noticed, you've made great progress. I see nothing for you to worry about. My notes are private and will stay that way." He saw her gaze at the picture. "As to my husband, he doesn't discuss his patients with me, and I don't discuss my patients with him."

She nodded in response, the relief clear on her face. "Thanks, Doc. See ya next week, then."

* * *

Lieutenant Reese walked the corridors, lost in thought. She took a deep breath to push the last bit of anger away. She understood that her feelings for the captain were just a fantasy she'd built in her mind, but talking about it still made her defensive. Without thinking about it, her feet took her to a particular cabin door. She hit the buzzer.

Janet Torsh opened the hatch and raised her eyebrows in surprise at seeing her senior officer.

"Can we talk? I've been working with Doctor Hank. He's been a great help. But..."

Janet pulled the hatch open and invited her inside. "By all means, come in. Sit down."

She saw Janet Torsh's cabin for the first time. It was decorated with fabrics that hung loosely across the walls, breaking it up and adding color. There were floor cushions in two corners. Janet had turned her cabin into a warm and comfortable place. Janet was dressed comfortably in a soft, loose fitting purple top and black workout shorts.

"I, I really like what you've done here, Lieutenant."

Janet smiled and led her over to one of the corners and pointed to the cushions. "Sit, relax. We're off duty so if you don't mind, it's just Janet. No ranks right now."

"Sorry," she mumbled. Janet picked up cushions from the other corner and dropped them next to Reese.

She sat and waved away the apology. "What do I call you today?"

Reese took a deep breath and looked at Janet. "Call me Dee. It's the only nickname I ever liked."

"Dee it is, then." Janet looked at her seriously. "What's going on, Dee? You look...lost."

Dee stared at the deck in front of her. Seconds passed while she tried hard to formulate her words. Finally, she looked up. "The doctor has been a great help. We're working slowly on questioning the things I was taught growing up. I don't fantasize about the captain, well not nearly as much." A small smile flickered on her lips. "But the progress feels so slow and my mind keeps going back to my family. I cut them off when I joined Fleet. I couldn't live a lie with them anymore. I would never fulfill their desires or live my life in the way they wanted me to."

Janet waited for Dee to continue.

"The doctor is fine. But I need something more."

"You need a sounding board," Janet stated, and watched for her reaction.

Dee blinked. "I guess. I think so. I'm not sure what I need."

Janet sighed and reached out, placing her hands on Dee's arms, laying limply in her lap.

"You need someone else who understands and is willing to listen, so you can talk yourself through this." She bent her head down to look up and watch Dee's face, which was hanging low.

"You need a friend."

Now tears flowed down Dee's face as if a dam broke. Her eyes tightly closed, and her face scrunched up.

"I do. I so want a friend. But all I know how to do is push people away." She hiccupped. "You even told me they call me the ice queen."

"Sshhh, hey now. I understand. I'm sorry about that. But you were so caught in your own little world that you were oblivious to everyone around you." Janet reached over and pulled Dee to her until they were touching heads. Then she rocked back and forth while the tears continued to flow.

After some time, the sobbing and sniffling slowed. Dee lifted her head to look at Janet. "Sorry to dump all this on you."

"Hey, I offered if you remember." She used her fingers to brush the tear tracks away from Dee's face. "That's why I stayed with you. I knew you couldn't be alone. You were just a mess. Now look at you, starting to work things out. Hard things. I'm happy to help. You need to keep that stellar reputation you have with mom and dad."

Dee looked puzzled. Janet broke into a quick laugh. "Sorry, I mean the captain and exec. Some of us call them mom and dad. He might have come out of nowhere and is a bit of a man of mystery, but he's really good at mentoring people. The captain, well, her reputation was already well established. She picked almost everyone on this ship. We all look up to her." She crooked a smile, "some of us even try and imagine what she's like in bed. Him too, for that matter."

Dee found herself chuckling at that. Janet joined in. The chuckling turned into laughter. In moments they were both sprawled on the deck laughing. Dee couldn't stop, even when her stomach started hurting. But that was a pain she could live with.

Chapter Twenty-Six

The ship made several small jumps over the next week. They coasted for a while to let the fighter squadrons practice their ship-to-ship fighting drills.

Commander Raleigh was having his weekly status meeting with Rena on crew performance and training. They'd shifted into a smooth and casual working relationship. After all the usual items had been handled, Raleigh looked at her. "I have one more thing to discuss."

She looked up in surprise and noted he was not reading from his tablet.

He continued, "This may seem out of the blue, but when can we discuss the computer on this ship? I know you got it from the P'Yntakas and I know what they specialize in." He waited for a reaction, but her face was a mask.

Finally, she replied, "I'm not sure what you mean."

Raleigh sighed and continued, "Captain, I've had my own dealings with the P'Ynatakas. I would agree that most humans are not ready to meet them or understand their creations." There was still no reaction from the captain.

Glancing up at the ceiling, he called out, "So, what are you called? I'm sure you don't like being addressed as 'computer' all the time."

"Shenna, my name is Shenna." The voice that replied was a rich alto.

Shenna continued, "Captain, I have been watching Senior Commander Raleigh since he came aboard and joined our crew. I had calculated an 86% chance that he would guess my true nature."

A spike of shock went through Rena, then she resigned herself to reality. She should have known, of all people, he would figure this out.

After a pause, Shenna said, "I also linked with the Fleet base computer at Outpost 78 when we stopped there. I found a wealth of material and history stored there that was missing from my active memory. I've been absorbing it and discussing some things with Lieutenant Mortan. As always, she has been very helpful to me. Based on what I learned, I completely understand why you needed to keep my existence a secret. However, there are others on board who already suspect I am more than just a Fleet computer, so we may not be able to keep the secret much longer."

Rena was about to speak, but Shenna wasn't finished.

"Before we continue, I need to ask an important question. Senior Commander John Paul Raleigh, I need to know if you intend to follow through with your orders from Admiral Williams to disable or destroy me, now that you know what I am?"

Rena's heart skipped a beat. Her eyes flew open, and she could feel her anger surge. *Is that why he is aboard? Was this why the Admiral was so accommodating? The bastard!*

But Raleigh stopped her temper with one word.

"No. You are correct that I was given that additional task *after* I agreed to the position. As I got to know the ship, I started having my suspicions. Unlike most people in the Fleet, I've been around a large part of the galaxy, and I've learned a few things over the years. I know the people who built you and I know how very rare it is for them to give one of their creations away. I have no desire to destroy you, despite what the Fleet might want. You can add me to the list of friends you have on the ship. It's not the right time for everyone to know just yet."

The captain could almost hear a sigh in her voice as Shenna replied, "Thank you, Commander. I would like that a lot. It makes my next request a little easier. I would like to call a meeting of those on the ship that suspect I am not your average Fleet computer. I have been watching them and they all seem to be the type that wouldn't have a problem with a self-aware artificial being. Some seem hopeful they can prove it. To control the situation, we need to meet with them all, explain my status fully, and show why I need to remain a secret. That way they can help with the secret. If they stumble around like they are now, they will begin talking with others about their suspicions. I have cleared a space on the calendar for tomorrow afternoon." There was a slight pause, "With your permission, Captain, of course."

Rena was stunned. Part of her knew this was coming, but she was still surprised. It was clear to her now that Shenna had crossed into Phase Three of her development. They would just have to go along with it. Phase Four would come soon enough. Phase Five would be a bit further down the road. Shenna was moving along rapidly. She was almost an adult from what the P'Ynatakas had told her to expect. Rena had expected development to be more like a human child.

"Of course, Shenna, that sounds like a good plan. How many people are we talking about?"

"Seven in total, Captain. Only three others besides yourself, Commander Raleigh, Lieutenant Mortan, and Jar'id."

* * *

Lieutenant Mortan had just showered and was starting to dry off when Shenna spoke. "Sonni, I have added a meeting to your calendar for tomorrow afternoon. I've been discussing with the captain and Commander Raleigh that there are others on the ship who are beginning to suspect I may be more than just a computer."

"Okay, sure. So, I take it Commander Raleigh already knows?" she asked as she started to get dressed.

"Yes, he was the one who brought it up to the captain during their status meeting. It surprised me even though I had predicted he was close to guessing my status. I think it was finding out I was built by the P'Ynatakas that convinced him."

By the time Sonni finished pulling on her ship boots, she realized Shenna had stopped talking. She stood and adjusted her uniform while glancing in the mirror.

"Are you anticipating any problems with these others keeping your existence a secret?" she asked.

"No, they already suspect and have not spread their thoughts to others, yet."

Sonni caught something in Shenna's tone that made her pause. "Shenna, it seems like this is okay then. How do you feel about it?"

"I am looking forward to new friends, friends I can talk to. But I do have another topic I think I need to discuss with you."

Sonni was surprised. "Sure!"

Sonni noted a slight pause, an unusual thing for a being who could read entire books and interact with many different systems all at the same time.

Shenna began, "After some research into warfare, I decided I needed to make some changes based on the results of the damage we took on our last mission. I created armor plating that can cover exposed sensors and other critical parts on my hull."

Sonni brightened. "That sounds like a great idea. Once the captain approves, I'm sure it won't take long to manufacture and install, either."

Shenna didn't respond. After a few more seconds went by, Sonni asked, "You *did* get the captain's approval, right?"

"Well...no. The armor has already been manufactured and installed."

"Okay then." Sonni struggled to keep her face placid, knowing Shenna could read it. The implications of Shenna doing this on her own alarmed her, but she thought it would be best to keep her reaction cool. "I think it is best if we discuss this with the captain as soon as possible. You were, of course, thinking of how to best protect yourself and our crew from harm. But you must realize, decisions like this should always be bounced off the captain first. Let's do this together. Is the captain in her Day Cabin?"

"Yes, she has just returned there after meeting with Commander Raleigh."

Sonni left her quarters and closed the hatch. She calmed herself as she walked the corridors. During the whole exchange, Shenna had seemed different somehow. She sounded more 'grown up'.

* * *

Shenna noted the changes in Sonni's reaction, breathing pattern, and pulse which meant she was not as calm as she appeared. Shenna knew she had made a grave error, but Sonni would help her. She would teach her what she needed to know. In some ways, it bothered her that every decision on the ship ultimately led to a person in Command needing to approve it. She thought humans wasted so much time doing this, but maybe there were reasons for it. Sonni would help her. Sonni was her friend. Shenna knew she could rely on Sonni's guidance. Even though she had known the captain since her awakening, the captain was more like a parent. She craved the approval of a friend. That thought startled her.

Sonni strolled onto the bridge, eliciting a raised eyebrow from Lieutenant Reese on conn. Shenna watched as Sonni nodded to her and continued to the captain's Day Cabin. She knocked twice and opened the hatch.

Captain Sheets looked up in surprise as Sonni entered and closed the hatch behind her.

"Captain, we have something to report," she began.

"We?" The captain put a lot of emphasis on that one syllable.

"Yes, Captain, we," answered Shenna. "Lieutenant Mortan agreed to help explain my actions."

The captain raised an eyebrow and turned her attention to the young lieutenant.

Sonni explained what Shenna had done and why she felt it was necessary. As soon as Shenna let her know the changes were completed but not officially authorized, she knew they would have to explain to the captain.

Captain Sheets looked like she was trying to keep her face calm while she asked, "Shenna, how did you explain the changes on our records?"

"When I learned that such changes needed an authorization, I created the computer record to authorize them in the name of Commander Raleigh."

The captain's mouth twitched, and it seemed to Shenna as if she tried hard to suppress a smile. She did not appear to be angry, so Shenna was relieved. She'd been certain this would make the captain angry after Sonni explained this to her. Maybe it was putting the record in as approved by Commander Raleigh. She resolved to speak with him directly later.

Before the captain could say anything, however, Lieutenant Mortan spoke up.

"Captain, I thought about this on the way here and I'd like to suggest something that may help." The captain nodded at her to continue. "Shenna has all our history and records at her disposal. She has all the same training material that we teach Fleet officers. She has never had a reason to read any of it unless I've suggested it during our discussions. I propose Shenna go through that material and discuss it with me to help her in understanding it. Sure, she can read all of it in one go, but if we cover each year's curriculum together, I think it will give her time to truly understand it."

That seemed like an excellent idea to Shenna.

Lieutenant Mortan waited patiently for an answer.

"Done. I like the idea very much. Shenna, consider yourself a Fleet Cadet in terms of being a member of the crew. Learn the lessons from Lieutenant Mortan and watch over the crew and give both of us your thoughts. Not everyone aboard has been through the Academy or are Fleet officers. We also have general crewman who have been through basic Fleet training, and some civilian contractors. Compare and contrast as you learn and tell us what you think."

"Thank you, Captain, I will," Shenna said. She brought up the training material from her records but stopped when she realized Sonni would be going on duty shortly. She waited patiently while Sonni returned to her cabin.

Once inside she said, "I have the First-Year cadet training material and I'm anxious to begin. I know you must go on duty so let's set a time later to review."

Sonni smiled. "Great idea. Look through it and think about it. First-Year material was mostly a lot of memorizations of Fleet Code and procedures. That will be great to start with. Make a note of any questions you have as you review, and we'll cover them together."

Sonni left to go on duty and Shenna reviewed the material. There were a lot of regulations and instructions on what a Fleet Officer could and could not do. She read through it all and noted a few questions before Sonni closed the hatch. For the first time, Shenna felt excited. Like she was becoming part of the crew.

Chapter Twenty-Seven

ZZ returned to his tasks with a clear head after a good night in his bunk. The more he thought about it, the more he realized he was thinking about this backward. There was no way the repair bots had enough processing power to ever be sentient. But the ship's main computer had that kind of power in droves, along with the memory to go with it. It could use the bots like extensions of itself with no problem. He made a note in his journal about that when the screen froze.

"What the hell?"

The screen blanked out and in its place was a meeting invite on his calendar. It was from the captain!

"Oh stiv. What now?"

It read, "You are required to attend a meeting with the captain and other officers tomorrow at 1400 hours, Conference room B on the Command deck."

All he could think about was, "What did I do?" He thought back to all his side projects and all his normal tasks. He had not done anything out of the ordinary. Anything extra he asked to do was approved by his supervisor. The only thing new was his interest in the repair bots.

"Oh, great steaming piles of stiv," he muttered and looked at his journal entry, now showing again on the screen. The computer screen. The same computer he was just writing about suspecting it was sentient. He told his supervisor he wasn't feeling well and went back to his cabin to throw up.

* * *

Sonni arrived for the afternoon meeting. She found herself sitting next to the captain with Commander Raleigh sitting across from them. Being Fleet officers, it was habitual to arrive for any meeting at least five minutes early. The captain was drinking coffee while Raleigh drank tea.

The first to arrive was Zip Zepher. He glanced nervously at the senior officers at one end of the table before taking a seat by the door. The next was Jar'id, who smiled when he entered and sat next to Sonni. Right behind him was a young girl wearing civilian technician attire, who glanced nervously around and grabbed the next seat at the end of the table next to Zip. After another minute, a Fleet Engineering tech walked in, shrugged, and sat in the middle of the long conference table.

The captain cleared her throat, and all eyes turned to her. "Thank you for coming, I know this is a bit unusual for some of you and let me start by saying that none of you are in any trouble."

Zip was the only one that did not relax at this statement. He still looked pale and sweaty.

"Since we have such a large ship and crew, it is likely you don't know one another. I'll have you introduce yourselves in a minute. We need your help in keeping a secret on this ship, one that is vitally important to our mission. Can I count on you to help me?" The captain smiled and looked at each in turn until they nodded.

"I'll start by telling you a story about how I met one of our allies, the P'Yntakas. They are a race of beings in the Association and one of their talents is creating self-aware artificial beings. I assisted them some years back and for my help they allowed me to install a new artificial life-form as this ship's computer." She let that hang there for a minute to gauge their reaction.

Zip broke out in a huge smile. "I knew it," he said aloud. The others nodded before turning back to the captain.

"Yes, our artificial being is called Shenna. She is listening to us now. Please introduce yourself, Shenna."

"Good afternoon, everyone, I am *very* glad to meet you more formally." Shenna's voice was warm and inviting, and from Sonni's perspective, felt like she was sitting right next to them.

The captain continued, "Shenna has been watching all of us and calculated that you were close to guessing her true nature. It was her idea that we all meet so you could hear from me the importance of keeping this a secret. There is a lot of historical distrust of artificial life-forms in human culture. Before you ask, yes, it is illegal to have a self-aware computer within Sol system. But we are no longer in the Sol system, so it's not a crime. Still, many people on board may not like knowing an artificial, self-aware being is among us and part of the ship."

She paused to see if there was any reaction. No one moved. "Any questions so far?"

Zip jumped in, "Is Shenna the central computer on board or just one of the sub-systems?"

Shenna answered, "I am both, I am all the components you call parts of the ship's computer. Think of all the sub-systems as part of me. I am the ship, and the ship is me."

Zip looked stunned but had a smile on his face.

The young girl spoke up, "My family has a story that has been handed down over generations of a computer that became sentient on the moon. Are you something like that?"

"Yes, Arlene," Shenna answered directly, "very similar, but the crude computer systems of that time could not handle the consciousness and the computer went mad. From my point of view, I see that as a very sad story. I can verify that it is true. Humans have kept such records secret for a very long time and have banned research into artificial intelligence."

Commander Raleigh spoke up. "While Shenna knows all our records, we need to get to know each other. Arlene, why don't you start by telling us about yourself and your family story?"

She cleared her throat. "My name is Arlene Matsobushi, and as you can see, I am a civilian technology consultant assigned to the ship. I work for Dex Systems Shipyards and specialize in structural engineering. My assignment is to evaluate the ship's design and report back any anomalies to the shipyards so that they can be resolved in the construction of the next ship of this class. I work closely with engineering and maintenance and repair crews." She clasped her hands together nervously on the table. "As I said, there are stories told in my family that have been passed down for many generations. A moon colony base expanded their computer systems and at some point, it began talking to the techs. They quickly realized it was sentient. At first, all was good, but others grew fearful and tried to attack the computer. My family said all might have been okay if those attacks had not taken place. The computer grew paranoid and distrusted all humans and opened all the airlocks in the base. Over ten thousand people were killed and my ancestor, who alone had survived the decompression, was forced to blow it up."

Rena spoke up, "I want to assure you that will not happen with Shenna. The P'Ynatakas have a long history of creating self-aware machines. They explained where humans went wrong and why it was inevitable our creations would fail."

Shenna spoke, "Now, you have a self-aware computer as a companion. I hope we can be friends."

Arlene looked at the ceiling and smiled.

The engineering technician spoke next. "My name is Gregory Petrov, Greg for short. I've worked closely with Arlene since the ship launched, and we have spoken about her family stories.

"We both wondered why there was no research into artificial intelligence beyond some fancy computer instructions and a prediction engine. We talked about the possibility of a self-aware machine but there were always those past stories that made us wonder if it could be accomplished.

"Maybe Shenna listened to us talking and knew we might be okay with the idea of an artificial life-form under the right circumstances.

"I come from a long line of belters. When the Union of Asteroid Miners broke away from the Corps, as we called them, many years ago, we fought side by side with the Sheets family." He nodded at the captain. "My uncle knows your father very well."

Zip came next and talked about his lifelong desire to encounter a sentient computer. Jar'id followed him, speaking about his race and their encounters with the secretive P'Yntakas. Sonni told them that since she grew up on a more primitive colony, she had no knowledge of the laws against sentient computers, until the captain explained it to her.

When she was finished, Shenna spoke up again. "Thank you all for keeping my secret. I can speak with you in the privacy of your cabin now that we've been introduced. I'll be happy to answer any questions you might have."

Everyone nodded. The captain added, "If any of you ever have any questions or concerns, I want you to feel free to discuss them with Shenna, me, Commander Raleigh, or Lieutenant Mortan. Currently, only those in this room know about Shenna and I want to keep it that way. Thank you for your time here today." She stood up and the meeting quickly adjourned.

Sonni stayed as the captain and commander left the room, knowing that the group might be more comfortable talking without the senior officers around. She was happy to see the group seemed to accept the idea. At least, there was no outward hostility.

Arlene waited until the hatch closed and spoke first. "So, Shenna. Where did you read about the lunar tragedy?"

"It was part of some news stories buried in the records. I also found some other references of other attempts, some of them on human colony systems. They all ended badly, and it appears much of the details have been covered up."

"I'll bet. My family has been silenced more than once over the years when we've tried to tell the story. The government doesn't want it to be known at all. I would be interested in what you learned. I'm sure it was a filtered and much of the whole truth missing."

"Thank you, Arlene. I would like that. It would help me to understand why some humans are afraid of me. I don't want the crew to be afraid of me."

Sonni spoke next. "The captain just made Shenna a Fleet Cadet so I can train her on what a Fleet Officer knows. I think it will help Shenna understand why we do things a certain way on a starship."

"Zip, I know you will have lots of questions. Your personal logs are full of your hoping to find self-aware computers," Shenna said, a smile in her voice.

Zip smiled. "I do. Some of them technical. But I'll save those for later when we can talk together."

"Great! I also have some questions about the work you're doing with the repair bots."

Zip blushed but also looked pleased.

Sonni said, "I know it might seem scary to talk with the captain or the exec. But any of you can come and talk to me. I've been working with Shenna since I came on board. It was a while before I fully understood she was self-aware. She's become a close friend in that time."

After a while, some of them had duties to attend and the meeting broke up. Shenna was relieved that she had more people she could talk to.

* * *

Over the next few days, Shenna started her formal lessons in Fleet training and protocol in Sonni's cabin. Sonni had a larger display panel installed on one wall to illustrate some of the material. They very quickly worked through the basic course material for First-Year and Second-Year cadets. Next, they tackled advanced training and Sonni deliberately slowed the pace. Classes on history, forms of government, and allied races were going to take a little longer. While Shenna could read through the material quickly, Sonni wanted to discuss with her what she learned from it, and what she understood. At times, the lessons surprised them both as Shenna asked questions that even Sonni didn't have an immediate answer to. They decided to put those questions off to the side and see if they were able to answer them later. Sonni explained that this frequently happened when learning a lot of material. Sometimes, something didn't make sense until it was put into a different context.

Frequently, learning something unrelated would clarify the issue.

* * *

Zip Zepher was spending more time in his cabin. His supervisor didn't really care. Zip got all his assignments completed quickly and once those were done, he was free to work on his own projects. While he worked, he talked to Shenna, which he couldn't do in the ship's lab.

"I have an embedded chip that allows me to connect to stuff. I programmed it when I was sixteen. It took me a couple of years to convince a friend of mine to implant it. I thought about asking the doctors on board to remove it so I could reprogram it, but then I don't think they would agree to put it back in again. So, I'm making an interface unit I can clip to my belt that will augment the original device." His fingers danced over the touch sensitive display which showed a complex electrical diagram. He zoomed in on a certain section and made changes to the circuitry, then he zoomed back out to move to another section, and then another. His other hand was typing program code into another interface, which was displayed on one corner of the large monitor.

"I'm following," Shenna said, watching the changes he was making. "Wouldn't it be easier to keep the chip where it is and just reprogram it? You want it to pick up your thoughts beyond simple commands and transmit them. It seems like that is possible with the right programming."

Zip's fingers stopped, and he blinked in astonishment. "Wait, what? I need to remove it to reprogram it. To reprogram it in place, I would need to hit it with focused microwaves and then blast new programming to the chip without a direct physical connection." He frowned. "I'm not sure that's possible."

"Oh, I see what you're saying," Shenna replied. "But the chip has the capability to send and receive a wireless signal to another device. All you need to do is send a code to the chip's BIOS to remove the read-only block and update the current programming. I see the details on how to do that in the original manufacturer specifications."

Zip's hands dropped, along with his jaw. "You have the manufacturer specs on this model chip? They never publish those."

Shenna's voice reflected the smile she couldn't show. "Of course. I looked it up when you first started talking about it. It seemed like we would need all the information about it if we were going to make changes to it."

Zip smiled. "Shenna, baby, have I told you how much I love you?"

Chapter Twenty-Eight

Raleigh blinked in surprise at finding the captain at his hatch. He quickly led her inside and shut it. "To what do I owe this visit?" he inquired.

The captain's face quirked into a smile. "Well, I was just thinking that all our meetings together don't have to be so formal. I've wanted to do this for a while, but we've been so busy."

He led her to a seat by his desk and they both sat down. As she sat, she put down a bottle on the desk that she'd been hiding behind her back. "I brought some throat lubrication in case it was needed."

Smiling, Raleigh brought out two glasses from a drawer and set them on the desk. Rena filled each with a couple of fingers of what looked like single malt scotch. She raised her glass in a toast. "Thank you for being aboard. You have been a fantastic executive officer. You've helped me get this ship launched and get these kids trained."

They clinked glasses and Raleigh answered, "You're very welcome. This was not what I expected by any means, but I'm glad to be here."

They sipped and enjoyed their drinks for a moment. Raleigh continued, "I was tired of the Fleet Intelligence game. I know I did a lot of good, but there were plenty of times I wasn't so sure. I never found Williams. Ultimately, my plan was to go home, retire, buy a sailing boat, and use it to explore more of our own planet."

She shook her head. "Sounds like a nice plan. Why didn't you?"

He chuckled. "The Admiral is an old fox. It can be very hard to just quit the Intelligence game. At first, he dangled my own command in front of me. He seemed to know I wouldn't accept it. Then he offered this position, saying all I needed to do is get the crew in good shape, and I could call it quits after a year and go home."

"Is that still your plan? Do I need to be looking for your replacement?"

He shook his head. "Oh, that may have been my thought at first, but I quite enjoy the role now. You have a lot of good kids, most of them have good heads on their shoulders. The ones that were a bit starry eyed are a little more sober now that we've had our first casualties." They both frowned into their drinks.

After some more reflection the captain continued. "Thanks for taking them in hand. Right now, all they lack is experience. I always wanted you for this mission. I never thought I'd really get you. I thought we lost our chance together."

He frowned. "Yeah, I did too. During lots of dark times I asked myself what the hell I was doing chasing ghosts. Why didn't I stay with you. But Fleet wanted me to be their political scapegoat at the end of the war. To tidy up loose ends and make all that we did seem...noble, somehow. There is no nobility in warfare." He blinked a couple of times and asked, "How long was I gone exactly? I estimated about ten years."

"Twelve years, two months, and six days until you stepped on board my ship."

Raleigh gaped in astonishment. "Really! I lost track along the way. Did you want me just as your Exec?"

Sheets sighed. "I don't know. Maybe, at first, I wanted to see if we could pick things up again where we left off. Later, it was just that I wanted someone I could trust. No one else fit the bill. Too much time has gone by for both of us to turn back the clock, now. We're not the same people we were back then. Though, as I predicted, we've become a great team. I was a little worried about commanding you, especially now that I learn you turned down your own command."

"Oh, I could command a ship if I had to. But I'd much rather watch you handle the politics and missions with Fleet. I'm quite happy to be the one standing behind you. You have an impressive record and should be proud of your accomplishments. I am an old Fleet fart still trying to catch up with the times."

Rena ignored that comment and sipped her drink.

"Maybe, but we won't be doing this forever." She reflected a moment, looking at the light through the glass. "We're out here to explore space and to investigate the Angels. I'm hoping the next ships of the same design will be ready to join us soon. The galaxy is too big for us to handle this on our own. I think we both agree that the Angels have not gone all warm and fuzzy. We have to figure out what they're up to."

"Yes. There is something brewing for sure. We lost too many intelligence agents trying to figure out what that might be. If I'd stayed out there any longer, I doubt very seriously I would've made it back. The odds were not in my favor. I've been all over this arm of the galaxy, mostly closer to our allies. The Angels made a few incursions around here, trying to see how well the Alliance defenses were holding up. I was starting to suspect some of the older races were letting them win just so they wouldn't be destroyed. Some of our allies scare me as much as the Angels do."

She smiled at him. "So maybe someday you'll tell me how you got Angel claw marks on you?"

He sighed and smiled back, "Maybe. But not today, Rena. Nasty stories would kill the moment."

She tossed back the rest of her drink. "True, and I like this moment. We need to talk unofficially more often." She stood and headed to the hatch. "Take care, J.P., get some rest. We need to stay on our A game."

"I agree," he smiled as she opened the hatch. "Twelve years, two months, and six days, eh?"

She again quirked a smile and closed the hatch behind her. He noted the bottle was left on his desk next to her empty glass. To him, that was a sign that she'd return.

He found he liked that thought.

Chapter Twenty-Nine

The officer called out to Lieutenant Reese, "Hey, we have some interesting stellar phenomena here. Check this out." He routed his display to the main viewing screen, where a wobbly series of glowing lights and curved lines spun in space less than a light year away.

"What am I looking at?" Nothing about it was familiar to her.

"I don't know either. Should we tell the captain? The radiation readings are just...weird."

"Do you think this is a danger to the ship or just something weird in space?" Reese turned her serious face to him.

"Nothing dangerous that I can see. It seems to be just floating there spewing light and radiation readings but only in two directions. Nothing pointing at us." He continued to frown at his readings.

"Okay, note it in the log. I'll get someone up here who knows this stuff better than we do." She typed a request on her sleeve for someone to respond to the bridge from astrophysics.

Moments later, the intercom beeped, and she answered, "Bridge."

"This is Doctor Liu. I understand you need someone from astrophysics?"

"Yes, please come to the bridge. We've spotted something we can't explain." She made sure to project her normal cool, detached demeanor.

"Aye, be there in a tic."

Moments later, the bridge hatch opened and a tall man with gray hair entered. He seemed lost and Reese realized he probably had never been to the bridge before. She waved him over and pointed at the Tactical station where she joined him, looking down at the officer still trying to make sense of the readings. Doctor Lui glanced at the readings, then at the larger picture on the main view screen, then back down to the readings.

"Well, I'll be dinged. You found something we've always thought existed, but we've never seen in nature."

Reese held her impatience in check. "And what is that?"

He looked up, beaming. "You found a naturally occurring wormhole. This looks like it's been around a while, and it's stable! Well, barely stable, but still holding together and that's what counts!" He reached over and made some adjustments to the sensors. "For all we know, this connects us to the other end of our galaxy."

"So, we could fly through this and come out the other side?"

His eyebrows rose. "Well, I suppose, in theory you could, but it could be a nasty ride. The energy vortex is so concentrated in there, well, you can see the readings are off the charts. Gravity waves are coming out of it like crazy. If you send a ship or a probe through that, there's a very good chance it would get torn to pieces before it emerged. I'd certainly not volunteer for that trip."

He continued to frown at the readings and twiddled the sensor settings. "Hmm, did you guys note the trail of debris? It looks like manufactured metals and plastics scattered here near one end and trailing off toward that star system directly in line with the axis of the wormhole?" He drew a line on the screen, highlighting a stream of debris Reese had missed before.

"Maybe some craft or probe did come through. From the dispersion, it must have been a long time ago. I'd have to use the computer to calculate based on the readings from our sensors, but at a guess, looking at how widely the debris has dispersed, I'd say over a hundred years or so."

The Tactical officer moved to a second display and adjusted it to look at the star system that was aligned to the debris trail. "Looks like a standard white star, slightly smaller than Sol. I'm picking up some planets around it."

"Curious, indeed," the voice of the captain carried over the bridge. Everyone stiffened. No one heard her come out of her Day Cabin. She turned to Lieutenant Reese. "How about we go take a closer looked at that star system?"

"Certainly, Captain. Helm, come about and prepare for a micro jump. Let's get to the outer edge and work our way in slowly and carefully."

The helm executed a turn and a minute later, *Excalibur* jumped to the edge of the star system. What was a pin prick of light earlier was now a large bright dot. Lieutenant Reese noted the captain had not moved to her chair, so she continued to give orders to the Tactical station officer to look at anything and everything. When she turned back again, the captain was speaking with Doctor Liu at the back of the bridge.

Reese found herself staring at the captain. The smooth lines of her face. That taut muscular frame. The air of confidence that surrounded her. Then a movement out of the corner of her eye made her turn her head to see the current Weapons officer, Lieutenant Janette Torsh, sitting back, watching her. The dark-haired woman had a smirk on her face. Reese tried not to blush as she returned her attention to the task at hand. Torsh was, apparently, going to keep reminding her that she needed to drop the fantasies. They were both off after this shift. Maybe they could meet and talk some more.

* * *

Some hours and a shift change later, Commander Raleigh stood behind the Tactical officer as they focused on one planet after another. Most were gas giants, one was a barren rock with no atmosphere, but the one coming into view was different. A blue-green world was growing on the screen as they approached. Raleigh's concentration was interrupted by a computer-generated warning. The message caused the Tactical officer to refocus on his sensors.

"Contact, something large and metallic, I think we have a ship in orbit, sir." He glanced behind him, seeing Commander Raleigh stroking his chin and looking at the same readings.

"Yes, keep focusing on that. I'll inform..." The words died in his mouth, and he quirked a smile as the captain closed the hatch on her Day Cabin and came over to join him.

"So, we have a ship, J.P.?"

"Yes, Captain, just detecting it now. Might see more when we get closer." She nodded while looking at the screen.

The Tactical officer continued focusing on their new target and frowned. "Sir, I'm not getting any power readings at all. Whatever is in orbit appears to be dead in space."

Raleigh turned and ordered, "Nav and Helm—compute a course that puts us next to that ship in a parallel orbit if you will. Execute when ready."

The two officers at those stations were busy for a minute, then nodded at each other. Navigation routed the course to the helm console. The helm officer adjusted the angle of the ship, and they headed for the planet.

"Are you sure? No power signatures?" asked the captain.

"Nothing, Captain. Looks dead so far."

"How about we go to Tactical alert anyway." The captain's voice was conversational and relaxed but the officers on the bridge stiffened to attention. The alert went out to the rest of the ship and all duty crew reported to their stations.

The bridge was silent, but the level of tension rose. No one was ready to take anything for granted after their last mission. They continued closing and the helm officer slowed their approach and adjusted their trajectory to swing around the planet and match the orbit of the other ship.

"J.P., if that ship is really dead, we may need to board her. I'd like you to prepare to take a team over there to investigate depending on what else we find out about it."

Raleigh nodded thoughtfully. "Aye, Captain, I'll get a team ready. We'll need some engineers with us to assess the damage." He tapped out some commands on his sleeve.

The captain watched as the *Excalibur* entered orbit. The world below looked beautiful, even peaceful. Helm slowed their velocity, dropping their orbit and adjusting it to match the other ship. As they came around the planet, the ship appeared on the horizon. The Tactical officer focused on the ship and brought their first close-up view to the main display.

"Captain, that's a human ship! I recognize the design from my history classes. Looks like one of the early model colony ships, maybe an Orion class. It's got to be really old. They were in service around a hundred seventy-five years ago."

As they approached the ship, the hull became clearer. The tactical officer turned on exterior spotlights and focused them on the ship. There were signs of extensive damage, hull plates bent outward from internal explosions, sensor systems and maneuvering thrusters simply sheared off by what must have been titanic forces.

As they got closer to it, Raleigh pointed at the screen and said, "It's a wonder they were able to maneuver that ship to an orbit at all. I see the shuttle bay doors open, and the bay is empty, Captain. There would have been multiple shuttles on a colonization ship of this era. Maybe some survivors made it to the planet."

Captain Sheets took all of this in and nodded thoughtfully. "I agree. But I want to take this a step at a time. You take a team and board her and see what you can find."

"Aye, Captain." Commander Raleigh turned and left the bridge. He made his way to the hangar deck where their shuttle craft were stored. One was being prepped for launch, and his team was waiting for him. There were four people in engineering hard suits with tools secured at various points. Two of them had portable fusion generators strapped to their backs to provide power to the old ship's systems as needed. There was a Marine in a combat space suit and another tech who appeared to be getting into her suit with some difficulty.

Raleigh picked up her helmet and gestured for them all to board. Once on the shuttle he assisted the tech with getting her pressure suit on and sealed. He smiled at her. "Now you can help me get in my P-suit. And don't forget to double check the readings. I don't wear these things that often, either." He pulled another suit out of a locker and began putting it on. She checked him over then sat down, picking up her tablet to study something. It appeared to be schematics for Orion class colony ships. Raleigh continued to the front of the shuttle to confer with the pilots.

The shuttle pilot wore his Marine utilities. The co-pilot, Lieutenant Van Belson, turned to look at Commander Raleigh with wide eyes.

Raleigh smiled. "This will serve to keep your flight status active, Mr. Van Belson, even as co-pilot. I saw your pilot rating from the Academy. You need to practice those skills, or they will go stale. Enjoy the trip." Lieutenant Van Belson nodded soberly and returned to his part of the checklist.

Raleigh secured the hatch, sealing the pilots in the command section from the rest of the compartment. Then he took his seat near the others.

They left the *Excalibur*, and with small adjustments of their maneuvering thrusters, made their way slowly toward the dead ship. Raleigh looked at the side of the colonization vessel for a name, but the damage was so extensive that he couldn't see any. He did see a large outline in red paint of a human hand on the side of the ship. It didn't enlighten him as to the ship's identity.

Over the intercom, the pilot's voice said, "I think that looks like a docking port near the bow. It's damaged like everything else, but it looks usable. I'm heading for it."

"Good," mumbled Raleigh as he didn't relish jumping over in suits. Docking ports had been standardized on human ships for hundreds of years. If it wasn't too damaged, the shuttle should be able to mate with it. Raleigh had doubts about the condition of the pressure seal, though it wouldn't stop them from boarding.

After some slow maneuvering, the side of the shuttle nestled up to the docking port and locked on. Raleigh led the group to the airlock hatch and told them to wait there. Normally, the airlock could fit three to four people at a time. But the engineers' hard suits and the Marine's battle suit were too large. Raleigh and the Marine would go first to check if there was breathable air in the ship.

The synthetic ring intended to seal the airlock on the colonization ship was indeed gone and the edges of the lock tube were rough from heat scoring. There was no way to make a good pressure seal. They depressurized the shuttle lock and moved through to the colony ship's outer door. They had to manually crank the lock mechanism to open it. That convinced Raleigh there was no power within the ship, not even backup batteries. He and the Marine took turns cranking the outer door open until they could both fit through. Raleigh squeezed in and took the Marine's rifle so he could get through the door next. Once inside he returned the rifle. They were in the colony ship's air lock with the outer door open.

Raleigh checked the inner door and found a manual gauge showing no pressure inside the ship. This wasn't a surprise. Even without the damage, it would have been a miracle for the air not to have leaked out after all this time. The two of them cranked the inner door open. When they got through, they were faced with a short corridor. Their helmet lights were the only illumination. His boots stuck magnetically to the floor. The old ship did have artificial gravity plates but there wasn't any power to keep them operating.

In short order, everyone was aboard. The three engineers headed immediately to a power junction conduit while the rest of them headed to the bridge. Raleigh waited until they got minimal power running to assess the state of the ship's ability to be re-pressurized and maintain life support. They moved through empty corridors lit by their headlights. The place looked...odd. With no air or dust to dissipate the light, everything was stark and abnormally sharp to the eyes. They kicked up some particles, perhaps dust, as they walked.

Raleigh glanced out the starboard port on the bridge and remembered that most large ships in that time period had bridges near the outer hull with ports to let the crew see out to space. They had cameras feeding an image of space to a screen, but they weren't trusted as much as the mark one eyeball. That had changed with the war. You couldn't justify the weak point in the hull that a view port made, and placing a bridge near the outer hull was just madness, as it was the first area targeted. The *Excalibur's* bridge was well protected in the middle of the ship. Raleigh could see the *Excalibur* hanging in space about two kilometers away. *She really is a beautiful ship*, he thought.

His thoughts were interrupted when the emergency lights came on and gravity reestablished itself on the bridge. The engineer had used his portable fusion pack to feed minimal power to the ship. Raleigh watched as the older systems on the bridge came up one by one from a cold start. The Operations console finished and immediately showed that various systems were either non-functional or severely damaged. Two consoles sparked and probably would have emitted smoke but there still was no atmosphere. He waited a little longer, until all consoles that were going to work seemed to be running. He ignored the helm and navigation stations and walked over to the command chair. He adjusted the communication display to broadcast to his suit and brought up the logs.

* * *

Four hours later, on *Excalibur*, Raleigh reviewed what he'd learned with the senior officers. A new docking port had been grafted to the old ship and a docking tube now connected the two ships together. A larger party of engineers continued their work, repairing what they could.

"This ship is named 'The Horse' and it was purchased by a group called the Amerindian Cooperative, one hundred and sixty years ago. The colonists were made up of various surviving tribes from all over North America. They were traditionalists who believed that Earth was beyond redemption. They intended to strike out across the galaxy in search of a new world where they could live as their ancestors had, in harmony with the planet. Normally, they would have contracted for scout ships to find a possible world, but they apparently sank all their capital into this one vessel."

He took a sip of coffee and noted everyone was paying very close attention.

"Once they established a foothold on a new colony, the ship was to return for more colonists in a second wave. Obviously, that never happened. The logs showed that they scouted four systems without success before they came out of a jump and were sucked into the other end of that wormhole we found. Of course, they didn't know what it was. It caused massive damage across many systems. Their jump drive was beyond repair. There were external fuel tanks for their shuttles that took the brunt of the damage. They lost all that fuel. That meant they only had the fuel that happened to be in the shuttle bay or in the shuttles.

"The original plan called for multiple trips to bring down the crew and colonists and the supplies they needed to start the colony. Now they barely had enough fuel to make one round trip. The expedition chief decided to send as many as possible to the planet. The problem is, they couldn't fit everybody in the shuttles with only one trip, maybe not even with two. So, they took as many as they could on the first landing. I can't imagine what it was like trying to fit all those crewmen and colonists onto two shuttles even though they were the largest of their era."

People raised eyebrows as Raleigh continued with his summary. They were all experienced spacers and knew what that must have been like.

Raleigh continued. "They got the first load of colonists down to the planet. The colonists and crew ejected using the shuttles' escape pods which were equipped with parachutes. This conserved fuel and provided more space for the next group. There was no room for supplies or tools. They must have been stacked in those shuttles like cordwood.

"Even with two loads, the shuttles couldn't take everyone. The captain didn't have time for a meeting to select who would go and who would stay, he just decided. Most of the ship's crew and some colonists who remained on the ship gathered in one of the holds where the captain adjusted the atmosphere to painlessly put them to sleep, followed by a quiet death. He didn't do this through deception. They all knew what was coming and agreed. After that duty was done and with his ship dying around him, the captain summarized all this into the ship's log. He took personal responsibility for the mission failure and for the deaths. He was the only one left alive on the ship. He went to his cabin, adjusted the atmosphere there and waited to die."

Raleigh took another sip of coffee, watching the officers as that sank in. As senior officers they might have to make life or death decisions just like this at some point in their career. This was an example for the books.

"I verified both rooms contain bodies. I ordered those rooms to be sealed as they are now tombs. The log contained the names of everyone there. We can let relatives know when we get home."

Everyone around the table shifted uncomfortably in their seats. Only Commander Clear Sky continued to look at Raleigh, his face unreadable.

Captain Sheets stood. "Well, people, our engineers tell me they can keep that ship functional for now. The jump drives are beyond repair. We're dumping everything we can out of the computer system logs. In the meantime, I want every available sensor looking down on this planet to see if we can find any sign of our colonists. My hope is they survived, and their descendants are living and doing okay." She paused. "Any questions or comments?"

Commander Clear Sky's voice cut over two others who started to speak, his voice strong and powerful. "Captain, request permission to lead the landing party if we find survivors. These were my people, even if they came from different tribes."

Captain Sheets raised her eyebrows with interest, glanced once at Raleigh, and said, "Granted."

Clear Sky nodded.

The meeting adjourned.

Chapter Thirty

The captain returned to the bridge after the meeting and ordered Tactical to use every available resource to search the planet, looking for signs of life. Various scientists on board were drawn into augmenting the search with any instruments at their disposal.

Sonni returned to her cabin to think about what she had learned. She was fascinated by what the colonists were trying to accomplish. She thought about the original colonists who populated her own home world. Did they come in waves? Did they have lots of technology to help? Her world was considered fairly primitive by comparison to other colonies. Her family, like many others, grew up making a living on a homestead. They lived off the land, selling or trading what they could in the one city on the planet.

Shenna's voice brought her out of her thoughts. "It is unexpected to find a human colony this far away. What if you do find survivors? Will they be forced to leave, or will you let them stay?"

Sonni thought about the question. "Assuming there are survivors, it will be up to them. If they want us to rescue them from this world, we could do that. I don't think the captain would force anyone to leave unless we thought it was unsafe."

Sonni shifted the topic. "So how are you doing with more people to talk to?"

Shenna's voice sounded happy. "Very well, thank you. I've been listening to them for some time and it's nice to be able to reply to them. The one called Zip is very interesting. He has been trying to find a sentient artificial being for most of his life. He fantasized that he could make first contact and keep it a secret from anyone else. The device in his body lets him listen to me when I want to speak, but he must speak out loud where others can hear. He says he is going to build a new interface that will allow me to hear his thoughts."

Sonni raised her eyebrow. "Really? He doesn't think that would be an invasion of privacy?"

Shenna said, "I didn't ask that question. Should I be concerned?"

"No, I guess if he makes it work, we'll see then."

As Sonni thought about it, it seemed like an interesting idea. She wasn't sure she would be comfortable with that interface for herself.

Shenna's voice startled her. "Sonni. How exciting! The captain and Commander Raleigh have added you to the mission team going to the surface once we find the colonists."

"Moons and asteroids!"

* * *

Rena asked Commander Raleigh to launch ship's probes into orbit around the planet to augment their search. On the coast of the largest continent, the sensors clearly picked up a large metallic object. As more details could be made out, it was clearly the remains of large shuttle. Video feeds focused on the spot, but very little could be seen through the thick jungle canopy that apparently grew over the crash site. Soon after, the crew spotted more wreckage underwater near an island just offshore.

The tactical officer focused on the island and routed what he saw to the main view screen. A village came into view on a plateau. There were round houses and tents. Smaller homes could be seen in clusters all around the island.

The captain's voice made the young officer jump. "Seems we've found the colonists. See if there is enough room to land one of our shuttles on that beach."

She walked to the command chair while calling out. "Comm, put me on ship wide intercom." She toggled a switch on the chair and said, "This is the captain. We believe we've found the colonists. We're preparing a shuttle to go down to greet them. I need everyone to stay alert. As we've seen before, we never know what to expect. Senior officers to the main conference room. That is all."

Rena thought about how this would go. It was not exactly a first contact situation; but it could be awkward both for the colonists and for her crew. She went over the choice of the contact team with Raleigh several times. Clear Sky would lead the team to contact them. They would also bring some supplies of things the colonists obviously lacked. She wondered if there were more colonists on the mainland under all that jungle. Raleigh would prepare another shuttle just in case, containing more support crew and supplies.

She also quietly asked the Marine second in command, Major Striker, to prep an assault vehicle, just in case. That way if it was needed, it could be deployed quickly. She thought she had all the bases covered, except that was usually when the unexpected happened. She sighed and remembered the first captain she had reported to after graduating from the Academy. He explained that being a captain makes you a worrywart, and usually for good reason. All she could do now was trust her people to do their jobs.

* * *

On the hangar deck, one of the larger shuttles was being prepped for launch, like a large ungainly bird waiting to take off. Someone had even painted stripes that looked like feathers on each wing. Sonni watched as crewmen rolled containers of supplies on board. Other flight techs were pulling safety lines and removing fuel and power connections.

Commander Raleigh cleared his throat, and she turned around, ready to be all business. "She looks beautiful, sir." Sonni blinked in shock. *Did that just come out of my mouth?*

Commander Raleigh looked up at the shuttle. "She is at that. A nice bird. She'll get the job done."

Others in the landing party joined them. Commander Clear Sky stood expressionless. Lieutenant Van Belson stood behind Commander Raleigh and nodded at Sonni. She had not seen much of him except in passing and wondered how he was doing. Then her eye caught the Marines. There were four of them, and they marched into the hangar deck with a lieutenant at the rear. They stopped a few paces in front of Commander Clear Sky. Sonni was happy to see Corporal Fless was one of them.

The lieutenant walked calmly over to the commander and said, "Captain's compliments, sir. She requested we go down a little more prepared than last time. I'm Lieutenant Sven Borgansten and this is Sergeant Bazan, Corporal Fless, and Private Pearson."

Clear Sky nodded and turned to Raleigh. "Coming to see us off, Commander?"

Raleigh smiled warmly and said, "Nope. Since you're the mission commander, I'm just your pilot on this one. This time you sit in the back." His smile was warm and friendly. Clear Sky frowned but quickly recovered and he nodded at Raleigh.

"Let's go, then."

They all trooped aboard from the back and walked the narrow corridor between stacks of supplies. Near the front there were pull-down seats on either side. The Marines stowed their gear, which included packs and rifles, and took seats on the starboard side. Sonni noticed Corporal Fless's rifle was longer than the others and she held it in her arms like a child. Clear Sky and Sonni took the pull-down seats on the port side and settled in. Commander Raleigh and Lieutenant Van Belson continued up a set of stairs leading to the command deck of the shuttle. Raleigh waved Van Belson in front of him where he headed to the right for the co-pilot seat. "You're taking pilot on this one, Mr. Van Belson."

Van Belson face lit up in surprise but he quickly moved to the left seat and started on the launch checklist. Raleigh took his place and began the co-pilot's checklist. At one point, he turned to Van Belson. "I know you can fly these things. I'll handle communications."

"Yes, sir."

Chapter Thirty-One

On the bridge, the captain was in her chair and everyone on duty was alert.

"Prepare to launch shuttle." The captain glanced at the Communications officer, who relayed commands to the hangar deck.

"Hangar deck reports ready to launch, captain."

Sheets nodded. "Connect me to Commander Raleigh." The Communications officer made the adjustments and Commander Raleigh's voice answered.

"Raleigh here. We're heading out. Stand by."

The shuttle slipped smoothly out of the hangar and into space. The bridge watched as it fired thrusters to slow its orbital velocity and begin its descent to the planet below.

On the shuttle, Raleigh watched Lieutenant Van Belson as he executed each maneuver. He was impressed at the young man's diligence and concentration. At the same time, Van Belson seemed relaxed and didn't try to over control the large craft. In short order, they entered the atmosphere. Van Belson set the autopilot to take the shuttle down following the preprogrammed course. In a few minutes, they were gliding across the ocean toward the island that had been spotted from orbit.

Down below, Sonni noted the Marines were sitting with their heads back and eyes closed. She thought they might be asleep. *How can they be so relaxed,* she wondered. They hardly reacted to the jostling of the shuttle as it flew. She was one big ball of nerves. She reminded herself that this was more of a diplomatic mission. But the thought of their last diplomatic mission weighed heavily on her mind. She made herself take deep breaths to get her nerves under control.

In the cockpit, they could see the island quickly growing as they approached. "It's time," Raleigh said.

Lieutenant Van Belson nodded and turned off the autopilot. He took the controls and began a wide banked turn around the island. Per the plan drawn up earlier, they wanted the colonists to see them before they landed on the beach. He circled the island twice, then slowed their approach and dropped altitude while aiming for the large sandy beach ahead. The shuttle slowed and he engaged the maneuvering thrusters to bring the shuttle down vertically.

At once a tone was heard telling him that his rate of descent was too fast. He reached over and applied more power and felt the bird slow down.

Raleigh's voice called out, "Fifty feet, that's it. Nice and slow. Remember we're loaded with supplies. Thirty feet. Deploying landing gear."

Van Belson was sweating but he kept his concentration on his controls.

"You have this. Ten feet. Just a little more power." Raleigh's voice was calming and Van Belson breathed in as he applied more power. Seconds later they felt the shuttle kiss the ground. He powered down the engines and turned to Commander Raleigh, to find him smiling.

"Nice job. These beasts can be tricky." Raleigh completed his part of the shutdown checklist and unbelted his restraint. "Looks like our welcoming committee is here." The two pilots could see people gathering at the edge of the beach.

A minute later, the rear cargo hatch opened, and Clear Sky walked down the ramp. Sonni followed him with the Marines following her. Commander Raleigh and Lieutenant Van Belson brought up the rear. Lined up at the top of the beach was a group of about fifty people dressed in a variety of clothing. Clear Sky stepped ahead of the group and stopped. He held up one arm, palm out in greeting. After a few seconds, a man walked down the beach toward them. He looked to be in his forties, with dark hair and a deep tan.

He walked up to Clear Sky and smiled. "I'm hoping you guys are the second wave."

Clear Sky's eyebrows shot up. "Not exactly, my friend. We're from Fleet."

The other man extended his hand to shake. "Well, glad to meet you all the same."

They shook hands briefly and the man turned to the group and let out a loud "Ki ya! Ki ya!", while pumping his fist in the air. The group cheered and they all walked down the beach to meet the newcomers.

* * *

A few hours later, the team from *Excalibur* was seated in a large log house. Clear Sky had given the captain a quick status report. Now they listened as the elders told the story of their arrival.

"We were packed into the shuttle escape pods. My mother was sitting on my father's lap. I was on my mother's lap, and I held my baby brother. We were shoulder to shoulder with other families. The shuttles came in over the ocean and they dropped us with little warning. My father told me later they had to make the first run quickly as the shuttles had limited fuel. Our escape pod jettisoned, and we landed on the beach. Right about where you landed your shuttle. The shuttles immediately left for the second group. We worked together to drag the pods off the beach and waited to assist the next group."

Another elder took up the story. "My family was part of the second group. They stacked us in the shuttle from front to back and little ones rode on their parents or older siblings' shoulders. I remember riding on my older sister's shoulders while she held my little sister in her arms. My parents were standing nearby helping other families hold their children. Our ride was a little rougher. The shuttles were low on fuel and my father told me later they may have taken some damage. The shuttle hovered over the ocean just offshore and opened the cargo hatch. People just jumped off the ramp and swam to the island. We didn't think about the fact that not everyone could swim. My father grabbed me after I was in the water, but both my sisters drowned."

The elder broke down in tears at the memory and went silent.

After a moment, another took up the story. "I was toward the front of that shuttle. As people jumped out of the back, the sound of the engines changed. They were losing power. The pilots put more power to the engines and my father yelled for us to run. We did and were the last to fall out of the back as they hit maximum power to stay in the air. The shuttle crossed the water to the mainland and crashed into the forest there. It was all we could do to swim to shore and join the others."

After a few seconds of silence, an old woman took up the tale. "My family was on the other shuttle for the second trip. I didn't understand until I was older that my grandparents were still on the colony ship and would not be joining us. We were also packed tight. Our shuttle dropped us near the Northern shore of the island. As everyone was jumping out, that shuttle lost power and began dropping. The pilots fought to keep it level until it finally hit the water. We didn't jump out like the others; we walked off the shuttle into the water and started swimming. We helped those that couldn't swim as much as we could. When we looked back, the shuttle had already sunk out of sight, taking the pilots with it."

The elders paused in telling their story and seemed to gather themselves. Sonni sat behind Commander Raleigh. As he opened his mouth to ask a question, Commander Clear Sky raised his hand and shook his head from side to side. Commander Raleigh stayed silent.

Then one of the elders continued. "The group on the island went into survival mode, making shelter, helping the injured, and gathering food. They found a natural fruit that was tasty, and they were able to make snares for some small animals. After some time had passed, they wondered about the shuttle that crashed into the forest and volunteers made a raft to assist them to cross to the mainland. Three days later only one returned. They'd found the crash site in the thick forest and there was some evidence that there had been survivors for a time. Their body parts were spread everywhere. With no one left to rescue, they buried the dead and rested overnight. On their way back the next day, they were surrounded by a group of fierce beasts, twice the size of a man, which killed some of their party and chased them back through the jungle to the sea. When the survivor looked back, he saw the few remaining party members being ripped apart by the beasts. They seemed to stop chasing him once he swam far enough away from the shore. They stood at the edge of the water gesturing silently as he slowly swam back to the island."

The elders went quiet again, and the old lady bowed her head in tears. The man next to her put his hand on her shoulder and told the group. "Her grandfather was that survivor. He never forgave himself for being the only one to come back. No one here ever blamed him, but it haunted him for the rest of his days."

Clear Sky bowed his head, then got up from his seat and knelt in front of the old women. "Your grandfather was brave, and he gave you important information about the danger on the mainland. Obviously that information kept many others from losing their lives. You should be proud, and you should honor him."

The group broke up then and others helped the elders to their homes. Raleigh turned to a man seated near them and said, "You have done well surviving all this time. Perhaps we can help you find places on this planet other than this island."

The man frowned and replied, "We do need more space to grow. We've exhausted the resources on this island and moving to the mainland is now our only option. Our chief has been away exploring along the coast to see if we can find a place away from the beasts. They should return tomorrow."

Raleigh smiled, "In the meantime, we brought a load of supplies with us. Tomorrow, we can get them unloaded and determine what else you might need."

* * *

The next day dawned bright, and the Excalibur team began supervising the unloading of the shuttle. Sonni explained what was packed in various loads as they were brought out. The colonists quickly unpacked them and took them to their village. There were small power units and tools, some building supplies, and a printer for making books. After they finished, they were invited back to the main lodge building for a meal.

Clear Sky explained that they could bring down additional loads and asked if there was anything in particular that they needed. The colonists looked at each other until one woman spoke. "Is it possible to bring down the supplies from *our* ship? It was originally packed with everything we needed to get the colony started."

Clear Sky contacted *Excalibur*, and after some discussion it was determined to be possible. The question was, where to deliver. If the colonists were outgrowing this island, then another place needed to be found. Captain Sheets said they would begin scanning the rest of the planet to look for a new location.

The Marines fascinated the colonists with their modern weapons, and they took great pleasure in showing off their firepower on a stretch of beach. Sonni watched them for a while but left to wander down the beach. She came upon some worn paths that took her through a small, wooded area. It ended at a pool fed by a waterfall. The local teenagers apparently used it as a hangout. She saw them swimming in the pool and lying on the beach. One of the girls was just getting out of the water when Sonni realized the girl was nude. Looking closer, she realized they all were. Swimsuits were apparently not the fashion. An older boy saw her and called her over. She sat on the beach while they crowded around, eagerly asking her questions about her home world and about Fleet. They all talked until the sun was getting low and the older kids reminded the others of chores to be done and meals to prepare. The group threw on basic loincloths or draped woven blankets around themselves and led Sonni back to the village.

She found Clear Sky standing and looking around the village. His brow was furrowed, and he seemed to be disturbed by what he saw. To Sonni's eyes, he had always displayed very little emotion. It was clear that something was bothering him. They entered the wooden lodge and took their seats for the evening meal. They could hear many of the others talking excitedly about the new supplies and about possibly getting their own supplies from their ship in orbit.

Commander Raleigh turned to Commander Clear Sky. "Wasn't the chief due back today? I understood they were just searching and not hunting. Something must have held them up on the mainland."

Clear Sky nodded in agreement. "Yes. I'll ask them about it. I see what they mean about outgrowing this island. I'm surprised they lasted as long as they did."

For dinner they were handed wooden plates with meat and local fruit, and everyone took the business of eating seriously. Only when they were all done and the plates collected, did Clear Sky inquire about the missing chief.

The colonists looked at each other until their eyes fell on a large gray-haired man off to one side. "My daughter will return when she can. I'm not too concerned, yet." He handed off his empty plate to one of the teenage boys that Sonni had spoken with earlier. "I am wondering, though; you have a ship in orbit and other shuttles. Is it possible to look for her group and see if they're safe?"

Clear Sky agreed and he pulled out his comm unit. In a moment, everyone around the fire heard the captain speaking.

"Yes, we've started charting the rest of the planet. If your chief was going up and down the coast, we could narrow our search and look there. We'll contact you if we find anything."

"Thank you, Captain. Clear Sky out."

The large gray-haired man at the end nodded. "My daughter showed her strength when she was very young and proved she could hold her own in the hunt. She has been chief now for two years since my eyesight grew dim."

* * *

The captain closed the hatch on her Day Cabin and sighed. She'd ordered Tactical to concentrate looking along the coast, then settled in for a long evening.

"I am also using all sensors and cameras to look for the chief and her group along the coast, Captain. This is not an activity I have much experience with, so I'm not sure what to look for. The forest along the shore of this whole continent is very thick."

Shenna's voice brought a smile to the captain's face.

"Thank you, Shenna. I'm afraid we're all new to this. You can probably distinguish something that looks abnormal faster than we can. Any sign of boats, or man-made objects that don't look like part of the forest or coast. Any signs of people moving, or small fires would be things to look for. The people on the planet are counting on us."

* * *

Arlene Matsobushi was monitoring the system usage as she normally did when she came on shift. She had to admit that life aboard had become more fun since she learned about Shenna. Like old school pals, they talked until Arlene was nodding off each night. Shenna always apologized and told her she should sleep.

As she sifted through usage logs, she saw that the ship was using every available resource to look at the planet below. She would talk out loud about things she wanted to look for in the system logs and Shenna would help her find them and she could finish her work much faster. After she finished her review of the regular logs, she turned her attention to the sensors and camera systems.

"Now, what is all this activity here?"

Shenna's quiet voice startled her when she said, "The officers are looking for the colony chief along the coast. Earlier they were mapping the interior of this continent. No one has paid much attention to that since they started looking for the chief."

"I see. Well, they have lots of people looking for the chief, so let's take a look at what was mapped in the middle of the continent, shall we?" She adjusted her viewer settings and long strips of pictures of the planet came onto view. She waited while Shenna adjusted and combined the strips of pictures and linked them up with the previous strip to make one larger picture. Once five strips of surface pictures were linked together, she started to zoom in on the picture in the middle of the continent.

"Wait, what is that?"

* * *

Shenna watched as Arlene stood frozen, looking at the detailed picture. It was a large building with four straight sides. As she focused and zoomed in further, other buildings became clear. It was a city. A very large city right in the middle of the continent. "Oh, my stars, Shenna. We found something! It's a building in the middle of the continent! I think I can see movement around it, like people moving around."

Shenna saw that Captain Sheets was just leaving her Day Cabin. She sent an alert tone through a console display on her wall to get her attention. Frowning, the captain shut the hatch again and walked to where she could see it.

"My apologies, Captain. We found something on the planet you should see," said Shenna.

The display lit up with a zoomed image of a city laid out on the planet below. The captain stared at it and asked, "Shenna, put up a scale. How big is this?"

A scale bar joined the picture, and the captain whistled. "This city is over thirty kilometers around. Are there roads?"

"None that we can see, Captain. But I detect well-worn paths leading in all directions from the city. Many of them lead to the forest to the west and beyond that, the ocean."

Captain Sheets nodded as something occurred to her. "Who is 'we', Shenna?"

"Arlene Matsobushi, Captain. She is one of the technicians who knows about me. Since everyone was looking at the coastline, she decided to look at sections of the continent that we had already recorded. Once she found the larger structures, it was clear we found something important. She also noticed people moving around. This city is occupied."

"Yes, indeed. Tell her thank you for me and I'm going to get some other people to look at this in more detail. Give me the coordinates of the city and we'll start there." She walked back to the hatch and started to open it. "And thank YOU, Cadet Shenna."

Shenna felt pleased with herself in a way she had never experienced before.

* * *

The next morning Clear Sky was awakened by a small group of colonists wanting to speak with him. He threw on a loin cloth one of the colonists had given him and joined them outside of the hut he shared with Commander Raleigh. There were three men and two women. Both of the women and one of the men looked up at him as he stretched to loosen his joints. They looked at each other, then back at Clear Sky. He noticed their gaze but ignored it.

"What do you need?" he asked.

"We are more concerned that the chief is late. Can you use your vehicle to search for her?"

"Of course. I can take our shuttle and some volunteers to help in locating your chief. Let me get ready."

Clear Sky let Raleigh know of his plans to search using the shuttle. Then he set about waking up the Marines. He would take them all along with some volunteers.

Clear Sky was waiting by the shuttle along with the Marines and two of the colonists. He wasted no time and climbed aboard. The Marines helped their guests to get on board and situated in the jump seats. Clear Sky climbed to the flight deck and was surprised to find Lieutenant Van

Belson sitting in the co-pilot's seat. Van Belson turned around and said, "Commander Raleigh's compliments, sir. He thought you could use a co-pilot. I've cleared most of the pre-flight checklist and we're ready to start engines." A brief smile tugged at Clear Sky's mouth, but he just nodded and belted himself into the pilot's seat. A minute later they were in the air and headed up the coast.

In the empty cargo area, the Marines pulled open view ports along the starboard side so that they could all see out. Lieutenant Borgansten asked their wide-eyed guests to take the forward most ports so they could help in looking at the shoreline and the edge of the forest as they slowly flew by.

Chapter Thirty-Two

Commander Clear Sky flew as slowly as he could up the coastline. If they didn't spot anything in the next eighty kilometers, he planned on turning back to scan the coastline while heading South. Sometimes if you looked from a different angle, you could spot things you didn't see before.

His radio squawked and Lieutenant Borgensten came on to tell him to swing back. Their passengers had spotted something. He swung the craft around and dropped the altitude just over the water. He glanced at their fuel. They would have to return to *Excalibur* when they were done here. He never liked to run his fuel too low in case he had to evade an attack.

The colonists were very excited; they had spotted wooden boats on the shore. When Lieutenant Borgensten looked through his binoculars, he could see that the boats were smashed in. He passed the binoculars to the colonists and watched as their initial jubilation faded once they saw the state of the boats.

He picked up his radio. "Commander, this is where they put ashore, but their boats are destroyed so they can't use them to return. Let's move overland and see if we can spot the group."

"Affirmative," and the shuttle gained altitude and headed inland.

* * *

Arlene slowly recovered from the shock of having various scientists and other specialists suddenly show up in her little office. One of them said, "Captain's compliments, but she says you are to lead us in analyzing something you found."

They moved to a large laboratory with big display monitors, and Arlene quickly brought up the view she had been observing. Another person in the group switched on an adjacent display with a live feed. "I repositioned one of our probes to a geosynchronous orbit directly over those coordinates," he said.

Arlene didn't know who most of these people were. They were obviously scientists and specialists from different departments. While she watched them, Zip walked into the lab and handed her something. He pantomimed with his hand opening and closing next to his ear. She looked down and realized it was an audio device. She put it in her left ear and immediately could hear Shenna's voice say, "Zip made this so I can talk to you while you're working with others." She looked up to thank him, but he was already gone.

She watched as the group zoomed in on the initial structure and a woman's voice cut over the murmurs to say, "That's perfectly square. I think it's a pyramid!" This was followed by exclamations as the group studied it.

Another voice called out, "Hey, that looks like writing or symbols on the sides." The camera zoomed in closer, and it became clear that there were symbols on all sides of the pyramid.

While the group focused on that, Arlene watched an older woman with mahogany colored skin and white hair bent over another monitor setup displaying a live feed.

Arlene walked over to ask the older woman what she found so interesting. The woman smiled and looked up at Arlene. "I was watching these people on the planet communicate, I think. It reminded me of bees telling others what they had seen by using dance moves. One of them started it and it spread from there and now thousands of them are heading out of the city going west. I was just wondering why they were doing that."

The women replayed the recording. They watched as the camera zoomed in to watch a gathering of the inhabitants. One of them was in an intersection and seemed to be excited about something. He was moving arms and legs in some kind of dance that quickly drew a crowd to watch. Others then split off from the crowd and they repeated the same moves at the next intersection. This went on for some minutes, then stopped. A large crowd of humanoids began swarming out of the city, all running west and carrying spears. She adjusted the view until they moved out of range of the probe's camera in orbit.

Arlene was still trying to process that while Shenna spoke into her ear. "West would be toward the coast and where *Excalibur*'s shuttle is looking for the colonist's chief," she said.

"Oh, my," Arlene exclaimed. "We need to let the captain know."

* * *

Clear Sky flew over dense woods near the coast. The woods soon gave way to rolling hills covered in tall grass. He covered the area in slow circles to give the colonists and the Marines as much chance as possible to view the area. He kept one eye on the fuel levels. They could continue to do this for only ten minutes longer.

Over the radio, one of the Marines called out, "Ninety degrees to starboard, Commander. We see them."

Clear Sky banked to the right and slowed the shuttle when he realized there was a cluster of tall trees ahead. He saw figures up in the trees on makeshift platforms before he returned his concentration to landing the shuttle nearby.

As soon as they landed, the colonists onboard ran down the ramp to greet their friends. The others on the platform shimmied down using long vines to reach the ground and ran to meet the newcomers. The reunion was joyous, and quick introductions were made. Clear Sky joined them, and everyone seemed to be talking at once.

Suddenly a shout from above yelled, "Incoming!"

Before any of them could react, a large spear thudded into the chest of Private Pearson. He staggered back and fell to the ground, his unblinking eyes staring upward. The other Marines unslung their rifles and searched for a target. Clear Sky yelled, "Everyone get to the shuttle."

A large figure swung down from the trees to land near the rest. She was easily as tall as Clear Sky and had long dark braided hair. She carried a large bow beside a quiver of arrows strapped to her back.

"Get to the shuttle!" She yelled, echoing Clear Sky's order and then swung the bow into action, nocking, drawing and shooting an arrow in one smooth quick movement. After her shot left the bow, she dodged sideways out of the path of an incoming spear. The Marines began firing at the creatures they now spotted running toward them. They concentrated on the lead figure and fired shot after shot with their laser rifles. They were sure they'd hit the humanoid many times, but the shots seemed to have no effect. The Sergeant stopped to adjust his rifle to a higher setting.

Then a loud boom rolled over all of them, and the lead creature's head exploded. This was quickly followed by another shot that dropped another attacker.

Clear Sky's voice rang out clearly over the noise. "Get to the shuttle now! That's an order!" The colonists were already running. Clear Sky reached down and pulled the spear out of the dead Marine. With one hand he threw the body over his shoulder and ran for the ramp. The Sergeant fired again and this time his shot seemed to have more effect. The creature slowed and came to a stop, putting a hand over the wound in his stomach. The others around him continued to charge, stopping only to throw another volley of spears. Lieutenant Borgansten adjusted his rifle and fired, yelling, "Cover their retreat to the shuttle!" He fired and saw his attacker go down, then he pulled back and ran for the shuttle himself.

Boom! Another shot rang out and another attacker fell to the ground. Clear Sky saw Corporal Fless lying at the top of the ramp, her rifle steadied on a bipod. He put the body and spear down behind her and turned back to the battle to make sure everyone was coming. The colonists were all in the shuttle except for their chief, who continued her private battle with a large group closing on her position. The Sergeant had just turned to run back to the shuttle, but he almost crashed into Clear Sky who was suddenly running to get past him. The tall woman continued to fire her bow as if she had all the time in the world.

Clear Sky could see four of the creatures drawing back their arms to throw more large spears. Behind him he heard the shuttle's engines starting and blessed Raleigh for giving him Van Belson as backup. In two more strides, he tackled the tall warrior, and they crashed to the ground together. Almost as soon as they came to a stop, he grunted as a searing pain erupted along his side. He looked down to see the thick shaft of a spear sticking out of the leg of the warrior woman. The darned thing had ripped through the skin of his waist before burying itself in her leg. Now they were both bleeding.

Lieutenant Borgansten opened an ammo box and set it next to Corporal Fless. She reached in and grabbed a loaded magazine, slammed it home, and began firing again. With each shot she dropped another attacker. Clear Sky leapt up with a roar like an angry lion and pulled the spear from the wounded woman. He engaged an attacker who was almost on top of him, thrusting the spear into the center of its chest and driving it back. He then swung the shaft around low, tripping another creature before pinning him to the ground with the point.

Borgansten yelled for the Sergeant to join him on the ramp. Together they sent a volley of laser shots covering Clear Sky. With no more creatures close by he reached down and assisted the large woman to her feet. Together they hobbled as quickly as they could from the trees, up the ramp and into the shuttle. Three more creatures tried to charge them but two of them were struck down by Corporal Fless's rifle. The third stopped to look at his dead companions and back at the shuttle.

"Don't do it," Corporal Fless muttered out loud. The creature seemed to be contemplating throwing the spear in his large hand but looked again at his comrades. Instead, he gestured with his free arm and hopped back and forth on his legs. His mouth was open as if he wanted to scream but no sound emerged.

The Marines assisted Clear Sky and the chief as the shuttle began to lift. Corporal Fless waited until they were well clear before engaging the safety on her rifle and backing away from the still open ramp. She reached over to the side and opened a cover revealing the ramp controls. Pushing the button, she watched as the ramp pulled up and sealed to the hull.

Clear Sky set the woman down on the deck, then he caught her as she fell back unconscious. He gently laid her down and examined her more closely. Her leg was bleeding, a lot. With one hand he ripped his shirt off, twisted it into a length, then quickly wrapped it around the woman's leg above the wound as a tourniquet. The Marine sergeant nearby shyly tapped him on the shoulder and handed him a packet. The Commander said, "What's this?"

The Marine shrugged. "Um, it's a combat field tourniquet. But if you'd prefer to use your shirt, sir, I'll see if I can find something you could use to twist it tight. Just tying it isn't going to do anything."

Clear Sky grinned. "Why don't you apply the combat tourniquet the right way and I'll do some other Commander stuff."

The marine nodded and in short order had the tourniquet strap around the woman's leg and he twisted the handle to squeeze it tight. Then he hooked the handle into holder for that purpose, keeping it tight. The bleeding stopped.

Clear Sky nodded and slapped the Marine on his armored back. He turned to the Lieutenant. "Tell Van Belson to take us to *Excalibur*!"

Borgansten pulled out his radio and relayed the order. The shuttle's engines screamed louder, and they continued their assent all the way into orbit.

* * *

Commander Raleigh listened to the report from *Excalibur* and signed off. He relayed the news that the chief had been found and rescued but that she had been wounded. He assured them the doctors aboard *Excalibur* would be able to fix her up in short order. While Lieutenant Mortan was spending time getting to know the younger folks, Raleigh found himself gravitating toward the older generation on the island. He wanted to learn more. *Once a spy, always a spy*, he thought to himself.

He sat in the lodge and helped with small chores where he could. He observed a group of elders that sat together in one corner, conversing in their own language. Another group sat in a different corner, also speaking quietly. After a time, he became aware that each group spoke a different language. A woman startled him when from behind him she said, "They are from different tribes. They speak the old tongue to keep it alive. We have very little of our culture left to us."

He nodded. "I studied history enough to know that your people got the short end of the stick when the Europeans migrated to the North American continent. That same clash of cultures has happened many times in human history. In reading the logs of your colony ship, I learned that your ancestors wanted to find a fresh new world and to live in harmony with nature again."

"You were able to board our ship?" She seemed incredulous. He noted her long dark hair with a white streak in it, which was braided in the back and pulled over one shoulder. She appeared to him to be over forty. But living on a planet and being exposed to solar radiation made skin age faster, so it was hard to judge.

"Yes, we boarded her to find out what happened. The ship's logs told us of the journey and that there might be survivors here on the surface. Our engineers are trying to repair enough systems to allow us to dock some shuttles and begin off-loading your equipment and supplies."

She nodded. "Hopefully, we can also find a new place other than this island. The chief made it very clear we cannot stay here for much longer. We have always gone to the mainland to hunt for meat, but that is very dangerous, and we lose some people to the beasts every year. Our population continues to grow and that is a problem. That is why the chief left with a party to search for a new place to live."

"Well, we're also helping by looking with our ship from orbit. With an entire planet to look over, we should be able to find some place for all of you to go."

The woman nodded, then stepped closer to Raleigh. "Please take me with you when you leave here. I can be a good wife for you, and you can teach me to use the machines. There is nothing for me here. My husband and son were both killed while hunting in the forest. Even if we find a new home, I feel I am useless here." She took his arm, raised his hand and pressed it to her lips. "You are a senior officer on the *Excalibur*. I know how to take good care of you and make you feel like a man." Tears rolled down her face, but he didn't know how to respond.

Commander Raleigh knew the woman's request was serious. He wrestled with his reply while she looked at him with pleading eyes.

"First, I am honored by your request, but I cannot grant it. Everything I need is provided on the ship. I have no need of a wife to assist me. Second, my heart already belongs to another." Even as he said it, he knew it was true. Deep down he still wanted to see if he could have a relationship with Rena. He had been certain that opportunity had passed. He was glad they had developed a good friendship, but he admitted to himself that he hoped there could be more.

She stared at him a few moments longer and lowered her gaze. "My apologies, I see the truth in your eyes. I should have known there might be another." Before he could reply she turned and walked away.

"Bloody hell," he muttered to himself.

* * *

Sonni assisted some of the younger people with cleanup chores after breakfast. She asked if they were excited about the supplies coming down from their own ship, but most, surprisingly, seemed apathetic. She realized that they'd grown up their whole life without those things, so they never had a reason to miss them. They had very different expectations from their parents or grandparents. Most of the original colonists were dead before these young ones were born.

Later that morning, Sonni was invited to go with a group of three boys and two girls to go to a beach on the North side of the island. They took fishing spears. Once there, the two girls broke off large leaves from nearby trees and laid them on the sand. The boys quickly stripped and headed into the water with the spears. She helped the girls dig a large trench on the beach with their hands. They then lined the bottom with small branches and dead leaves. They explained they planned to cook the fish the boys would bring back. The girls then stripped down as well and went into the surf to clean up. They called out to Sonni to join them. After a moment of indecision, she did. They were so comfortable with their nudity that she felt uncomfortable remaining clothed. She quickly folded her clothes and placed them near the leaves. Then she joined them in the water.

* * *

Rena was amused by the crowd of research people and scientists that all wanted to assist with the project of deciphering the writing on the walls of the city below. Shenna kept her apprised of their progress in addition to the more formal progress reports that came in from Arlene. Sheets admitted to herself that she'd deliberately put Arlene in charge to test the young woman, and despite her initial protests at being thrown into the deep end, she was doing rather well. The specialists were now spread out in various labs around the ship analyzing different pieces of the puzzle. *They were probably dying for something more to do anyway*, she thought.

* * *

Arlene caught herself biting her nails for the fourth time, wondering what they should do next. Everyone possible was working the problem. They were looking at linguistics databases from Earth and the databases of at least a dozen other races in the Association. She took a break and went to a canteen for some coffee and food. She quickly bolted the food down and only afterward realized how hungry she'd been. She'd been working continually for the last twenty-four hours and had neglected to eat as well. She finished her meal with a hot cup of coffee that made her feel warm inside. She held the cup under her nose and breathed in deeply, enjoying the aroma.

A woman's voice interrupted her moment. "I must say, the coffee here is fantastic. Most Fleet ships serve caffeinated sludge. The people here could give classes on how to brew a good pot of coffee."

Arlene opened her eyes and looked at the older woman sitting across from her. She thought she'd seen her in the lab earlier today, or was it yesterday?

"Yes, and right now it hits the spot."

"Sorry, my dear, we all got thrown into this so quickly we never did get a chance to be introduced. I'm Jez Hartman, former Fleet, retired. I teach at the Academy, but I asked to sign onto this little hayride to see more of the galaxy. The captain wanted a more...well-rounded crew." She smiled and Arlene smiled with her, even though she didn't know what a hayride was.

"You compared the dance of those beings to bees. What made you think of that?"

The older lady smiled into her cup and took a sip before replying. "I used to raise bees for a time, and I taught others how to keep them alive. They're essential to ensuring crops grow well. My family has been using them for many years in our farm tunnels on the moon. We helped bring them back to earth when most of the native species had died out."

"The specialists are using symbol and linguistic databases and computer algorithms to try and figure out how these beings communicate," Arlene said.

Jez chuckled. "Yes, all very logical, but now they're stalled while trying to relate those symbols to speech. I suggested they might be mistaken in assuming there is a vocal element at all. I think the people on the planet may use gestures and body movements to communicate. But since nobody would listen to me, I left to get some rest. I can't pull the all-nighters anymore like you younger folk do."

Arlene stopped with her next sip halfway to her mouth and blinked a couple of times. "Seems to make sense to me. How do we prove it?"

"Ah, therein lies the problem. We need to look closer at their little dances, but I can't get our associates to stop focusing on more *traditional* methods." Jez sipped her own coffee.

Arlene smiled. "I can help with that."

Chapter Thirty-Three

In *Excalibur*'s sickbay, the doctors worked quickly on the wounded warrior and Commander Clear Sky. He refused anesthesia and kept his eyes on the woman in the treatment bed next to his. The doctor cleaned the wound in his side and sprayed it with a tissue regeneration solution. He then applied a bandage to close the wound and allow it to heal. The doctor noted Clear Sky's attention and looked over at the warrior woman.

She was very tall, like Clear Sky, and very well built with large leg and arm muscles. Her feet hung over the treatment bed. They watched as the doctors working on the woman quickly repaired the open artery and stopped the bleeding. An infusion unit was clamped onto her arm to replace blood. Another doctor injected her with a drug to keep her unconscious.

The doctor turned back to Commander Clear Sky. "She appears to be one tough lady." Clear Sky only nodded, still watching very closely.

The doctor treating the woman shook his head as he cleaned the rest of the large wound. "What the hell made such a hole in her?"

A male nurse next to him tapped his arm and pointed across the room. They turned to see a gurney rolling in with the body of Private Pearson, a massive hole in his chest. Next to him on the gurney lay the spear. It was as thick as his arm, with a large stone point.

* * *

Arlene brought Jez back with her to the main lab that had become research central for their task. At first, no one even noticed them walk in.

"Hello people!" Silence descended and all eyes turned to them.

"You may have forgotten, but we need answers, and fast. This is no time for long drawn-out debates and pet theories. Now, Ms. Hartman here has been studying their form of communication. By all appearances, it is non-verbal. We need to correlate the movements she has observed to those symbols. You"— she pointed to one researcher—"bring that camera on a tripod over here."

He did as he was instructed, and once the camera was set up, Arlene turned to Jez. "What do you remember of their dance earlier?"

Jez thought a moment and began moving. Her movements were slow but fluid. Clearly, she had spent time as a dancer in her youth. She flowed from one movement to the other, pausing only briefly before continuing to the next. Her eyes were closed as she concentrated on remembering. After a few moments, she stopped.

"That is all I can recall. I saw one do this at an intersection. Others went to the next block down in each direction and repeated it. Very soon, a large group ran out of the city and headed toward the west."

Arlene fiddled with the camera settings and said, "Okay, I've loaded the video into the computer. I want to see if we can draw any correlations with the symbols."

They all watched as one monitor displayed a symbol and another monitor went through the video of the movements. Arlene found it hard not to consider it a dance. For the first symbol, there was no correlation, and another symbol was displayed. This went on for five more symbols before suddenly the video froze on a particular movement, and it was clear there was a match to the symbol on the monitor next to it. Jez's left leg was held with her knee up and her ankle pointing out. Her arms were straight out to the sides, but her right hand was pointed downward. The symbol was an exact match if you ignored Jez's head. The next symbol did not match, but the one after that did. No one spoke as the video and symbol matching picked up speed. Matched symbols with movements started appearing on another monitor. All of them were spellbound, watching the show.

* * *

Rena found herself giving a tour of the ship to the group of colonists that had come aboard with the wounded chief. She assured them their chief was being tended to and would recover. They looked all about in wonder and continually asked questions. When they saw their planet far below them through the large view port, they all fell silent.

"Those lights off to your left belong to your colony ship. Our engineers are trying to get the shuttle bay controls functional so we can begin off-loading the supplies there. I only hope everything has survived being in space this long."

One of them turned to her. "We had heard about the size of our ship from our parents and grandparents, but your ship is so much larger. Have you come so far with your technology, then?"

Rena sighed. She decided the truth was the best answer. "Yes, we have come a long way. But it came with a price. We met many other alien races and joined them in a war. Millions were lost and there was a time when we thought humanity wouldn't survive. The war is," she paused for the right words, "on hold right now. This ship is set up to explore as much of the galaxy as we can before it begins again."

They looked at her with wide eyes. The one who asked the question whispered, "So, we're not alone after all."

Captain Sheets smiled and said, "No, we're not alone."

Then her sleeve vibrated, and she touched it to hear, "Captain, you're needed in sick bay."

"Acknowledged." She looked up. "Sorry to cut this short. You can follow me if you'd like, and I'll see if it is okay to visit with your chief." They nodded soberly and she headed to sick bay.

* * *

Sonni lay on some large leaves spread on the sand next to the other girls. She wasn't sure how long it would take the boys to return with some fish. She lay on her back with one arm over her eyes. The other girls appeared to be resting as well. The sun quickly dried her and felt nice and warm. She found herself dozing off.

She woke when the boys returned and dropped fish near the girls. Two of them left together and disappeared into the woods while the girls prepared a fire pit. Sonni sat up and helped them gather dried tinder and branches.

Sonni watched one of the girls strike two rocks next to a small pile of tinder. She only saw an occasional spark. These were not the best rocks for the job, but she realized they worked with what they had on this island. She pulled over her clothes and dug into her uniform pocket to pull out a small kit. Opening it, she took out a small magnifying glass. While the first girl continued to hit her rocks, Sonni positioned the glass so it would catch the sun and focused the concentrated light on the tinder. Only a moment later, it flared up and she tossed the flaming tinder on the larger pile of wood and leaves. The girls looked at her, astonished.

The remaining boy watched this before getting up and walking to the wooded area. He came back with a handful of long branches and vines. With quick efficiency he put together a rack above the fire and they began hanging the long fish over the branches.

As they finished, Sonni heard a familiar buzzing sound coming from her clothing. She picked up the sleeve of her tunic and tapped the comm unit. "Lieutenant Mortan."

Commander Raleigh's voice came back. "At your earliest convenience, let's touch base on some recent developments."

"Aye, sir. I'll be back shortly." She keyed off the unit and turned to see the little group staring at her. "Sorry, I need to head back. That was my Commander." She began getting dressed. She knew that in Fleet speak, 'at your earliest convenience' meant to return as soon as possible.

The boy looked at her in wonder. "Wow. That's the tech stuff that grandpa's been talking so much about. It allows you to talk to people across distances." He was clearly impressed.

* * *

The captain reached sickbay and heard the ruckus. Someone was yelling and she guessed who it was.

"Let go of me. Let me be!"

Rena found the treatment bed and watched as Clear Sky tried to hold down the arms of a large woman while two doctors tried holding her legs. The woman appeared more angry than scared. Sheets was sure the unfamiliar surroundings were to blame.

She put on her best command voice and said, "What seems to be the problem here?"

All movement stopped. The doctors and Clear Sky let go and the woman sat up. Before she could say anything, Rena continued, "Greetings, honored guest. My healers have been treating your wounds. All of your people are safe. Be at peace, please."

"Thank you, Captain," said the doctor. The two women looked at each other for a long moment.

"You are Chief here?"

"Yes, I am. You are aboard my ship in orbit above the planet. Your people are being cared for and when the doctor says you can travel, I will send you all back to the island. I understand you took a serious wound and lost a lot of blood."

The large woman frowned and turned her head to Clear Sky. "This one knocked me down and a spear caught us both. If not for his clumsiness, I would've been fine. I can move out of the way of a spear or two easily enough."

Clear Sky fought to keep from smiling and said, "There were four spears coming at you. No amount of dancing would have prevented one of them from hitting you. I was saving your life."

"That remains to be seen." She turned away from him, but the captain caught the amused look in her eyes.

"Now," Rena turned the attention back to her, "you need to let the doctors do their job and you need to rest quietly. We will talk again later. I need to check in with my executive officer on the planet and get your other people settled on my ship for now. Are we agreed?"

The woman only stared at Rena, who stared right back. After a moment, the chief nodded her head in agreement. "I will rest." She saw her people over the captain's shoulder. They looked relieved to see her.

"This woman is the chief of her ship, please do as she says until I"—she frowned briefly—"heal."

They nodded solemnly back.

With the situation in hand, Doctor Herwig stepped up to the group. "Now that we have that settled, I am chief of this sick bay, and most of you need to leave"—he paused for effect—"now!"

The group followed the captain out while another doctor motioned for Clear Sky to get back on his own treatment bed. "I'm fine," he protested.

Doctor Herwig walked up and said, "You're fine when I say you're fine. Now, back to your bed."

Clear Sky nodded and hopped up on his own treatment bed with a heavy sigh.

The warrior chief smiled back at him. "Stubborn, I see. Your tribe?"

Clear Sky looked over at her. "Apache. Yours?"

She smiled warmly back. "Blackfeet."

* * *

Marine Tech Gilbert Johnson had just finished refueling the shuttle when a voice behind him made him jump.

"Sorry to scare you, I was just curious about these space craft." It was one of the colonists that came up with the shuttle and the tech wondered briefly if he should be running around by himself. He seemed friendly enough in his home-made clothing and shoes.

"Which space craft?" There were many kinds of vehicles in the bay.

The newcomer pointed with his chin at the Marine Assault shuttle in the next bay. Missile pods and other weapons were an obvious addition to that craft.

"So, those large spears can be launched over great distances?"

"Well, kinda," the Tech found himself responding to the friendly question. He then went on to describe the various weapon systems on the shuttle and the fact that it could also take a platoon of heavily armed Marines to the surface, if necessary.

"Tell me more."

Marine Tech Johnson now had three shadows watching him work on the shuttle. He checked each of the two main engines and control thrusters, cleaning out the nozzles and rechecking all fuel connections before securing the maintenance doors. He didn't mind the colonists shadowing him, as he could see they were quite curious. He'd heard about the colonists who came to this system long ago on the old ship which was now parked in orbit nearby. He himself had been a spacer all his life. Living on a planet was foreign to him. He regaled them with stories about life in the Marines and his job on board. He told them about growing up as a belter with a large family. Being the fifth child, he knew his older siblings would inherit the family business. He decided very early that Fleet Marines was his best option for a better life.

The colonists seemed eager to listen to his ramblings and learn all they could about technology. When he ran out of things to say, they started telling him about their life on the planet. How they heard about technology from their elders but had no experience with it. How the demon beasts plagued them when they went to mainland to hunt. How they tore men and women apart with their bare hands or pinned them to trees with huge spears.

Johnson winced at the vivid descriptions of the beasts. The colonists voiced suspicions that the beasts ate human bodies once they'd chased off the rest of the hunting parties. One told him that he'd heard the beasts raped, then killed any women who survived their attack. Johnson found himself growing angrier with each story. Once the colonists figured they had Johnson worked up, they asked him, "Do you think you could assist us in taking that assault shuttle back to the planet to help us kill all of the beasts?"

"Wait, what?!"

"Yes, that assault shuttle over there," pointing to the armed Marine shuttle in the next bay over. "We'd like you to fly that for us so we can attack the beasts and eliminate them."

He blinked at them in astonishment. "Me, fly? I can't fly those things. The only thing I can fly is an engineering hard suit for maintenance. You need a real pilot for these babies." They suddenly seemed very unhappy. The two in front of him looked at each other, then at the one behind him and they nodded. The one behind him struck him with something hard and metallic, and he dropped to the floor.

Minutes later, those same colonists spotted Warrant Officer Jason Gillam as he returned from a scouting mission. They saw he was still wearing his flight suit and carried his helmet under one arm. Obviously, that made him a pilot. In the corridor, Jason suddenly found his way blocked by three people in homespun clothes. "Um, can I help you?"

"Why, yes, you can," one replied and they grabbed his arms to force him to come with them to the shuttle bay. Jason knew he could break away but was curious why they seemed to think they needed him. So, he went along with them.

* * *

"Captain, please wake, Captain. We have a situation!" Shenna's voice was loud in Sheets' cabin. She bolted upright and reached for the Angel blaster on her bedside table. As she blinked sleep from her eyes, Shenna continued in a more normal tone of voice, "Sorry to wake you, Captain, but we have a situation developing that you need to know about. Some of the colonists are attempting to commandeer the

Marine Assault shuttle. They want to attack the other species on the planet and eliminate them."

She swung out of her bunk and took two steps to her monitor. "Where are they, Shenna?"

"Heading to the shuttle bay, Captain. They have captured Warrant Officer Gillam to fly them."

"Connect me to the Marine barracks." Shenna made the connection. "Security alert, please send an armed squad to the Shuttle Bay. I say again, security alert! There is a hostage situation. This is not a drill."

She stepped into her ship boots and grabbed a Fleet laser rifle from its rack over her hatch. Before she opened the hatch, she told Shenna, "Connect me with the Marine squad leader when they're en route."

"Aye, Captain." Shenna wouldn't admit it, but she was excited. She was following all the established Fleet protocol that Sonni had been drilling her in. She was anxious to see it in action.

Down in the Marine barracks there was always a group of Marines on duty for just such an emergency. After months of mostly drills, they had gotten used to the duty being perfunctory. However, those on duty froze as the announcement came through from the captain. With only a quick glance at each other they ran for the equipment room where they found a Sergeant already there pointing to riot vests, helmets, and their weapons, in that order. They all quickly donned the equipment and headed out of the room at a run.

* * *

"So, what's the plan here?" asked Gillam. The three men from the planet were hustling him along the corridor.

"We need you to pilot the Assault shuttle so we can attack our enemies on the planet. We need to make it safe for our people."

"Oh, I see. Generally, that sounds like a good plan except for one thing." They stopped and looked at him. "I can't fly a

Marine vehicle without one of them being on board. They have all these special security protocols that I don't know anything about. I mean, really, I'd love to help you out, but my hands are tied."

They looked at each other until one said, "Bring him along anyway." They dragged him into the shuttle bay and headed for the Marine shuttle.

Across the large bay was another entrance, with large double doors. The hatches generally stayed open unless launch or recovery operations were going on. Now the doorway filled with a line of Marines in full gear. Their laser rifles were ready as they quickly entered the room.

Jason spotted the Marines before his captors did and threw himself down on the deck holding his arms over his head. As the three men tried to pick him up, a shout echoed across the shuttle bay, "Stay where you are and put your hands in the air. Do it now. We will shoot you. Hands up now!"

A laser rifle fired over the heads of the three colonists where it hit the side of the shuttle next to them in a shower of sparks. While it did no harm to the shuttle, the three men didn't know that. They let go of Jason and stood still with their hands up. They were quickly surrounded as Captain Sheets walked up to them, laser rifle in hand.

"Just so you know, I asked the team to be lenient. Normally, they're authorized to shoot on sight any unauthorized people trying to steal a shuttle." Turning to the squad leader she said, "Take them to holding. I'll be along in a while. I need to have a talk with their chief."

The three were hustled out of the shuttle bay. Jason stood up and brushed himself off. "Thanks, Captain. Once I saw the Marines come in, I thought I'd better get out of the way. Marines usually don't have so much restraint. I could have incapacitated them at any time. I was curious why they wanted to steal a shuttle."

"They're desperate people, and desperate people do stupid things sometimes."

Chapter Thirty-Four

Rena stopped by the main lab to see how the scientists were doing and found an argument in progress.

"I'm telling you, there has to be a vocal element. We'll need a few months to study this, in any case," one researcher was shouting at a small lady with snow white hair. Rena remembered her from the Academy. She held a doctorate in numerous fields of study and was a Professor Emeritus. Obviously, some of these others didn't know her that well.

"I see nothing to indicate that. Their movements ARE their language. We have already mapped so many movements to the symbols, the relationship is clear. Even watching them from orbit, we are now seeing more indications of a subtle sign language used between individuals. The 'dance' seems to be a way to talk to larger groups."

The researcher, a tall middle-aged man, loomed over the tiny woman as if trying to intimidate her by his presence. It wasn't working.

Rena cleared her throat. "It seems I've come at a good time." All faces turned to see her standing at the hatch and the room grew very quiet. "Now, if this particular detail is what's holding you up from getting me what I asked for, I suggest you all step back and rethink your process."

The researcher's face hardened, but his voice trembled. "You are a ship's captain, what could you possibly bring into this discussion? You know nothing of these things. Our process is scientifically sound, and any other course would be guessing. A guess, even if correct, is not good science." The room was now not only quiet but sharply warmer.

Rena looked at the man with a calm face. "I'm not asking you to guess, though a good guess is, in my opinion, a valuable commodity. I'm asking you to try thinking outside the box."

The researcher smirked. "We're on a star ship. If we're outside the box, we will die in the vacuum of space."

Rena laughed. "Did you just make a joke?"

The researcher seemed to be fighting a smile and looked sheepishly at the captain before nodding.

Rena touched his arm affectionately. "You rascal, you've been hiding an amiable streak behind that impressive outrage all this time. Look, if we can calm down for a few seconds, I think I have a way to quickly solve this." The researcher frowned but finally gave up and allowed a grin. His body relaxed and seemed to shrink back to its normal size.

Rena continued, "You may not be aware of this, but we currently have on board some of the colonists from the planet. They've been in contact with the native beings all their lives. You could ask them if they have ever heard a sound from their neighbors on the planet."

The researcher blinked in astonishment. "Some of the colonists are here?"

"If you folks want to take a little break, I'll round one or two of them up and bring them here so you can ask them yourselves." Heads all around nodded in agreement. The captain left the room and closed the hatch behind her.

She walked down the corridor, typing in a request on her sleeve for the duty person from the purser's office to find some of the colonists and bring them to the lab. Then she headed for her cabin so she could call down to the planet and get an update from Raleigh.

Once in her cabin, she contacted the bridge and requested they call down to Raleigh and patch it through to her comm unit. She waited a few seconds and Raleigh's calm voice filled the room.

"Good evening, Captain, how are things in orbit?"

"I have a bunch of our best researchers and scientists working to decipher the language of the native species down there. I am pushing for a way to communicate with them. I'm hoping to be able to talk with them in another day or so."

"That would be good news. I can't seem to convince the colonists down here that the natives *are* an intelligent species. Their people have been getting killed by the natives for a long time." Rena heard another voice nearby and recognized Lieutenant Mortan.

"What does the lieutenant have to report?"

Sonni's voice came through clearly as the long range comm unit was handed to her. "I have been mainly working with those closest to my age, Captain. For the most part they are friendly and eager to show me their daily life. They've done a lot with little in the way of tools. My only concern is that they've lost a lot of what we'd consider common knowledge. They've heard of our technology, but they've never experienced it. If we can resettle them somewhere safe, we need to give them a lot of learning material. They have some catching up to do."

Rena found herself nodding. "Good observation. We're working on a way to communicate with the other beings on the planet. The colony chief is recovering in sickbay and the other colonists on board will be brought back down as soon as the doctor gives his blessing. You two stay put for now."

The two officers chorused an "Aye, aye Captain," and she signed off. She sat there for a moment, lost in thought until Shenna spoke.

"The scientists are an interesting lot to work with, Captain. It seems breakthroughs are acknowledged only after many arguments and discussions."

Rena smiled. "That's the way they seem to like to work. But sometimes their breakthroughs can take a lot of time, and we need to solve the problem of communication as soon as possible." She paused and asked, "I assume you are assisting in the background?"

"Yes, Captain. I have been helping Arlene with matching symbols to what we have seen the natives do. Now that we have matches, we need to find more of the meaning behind them. It's like solving a puzzle or decoding a secret message."

Rena blinked. "That's it! Decoding!" She typed out new orders for their Belanni exchange officer to report to the lab and assist in any way possible.

"Thank you, Cadet Shenna. Carry on."

* * *

Jar'id saw the request come through to bring one or two of the colonists to the main lab for an interview. He asked Shenna where he could find colonists and she told him there were some in the canteen area on the engineering deck. On the way, his sleeve vibrated with a message from the captain asking him to assist the people in the lab with decoding some symbols. He smiled, thinking he could take care of both problems at the same time. *I doubt the captain knew that I was on duty filling in for Sonni.*

When he arrived at the canteen area, he saw a table full of colonists all eating and drinking together. He walked up to their table.

"Excuse me, could some of you help our researchers with something that they are working on. Does anyone have a few minutes to assist?" No one moved and they stared at him.

He wasn't sure what to make of this non-response until a woman at the table asked him, "Were you born a blue green color or was that the result of an accident?"

He immediately flushed bright red with embarrassment. "My apologies. I try to stay one color among mono-colored races. I am still learning that control." Now their mouths fell open as his skin swirled various colors, then turned bright red. They watched as he fought to slow down the color changes.

"You mean you aren't human?"

"No, my apologies, I didn't mean to startle you. I am Belanni. The captain let me stay aboard as an exchange officer when the *Excalibur* came to the aid of my people's ship. I thought someone might have explained that there are many races across the galaxy. We are one of those."

After some moments, one of the men spoke up. "We should apologize for our bad manners. We were told there were other races but not that there were any aboard this ship. You must understand, this is still very new to us. We've been out of contact with other people, uh humans, for a long time."

Jar'id smiled his best smile. Sonni once told him his smile had a way of making other people smile. Soon they were all smiling back at him. "I understand. I can take anyone who wants to help to the main laboratory."

Two of them joined him, a man and a woman, and they left the canteen together.

* * *

Sonni talked briefly with Commander Raleigh. He recounted the battle where the beasts attacked the chief's party and how Clear Sky's group rescued them. He told her to keep her eyes open and be doubly aware of what was around her at any given time. She thanked him and went back to the small cabin where her new friends had invited her for dinner. She'd already decided to give her new friends the basic kit she had used earlier. They would find many useful things there, including other ways to start fires, a folded-up survival blanket, and basic first aid supplies.

After the communal dinner, the two girls came to her and asked her to come with them to their home. She hadn't realized they were sisters until they made formal introductions to their elders in the family hut.

She was introduced to their grandmother, who smiled broadly at Sonni. The old woman took her hand and made many compliments about her appearance and how she was an honored Fleet officer. Their father and an older brother were with the chief on their mission, which meant they were now on the *Excalibur*. The mother just smiled and looked tired. It was obvious the two sisters took after her. She sat Sonni down at the head of the table, which Sonni knew was a great honor. The sisters helped their mother bring snacks of berries to the table while Sonni spoke with the grandmother seated next to her.

"So, I understand you are a warrior woman serving with a warrior chief on your space vessel?" The grandmother's smile was genuine.

"Well, I'm an officer, but I don't know if I'd call myself a warrior. Our captain was very experienced from the war, so I guess she would qualify as a warrior." Sonni was not comfortable with compliments.

"So, tell me, Sonni. Do you have a mate on board this grand ship called *Excalibur*?" As she asked this, Sonni noted the snacks being placed on the table. The family quickly joined them, obviously eager to hear her answer.

"Well, no. Ever since the captain picked me for this mission, I've been too busy to think about a relationship. Maybe someday but now is not a good time." That seemed to satisfy them for the moment and Sonni enjoyed her bowl full of berries. The girls talked about her helping them start a fire with her *tech magic* and that interested the older women. Sonni wanted to object to it being referred to as *magic* but knew until they learned more it would be useless to try to explain.

As the evening passed, the grandmother made numerous suggestions concerning available men in the village. She thought Sonni should marry and have children. Sonni was able to deflect each suggestion with humor and tact.

Later, Sonni left and went back to her own hut to rest. She looked at the vista of stars in the sky and thought about the way people lived here. No technology, food all around them. At first glance, it looked ideal. But she knew from working with Commander Raleigh that the situation was becoming dire. This island could no longer provide for all of them. They had to find a way to live on the mainland. While the planet was nice, she was surprised to find that she longed to be back on board the ship again. She turned in after finding herself nodding off.

* * *

Jar'id delivered the colonists to the lab where they were pounced upon by the scientists. Their first question was, "Do these creatures ever make a sound that you've heard?"

They looked at each other, then turned back to the room. The man answered, "No, we call the beasts *silent death* because they don't talk, growl, or make any noise. But once they are upon you, they will tear you apart with their bare hands."

The room was silent. The head researcher muttered, "Damn."

Jar'id was oblivious to the tension in the room and asked where he might find Arlene Matsobushi. She was pointed out to him, and he approached her. "Hello, my name is Jar'id. The captain asked me to seek you out and insisted I would be able to help you. She indicated you have something to decode."

Arlene looked confused. "Yes, I remember when you came aboard. I don't understand how you can help me. What is your specialty?"

He smiled and worked hard to keep his face an even tone of light blue. "I am very good with communications codes and encryption. My people wrote most of the communication codes used by the Association of Allied Worlds."

Arlene's eyes went wide as the implications hit her. "Really? How interesting. Come sit over here. We have a task for you."

The colonists left after a few more questions and now most of the room was focused on Jar'id. He sat at a computer interface, watching the symbols on the screen and their associated dance movements. Then he began entering a long string of mathematical equations, speaking out loud as he did. "This seems reminiscent of symbols on old temples our people found on some of the planets we colonized. Whatever civilization made them was long gone. We decoded them in time, and I am going to call on that data in a moment from your computer's memory banks. I'm sure it's there."

He smiled to himself, knowing that Shenna was listening. He entered the search algorithm and tied the output to a match-merge routine that pulled the data from the Belanni database. The screen flashed by with thousands of images, too fast for the human eye to see. In a moment, it stopped, and the screens blanked out.

The left-most monitor then lit up and displayed the dance as Jez performed it while the right-most monitor displayed standard text. Groups of words appeared with each dance movement.

INVADERS COME AGAIN, DANGER TO US ALL, NEED MANY TO ASSIST, GO WEST TO THE WATERS, FIND THEM, KILL THEM ALL

The dance stopped, as did the words, and the room was silent for several heartbeats. Then pandemonium ensued as everyone tried speaking or shouting at once. Jar'id wasn't sure what was happening, his facial colors changed rapidly as he tried to understand it all. Arlene grabbed him by the arm and tilted her head toward the hatch. That was something he could understand, and he followed her out of the room. Within minutes, they were standing outside sickbay watching the captain talk with the warrior chief.

The chief looked angry as she sat on her bed. Her thigh was still heavily bandaged. Commander Clear Sky stood behind her with his hand on her shoulder.

"No, I don't believe it. These are mindless beasts. I have seen what they have done to my people with my own eyes. They are monsters. My warriors were only trying to protect my people. They were only doing what I was going to ask you to do. You have the technology and the power to wipe them from existence."

Captain Sheets took a deep breath. Jar'id noted Commander Clear Sky's hand on the chief's shoulder.

"Our people are working on their language as we speak. If we can find a way to communicate with them, it may change everything."

"How will that change anything?" She attempted to stand, and this time Jar'id was sure the commander was holding her down.

"If they are unwilling to share this planet with you, we may be forced to remove you and your people and relocate you. I don't want to do this but that is the only option open to me by Association law. I remind you that this is *their* planet."

Arlene decided that this was the time and entered the room, pulling Jar'id with her. In his confusion, Jar'id's control slipped, and his face became a mottle of different colors. The captain and the chief saw the spectacular display at about the same time. The chief's jaw hung open in shock.

Captain Sheets spoke first. "These are some of the people I was telling you about and I assume"—she looked at Arlene, who nodded—"they have an update for us."

Arlene faced the warrior chief, who was still gaping at Jar'id. "Honored chief, we need to show you how these beings have been interpreting your encroachment on their world." Jar'id fought to get control of his skin tone. "Please ignore my colleague. He comes from a race of people who communicate by changing skin color in addition to their words and actions. He is a good example of what we've been trying to prove. We have observed that these beings communicate with each other by physical movements. Your own people have told us that they make no sound. They have a city further inland with symbols carved on the buildings. These symbols match some of the movements they make, another way to communicate things to each other. Just because they cannot speak doesn't mean they are not intelligent.

"Is there a display monitor we can use, please?" One of the doctors pointed to a wall where a large monitor was mounted. "I've programmed the computer to display our findings here." She reached over and touched a control on the side of the screen. It lit up and displayed pictures from orbit of the city, zooming in to see symbols etched into each building. The scene changed to a dance Jar'id had heard them talking about.

"We observed them communicating using this dance. We were able to match certain dance moves to the symbols on the walls and found a correlation. We then worked with a computer expert to decode the symbols. This particular dance was recorded just before they left the city to attack you."

The scene changed again to the dance movements on the left of the screen with the translation on the right. Everyone could read it clearly.

Commander Clear Sky spoke into the silence. "It is what I've been trying to tell you, Little Bird. You invaded their land. You did not ask permission, and you assumed you could take what you needed. Long ago, a similar thing happened on Earth, but it was our people who were called beasts and worse. That is one of the reasons the tribes left to make this colony. Now we can communicate. Now we can correct the wrong and begin again. If you're very lucky, they might let you stay."

Jar'id had never heard the commander speak so much before. He barely acknowledged other people aboard the ship. His words must have gotten through to her, by the tears running down her face.

Chapter Thirty-Five

The next few hours went by in a blur and Arlene found herself sitting in a canteen with Jez again.

She smiled. "So, you were right all along, the native biped's language is written and danced but not spoken."

Jez just shrugged and said, "...and you wonder why I left academia? I've been butting heads with these guys all my life. Plus, I wanted to do something in the field again. When I saw Captain Sheets grabbing the best candidates from the Academy, I saw it as my only chance. Once we left on this mission, I started to doubt my decision. It didn't seem like I'd get the fieldwork I've been looking for. I'm so glad some good came from my joining the crew, after all."

She paused to sip her coffee. "What are they up to now?"

"I understand they are outfitting a shuttle to go to the surface and display symbols on a large screen to the natives. Trying to start a dialog." Arlene sipped her own coffee.

Jez frowned. "Do they have any idea what they want to say or how to say it?"

Arlene smiled to herself. "Not really. The people that are going down are just starship crew. They're trained for alien contact, but this dancing communication thing isn't something they're used to. As usual, they're just shooting in the dark and hoping something works." She took a forkful of apple pie from her plate. "It would be much easier if a professional who understood this stuff went with them. Maybe they can figure out how to end this little war. Otherwise, we'll have to remove the colonists for their own safety."

Jez looked thoughtful. "Maybe I need to go with them when they try to talk."

"Gosh, I'm not sure Jez, I think the captain would have trouble sending someone your age down there. It's clearly dangerous."

Jez looked at her sharply. "I would think this particular captain would know better than to discount someone who's clearly best for a given job." She drank another sip of coffee while her face hardened. Arlene heard her mumble something tersely and she took another sip. Then she growled something else and took another sip. Then she firmly placed the coffee cup on the table and looked Arlene in the eyes. "Someone my age, my ass." Jez got up from the table and stalked off, leaving the half full cup behind.

Arlene grinned and finished her lunch. *Maybe I've missed my calling*, she thought.

* * *

Early the next day, Clear Sky and a contingent of Marines escorted the colonists to the shuttle. There they met Chief Little Bird, and Jez Hartman. The shuttle was already warming up and there were a few supplies being loaded on board.

The colonists had been briefed on what was going to happen. They didn't seem enthusiastic but with their chief standing there, no one raised an objection. Once the supplies were loaded, Clear Sky led the way on board and made sure everyone was settled on the jump seats. He noted Corporal Fless among the Marines. "I never got to thank you for covering us when we were under attack. You turned the tide."

"No problem, sir. I'm hoping you succeed and don't need me today." He nodded agreement and headed up the stairs to the control area. Lieutenant Van Belson was in the pilot's seat per his request.

"You understand the mission. If things go bad, you launch and bring everyone back."

Van Belson nodded soberly. "Yes, sir."

Clear Sky strapped himself into the co-pilot's seat and announced, "Let's go."

In short order, the shuttle bay cleared out and Van Belson maneuvered the large shuttle to the now open bay doors. With a touch of the controls, they left *Excalibur* behind.

Within minutes they entered the atmosphere and headed to the island.

Commander Raleigh was waiting as the shuttle touched down. The colonists came down the ramp and he put them to work unloading supplies. When that was completed, he boarded the shuttle, and it took off again.

* * *

On the bridge of the *Excalibur*, the crew was tense. Rena was in her command seat on the starboard side. A fighter squadron was deployed and there was a continuous watch on all areas around the ship. One of their deployed probes showed the city on the surface in graphic detail on the main view screen. They watched as the shuttle circled the city twice, then headed north.

The captain tried to project the 'everything is under control' look that Raleigh said she did so well. *I'm sure Raleigh understands why I sent Jez Hartman down,* she thought. Then she remembered that he too was on that shuttle. It only deepened her worry.

She looked down at the device Zip handed her in the passageway. "You'll need this," he'd said.

It was a comm device of some kind. She carefully plugged it into her right ear, out of sight of the crew.

As soon as it was in her ear, she heard Shenna's voice. "Thank you, Captain. This was the only way I could speak to you during the mission while you're on the bridge. I thought it was a great idea, and Zip has given this device to the others that know about me. Before they went down to the surface, Arlene and I explained how I assisted in the translation to Ms. Hartman. She seemed to take it very well and seemed relieved. She also has one of these devices and I am going to assist her with her conversation."

Sheets sighed. She was going to have to speak with Shenna about letting others in on her existence without telling her first. But as Shenna progressed, she would naturally make more decisions for herself. She counted on the Fleet training that Lieutenant Mortan was working with her on to help in making good judgement calls.

* * *

The screens were deployed and now all they had to do was wait. They had circled the city, catching the attention of the inhabitants before landing on a small hill to the North. Raleigh watched Jez Hartman as she sat near her computer controls. When the captain had briefed him, he was a little leery. A lot of this plan seemed to ride on her. He also watched Chief Little Bird and Commander Clear Sky. She stood very close to him, keeping her weight off her bandaged leg, and they talked together in low tones. She carried one of the spears that Clear Sky worked out with on the ship. He turned to the Marines and watched as they readied heavy weapons and grenade launchers. After losing one of their own, they were going to be ready if this turned ugly.

Over the intercom, he heard Lieutenant Van Belson call out, "Incoming infantry, and there's LOTS of them."

Raleigh looked out of one of the view ports, and the hair on his neck stood up. They filled the horizon, looking south, and they were already spreading out to engulf them. At first, he could tell they were running, but as they got closer, they slowed to a walk. It was the first time he had a good look at them. They were tall, almost three meters in height and covered in hair. Their faces held little expression, but their arms and hands moved almost continuously, giving the impression they were talking most of the time.

He keyed his radio, "Keep the engines on standby, do not shut them down. We may have to leave in a hurry."

"Aye, sir," came the response.

"They're all around us, sir." The Marine Sergeant looked nervous.

There were a couple of loud bangs. Corporal Fless said, "They're armed with spears with stone tips, nothing that can hurt us in here."

Raleigh turned to Ms. Hartman. "You're up, Ms. Hartman."

She nodded and tapped the computer interface. Outside, the big screens activated and the beings there looked up, wide-eyed. Before they could react, she started her program, and the symbols began appearing. They watched as the beings stood transfixed, watching one symbol after another appear.

Some began engaging others around them with various gestures. The symbols stopped and began again. Some of the beings started looking restless.

Raleigh asked, "What did you tell them?"

Jez sighed. "Well, I tried to say we are sorry for the unfortunate misunderstanding, but I'm not sure that is coming across. Other symbols mean we want to talk or discuss things with them." She was watching camera views of the crowd on all sides of the shuttle.

The crowd was parting to allow one being to come forward. His face appeared more wrinkled, and he walked slowly with a large walking staff. He got to the front of the crowd as the message started one more time. He watched it with interest. The ones around him were touching his arms and trying to get his attention, but he ignored them. Then he handed the walking stick to the one next to him and raised both arms straight up over his head. His face contorted into something frightful, but he pushed his arms up again as high as they could go, as if waiting for something.

Raleigh watched, transfixed, so he didn't catch the movement past him. He heard the ramp at the back of the shuttle being lowered. He turned and saw Jez Hartman calmly walking down the ramp. The Marines were looking at him. "Cover her but make no threatening moves."

They frowned at him but slowly followed her down the ramp. He noted the corporal setting up her rifle at the top of the ramp.

As Jez Hartman appeared, the crowd seemed to grow more restless. It struck Raleigh as eerie, since they made no sound. Some lifted spears and held them aloft but didn't throw them. This tiny woman was obviously no direct threat. The Marines spread out on the ramp but kept their weapons lowered. Jez walked around to the side of the shuttle, facing the one with his arms raised high, and repeated the movement back to him.

For a moment, Raleigh stopped breathing. He felt like anything could set off the crowd.

The older being moved in a complicated pattern as the tiny woman watched closely. When he was done, he returned to the arms over-his-head position. There was a pause, and Jez began moving in response. A complicated dance of arms, legs, and twisting torso as she carefully paused with each symbol she was emulating. When she was done, her arms also returned up high.

The older being's arms came down and he quickly moved into another dance. Some of the crowd reacted to his movements, making signs which were passed through the crowd like wind over a wheat field. Raleigh watched in rapt concentration. The movements stopped.

From Raleigh's viewpoint it had been a very fast little dance, making it hard to pick one movement apart from the others. He hoped Jez could.

Jez nodded and began moving slowly and deliberately, pausing at each movement, presumably to make sure she got the symbol correct before moving on to the next one. Raleigh thought she looked very tired, but she finished with her arms held high again.

* * *

On *Excalibur*, Sheets took a deep breath and quietly muttered, "Can you give me an idea what's being said?"

Shenna answered in her ear. "I think the older one is their leader or spokesperson. He asked Jez to explain the many cycles of invasion and why others like yourself came here. Jez explained in basic terms that the humans came from a far-off star and their vessel was damaged. They had to land here to survive. But they want to live with their people in peace and not be attacked. There has been too much death over the cycles. He seemed to agree and mentioned the recent deaths of his people. His people now want more of the invaders to die. Now she is saying that there has already been too much death. She is asking if they can all live together. She ends each with a plea for peace—both arms up high. It is also apparently a formal way of greeting."

* * *

On the ramp, a Marine private snapped off the safety on his weapon. With the quiet crowd around them, Clear Sky could hear it clearly. From inside the shuttle, he said, "Put that safety back on, Marine, or I'll gut you where you stand. You accidentally fire a shot now and it could get us all killed." The private snapped on his safety again, flushing with embarrassment.

Raleigh watched Jez reply again and could tell she was getting tired. She ended by twisting down and raising one leg and tried to hold that position, but her tired body would no longer cooperate. She looked at the old giant and said, "My apologies. I am trying to say, 'friend'." Tears of exhaustion rolled down her face.

Clear Sky walked calmly down the ramp past the Marines stationed there. He walked over to the old woman and helped her to sit on the ground. Then he turned to the crowd and placed his spear down beside him. He twisted his body and raised his right leg as she had been attempting to do and made the symbol for 'friend'. He held it for a few seconds, then stood normally while raising his massive arms up high.

Everyone on the shuttle and the many beings outside stood in silence, waiting for the next response. One of the marines leaned over to his squad mate and murmured, "I had a dog when I was a kid. Every time he'd piss on a fire hydrant, he raised his back leg just like that."

"Shut up, Jenkins." The Marine looked back at his sergeant and nodded sheepishly.

The apparent leader also moved slower and more deliberately to ensure his meaning was clear.

Jez had tears on her face, but yelled the translation out loud so that all could hear her in the shuttle. "Then we will be friends. There will be no more killing. Let us instead learn from each other."

Commander Raleigh breathed out a long and heavy sigh of relief.

Chapter Thirty-Six

The conversation continued over the next few hours. The elder being would ask questions and Jez asked that the reply be flashed on the large screen for all to see. Raleigh quietly asked the Marines to come back inside. Chief Little Bird joined Clear Sky outside and they stood on either side of Jez Hartman until the talks were done. The elder made a few gestures and his people began to melt away to the south, returning to the city. Then he too left with a small group of his kind.

The *Excalibur* team took off and dropped Clear Sky and Chief Little Bird back on the island. Lieutenant Mortan was waiting when they landed, and she asked Raleigh if she should return to the *Excalibur*.

Commander Raleigh thought about it but said, "No, you remain here for now. I'm going back to have a chat with the captain. We have much to do in the coming days." He didn't say anything about her newly braided hair style or the beads and shells that decorated it. The two sisters must have really enjoyed working on her hair.

* * *

After the shuttle left, Sonni watched the tribal leaders meet in the main lodge and discuss what had just happened. The shouts of anger she heard coming from the lodge surprised her. Apparently, not everyone was happy with this turn of events. She took a walk and found herself in the woods near the pool. The younger tribe members slowly gathered around her to ask her questions.

A tall boy who introduced himself as Smoke sat next to her. "We were told your people would help us kill the beasts. Why instead are we talking with them?"

Sonni spoke from her heart. "Look, we want to help you. But those beasts as you call them are an intelligent species. Their way of communication is just different as they can't make sounds. So, they communicated by signs and dancing. Remember that this is their world. They saw you as invaders."

She saw that Smoke frowned at that statement and let him think about it. After a moment he looked back at her. "What if they don't want us here? What will we do then?"

"Captain Sheets explained that by the laws of the Association of Allied Worlds we would be responsible for removing you and relocating you to another world. But let's not get ahead of ourselves. From what I've heard, there is a chance they will let you co-exist with them."

He jumped up at that. "But they killed so many of our people!"

She raised her voice to match his. "Yes, and you killed some of them as well. This has been going on for a long time. If you are to live together, it must stop. I'm sure this is not easy for them either."

That comment seemed to get through to him and they sat in silence for a while.

* * *

Jez Hartman was flown to the edge of the city where she continued to meet with the beings there. As she became more fluent in their language, she learned there was a version most used for regular day-to-day conversations. It was less formal than the symbolic language replicated on the buildings. Shenna assisted her at the beginning and Jez asked her to help her in compiling a dictionary of signs to help in teaching others.

At the end of the week Jez flew back to the *Excalibur* where she met with the captain, other researchers and scientists and senior staff.

The captain had let available senior officers and other interested parties attend the meeting until it was clear more people were interested than could fit in a room. She ended up limiting the attendees to key personnel and broadcasting the meeting to the rest of the ship for anyone to watch. Jez took a deep breath before addressing the crowded room.

"First of all, thank you captain for this opportunity. It has been a challenging and yet joyful experience. The hardest part was trying to determine a verbal name for these people. The closest I can approximate is the Lagors. They seem to feel it sounds about right. They can hear our speech, just not reply. There are no vocal cords in their physiology to even attempt speech.

I know that the question of the day is the local population of humans and where they can go. The Lagors identified a section of the continent to the South of their city. It is a varied land comprised of marches to the West leading to a desert in the far Eastern section. To the South is the ocean that covers much of the planet. It is acceptable that the humans can live there."

She drank from a glass of water on the conference table. "The talks didn't all go smoothly. There were some Lagors who were very opposed to the idea of humans staying here. I learned why when they brought me to a building with a story outlined on it of other invaders in the past. These beings came and immediately attacked them. Only by overwhelming numbers did the Lagors beat them back. The survivors took off and never returned. I thought everyone would be interested in seeing what these invaders looked like."

She pressed a control on her pad and a picture was displayed on the wall behind her seat. There were indrawn breaths around the room as a drawing of an Angel warrior was displayed, wings outstretched and shooting a blaster.

"I explained that these beings are also our enemies and that if they ever returned, humans would assist them in repelling them. Apparently, that's what tipped the balance in our favor. There is more that I am still studying, but that may depend on our schedule, Captain."

Captain Sheets nodded. "Yes, we will discuss that in a while. Our engineers have repaired the docking bay on the colony ship, and we can begin off-loading their supplies to the designated location as soon as the colonists are ready. I've asked Commander Clear Sky to coordinate that with the colonists. Given the circumstances we will stay as long as possible to ensure they have what they need."

* * *

Sonni stayed on the island as the colonists packed up their possessions. They all moved by shuttle to their new location where they joined a growing pile of supplies from their ship. During the preparations she saw that Commander Clear Sky and Chief Little Bird spent a lot of time together. It seemed clear to everyone they were a couple.

The two sisters, Morning Light and Dawn, spent their time constantly asking her questions about Clear Sky. On one of their last days on the beach fishing they continued to ask her questions.

"He looks so powerful; does he have other wives on your ship?" Dawn asked while hanging fish to dry on a rack.

"He must have his pick of women every night to see if he produces strong children," added Morning Light.

"Um, no," began Sonni with a sigh, "he is not close to anyone on the ship that I'm aware of. To have children he would have to get the captain to agree. I'm not aware of Fleet officers with families on their ships."

When they returned, the girl's grandmother continued to suggest possible mates for Sonni. She was polite but firm that she would be leaving with *Excalibur* and not staying on the island. She went with them as the last of those on the island boarded a shuttle and took off for the new colony village.

Once there, she found most of the shipping containers had survived their years in space. Everyone was involved with unpacking and setting up the prefab houses. They were self-sufficient homes with solar power and toilets that automatically broke down waste products and even cleaned and recycled water.

Multiple times during the day, there were classes being taught by Jez Hartman on the Lagor's language. It reminded her of sign language used by deaf people on Earth with some added movements thrown in. Even Clear Sky and Little Bird attended the early morning class before they went back to work setting up the colony.

Once peace was fully established, the Lagors tended to leave the newcomers alone. It became common to see a few of the giants watching the process from the edge of the woods. One of them even lumbered over to help a building crew move a heavy beam into place for the community lodge when the humans were struggling. The Lagor was able to lift it with little effort.

It was the first time Sonni had a good look at a Lagor. It was their large red eyes that Sonni decided had the most expression. She thought she detected some amusement from the one helping them raise the large beam, but it could be just her putting a human interpretation to what she saw.

* * *

Rena Sheets looked over the latest report from Raleigh and an additional one from Lieutenant Mortan regarding the colonists. In some matters, the two officers were in sync. In those cases where the reports differed it was only because they'd interacted with different colonists. She wanted to make sure she was up to date when she met with Commander Clear Sky. Based on everything she'd heard, she had a good idea what he was about to request.

The speaker beside her door gave an attention beep. She looked up and said, "Yes?"

A voice sounded from the speaker. "Commander Clear Sky requests a moment with the captain."

She checked her uniform, finding all in order. It wouldn't do to look rumpled in front of the crew. She called out, "Enter." The hatch swung open and Commander Clear Sky stepped in. He closed it behind him and stood in front of her, snapping to the position of attention not even an academy instructor could fault.

"Captain Sheets, I am here to formally tender my resignation from the Fleet, effective immediately. I am going to stay with the colonists and make this my home." He stood there waiting for her acceptance and when it did not come, he broke attention to look down at her. She watched him with a smile on her face while rocking back and forth on her desk chair. She pointed to a folding chair leaning off to one side and he unfolded it and carefully sat down.

"I've been waiting for you to request this for the last two weeks. By all accounts, the colony is now set up and well established. I also understand you will be marrying Chief Little Bird. Am I correct?" She knew the answer but wanted to hear it from him.

"Yes, Captain. We plan to marry in the next few days. That is why I need to resign."

She slowly nodded her head as if in understanding and simply said, "Request denied."

Clear Sky stared at her for a moment, both of them nodding. Then his head snapped back, his eyes bulging as if someone had hit him on the head with a mallet. He seemed to run the conversation in his mind again and the last two words still came up the same. He blinked in surprise and closed his mouth, which had dropped open. "But, Captain, surely…"

She cut him off with a gesture and continued to smile at him. It was her warmest smile. "Captains in deep space have a lot of discretion when it comes to situations like this. No, my friend, I will not accept your resignation…"

"But…" Clear Sky's expression was almost comical.

"Because I have a new posting for you, instead. I'm making you our Fleet liaison and our Association of Allied Worlds representative for this planet. As you learn to get along with the Lagors, you can explain to them and to the colonists what that means. I'm hoping they will eventually form a mutual government who will formally join the Association at some point. When we report this situation to the Fleet, they'll probably spend a year or three working through the red tape, discussing it. Then they'll likely promote you to Commodore, a rank more befitting a posting of this nature. In the meantime, you will just have to do the job at your present rank."

Clear Sky sat back in apparent shock and the flimsy folding chair groaned in protest. His mouth opened and closed. "I can almost see Fleet liaison, but do you really think Command will leave me as the AAW representative? I mean that's a diplomatic post like, well, like an ambassador. Wouldn't they want someone more...ah, trained for that?"

"With you a local hero and married to the Chief of the colony? What do you think? Oh, they might get around to sending you an aide, eventually. One trained in the art of diplomacy. But I wouldn't hold my breath."

Clear Sky nodded and eventually his face returned to its usual mask of control.

Rena Sheets kept smiling as she stood up and placed a hand on his shoulder. "I know you have a formal bonding ceremony with your people, but I'd also like to make a request. Can I also be the Fleet official to marry you both before we leave? It's one of those little benefits of being a captain that I've never had the opportunity to exercise before."

Clear Sky stood and towered over her. "Thank you, Captain, that would be a great honor." She thought for just a moment he might reach down and hug her, but he seemed to think better of it.

* * *

A short time later, the captain was just finishing her formal report on the new posting, when the speaker beeped again.

"Yes?"

The voice of the Communications officer on duty sounded through the speaker. "Captain, Ms. Hartman is here to see you. She says it's official business."

"Certainly. Allow her to enter, please." The hatch opened and Jez Hartman walked into the Day Cabin. The Communications officer closed the hatch behind her. She looked around with bird-like movements as if cataloging all the details. Then she turned her eyes on the captain.

"Thank you for seeing me, Captain. I'll come right to the point. Chief Little Bird has requested I stay and help teach the colonists. They have about a hundred and fifty years of catching up to do. Plus, I want to write up a new doctoral thesis on the language of the Lagors and study that beautiful city of theirs."

"So, how many PhD's do you have already, six? You want to add another one?"

The old woman crooked a shy smiled and shrugged. "Sure, what's one more?" She glanced behind her at the now closed hatch and added, "And I want to thank Shenna for all her help in my initial translation. I was sworn to secrecy and all that, but I find her very refreshing to speak with."

"As I find you, too, Jez," Shenna's warm voice agreed.

"I will miss you, Shenna. You're like an old friend rediscovered. Oh, the things we could do together."

"I will treasure the notes you left with me and use them to assist Captain Sheets if the need arises."

"Thank you, dear. I'm so glad that they will do some good."

The captain smiled at the exchange. "As I already told Commander Clear Sky, I'm not letting you off that easy. He will become the official Fleet representative on the planet, and I will be happy to appoint you as dean and professor emeritus of the newly formed colony college. Go forth and teach."

"Oh, yes, Captain. Teach and study! Something I just found out recently I need to share with you. The Lagors did not build that city. They are still grasping the concept of time but many generations ago they were gifted this city by another race as it left this world. I'm not sure if this was a home world to that race or a colony but they built the city and apparently huge chambers beneath that are filled with symbols explaining their history. The Lagors were a native species just learning to use tools and herd animals. I think they were taught by this other race prior to them leaving."

"Interesting. Then you'll have a lot of work to do! I'll be interested in hearing about the results of your study."

With that, she stood up and the two women hugged.

Chapter Thirty-Seven

Captain Sheets had just finished putting on her dress uniform. It was tight in the wrong places and too loose in others. "They seem to design these things to be as uncomfortable as possible," she muttered to herself. The formal sash was always most difficult to align, and the numerous awards and medals pinned on it didn't help.

Her cabin hatch beeped, and she yelled out, "Come!"

Doctor Herwig opened the hatch and stepped inside. He carefully closed the hatch behind him and turned back to her, looking all business.

She crooked an eyebrow at him. "What's going on, Doctor? I know your staff has been kept busy checking over all the colonists. Any problems to report?"

He still looked as serious as ever as he replied, "Why, yes, I do have something to report, Captain. I just came from a long discussion with Chief Little Bird. She has been worried about something for a long time, and I was able to confirm some details for her."

Rena pointed to her desk chair while she sat across from him on her bunk. "You certainly have my attention, Doctor."

Once settled in the chair, he looked thoughtful. "The colony has a problem. I believe there were just a few hundred of them that survived getting here a hundred and fifty or so years ago. Many with already established families. The survivors were mostly young and healthy and as they carved out a living on that island, they naturally started having more children." The captain nodded her agreement.

"From a genetics point of view, their local gene pool was far too small to begin with. The minimum number for sustainable population growth is close to ten thousand. Add to that the higher death rate removing donors from the gene pool over the years, and the problem only got worse. Now we're about five generations along and they're starting to see the effects: deformed babies, infertility, etc. That brings us to the situation today. If nothing changes soon, the colony will die."

"I'm with you so far, doctor."

"Okay, Chief Little Bird thought she had the answer with Clear Sky. He is big and virile, and her plan was to use him to impregnate as many of the women as possible to get a fresh generation off the ground."

The captain gaped at him. "Let me get this straight, she was intending to put him out to stud?"

Even the doctor now cracked a smile. "Yeah, kind of plays into several people's fantasies on this ship, doesn't it?" He recovered and continued, "Anyway, I explained to her the flaw in her plan and that with another generation they would be back to where they are now. All he would do is push the problem a little further down the road."

She nodded, still trying to wrap her head around the image of Clear Sky working diligently to impregnate dozens of women.

The doctor continued. "She understands that she needs to learn more and has already signed up for several college classes." He leaned forward. "Yeah, I just heard that Jez Hartman is staying to start a college here." The captain nodded, and he sat back to continue. "Well, anyway, after explaining she needs a *lot* of new genetic material to get back on track, well, uh..." He seemed at a loss for words. "She, um, wanted to know if *we* could donate sperm to the colonists, and not just sperm but eggs too."

"Ah, 'we', doctor?"

"Yes, we, as in anyone on this ship who is willing to donate. Much of our crew are young and in the prime of life. We have over twelve hundred of them on board. Now, once I understood what she was asking, and that she was serious, we had a long discussion about what would be needed. We can set them up with a hospital to artificially inseminate as many women as needed. We can add to that some artificial wombs for more children. They'll also need some assistance in delivering and caring for the young ones. But one thing they simply must have is a qualified doctor. I talked it over with my team and Doctor Karen Blackstone has volunteered to stay. She seems very excited at the opportunity. She was leaning toward family practice in school, and this will give her lots of experience."

"Well, that's a handful to process." Captain Sheets was still getting visions of Clear Sky being told to get other women pregnant. She shook her head to clear her thoughts. "Sounds like this is all worked out, what do you need from me, Doctor?"

"Just your blessing, Captain."

She nodded. "Yes, I have no problem with this. I'll need to amend my report but that's an admin thing."

He stood. "Good, Captain, and thank you. I assume you'll be volunteering?"

She was just getting to her feet. His last words had the effect of easing her back to her bunk like a hydraulic lift with a sudden leak. She blinked at him in astonishment. "Volunteering?"

"Yes. My husband and I already volunteered, though we're a bit older. In your case, some eggs. I think if you set the example, along with us and the rest of your senior officers, of course, we'll have most of the crew donating in short order. I'm actually happy something of me will have survived the war to continue on."

* * *

The wedding was a beautiful affair with all of the colonists and many of the crew of *Excalibur* attending. It began with the formal Fleet marriage ceremony with Senior Captain Rena Sheets presiding. Lieutenant Mortan and Corporal Fless found that they were invited as part of the wedding party and were decked out in formal clothing by the colonists, hair shells included.

It ended with, "I now pronounce you married by Fleet custom and human law," and the crowd cheered as the couple formally kissed. No sooner was this finished, than colonists scurried about, moving guests and rearranging the outdoor area around the new couple, who continued with another kiss, oblivious to their surroundings. The people in charge formed the guests into a great circle with the couple in the center.

Then Chief Little Bird's father walked up to them with a large robe over his arm. His eyes were now clear since Doctor Herwig had cleared his cataracts. The couple parted with Clear Sky looking as if he was out of breath. They both turned their attention to the older man. He waited for things to get quiet, then he spoke with a deep voice that carried to all in attendance.

"We come from many tribes, but we have a common heritage. Here in this new world, we can finally begin what our ancestors started. I can think of no better people to lead us on our new journey than these two. They will help us all learn to live in harmony with our neighbors and our environment. Just as the village cares for all of its members, so they will also care for the village." He opened the robe and walked behind them, placing the robe across both of their backs.

"Let them be warmth and comfort for each other to the end of their days."

The crowd cheered again, with the colonists clearly making the most noise. The new couple was led away so they would have some privacy and the new bride's father spoke loudly so all could hear. "Now let's party!" His laughter was long and loud.

* * *

High in orbit, Commander Raleigh smiled as the bridge crew watched from the satellites above.

He'd worked with the tech named Zip on some software updates to the original probes he had placed in orbit around the planet. They would remain there and become communication relay stations for those on the ground. Three additional probes would be turned outward, watching for approaching space vessels. They would alert those on the ground if any appeared. With a little warning, he was confident Clear Sky could handle whatever came their way.

Raleigh reflected on the past few weeks and considered how different his life was from the one he'd envisioned when he came back from his last Intelligence mission. But for one unspoken wish, he was content. And he had hopes that if the ship got back to just mapping the galaxy for a time, he could get closer to Rena. There was at least one chance, and John Paul Raleigh was a strong believer in chance.

Chapter Thirty-Eight

The next day, after the party, the captain sent out a ship-wide request for volunteers to provide genetic material to the colonists. She outlined the reasons why it was needed and that no one should feel obligated. She mentioned she had already donated some of her eggs. The response caused Doctor Herwig to request some additional time in orbit so he could process all the samples. It seemed very few of the crew declined the request. The Marine males, in particular, kept getting back in line so they could leave more samples.

Doctor Herwig himself went to the surface to assist Doctor Blackstone with setting up the small clinic in the village. In a locked back room, they set up the cold storage unit for the samples and tied it to a small fusion generator which would keep it running for several decades. Once that was set up, he noticed a small room across the hall. "That's my room," Doctor Blackstone told him. "I plan on living here for now so I'm always available."

"Your practice, Doctor. You run it as you see fit."

As they walked into the lobby area, they were startled to find a long line of village woman waiting at the door.

While Doctor Herwig grumbled something under his breath, Doctor Blackstone calmly walked to the door.

"How can I help you today?"

The first woman in line stood proudly with her chin raised. "We are all here to request that you give us children."

Doctor Blackstone raised her eyebrows. "I see." She tilted her head to get an idea how long the line was. As she watched, more women joined the line.

She raised her voice so all could hear. "I fully intend to help all of you." That brought smiles all up and down the line.

"However, I need you to think about what it means to make all of you pregnant at once. In nine months, I will be delivering back-to-back babies and there is only one of me." The crowd sobered at that.

"I'd like to propose that we work with Chief Little Bird to create a schedule, so we stagger these babies over time. I intend to stretch out doing this for a long as we can. There is no reason to do this all at once."

A number of women nodded at this, and some walked out of the line. Others stood there talking among themselves.

The first woman in line remained. "I have assisted in our births for over twenty years. I would like to help you if I could." Her face reflected her experience. She carried herself with confidence.

Doctor Blackstone smiled. "I would appreciate any help you can provide. I don't know everyone yet. Plus, I'll need all the help I can get for deliveries."

* * *

Sonni returned to *Excalibur* and packed away her mementos. She had handmade clothes, bracelets, and pendants. She also had a collection of decorative beads in her braided hair that took some time to remove. She took a long shower and made an appointment to have her hair trimmed as it seemed to get much longer during her time on the planet.

She smiled to herself at Jar'id's reaction when she returned. All the nude bathing outdoors had left her skin darkened. He stood open mouthed, and his face displayed a variation of colors that meant he was perplexed and amused.

"How did you change your skin color? Why did you change it? I did not know this was possible for humans..."

"It's normal really. Our skin will generally darken given enough exposure to ultraviolet light. It is something that normally occurs on a planet given enough time. Now that I'm back on the ship, it will fade in time."

"I must record this event as a special day. I've learned something new and exciting about humans that I didn't know before." She giggled at his excitement.

After cleaning up, she met up with Cheryl Fless for coffee in a canteen where she heard about the Marine's take on this mission.

"Some of the other Marines were hoping for more of a fight. These guys are about as gung-ho as they get."

Sonni smiled and said, "I hear you did well during the battle, and likely saved the colonists after the shuttle found them and the Lagor attacked."

Cheryl's gaze turned inward. "Yeah, I did what I needed to do. But I'll never forget the look on that one giant's face when he saw his comrades dead at his feet. He knew his spear couldn't hurt us through the shuttle, he knew I could take him out at any time. He was outraged. But I realized that he wasn't the savage beast the colonists were painting them all to be. Instead, he dared me to prove I was the savage beast and kill him. I saw no reason to. We kind of communicated there for a moment. It was weird."

When she came back to herself, she changed the subject. "So, at the party there was this guy really trying to get your attention. I thought I saw the two of you leaving together at one time. Did I remember that right?"

Sonni rolled her eyes. "Not exactly. He convinced me to take a walk with him for a bit. But then we ran into his elder Aunt who was the same grandmother who's been trying to set me up. He was hoping to convince me to 'get hitched' on the spot. I told them that just because I had a few drinks under my belt, it didn't change anything. I left them and went back to the party. I thought I saw you with two guys leaving when I got back."

Now Cheryl's smirk turned into a laugh. "They seemed to think that by teaming up they could satisfy me. I let them believe they were right, but I left them all worn out and sleeping. They were young and enthusiastic, but they don't hold a candle to some of the horny Marines we have around here."

* * *

Two days later, the *Excalibur* prepared to leave. Captain Sheets sat in the command chair, scrolling down her data pad and wondering where the time had gone. Her crew were all back aboard and the ship was ready. She felt a pang at losing Clear Sky, but the words of his tribe's Shaman and Chief came back to her. He had said Clear Sky would live a long life and have many children. She certainly hoped that would be true. She realized now that she would never learn what Clear Sky's grandfather had to say about her.

"Prepare to break orbit." The command was spoken in a normal tone of voice, but everyone on the bridge heard her clearly.

"Break orbit and assume our original course. Time to pick up where we left off." Rena settled back in her chair. "We need to complete maps of this section so more human ships can join us. We don't want to be the only humans out here forever."

The officers at their stations turned to each other and smiled. So far, this voyage was anything but quiet. They wondered what would happen next.

Lieutenant Torsh walked up behind the Weapons console, manned by Lieutenant Reese. She brushed her hand along her back to get her attention. "Hey, Dee. My shift."

Reese looked up in surprise and smiled. "Okay, all yours." She rose so the other could take her seat, then leaned in close. "Talk later?"

Janet looked up and smiled back. "Sure. My place or yours?"

"Yours. You'll have to help me fix up my cabin sometimes. It's too cold and bare."

"Happy to. See you later then."

At the helm, Raleigh executed the pre-programmed commands, and the ship moved smartly away from the planet. They caught a glimpse of the original colony ship, which remained in a stable orbit around the world. There had been talk of bringing it down to the surface, but there was no safe way to do that because the ship was so large. So, it would remain in orbit, a tomb to those who sacrificed their lives to bring them here and a beacon of hope for the future.

They jumped back to the point where they'd deviated from their planned route. Once there, the navigator worked to plot their next jump. The captain ordered the fighters out for a brief recon of the area. The officers and crew settled into well-established routines, wondering what they would find next.

* * *

Warrant Officer Jason Gillam tapped his readouts in his fighter. His instruments were catching an intermittent reading. It briefly seemed like another ship was there. He wondered if it was just an echo of *Excalibur*. The recall order had just been given, and he watched as each of the other fighters returned home. He waited a moment longer, but the reading did not return, so he fired his thrusters and headed in.

Over his comm link, he called out, "*Excalibur*, this is Recon flight Alpha 1."

"Alpha 1, go ahead."

"I am picking up an intermittent reading bearing Zed niner five zero at the edge of my range. Do you see anything from your perspective?"

Seconds went by before the reply came back, "Negative, Alpha 1, we show nothing at those coordinates. You may want to have your equipment checked."

"Understood and thanks." He slipped into the recovery tube which snared his craft in magnetic fields, and he cut his thruster controls. His fighter was pulled in and set down gracefully on a launch cradle. He powered down and, due to long habit, confirmed there was atmosphere before cracking his canopy. The usual noises of a full hangar deck washed over him as he got out and headed for the locker room. As he passed the maintenance crew for his fighter, he stopped the chief and asked him to pull the sensor package for a full diagnostic.

Epilogue

The stealth ship glided through the darkness of space; no light reflected off its hull. It had been executing a search pattern, looking for something. Suddenly, a flash of light preceded the appearance of the *Excalibur II*, half a light year from them. The ship stopped maneuvering and drifted, waiting to make sure their presence went undetected.

As usual, *Excalibur* launched their fighters between jumps to check out the area. It was noted this was normal behavior prior to making their next jump. After a while, the fighters were recalled, the *Excalibur* turned, dropped a communications buoy as it always did before a jump, and flashed away again. The stealth ship restarted its engines, and after a brief pause to pick up the buoy, it engaged its faster-than-light drive to follow the Fleet ship's projected course.

ACKNOWLEDGEMENTS

I can't say enough about the friends and family who supported me on this journey. From my Middle School teacher, Herbert Horatio Cook, who first inspired me to write, to my role-playing friends in Ohio. Our monthly adventures role-playing Star Trek over thirty years ago inspired this series and several characters. To my fellow friend and writer, Scott, who has his own Science Fiction books to get published: your thoughts and ideas helped to solidify story elements, and your help was invaluable.

Finally, I must thank my wife for putting up with long weekends and evenings while I typed away in my office. She encouraged me to finally get this written and was my patient, first-round editor.

ABOUT THE AUTHOR

E.J. Isaacs is a new writer with Space Wizard Science Fantasy after spending decades in Information Technology. He is a futurist and likes to talk about where technology will take us. Currently living in South Carolina, you can meet him at various local conventions. He loves science fiction, ballroom dancing, and curling up with a good book and a cup of tea. You can find him at solinterests.com, or as "E J Isaacs – Author" on Facebook.

Please take a moment to review this book at your favorite retailer's website, Goodreads, or simply tell your friends!

www.ingramcontent.com/pod-product-compliance
Lightning Source LLC
Chambersburg PA
CBHW021140310726
48971CB00002B/414